A Symphony of Wings

A Symphony of Wings

Heralds of Misfortune: Book I

Simon Williams

Simon Williams

Simon Williams

A Symphony of Wings

Heralds of Misfortune: Book One

A Symphony of Wings by Simon Williams
© Simon Williams 2023
First published 2023

All characters in this work are fictitious and any resemblance to any real persons, living or dead, is purely coincidental.
All rights reserved.

No part of this publication may be reproduced or transmitted in any form or by any means, without the prior permission in writing of the Author, nor may this publication be otherwise circulated in any form of binding or cover other than that in which it is published and without a similar condition including this condition being imposed on the subsequent purchaser.

Cover art © Slava Gerj
All rights reserved.
Map by Diana Hurwitz

| 3 |

THEYA
N
W E
S
Selyph's Cove
Summer Point
Traitor's Channel
Firemount
Ai Salar
Se'Hir
Bay of Slaves
Blood Peaks
Mountains of the Moon
Mirrordeep
Farwater Edge
HYLIOS
Farwater
WISTEREN
Ja'Har
Arakir
Serendar
Amben
Belath
Char
Port Hope
Deep Faering
The Barrens
ASQABAL
Wistmere
Midwood
Fenwood
Lower Faering
Northbridge
Qaan
SAANU
The Greatwater
Eastferry
Isle of Erin
The Greatwater
Aun
Timber Bay
Isaan
Toran
The Spine
Erin Point
GHARAAN
Eastcliff
Hopesfall
Point Marsh
Southwood
Dankwood
Fort Cailan
Southwater
Saintscastle
Winden
Aaler
Beggars Harbour
ANPHAY
Southport
Westport
Sun's End
Seal Island
Witherport
Barren Island
Blood Bear Island
The Frostwastes

I - The Singer

The blackened, parched earth shook with the force of distant yet powerful eruptions. Zei's feet hissed against the savagely hot surface as she jumped over deep cracks that split the ground. The pungent, sulphurous air hurt her throat and made each breath a struggle.

She paused every six or seven jumps and took short and shallow breaths, each one measured and as calm as possible. Her eyes stung. Blisters had appeared on much of her body, another effect of this poisonous environment.

The vast and ever-growing shape of the black mountain loomed before her, half a moon-hour distant, an ever-present reminder of the impending catastrophe that faced Ilentra. The *schiaan* race had named that peak Despair, because to look at it was to be reminded of their hopeless situation. Day by day this vast mountain grew, augmented by material expelled from deep under the ground. On the other side of that colossus lay the Far Abyssal Reach, a deep wound through Ilentra's heart. The violence wrought far below the surface had inflicted disastrous changes on the world. Vast heat and potent poisons leaked from those depths, and for eighty sun-cycles they had shown no signs of abating. The world, with the help of the *schiaan*, had fought against it. But over time the balance shifted, and now it had shifted too far.

Calamity was certain.

Zei, as a Singer of the *schiaan,* knew precisely how close she could get to the mountain without being burned beyond her ability to heal. Soon she drew to a halt, taking slower breaths now as the baking hot winds swirled around.

She stood with her tail curled upwards against her back, wings folded tightly, and looked up into the sky, golden eyes reflecting what little illumination remained. Ash and dust polluted the air so that only the very brightest stars could be seen, their light distorted. Near the horizon where the sun had set earlier, the Southern Guide shimmered blue and white, a distant fire around which other worlds might circle- as well they might around the Ageless Companion, a red-tinged star located higher in the sky and further from the dying daylight.

The *schiaan* would never unravel the mysteries of such places, never learn the secrets of the cosmos as they had once intended. Those hopes were a forgotten dream now.

The unbalanced world would, with neither malice nor intent, reduce their civilisation to a smoking ruin before at last the Reach covered all Ilentra. Starlight would shine down on fire, and finally on a black and dead world.

Zei had a task to carry out- a spell to slow the destruction, even if only by the tiniest degree. A spell that required the use of her voice, here near the heart of the savage fires. If she retained enough strength afterwards, she would fly part of the way back to Cloudwall, the *schiaan* capital.

Their bitter enemies the *xyrral,* whose lands lay north of the Reach, believed that the cataclysm that had forced open this gouge in the world was the work of their deity, the Shining Dark, a monstrous and omnipotent god that lived both in the bowels of the world and in the deep space between the stars- everywhere, but always in an abyss or void. The *xyrral* routinely sacrificed the weaklings and runts of their society to the Shining Dark, casting their entrails upon the smouldering rocks or burning those unfortunates alive as close as possible to the Reach- and, presumably, the all-seeing eye of their god. They believed such acts would dampen its fury, and perhaps even save them from the hell that Ilentra had become.

The Shining Dark was angry, and an angry God must be appeased.

The *xyrral* had always practised ritual sacrifice. The weakest of their kind were rooted out and destroyed, and those a little further up the natural order were predestined for a lifetime of slavery. The *xyrral* lived absolutely by their hierarchies.

Zei had studied the Far Abyssal Reach for more than twenty sun-cycles and knew that even if this mythical, supposedly universal creature existed, the bloody efforts of its faithful had been in vain. Ilentra's expanding wound grew ever more quickly, its infernal heat ever more terrible, almost as if the scorched meat of hopeful offerings fuelled it further.

If the abyssal God of the *xyrral* existed somewhere, it was either wholly vengeful and destructive, or as powerless as its subjects.

No hope remained for Ilentra.

But the *schiaan* Singer had a duty to her people. She faced the implacable blackness of the mountain and the red glow that lit the sky above it.

Then she began to sing.

As her clear, strident voice rose through the raging heat, Zei closed her eyes. The song-spell allowed her consciousness to ascend above the jagged peaks separating her from the Reach, and then over unquenchable fire, so that with her mind's eye she soon looked down into bright oblivion, a demon's mouth that would swallow the world.

The Singers were the most gifted of the *schiaan* magicians. Their songs, when perfected, had the power to change the weather, the environment, and help protect and balance the world. In the early days of the Reach, they had kept its devastating power at bay by making use of such transformations, bending environmental factors to their will. They had used every weapon possible to dampen or disperse the worst effects of this raging inferno.

But over time, as the Reach widened and grew more volatile, the Singers' efforts were blunted, and despair ate away at determination.

Such was the vast power of this roiling chasm now that Zei's song-spell had negligible effect. One by one the other Singers had abandoned their duties, allowed to by those in power who believed their talents would be better used researching ways to protect the remaining *schiaan* settlements. The Ascendant himself, leader of their people, had not dissuaded them in the years since, despite that research having done nothing to stem the tide of destruction.

Zei now made her journeys to this hellish wasteland alone.

She stared helplessly down into the heart of the Reach. How had it started? Might some unknown intelligence be driving it? The *schiaan* had long been the loyal custodians of Ilentra, committed to keeping the world in balance. Had they done something wrong in the past, to spark the annihilation?

Or was she trying to find a reason where none existed?

Had anyone else been present, they would have observed the golden-eyed *schiaan,* mouth wide open, delicate but fierce head upraised, scales shimmering in the faint combined light of stars, moons, and fire. Her wings rustled as the bone-dry wind lashed at her, blowing one way then the other, always hot and- when it came from over the mountain- unbearably so. Occasionally, the environmental conditions combined to cause flames to flare up nearby, but whenever fire drew close her body's natural defences would crush it.

When Zei finally withdrew back into herself, she stood with head bowed, exhausted, broken.

Her song had achieved nothing. It ought to have at least generated some moisture, changed the predominant direction of the wind, even caused a landslide of extruded rock back into the chasm. Something, anything, to delay the inevitable.

The effect of her efforts could not even be measured.

She was too exhausted to fly yet. It was all she could do to walk back across the charred and smoking plain to rest by the Hollow River, a dried-out channel that cut through the desolation. Once, water had flowed here in abundance, crops were grown, and animals reared. Communities had thrived. In the distance, the stony remnants of their towns still protruded starkly from the unstable ground, mostly formless rubble, a grim reminder of life's impermanence.

That occupation had been before Zei's time, and she found such an existence difficult to imagine. What had people done when such little peril infected their lives? They would have had time for so much more than survival's grind. What would have filled their thoughts each day?

Now, the amount of still-habitable land across Ilentra had shrunk dramatically, and the *schiaan* occupied all such areas south of the Reach. Beyond, only ocean lay. The *schiaan* were adaptable like no other race, but even they could not evolve to live on water, and no land masses existed either in or beyond the southern ocean.

Besides, even the sea would succumb to the Reach eventually, and boil away to nothing.

The Great Moon had completed its arc through the grimy heavens and reddish hints of the sun began to grow in the west by the time Zei finally arrived back in Cloudwall. As ever, the lurid colours of the rising sun spread like a diseased flower from the horizon, distorted by the permanent filth in the atmosphere. Zei flew low over the spindly, glass structures of the city's tall buildings and landed near the Hall of the Ascendant, the ornate pillars of which glowed in the emerging light as if a poisonous heat exuded from the stonework.

At first Zei thought herself alone, but in the shadows of the entrance a tall, lithe figure moved and descended two steps towards her as she dragged herself up the stone blocks.

"You are late." Oathkeeper Sherrim made no secret of his displeasure. He wore a ceremonial robe, which meant a full meeting of the Enlightened would convene in the Hall this morning. Zei had not been told of this.

Sherrim scowled when she gave no immediate response. "They are *waiting*. The Ascendant wished to hear from you before a Movement is made." The slight shake of his head made it clear that no matter the Ascendant's view, Sherrim would not have delayed a meeting with all the Enlightened for the sake of one stubborn Singer who still dreamed of making a difference.

Zei thought better of answering. If experience taught one thing, it was to think before speaking and sometimes forsake speaking altogether.

In any case, she was too tired to waste words.

Deep within the confines of the Hall where the Enlightened gathered, the air was cooler and far less disagreeable, particulate matter from the Reach having been filtered out at great cost.

Zei took her position within the tiered stands that circled the vast room. As a senior Singer, she stood close to the central floor, occupying a place on the second tier of eleven. She kept her gaze fixed resolutely ahead, aware of many eyes observing her bedraggled state, her wounds and burns from recent forays to the Reach. Whispers carried far in the Hall- the acoustics of this building were not conducive to secret conversations, nor were they meant to be- but with an effort she drowned out the sibilant, questioning noises.

Soon, as fire consumed the world, no one's opinions would matter.

The Ascendant, aged but still sturdy and with eyes like quicksilver, sat at the centre of the hall. Burnished scales shimmered in the firelight. The Ascendant's left hand held the mace of Movement, a device used only when decrees bound by law were made. Zei felt foreboding stir within her, as if a decision was soon to be made that her report would have no bearing on.

"Singer Zei," he said, and motioned for her to begin as a sombre hush descended on the Hall.

The Singer related her journey to the Reach in scant detail- descriptions of that desolate area had become commonplace and everyone knew the horrors involved. Then Zei told them of her song-spell, and the vision it had granted her of the Reach. Everyone in the Hall understood something of a Singer's art. A few had even been Singers themselves in their younger days.

Finally, Zei admitted that her song had not affected the Reach at all. She might as well have done nothing and turned back without a sound.

"We have no other means to fight it," she added quietly. Then she glanced at the Ascendant, wondering if a scheme existed about which she had been told nothing. It would not be the first time, although no previous ideas had worked.

She gestured with open palms to indicate she had nothing more to say, but it seemed that those around her did. The Hall swiftly became alive with fearful, even angry whispering.

"I fear you are right, Singer. You have done all you can." The Ascendant turned to address the Enlightened. "Ilentra is on the brink of destruction. That fate is inevitable. I have therefore commanded

Elim Har to widen and intensify his studies of the holes in the Continuum and find a place to which our people may go. That is our last remaining hope."

Even before he finished speaking, the Hall erupted into pandemonium. The very mention of that creature was enough to send many of the Enlightened into an apoplexy of fear and rage. Elim Har, according to the worst rumours, conversed with the formless, eternal demons of the void. Some said he committed unspeakable acts in the pursuit of powerful knowledge. Others claimed he made deals with abyssal creatures, allowing him to move objects from one place to another, distant location, in the blink of an eye, using peculiar machinery he had built in his fortress.

Zei didn't know how much of this was true, but fear rose like a wave within her *because* of the response from fully two thirds of the Enlightened. Even those who managed to retain an outer calm looked ill at ease. What use could we make of *him*, their expressions demanded.

She had met Elim Har once, years ago. Wizened and wingless, he was a little younger than Zei, and whereas most of the *schiaan* had golden or silver eyes, his were jet-black. Zei couldn't recall anything of their conversation. Maybe Elim Har hadn't said much at all. She had accompanied one of the Earthreaders, who needed to consult him about some technical matter, but she couldn't remember the reason for her presence.

Find a place to which our people may go. The Ascendant's words would not leave her thoughts. It was known that the *xyrral* had found ways to other realms and had supposedly gone to the fabled world of Theya, although the sorcery they used remained a mystery to the *schiaan*. Certain things those creatures guarded so well that *schiaan* spies had never gathered much information about them. They knew only that the *xyrral* had facilitated a link to Theya with the help of human sorcerers on the other side. But since the Reach had grown impossible to cross, the *xyrral* and *schiaan* had been permanently separated by the inferno.

Zei struggled to imagine what humans looked like. None of her people had seen any for almost a thousand years, and the few descriptions of encounters with those creatures gave rise to more questions than answers. They were supposedly an odd, contradictory race. They gave birth to young that could not defend themselves for years after their birth. They were poorly equipped to cope with changes in their environment. Some supposedly possessed intelligence almost on a par with the *schiaan,* but little wisdom and insight. A few sought to further their understanding of their world and the universe it occupied, but most did nothing more than fight amongst themselves.

Above all else, humans had a predilection for violence. In that sense at least, they shared a dark trait with the *xyrral.*

Zei quietly left, unnoticed, as fury spread around the Hall of the Ascendant.

II

That fateful day soon became known for the beginning of the Great Collapse.

The Ascendant was eventually usurped and executed- a rare punishment amongst the *schiaan*- and as they could not agree on a successor, a group of the six most senior Enlightened were appointed to rule over the *schiaan* territories. But as the damage wrought to the climate by the Reach worsened, little remained of their civilisation to lead.

In desperation, they summoned Elim Har and demanded to know what he could do to help.

Elim Har stood before the Judgement- the name now given to the six Enlightened- and gave an account of his research and findings. The Judgement listened in the faint hope that somehow, the mad creature might have stumbled upon their salvation, but also in the suspicion that he wasted valuable resources in his dark studies. Privately they even feared he had worsened their bleak situation.

The things he told them were troubling. Worlds existed to which escape might theoretically be possible, but the vast majority were so inhospitable as to make any kind of life impossible. Others were- in Elim Har's words- too *tenuous.* Their extreme distance across space made it difficult to maintain links to them. "The void is full of mathematical *noise*," he told them, which meant nothing to those who sought to give a verdict on his years of secretive research. "It is easier if they are close in space and time."

"Space and *time*?" one of the Judgement queried.

"They are much the same, or you can think of them as such," Elim Har said. "Time is a way to understand space." This only confounded them further.

"What about Theya?" another asked. "The world the *xyrral* have supposedly visited?"

"They intend to escape there, surely," a third declared.

"Theya." Elim Har smiled uncertainly. "Yes. In theory, it might be possible to find a way there, although I have not yet been able to. But as you pointed out, the *xyrral* have *already* found a way to that world, and there are far more of them than us. And we can no longer reach them to make peace."

It occurred to the six Enlightened, at long last, that they should have thrown every effort towards making peace with the *xyrral* long ago, no matter how difficult or far-fetched the prospect of a truce. They exchanged bleak looks as they silently admitted the failure of their collective wisdom.

The Judgement could not decide what to believe. The further long and rambling accounts that Elim Har gave of his research and visions confounded them, and they could give no verdict on something so incomprehensible. Often, he contradicted himself or lost his train of thought so completely that the Judgement abandoned their sitting in frustration.

But as no other option remained, they instructed Elim Har to do everything within his power to find a way to reach Theya, no matter the consequences.

In their hearts, they held out no hope. Soon they stopped meeting with him, for it became obvious that his research achieved nothing meaningful.

As the state of the world swiftly worsened the Judgement abandoned the idea of slowing their slide towards oblivion. They looked ever more inward and turned their attention purely towards maintaining law and order as much as possible and finding ways to temporarily protect the remaining *schiaan* settlements.

But no Singer remained to help them. Zei had gone, and the other Singers had died in the violence that engulfed much of their lands.

Left to his own devices, Elim Har immersed himself further in the work that had consumed him for so long. He had no family and certainly no friends, and so he remained alone with his research. This study of possible ways between worlds was all he had left, and he became abandoned to that fruitless endeavour, addicted to the distraction of his studies.

Ilentra slipped relentlessly into panic and chaos. A collective desperation infected all *schiaan-* an emotion their ancestors would not have known. From the marshy, flooded west to the icy spires of the Sky Mountains in the east, from the southern tundra to the Reach in the north, the proud empire collapsed.

Zei had gone to the distant south-east headland of Fallen Bay to spend the rest of her days. Her blood-clan had held this land for many generations, and she- the last of them- had inherited it along with the ancient fortresses built across that lonely expanse. As she flew over the area, she would sometimes see small bands of migrants in the distance, heading towards the far southern tundra. Some flew, others walked. Even here the air had become tinged with poisons, and it grew worse whenever the humidity was high.

She wondered how much time they thought to buy themselves. A cycle, perhaps. Two at the most.

Zei had made herself a makeshift home in one of her clan's abandoned strongholds. It should have been winter, but the paroxysms of the Reach had upended the natural cycle, and, on many days, it was impossible to tell the season from one moment to the next. One day a funnel-storm might tear across the landscape, then the next day would be still and unbearably hot. Sometimes, huge chunks of ice larger than Zei's fists would fall from the sky. Day after day the Singer watched the violence from the glassless windows of her lonely refuge.

The great empty halls, mouldering libraries and lonely watch-towers of this black-stoned castle at the end of the world nevertheless comforted her in the short term. Zei had never craved company and did not miss it. Likely the settlements had long since descended into anarchy, and she had no desire to witness the death-pangs of a once-great civilisation, a pointless emotional ugliness that served only to show how small they were, how insignificant in the universe's grand scheme.

The days passed. Occasionally, the former Singer would climb to the top of one of the observation spires and look far to the north, where violent storms created by the Reach now roiled constantly, raking the tortured land with continuous stabs of lightning. Even here in Fallen Bay, the air had grown unbearably acrid and the effects on the weather more pronounced. Savage storms built and spent themselves, over and again. Sometimes the humidity became such that Zei found flight impossible.

As time went on, she grew restless and curious about the fate of Cloudwall and everything that she had left behind for this silent life spent waiting to die. She could not understand why. After all, the world was beyond helping now.

But that morbid curiosity only grew stronger as she languished in her fortress home, until at last Zei could no longer bear the endless unease and restlessness. She ate and drank enough to last her through the long journey to Cloudwall, and then she flew northwest, sheltering between storms, back towards the city.

Five days later, Zei stood surrounded by the ruins of Cloudwall. Overhead, black clouds had gathered, and she could barely take a breath without lightning flashing through the hot, polluted sky. Dust filled her mouth and irritated her eyes. Lesions had appeared on some of her scales.

The Singer couldn't understand what had drawn her back to this place, once the centre of the *schiaan* civilisation. She'd sworn never to return. Now as she stood in the ruins, conflicting thoughts swirled in her head. The end was very near. The Reach had extended to less than half a day's flight from here- she had seen that hellish glow across the land during her journey. The sky's sullen darkness was almost like night. Every breath hurt. Although she could not see them, she knew the air contained tiny fragments of glass and other harmful particles.

Zei soon found the Hall of the Ascendant, or what remained of it. She walked up the cracked stone steps to the entrance arch, recalling that distant day when she returned from the Reach to admit the hopelessness of their struggle.

The Singer wandered through the half-standing remains of the Hall. If a block or beam fell to crush her then so be it. Despite the swirling storm, the rumbles that shook the ground, and the crippling pain that now assailed her, Zei felt an odd, detached sense of peace. The victory of their all-powerful and implacable enemy was all but complete. Some powers could not be defeated, and those who thought otherwise were fools.

Deeper into the ancient Hall she went, clambering over rubble and stepping across great dark chasms, until she came to a wide arena riddled with cracks and littered with fallen brickwork and timber. Zei knelt to look closely at the fragments and was mystified to see that some had partly melted. An immensely powerful force had been unleashed here- perhaps one of the lava holes that had burst through the surface in many other settlements. Yet she saw no evidence of lava flows.

She walked to the centre of the arena, whose surface had collapsed in on itself. In those twisted depths, something emitted a flickering white light, the illumination blurred by the thickness of particulate matter in the air.

Next to this phenomenon lay a badly burned body.

It still lived, Zei realised as she drew nearer, and the body twitched as if buffeted by unseen forces.

The head slowly turned, and Zei took a sharp breath, shocked. "Elim Har," she murmured.

He didn't recognise her- why would he? Yet this broken, dying creature tried to speak, desperation in his eyes. She couldn't understand his faint, croaked words at first. As she knelt closer, Zei listened attentively. "...worked," he whispered. "Path... but it's..."

He made a clumsy gesture with his horrifically burned arm, and Zei realised that he was trying to point to the pulsing light. She turned to look and saw that now the light flickered between various complex geometric shapes. "What is that? What have you done?" she exclaimed.

"Make... find them..." Elim Har's voice faded quickly.

"Make what? *Find* what?"

A wheezing sound emerged from him. Dark blood flecked his lips.

Zei looked again to the mad flicker of light and motion, and saw it fade. The surrounding gloom now appeared darker than ever.

Whatever Elim Har wanted to say, she would never know. His arm fell uselessly to one side, and a moment later his harsh, shuddering breaths ceased. He had passed on, perhaps to the Great Rest, or even one of the places in his visions.

"Or maybe nowhere at all," Zei added. Regardless, Elim Har's remains would rot away here in the ruins, at least until the Reach swept over everything.

The Singer clambered cautiously down towards the light source. The illumination had faded to a faint core, leaving an opaque white jewel, in which a faint movement flickered, as if a constantly shifting mist lay trapped within the stone.

Whatever this was, Zei decided she ought not to have anything to do with it. Elim Har had unlocked magics he couldn't control, and now that immense power had destroyed him. Had it even destroyed the Hall, or was that the work of the almost continuous earthquakes that shook the land?

Even as she pondered the matter, another great rumble shook the ground and dislodged some of the wall stones. Zei took flight for a short while before she judged it safe to land, whereupon she remained crouched on the ground, fighting for every breath. Here in Cloudwall, where the Reach was near and the air thick with poisons, remaining airborne was an immense challenge.

Why was she here at all? Frustrated and confused, Zei turned away. Better to return home and wait for the end.

Then she saw the sullen, fitful glow of the jewel again from the corner of her eye. Something about its uncertain light drew her in. She went to it and knelt.

The Singer abruptly decided that to return to her lands to idle away whatever time she had left would be torture. It would end only in painful and lingering death.

She seized the jewel, half-hoping it would make an end of her. She had nothing, and no one.

What difference would a few more cycles make, now?

Put me out of my misery, the Singer silently pleaded.

The world around her melted away into darkness. Shapes that she didn't recognise began to form around her, as if a new day came into view, in a new world. And yet she had not moved.

Was she dying?

Zei stared around in wordless fear as something materialised in the slowly growing light. A rip in the world, and beyond it, a pathway. She stared into this revealed space for an age.

The light grew more intense, casting back the ashen gloom. Zei sensed other *schiaan* drawing close, brought from the hiding places where they too waited for death.

"Where does it lead?" she murmured.

But where it led didn't matter.

It would take them *somewhere.*

II - The Passing of a Plague

I

As Martha bled slowly to death on the floor of her kitchen, she reflected, when the agony subsided, on the strangeness of life's twists and turns.

Things never end how you expect them to, her mother had told her, many decades ago. *Never.*

Her mother had been right, of course.

Every time Martha hoped to pass out from the sheer pain, and in so doing leave this world for good, the agony would mysteriously clear and slowly return. The two intruders- they had taken on human forms, but Martha knew better than to think those were their true skins- wanted her to remain aware as they ruined her body, pausing only to ask questions to which she had no answer.

"You are not from this world," she managed to say at one point during the afternoon.

The young woman- such a pretty creature, Martha found herself thinking, even though she knew something utterly inhuman hid beneath that surface- stared at her in wide-eyed innocence. "Did you hear that?" she exclaimed, turning to the man, who sat by the oven adding more wood to the fire.

"Many things are not what they appear to be," he said. He turned, and Martha felt her head being moved by an invisible force so she could look at him. Her blood stained his teeth and caked his lips and the surrounding skin. His eyes were a muddy dark brown.

His complexion was alternately grey and yellow-hued, as if parts of his skin were dead and the remainder bruised. He hadn't looked like that when Martha answered their knock on her door earlier that afternoon. Something was desperate to burst through that paper-thin visage. Their masks were slipping.

"Are you hungry?" he asked, and Martha realised to her horror that the smell of her own blood was making her salivate.

"Never mind what *she* wants." The woman sounded petulant as she looked down at Martha. "Are you going to tell us where it is? I am *so* tired of asking you."

The witch would have laughed had she the energy. A faint wheeze emerged from her lips. She couldn't imagine what these two creatures were after. An *artar*, they had said, but Martha had no idea what that might be.

A messy death and a small victory, she thought deliriously as her vision came and went.

The woman sank her teeth into Martha's thigh, but the witch no longer felt anything. She heard her flesh being tugged and pulled apart and the scratching of sharp teeth against her femur. Then her attacker sat back with a piece of fat flesh in her mouth. *Such a beauty!* was all Martha could think, even as she began to drool from the corner of her mouth.

The late afternoon sun poured through the west-facing window, by which Martha had spent many happy times watching the day fade. *My time's almost up now,* she thought. *No more sunsets.*

The female finished her impromptu meal and loomed closer. Martha detected an odour of deep, warm vaults and old earth. She heard her tormentor's joints slide and imagined bones and cartilage slipping past one another in fleshy darkness. *Show me your true form,* she wanted to say, curious to know exactly what sort of creatures these two were. Undoubtedly they were outworlders of some kind, possessed of great power.

Blood and spittle dripped onto her lips and found its way into her mouth. Fear and bewilderment swirled in her head accompanied by a hungry lust that Martha could not understand, transmitted by the creature whose angelic yet demonic countenance filled her view. She uttered a desolate cry that became a faint, low groan of primitive need as *something* within her assailant's leavings polluted her.

The unknown quantity drifted like smoke into her body. She felt the taint spread slowly like drops of ink in the reddish gloom of her insides.

"It transforms her," observed the female in hushed tones. "Will she talk now?"

Martha saw her oppressor's angular form through a haze of heat and blood, indistinct except for the shine of her teeth, which gleamed ominously in the fading light.

The witch's vision went. When it returned for a moment, the two creatures looked less human than before. They appeared taller, thinner. Their eyes bulged from almost skinless faces, the monsters behind the facades on the brink of breaking free. Even now, the woman's eyes reminded Martha of the endless sky, the man's of the eternal darkness under the earth.

Yes, she thought numbly. *I know what they are, now.*

They cut the limbs from her body, and still she remained aware.

They slit her open and rummaged through the softness of her innards, and even then she did not lose consciousness, kept lucid by the creatures' sorcery.

Martha's final sensation was of one of them caressing her peeled scalp as the other feasted on her meat. She could no longer hear, but as her melting, burning brain succumbed to oblivion- even demons could not prolong her wretched life any longer- she felt their words, their unearthly conversation.

She's tough. Tastes dark, somehow.

Why would she not give it to us? Had she forgotten where it is?

"Do the women of the Faering taste different to other humans?" Ishiya wondered aloud. The light of life had fled the old woman's eyes at last. *This* one did, she reckoned.

Her brother considered the question for a moment. "Less tender than I would have liked," he remarked. "But the taste is strong. *Earthy*, I would say."

"Children are sweeter." Ishiya crunched her way through a tibia and sucked the marrow from inside. "But there are no children here in the forest."

Had one of the other women of the Faering arrived at the house- unlikely, for Martha had been a determined recluse- she might well have fled in terror from the scene of the two *xyrral*, now naked and feasting as they squatted on the gore-strewn floor of the kitchen. They had abandoned their human facades. Angular and muscular in their natural form, with leathery, colour-changing skin, sharp claws and rows of long, needle-like teeth, they were truly monsters out of the scare-tales told across Theya- stories of demons that came from another world to feast on people.

Afterwards, with their bellies full of warm meat, Ishiya and Ichaan retreated to the bedchamber and copulated on Martha's unmade bed, feverish in their lust, laughing and biting and rolling around the room entwined.

II

The *xyrral* searched the house meticulously for a full day. They dared not rest for longer than they already had, given the importance of the artefact they sought, and the fact that the sorcery masking their nature from the *faer-* the ultimate custodians of the Faering- would soon fade. The *faer* would not run from them. They would relish the challenge of fighting two outworlders in their midst, interlopers in their sacred arbour. And if they descended on this place in sufficient numbers, the *xyrral* twins were as good as dead.

Eventually, their mood soured as their worry that they might not find the lost *artar* became a grim certainty.

Ichaan sat on the straw-stuffed mattress and contemplated the matter while his sister seethed and gnashed her teeth.

"The astromancers must have been wrong," he said at last. "We've looked everywhere. The *artar* is not here."

Ishiya snarled, her expression nothing short of venomous. "We should have kept the old woman alive for longer, tortured her until she sobbed and begged, until we broke her spirit."

"You saw her step outside herself," he pointed out. "The pain meant nothing. I doubt that she knew anything of the *artar*. And were the object here, we would have found it."

"So someone or something has *moved* it?"

"Or it was never here."

Ishiya swore and struck the wall so hard that a great crack snaked up the surface almost to the ceiling.

"Temper," her brother said, but looked away when she fixed her furious stare on him. Ishiya's rages could be formidable and had killed not only many of the meatsacks that inhabited this world but even two *xyrral,* in Ilentra.

That said, her mood had gradually improved over their years in Theya. They both knew how fortunate they were to be here, for Theya did not share Ilentra's state of alarming flux and geological peril. That did not mean a world in temperate statis, of course- there were volcanos, areas prone to flooding, vast tracts of desert and even larger areas where ice lay permanently over the earth- but Theya was a calm paradise compared with the hellish churn and mayhem of Ilentra, where even the seasons had fallen into chaos. Not even the greatest *xyrral* sorcerers could discern any pattern to the violent changes in the weather, the powerful earthquakes, earth-shattering volcanic eruptions and crushing tidal waves. Every creature on Ilentra, no matter how powerful, remained helpless in the face of that mayhem.

Most tellingly of all, the ever-widening, ever-deepening Rift, which some called the Abyssal Reach, now extended the entire way across the main continent. Already it had decimated much of the southern hemisphere where *schiaan* and other creatures had lived, partly due to the prevailing winds that caused the dirt and poison to move south more often than north. Those who worshipped the *xyrral* all-God, the Shining Dark, maintained that He was fighting through the Rift and out into the wider world. Whether to remake it or destroy it entirely, was a point of argument- but only academic.

Ichaan, like their father, preferred the theory put forward by the *xyrral* cosmographers, that their sun's previously dependable heat and light had grown more erratic over time, and forces emanating from it had wreaked havoc upon Ilentra. Of course, the logic and sense of that idea, backed up by observations and calculations, not only offered scant comfort but also enraged the theologians in their midst.

"What now?" Ishiya demanded pensively at last.

Ichaan stirred from his thoughts. "We must tell him the information was wrong. The measurements given by the astromancers were inaccurate. The *artar* may be *somewhere* in the Faering, but not *here*. It's too vast a place to continue searching."

"He will have their tongues and eyes out for this," Ishiya declared, but she sounded despondent.

The two of them fell silent. Neither wanted to deliver news of this setback to their father. To seize one of the fabled *arterrim,* the ancient objects of power supposedly made to protect and preserve the ways between worlds and the stability of those paths, would have been an immense achievement, no matter that they had no real idea how such things were meant to be used. Keeping it out of the hands of others who *might* find a way to use it was just as important. To not do so constituted an equally immense failure.

Ichaan and Ishiya feared little, but their father instilled a terror in them when one of his cold rages swept over him- no matter that his children were now full-grown. No one knew how to make other creatures suffer quite like Ihar, Chainmaster in the City of a Million Wings.

"We can't tell him," Ishiya said.

"But we must, because he'll find out anyway," her brother reasoned. "He will expect us to meet with him in Char, four days from now. We can't withhold the truth."

"You are always the sensible one," she complained.

The two *xyrral* easily hid all trace of activity that could be linked to them. Pieces of the old woman were left where they had been thrown- cooked, burned, gnawed and half-eaten. But there would be no evidence that *they* had killed, mutilated, and eaten the woman. The teeth marks would be human.

Meanwhile, the residue of their urgent fornication would have seethed and dried and vanished from existence.

Of course, women from the human settlements dotted around the Lower Faering- not to mention the *faer-* would sooner or later determine that outworlders of one kind or another had been here.

Even an obvious recluse like the woman who had lived here would have visitors eventually. But it would be far too late.

By the time anyone worked out what had happened here- let alone *why*- Ichaan and Ishiya would be many hundreds of miles away in the eastern land of Asqabal, where their kind were valued assassins and enforcers.

Night fell, and under a moonless sky they took flight.

III

A nameless, existential dread crept through Shaya, the Elder of Greenwood, stirred by the fearful news Merrilin and Thulinne had brought.

Merrilin had calmly reiterated the facts that had brought them here long after dark and following a long and tiring journey, as Shaya listened in grim silence.

"How long someone was murdered here?" Merrilin asked suddenly. The fire had gone low and sullen in the hearth and the table candles sent long and lurid shadows against the timber-panelled walls of Shaya's little house. The women had drunk some of the Elder's strong ale but had not eaten. Neither Merrilin nor Thulinne could stomach anything, and neither could Shaya after hearing their story. The meat and potatoes she had prepared for dinner languished stone cold on the back table.

The Elder couldn't remember any murders in the Lower Faering during her time here. The Lower Faering was a safe haven for women who fled persecution and those who chose to retreat from the societies of nations in search of a simpler, more natural life. Centuries ago, this part of the Faering was effectively loaned to the first group of women who petitioned the *faer* for the right to live here.

"I don't know," she said at last. "A long time ago. Are you certain that outworlders were behind this?"

"Undoubtedly." Merrilin grimaced. "Shapechangers, too. The creatures must have been cloaked with sorcery of some kind, subtle in a way that the *faer* could not have detected at the time. Something otherworldly shielded them- something more than their shapechanging ability. But the way they pulled apart floorboards and sections of the walls... they would need to have been stronger than humans."

"It seems to me that a great power amongst their kind went to immense trouble. They must have been looking for something vastly important."

Thulinne nodded. "They almost pulled the place apart, presumably in the hope of finding whatever they searched for. They were very thorough."

"But did they find whatever they sought?" Shaya mused. "What could they have been looking for in an old woman's cottage? Martha kept nothing of value. No one *anywhere* in the Lower Faering keeps anything valued by such creatures." She sat back, thinking on the chances of this incursion having been noticed at all. Merrilin and Thulinne had been visiting the smaller, outlying settlements and homesteads around the Lower Faering, to ascertain the welfare of the women who lived in those remote places. The tradition had existed for decades and took place each year. Merrilin and Thulinne had been chosen this time.

All had been well, they said, until they arrived at Martha's house.

"Did you know her?" Merrilin asked.

"Somewhat, although I hadn't seen her in a long time. Martha was one of us, loosely speaking, but she hadn't come to Greenwood for many years."

"What now?" Thulinne wanted to know. "What if they're still somewhere within the Faering?"

Shaya shook her head. "They won't be. You were able to detect something of their nature, so the sorcery that hid their nature has expired. They will have long since hastened away."

"Who sent them?" Merrilin frowned. "The Sentai lords of Asqabal have been known to make use of such creatures, no matter that they deny it."

Thulinne nodded. "The ruling family consorted with those demons for centuries. The Sentai continued to do so, even after the Queen's disappearance."

"Why send them here?" Merrilin wanted to know. "Why provoke the *faer*? They haven't openly thirsted for more territory, nor craved war with any other nation. They're nothing more than a collective regent still hoping for the return of their monarch. From what I hear, they struggle to maintain order in their own land. They're hardly in a position to expand their influence."

"Maybe the task was given by other outworlders," Thulinne suggested.

Merrilin nodded. "That's more likely."

Shaya sat back in her chair and thought. "We must find out what they were looking for."

"We should gather the Circle," Merrilin said, misinterpreting Shaya's words.

"No. The Circle cannot know of this yet." The Elder of Greenwood shivered and went to add another log to the fire. "A plea for audience must be made to the *faer*," she added, warming herself as flames leapt up. "They will have learned of what happened by now. They might even know why these creatures came to the Faering."

Merrilin and Thulinne exchanged worried glances.

"And I expressly forbid you from mentioning any of this to anyone else, until I give leave for it to be said."

Then Shaya turned away from her visitors, not wanting them to see the fear and indecision in her eyes- for the *faer* were not easily called upon, and had no great love for humankind, not even the women of the Lower Faering.

IV

Wind sighed in the trees, and the forest shivered in autumnal chill. Shaya drew her cloak closely around her aged body as she shuffled along the track to the Gathering Stone in the middle of Greenwood, where she would often sit to think matters through. The Elder preferred to be outside, even on mornings like this, but at her age she was disinclined to potter aimlessly about the village, and she thought best when seated.

The season was normally wet and mild in the Faering, but this year had seen touches of frost, which usually only appeared in the hillier lands of the Deep Faering. The unexpected cold made her bones ache and her temper fray. Shaya scowled as she carefully walked around the edge of the track to avoid the worst of the mud and leaf mulch.

Last night's meeting with Thulinne and Merrilin preyed on her mind. Shaya felt uneasy at keeping this matter from the Circle, the group of Greenwood's senior women who gathered very occasionally to make the most important decisions. But revealing what little she knew would only stir unease in the community.

A little knowledge was a dangerous thing.

Five years had passed since the last Grand Meeting of the Circle. What emergency had brought that about? Shaya couldn't recall, but then there were many things in her life she no longer remembered.

Her body had begun to deteriorate many years ago, but recently a vacuous torpor had begun to eat away at her mind- *the slow, slow dark* as her predecessor had named that resolute, unshakeable foe.

It was a quietly fearful state of being- to feel every one of her hundred and sixteen years. And although the Elder would never admit it, the last few months had also found her growing weary in a less physical but more troubling way- tired of life itself.

That was how Shaya knew she wasn't destined to spend much longer here.

She was not simply exhausted, but world-weary. She had accomplished much of what she wanted to. But it would never be enough.

Shaya stopped and watched for a moment as, some distance away, the young apprentice Anwynne hurried on her way somewhere, long ringlets of dark hair flowing behind her. Something about the girl seemed odd, Shaya thought. It wasn't the first time she'd seen her heading into the woods at an early hour, and Anwynne had every right to do so if she wished, but she always went the same way, when few others were up and about.

The Elder recalled that Anwynne had moved in with Merrilin some weeks ago- it was common knowledge that the two had become lovers not long after Anwynne's arrival in Greenwood. Maybe she would ask Merrilin about Anwynne's habits. Then again, maybe she wouldn't. Most things were an Elder's business, but not everything.

She observed Anywnne's progress until foliage obscured the girl from view, then shrugged and walked on.

Shaya maintained an air of detached composure as she eased herself down on the Gathering Stone, the place where an Elder would sit with other members of the Circle, during a Grand Meeting. The mask had long been second nature, a shield that she rarely let slip, even now as she felt the long shadow of intruders.

As Elder of Greenwood, the Gathering Stone had been hers for fifty years, a place where only she might sit. Shaya had led the women of Greenwood for longer than anyone else and maintained peaceful relations with the *faer* throughout that time. No matter what, acquiescence remained more important than anything else. Without the goodwill of the *faer*, the continued existence of communities like Greenwood would be forfeit. If they wished, the human women in their territories could be cast out from their lands.

Shaya's position afforded her a view across the wide grass clearing around which many of the buildings of Greenwood stood. She sat for a long time, observing as the morning light changed.

Later, two women came to the green to practice swordplay- Merrilin and Imogen. Soon the harsh clash of blades rang out in the still morning air and sun glinted on their surfaces. Shaya listened to the scrape and ring of metal on metal and faint grunts of exertion.

Merrilin had been Imogen's tutor in armed and unarmed fighting for the last three years. Not far shy of forty years, she looked at ease, graceful and fluid in her movements, her dark hair tied back and a faint sheen of sweat on her brow.

Despite Imogen's tender age- she was around seventeen years old, even younger than Anwynne, but not even the girl herself could say when her birthing-day was- she had shown herself to be talented in many areas. Such was the ease with which she learned some disciplines that rumours abounded (for which no evidence had been found) that she used subtle, undetectable sorcery. Shaya knew this to be nonsense, but the idea had lingered due to Imogen's unpopularity. She made little effort to work with others and remained aloof, speaking only when she had to. Some of the women wanted her cast out, but Imogen had never done anything so bad as to warrant that.

Merrilin had been one of her few supporters, and Anwynne- perhaps because she saw Imogen as a threat, though there was no evidence for that either- one of Imogen's most vocal detractors.

Many of the women interpreted Imogen's aloofness as self-superiority, and that served only to harden them against her. Green-wood, like all eight of the Lower Faering settlements, was a hardy, no-nonsense community where everyone was expected to pull their weight. Named as witches by the world outside this vast forested land, some of Greenwood's women fitted that title well enough, but others were hunters or crafters, or spiritual guides and mentors. Some came here not knowing what they wanted to be, and only found their vocation later. What they all had in common, however, was their choice or need to live unhindered by the insidious power structures of men- most notably the Church of the One God that held considerable power in Gharaan but also parts of Saanu and Asqabal.

Their resilience and self-sufficiency meant they did not suffer fools gladly and took a dim view of those who coasted on the hard work of others.

Imogen had been brought to the Faering as a ten-year old by a woman who claimed to be her mother. Shaya knew more about Imogen than anyone else in Greenwood- which was not a great deal- and when she first talked with her, it quickly became clear that the girl remembered almost nothing of her past.

An apprehension had taken hold of the Elder when she agreed to take the child into Greenwood, a feeling that she had made a momentous decision for good or ill. Perhaps a subtle power had been at play, something so intricate that she couldn't glean its nature or origin. She'd never believed that Imogen's companion was her mother- not only did she seem a little young to be the mother of a ten-year old, but she hadn't borne much resemblance to Imogen.

Shaya hadn't pressed her on the issue- after all, it certainly wasn't the first time that a girl or a young woman had been brought to Greenwood to be raised here, for reasons that were either untrue or overdone. Many fled persecution. In past centuries even one or two fugitives from the brutal desert realm of Hylios had arrived.

Imogen's accent- slight though it was- placed her from somewhere in eastern Gharaan, although Shaya had never been certain, and Imogen's memory of her origins had shown no sign of returning over the seven years she had spent in Greenwood. Her name was very common in that part of the world- assuming it was her real name.

Aside from Gharaanian, the girl had been fluent in the common Theyan language when she arrived, unlike some of the women who came here with only their native language and perhaps a smattering of Theyan words. Indeed, Shaya reckoned that Imogen spoke Theyan *better* than she spoke Gharaanian. She had no grasp of other languages, but that hardly mattered in the Faering.

With the passing of years Shaya's worries concerning the girl had faded, for nothing momentous happened. Meanwhile, the words of others appeared not to affect Imogen in the slightest. She learned obsessively, particularly the disciplines in which she showed promise. For that reason, she had earned a grudging respect from some quarters, but it had long been apparent that Imogen cared little for the respect offered by others.

What *did* she care about? Shaya had asked herself that question more times than she could count.

The woman who had brought Imogen to Greenwood had worn a necklace with the likeness of the Protectorate's star emblem when they arrived. Perhaps the Protectorate had sent her, or she was linked to them in some way. Dedicated to the defence of Theya against demon outworlders, the Protectorate ruled the far southern land of

Anphay, where winters were bitterly cold and summers miserably damp.

They could use the help of the Protectorate now, Shaya thought ruefully, although they seldom sent anyone this far north.

Anyway, when had any woman of the Lower Faering last asked for help from the outside world?

Maybe that was their weakness. Maybe they were blindsided by their determination to be utterly independent.

Shaya sighed as her thoughts returned to the troubling matter of the *xyrral* invaders, now certainly long gone.

It ought to have been impossible for any such creatures to enter the Faering without the *faer* knowing- and even if their cloak faded as they fled, and the *faer* already knew of the incursion, what would the guardians of this place do? They kept to their territories and by and large they had no dealings with any lands save Wisteren, where humans and *faer* had governed together for untold centuries.

One of Merrilin, Thulinne and herself must go to the *faer* and consult them.

If Shaya were younger, she would be the obvious choice, but the journey through forested uplands to the Deep Faering would be beyond her.

Thulinne, for all her admirable qualities, was too emotional and lacked the cautious nature needed when dealing with the *faer*.

Merrilin would need to go.

The battle came to a sudden conclusion. Through a deft move, Imogen had the point of her sword levelled directly at the other woman's prone neck. Merrilin dropped her blade and after a moment Imogen lowered hers. A faint sheen of sweat glistened on her brow, and she wiped absently at it, then untied her long, blonde hair. Imogen only ever tied it when she was training.

"Very good," Merrilin remarked as she picked her sword up.

"I've done better," Imogen said with a shrug.

Shaya abruptly decided to summon Imogen for a talk later. It was past time to find out more about her, or at least talk with the girl. She hadn't spoken with her at all for almost a year. "Imogen," she called out. "Come to me at sunset. I would like to speak with you this evening."

Imogen turned, gave a brief nod, and then continued to walk across to the far side of the green. Shaya caught Merrilin's eye and beckoned her over.

"I've been thinking about our discussion last night," she said without preamble.

"As have I."

Shaya drew her shawl around herself, shivering. "I need you to go to the *faer*, Merrilin. To the Arbor Wall and beyond, if they allow it. Plea for an audience, tell them everything you know. Ask them what we must do. If outworlders can find their way in and out of the Faering undetected, if they are seeking something here, then everything has changed."

She saw a flicker of fear in the woman's eyes for a moment, but Merrilin was calm by nature, and she simply nodded. "Today?"

"As soon as you can, yes. You know the path to the Singing Gate?"

"I do. It's been many years, but I remember the way."

Shaya stood up, wincing as her old bones protested. "Good luck. And come to me as soon as you return."

"Are you all right?" Merrilin enquired.

"I'm fine," the Elder lied as she walked away.

Merrilin told Anwynne about her mission when the younger woman arrived back at their house. After some hesitation she also told her about the findings at Martha's cottage, given that this was the reason behind her leaving. "Speak of it to no one," she warned. "Even the Circle haven't been told about this yet."

Anwynne, as Merrilin had feared, reacted less than calmly. "Why does the Elder need *you* to go?!" she protested.

"Shaya can hardly make the journey herself. It's a tough trail." Merrilin sighed. "Of course I don't *want* to go, Anwynne. But she has made her choice and it isn't my place to speak against it. Besides, I was at the cottage..."

"Thulinne could go."

"*I* am going, Anwynne. The Elder has decided."

Anwynne shook her head and opened her mouth to argue further, but Merrilin said quickly, "Let's not fight over this. I'll be back in less than two weeks."

She packed enough provisions she might need for the journey there and back. It would take at least four days to reach the Arbor Wall and Singing Gate, from where she would be accompanied by *faer* sentinels if they saw fit to allow her past that barrier. They would take her to one of the more southern gathering places of their kind, most likely Seir Haal, or perhaps that place no human could pronounce, which the women called Fallen Gorge.

And what then? She would tell them the little she could, but their response could not be guessed.

Suddenly, Merrilin felt so exhausted she could barely think. Old certainties had begun to break down. Dangers once reckoned unthinkable were now real. What would come next?

Anwynne stood nearby and watched pensively until Merrilin finished her packing. "Don't go," she murmured, and pulled her closer.

"And don't *you* make it more difficult," Merrilin said as gently as she could. "I'll be back before you know it." She kissed Anwynne, then warned her, "Keep the place tidy. I know what you're like."

Anwynne managed a weak smile. It had already faded by the time Merrilin opened the door and stepped out into the sunshine.

V

That evening, Shaya was standing in her garden to watch the last scraps of sunlight fall behind the tree-lined horizon when Imogen appeared, almost as if she had stepped from out of a different, unknown place. The Elder shivered suddenly, not entirely due to the plummeting temperature. She recalled again the moment when she had accepted Imogen into the community, as if the girl was a mysterious, dangerous gift from another world.

Imogen, still with her pack and crossbow slung over her shoulder- today's other lessons had centred on marksmanship- walked as far as the little wooden gate at the foot of the garden and then waited until Shaya beckoned. "You're a little late, Imogen. You may not think our talk is important..."

"I don't know if it is or not," Imogen pointed out. "You haven't said why you want to speak with me."

"That will soon become clear," the Elder replied sharply. She disliked the girl's flippant response, and her own weariness only made her more cantankerous. "Respect the time that others choose to share with you! Time can never be given back."

Imogen inclined her head, unperturbed by Shaya's change of tone. "As you say."

Shaya tried to appraise the girl's mood and found that she couldn't. "Are you ever afraid?" she asked finally, immediately surprised at herself. Where had that question come from?

Imogen looked confused by the question. "I don't know," she said finally. "Ought I be?"

"Sometimes. It's normal, Imogen. It can keep us alive. Indeed, that's what rational fear is *for*."

Imogen shrugged uncomfortably.

"I'll make some tea," Shaya said.

Imogen stood to one side after they went into the cottage, until Shaya motioned impatiently for her to sit, whereupon the girl chose the hardest and least comfortable of the carved wooden chairs- the one that Thulinne had sat on last night. Imogen put her pack to one side and perched on the edge of her seat like a nervous bird about to take flight. She averted her eyes until the Elder spoke.

"We were talking about fear. I'm sure you must have been afraid before in your life." Shaya placed a pot of fire-heated water and tea leaves on the stove to boil. "Perhaps it was a long time ago and you've forgotten."

Imogen said nothing, but for a moment the look in the girl's intensely green eyes changed abruptly. Shaya could not read the expression, but a chill came over her. She wondered again what strange course of events had brought the girl and her companion to the remote vastness of the Faering. Maybe she should have asked more searching questions when Imogen was brought here.

Shaya reckoned she might have been reckless in accepting her.

She listened to the water hissing over the fire, and after a short while she went over to the stove to lift the kettle of tea with a thick, grimy glove.

"It must be difficult," the Elder remarked as she poured two cups and placed one on the table next to Imogen. "Not knowing who you once were, or from which place you came."

"I don't think about it."

"Nonsense," Shaya said immediately. "Of course you do."

"I'm Gharaanian. You said so yourself years ago. My accent and fluency place me there. But Gharaan is a big land. I've seen maps of it."

A silence fell between them. Imogen looked consideringly at the Elder, and Shaya held that green-eyed gaze. Imogen was undeniably beautiful, but her eyes revealed a hard and brittle nature, Shaya thought.

"Did you run away from something or someone?" The breeze had strengthened outside, and branches from Shaya's apple tree scraped against one of her windows. A draught found its way under the door. For a moment, Shaya wondered if the candles might blow out.

Imogen appeared not to have heard the question at first. Finally, her lips moved. "Yes." Then the girl leaned forward. "Everyone who comes here is running from something. Ask me a different question."

There was something slightly menacing in her tone, but Shaya was not to be cowed by a teenage girl with an overinflated sense of herself. She also leaned forward and stared unblinkingly at her guest until Imogen looked away. "Is there something you want to tell me about? Something you've never told anyone else, perhaps?"

"I don't know." Imogen suddenly looked troubled. "I don't think I should be here with you."

Shaya winced at another stabbing sensation in her back- her aches and pains had been annoying her all day and certainly hadn't helped her mood.

"Who are you?"

Imogen remained tight-lipped.

"Perhaps I can help you," Shaya continued softly, recalling that pivotal moment seven years ago.

A sudden fury leapt in Imogen's eyes, even more startling for the resolute calm she otherwise displayed.

Shaya's hand reached out to touch the girl's arm, hoping to allay her fears, but Imogen snatched it away.

"Are you *ready* to be helped?" Shaya asked softly and surprised herself by both the question and the tentative manner of its asking. A sense of unease still nagged at her, but she forced it aside.

"Are *you* ready?" Imogen whispered.

Shaya took a deep breath and then winced as a sudden pain spread from her stomach up into her chest. The direction and manner of that movement was strange. The Elder exhaled softly and placed a hand over her heart. The pain ebbed away.

Just heartburn, Shaya silently scoffed. She would have some mint tea before she went to sleep later. If it worsened, she could go to the healer tomorrow.

But she didn't believe herself.

The wind picked up outside. Shaya glanced at the window and thought she saw something dark and slender as it darted along the path that led past her garden. The creatures of the woods had been busier than ever over the last few weeks, she thought. But this was not a good night to be out and about.

Somewhere from out of the surrounding forest came a deep groan followed by a cracking sound as if a tree had swayed and snapped in the wind, although conditions were nowhere near bad enough to cause such damage.

Abruptly a savage pain cut through Shaya's stomach, so powerful she could barely stand. Imogen sat up and regarded her pensively. "What's wrong with you?"

Shaya turned and headed slowly to the back room and the privy, closing the door behind her. A malignant, intangible presence was somewhere nearby. She couldn't tell if it was inside the cottage with them or somewhere outside, perhaps moving this way and that like the wind, or hunting for a way in and stopping at each corner of her dwelling as it circled restlessly.

What had she done?!

The agony grew so severe that Shaya collapsed on the stone tiled floor of the privy room, uttering a faint moan. Her knee cracked against the surface, but she barely noticed. Her bones and fibres were moving, she realised in horror, and not as they ought.

A convulsion wracked her body, and she ejected a long thread of blood and spittle. The Elder watched incredulously as her fluids moved in every direction at the same time to create a shape like a many-pointed star gleaming in the faint light. *Perfect geometry,* she thought, and would have laughed had she not been so terrified.

Agony scythed through her, and Shaya cried out. A moment later Imogen knocked on the door. "Shaya?"

The Elder tried to reply but almost passed out as another wave of pain swept through her.

A loud scratching started on the outside wall. The lantern light in the privy dimmed alarmingly. It threw dark and bloated shadows upon the walls, but already they were fading, as if they danced one final frantic routine before succumbing to the darkness that had settled over her home. "I don't... know what it is," Shaya whispered.

Her vision had rapidly deteriorated, yet she glimpsed something watching her intently from the corner before the light failed completely.

You fool, Shaya thought dismally as the last of her strength leaked away into the dark.

VI

Imogen rapped on the door more loudly but heard nothing from the room beyond. She took a few steps back and stopped, suddenly confused. *I ought to see if she needs help,* was the first thought that came, but another quickly countered it: *I won't be able to help.*

Then she blinked, staring at the door in front of her. She couldn't remember what she was doing here in Shaya's house. What had they been talking about?

Imogen ran at the door shoulder-first. She was strong despite her slender frame and managed to buckle and partially split the door, which had not been repaired in decades. She ran at it again and this time the door split down the middle.

Shaya lay on the stone floor. Blood dripped from her mouth, and a thin tendril of something- steam or smoke, Imogen thought dazedly- drifted between her lips. The Elder's eyes were open wide as if she had witnessed something terrifying at the moment of death.

Imogen looked to the lantern light in the privy. It appeared unusually bright, as if its light came from some unnaturally incandescent material. A faint tang of something remained in the air- sour and acrid like burned flesh, although Shaya had suffered no obvious burns. Imogen breathed in the odour. She recognised it but couldn't remember from where or when. It must have been long ago.

The girl knelt by Shaya's body and stared at her. Curious, she reached out to touch the old woman's cheek. Immediately she flinched at the heat of the Elder's skin.

Imogen walked swiftly through to the front room and went to the front door, intent on rushing into the heart of the village to raise the alarm and try to explain what had happened.

No! The frantic thought came as soon as her hand touched the door handle. She couldn't tell anyone.

Most of the women in Greenwood distrusted her. They would think that she'd killed Shaya. They wouldn't countenance any other version of events. It didn't help, Imogen fretted, that she couldn't recall anything much of what had happened- until she heard Shaya's pained cries. She remembered darkness and shadows and questions and muddled thoughts, but little more.

She snatched her hand away from the door handle, having seen that it was covered with the Elder's drying blood. How was *that* possible?

"I didn't touch her," Imogen whispered. "Not her insides."

She looked again, and her hand was unbloodied. "I'm going mad," she mumbled. "No. Imagining things."

Escape was her only option. She had her pack- she carried it around with her most days- and could take some of Shaya's provisions. The Faering would have plenty of food at this time of year. Clean rivers and streams were abundant, so she could collect and drink water at will. And the women of Greenwood and other Lower Faering settlements were permitted to hunt, so she would lay traps and catch rabbits and squirrels if she needed to.

The beginnings of a desperate plan took root. She would pick a direction and get as far away from Greenwood as she could. The rest she would need to make up as she went along. There was no time for anything more.

Shame mingled with fear as she filled her water flask with shaking hands and then rummaged in Shaya's cupboards for food. *What are you doing?!* a shrill voice in her head demanded as she stuffed hunks of hard bread, cake, dried fruit, and cured meats into her backpack. *They'll certainly think you killed Shaya if you run now. Stay, and they might believe you didn't.*

Yes, Imogen admitted. Some of the women might believe her story. A few.

But how could she make *enough* of them believe her when she couldn't properly remember the last few hours?

How could she tell the truth when she didn't know it?

Imogen stood on the doorstep of Shaya's cottage. A light breeze blew, autumnal but not as cool as yesterday. She slung her pack over her shoulder, quietly closed the door behind her and took a long, deep breath, allowing her senses free rein as she took in the sights, sounds and smells of Greenwood. She felt truly alive. A thrill rushed through her.

It was wrong to feel so *potent* as Shaya lay dead in the darkness of her home. But she couldn't help it.

The Elder's house was situated at the eastern edge of the sprawling village and only a few other buildings stood nearby. No lit lanterns glowed, and no sounds of activity could be heard.

Where could she go? Imogen quickly considered her options.

South or south-west would take her towards the large and sparsely populated realm of Saanu. That meant crossing the Greatwater river that cut through almost the entire continent from west to east, and then head through hilly, difficult terrain where violent rural tribes roamed.

In the west lay the Wistmere, a vast, dangerous marshland that occupied the entire south-west of Wisteren except for the coast. No sane travellers ever went there.

North and north-west led directly into the Deep Faering, forbidden to humankind. The *faer* would kill her without hesitation if she set foot uninvited beyond the Arbor Wall, an ancient stone barrier that cut through the Faering and separated the territories permitted to human communities from those denied to them. This warning was one of the first things of note the women had told her when she came to Greenwood. Stray beyond that wall without permission, even *touch* that wall, and death would come swiftly.

And beyond the Faering, north-east would eventually bring her to the inhospitable desert realm of Hylios, a brutal theocracy where women were enslaved. Hylios, Imogen knew, was the *worst* option of all.

Distant Asqabal lay far to the east, and Gharaan to the south-east. To reach either, she would need to negotiate the Barrens.

A vast area of land claimed by none of Theya's nation states, the Barrens was an inhospitable desert where few dared tread. In ancient times the nation of Caian had taken up much of this territory, but Caian had been torn apart by a war whose parties used sorcery so powerful the land itself became poisoned and unable to sustain much life.

Imogen had been taught that travellers and adventurers occasionally crossed the Barrens. But the stories of poisoned earth, mutated creatures, ghosts of ancient warriors and lingering fell magic persisted, and few people strayed into the area unless they had no choice. Even a thousand years after the events that gave rise to the legends of that place, no neighbouring nation had claimed the land. The soil was poor, unable to sustain much vegetation. The forgotten territory had been left to rot and crumble quietly.

South-east, Imogen decided. Through part of the Barrens and towards Gharaan. That was her land, after all, and she spoke the language. Furthermore, the women of the Faering were not well-liked in Gharaan, the kingdom where the Church held considerable power.

Imogen hurried along the east track that led away from the village. She looked back three times and paused, listening intently, but heard only the quiet night-time sounds of the surrounding forest.

Even now, as the enormity of her decision began to dawn on her, she didn't feel frightened.

Perhaps the fear would hit her tomorrow when she woke somewhere strange, a fugitive alone in the world.

VII

Imogen recalled almost nothing from before her arrival in the Faering seven years ago.

She remembered clinging to her companion as they rode along a wide, grassy track towards Greenwood. A memory had lingered over the years, of the musty sweetness of damp bracken, the rustling of the breeze in the upper reaches of the great, gnarly oaks, the soft and comforting thud of their horse's hooves.

Those things had stayed sharp in her mind, meaningless yet potent. But only vague shapes and sounds remained from before that day, like experiences from a fragmented dream which, when she tried to grasp their detail, only slipped further away.

Imogen and her nameless guardian had rested and eaten lunch in the shadow of a broad, ancient oak with the sun still high and the woodland basking in late summer warmth. The morning's rain had eased off, and the clouds gone east.

The woman asked her charge urgent, terse questions, some more than once. She might well have done the same before this day, but Imogen didn't know. To all intents and purposes, she may as well not have existed then.

Do you remember anything from before we arrived here?

No, Imogen had said truthfully.

Where are you from? Do the names of any places come to mind?

None, she had admitted.

All Imogen recalled from before their journey were faint concepts and ideas. She remembered that they'd travelled from a city, but she couldn't name it, nor could she properly describe what a city even *was.* She knew it only as a place where lots of people lived in close proximity- an exhilarating but frightening notion. Why would so many people want to be close to one another all the time?

When she thought back to that day, months and years later, she recalled those questions with perfect clarity, but no longer remem-bered her companion's face. Had the woman been young or old, or middle-aged? What colour had her hair been? Her eyes? Her skin? What had her voice sounded like? Imogen could recall none of those things, and that troubled her occasionally, because she felt certain it would one day be important that she *did* remember.

In the meantime, all she had was the urgent guidance with which her companion had left her- to say and share as little as possible.

She had adhered to those instructions. They were not difficult to obey.

But now they no longer mattered.

Imogen fled through the small hours of the night. Occasionally she took a detour and crossed streams and small rivers to confuse the trail, although surely no one followed. Shaya's body likely wouldn't be discovered until morning at the earliest, and Imogen reckoned it would be a while longer until her own disappearance was noted. For a moment she wondered uneasily if whatever had attacked and killed Shaya would come for her, but the fear passed. If it wanted to, she reasoned, then it could have done so in Greenwood.

She wondered again how she had remained so calm, almost detached, as she knelt by the Elder's ruined body. Shock, perhaps. Shock did that to people.

The moon rose high in the sky and stars glimmered in the gaps between trees. Small creatures scurried through the silvery undergrowth. Imogen slowed after a while, but still strode along with grim determination. She stopped at regular intervals, listening to the night but hearing nothing to cause worry.

Later she took a less well-trodden route where vegetation pressed close and dark on either side and knots of thick and thorny bramble attempted to thwart her progress. The moonlight remained good enough for Imogen to make her way along relatively unscathed, barely noticing the few scratches she sustained. She took care to step lightly around obstacles rather than cut a path through with her woodsknife. There was no sense in leaving obvious clues that someone had passed this way.

The girl rested only for a short while at first light. The day grew warm later that morning as she pressed on through the vastness of the Lower Faering. Later, she ate some of the provisions from Shaya's cottage, sitting on a boulder with her bare feet immersed in a stream, her boots put to one side. She listened to birdsong and the business of creatures in the undergrowth.

The vastness of the woodlands fascinated her. Very few people lived in this area, so it was possible to walk for many days through the Lower Faering and encounter no one. She would have liked to live here in the remote wilderness rather than Greenwood, but that would never be possible now.

Imogen finished eating and put her boots back on. With a sigh she slung her backpack over her shoulder and headed along the track as it curved gently between rows of tall larches. Old bracken and tangles of bramble rustled in the breeze, and ivy wound thickly around fallen trees and branches.

That afternoon, she came to a wide, slow-moving river, across which a series of large steppingstones had been placed. She squatted down on one of the larger and more stable rocks a third of the way across the river and refilled her water flask. At this point, she caught sight of her reflection in an area where the water was almost still, and the image stole her attention completely. Imogen felt a chill in her heart as the young woman in the water stared back at her. Behind the reflection's green eyes, something mad and depraved lurked, a creature capable of cruelty beyond measure.

Something that had been locked away inside her for a long time.

Had she done something terrible? Was that why she couldn't remember anything of her early childhood? Had someone placed her under a spell to cloud her memory?

"I'm not like that," Imogen whispered. "Go away." She disturbed the reflection with her hand.

Trembling, she corked her water flask and almost ran across the remaining stones, tears falling down her cheeks to be whipped away in the breeze.

That night, as she slept some distance from the path in a small clearing surrounded by thick tangleweed, Imogen dreamed she was at Shaya's cottage, but *outside* it. She half-ran, half-flew around the building like a fractious spirit, pausing only to stare through the windows, where inexplicably she saw herself sitting with Shaya.

The girl knew this was impossible, and she must be dreaming. And yet she also knew a terrible truth hid within this strange nightmare.

As she circled the cottage, Imogen looked down at herself and saw only a shadow. She glanced up into the sky. For a moment the stars appeared wrongly oriented. When she looked again, they shifted into familiar constellations.

Then she heard herself speak.

Inside the cottage, in the company of the Elder she uttered words that she could understand. But out in the cold night, came a breath-less jumble of sounds. Her speech became quicker, until she no longer lurked outside the warded cottage- *warded against such as me!* Imogen heard herself savagely exclaim- but *inside,* able to reach...

She woke suddenly with a faint cry. Sweat prickled her brow and her heart thumped madly.

Even as she hurried along in the cool morning air, the images from her dream would not let her be.

VIII

Five days later, Imogen stood on the threshold of that empty, ruined land, the Barrens. Before her, the ground fell away steeply towards an arid landscape where tufts of grass and withered bushes formed the only vegetation. The desolate scene stretched away into the distance, dotted in a few places with the sad and crumbling remains of ancient settlements.

Imogen sat for a while with her legs dangling over the edge of the slope. The breeze sighed faintly. If any creatures lived here, they hid themselves well.

Perhaps they came out at night when the air cooled.

She took an apple from her pack, ate most of it and then stared thoughtfully at the core. Food would be difficult to come by in the Barrens. Maybe she should have picked a few more apples, but they were heavy, and the season had grown warm again in the last few days. With no cover from the sky, the days would be warmer still and not pleasant for carrying a heavy pack.

Imogen took out her flask of water and tried to calculate how long its contents might last if she drank sparingly. She reckoned six or seven days, which might be long enough to reach Gharaan.

She kept the apple core rather than discard it and leave evidence that someone had passed this way. Then she drank some water and retraced her steps to the last rivulet she had crossed to top up her flask before walking back.

Imogen reckoned it might be more dangerous to sleep at night in the Barrens. Better to walk by moonlight if she could, then find the safest, shadiest place to sleep during the day.

The sun descended, its colour deepening as it sank into the western haze. Parts of the uneven slope into the Barrens already lay in deep shadow. Imogen took a deep breath and decided that even if it wasn't safer to travel by night, it would certainly be cooler. She clambered carefully down the slope, zigzagging her way through the loose dirt and scree. By the time she reached the flat land below, a bluish-grey dusk hung over everything. The silence felt almost intimidating.

A dirt track led south-east through the dusty wilderness and Imogen decided to follow it. Stark remnants of dead trees and ruined buildings occasionally loomed, murky and impossibly strange, their shapes monstrous and yet mournful.

Stars emerged in the darkening sky as the temperature dropped further. The moon had risen, so her way would soon become better-lit as it ascended and brightened. Imogen pulled her cloak more tightly about herself and walked resolutely onwards, concentrating on the arid, dusty ground ahead as she picked up her pace a little. The only sounds were her faint footsteps and steady breaths. She might have been the only person left in the entire world.

She would break down her journey by increments and stages. Wasn't that the way to approach seemingly insurmountable challenges?

As she rested later, Imogen looked up at the stars and silently recalled their names, along with the constellations they formed. In the east the reddish Bloodhunters glowed, three sullen lights that formed a triangle in an otherwise sparsely populated part of the heavens. High in the sky she observed the glimmer of Kingslight, a bright white star and a near-constant throughout the year. In the western sky, at a low elevation just above the remains of the gloaming, the blue-tinged Herald Twins glittered. Their faint light would grow as the last dark yellow scraps of sunset faded.

As she named each pattern and the stars that shaped it, Imogen listened intently to the soft night breeze sighing around the broken landscape. She couldn't recall ever seeking the company of others, but the sheer emptiness of this place preyed on her mind.

The boulder on which she sat grew uncomfortable. The girl shifted herself and had almost decided to sleep in a corner in one of the nearby ruins, when she heard faint footsteps.

The hunting knife found its way into her hand in a heartbeat. She stood and looked around in every direction, blood pounding in her ears.

A ruined tower stood on the other side of the track. The sound had come from there, she reckoned.

Full of misgiving, Imogen backed away and turned, intending to flee, her pack already slung over her shoulder.

A man stood in her way.

Imogen darted to one side and ran, intent on nothing more than putting enough distance between herself and this stranger. Adrenaline coursed through her. She was younger, faster. She could outrun him.

Then, inexplicably, her legs collapsed from under her.

Imogen cried out in disbelief, scrambled to her feet and realised that the man had already caught up with her. His lined, lean face creased with effort or pain, and beads of sweat prickled his brow.

"*Don't,*" he hissed, speaking in Theyan. "I'm here to help you. I was sent here..."

Imogen swore at him and brandished her knife, but he seized her arm so powerfully that she dropped the weapon. "Be *still,*" he repeated, and she blinked in bewilderment at the intense look in his eyes. "Are you alone?" he demanded.

Imogen felt a sudden presence- a shifting, subtle thing, without any true form, an unseen creature that moved like a shadow through her brain. She opened her mouth in terror, madly certain that she was about to split in half.

The stranger opened his mouth to speak again, but a confused look entered his eyes.

He collapsed without another word.

Imogen dared not move. She could run, no matter that she still felt as weak as a new-born fawn. Yet she remained where she stood, staring at the unconscious stranger.

Would he wake and come after her?

Was he even alive?

She breathed in the cold night air and stared at the unmoving body lying in the dust. After a moment she saw the faint rise and fall of his chest under the tattered cloak. Slit his throat and be done with it, she urged herself. If she didn't, he would come for her again.

Imogen found her knife nearby and picked it up. She stared for an age at the man's neck, then cursed in frustration. Against her better judgment she couldn't kill him in cold blood.

Why had he pursued her and then simply collapsed? Was he ill?

It dawned on her how few men she had met in the Faering. Traders and peddlers would come to Greenwood occasionally, if the *faer* allowed them to pass through the Lower Faering on their way to other places, but they tended to be few and far between. Had she ever spoken to a man during her time in the Faering? Imogen didn't think she had.

As far as she knew, she might *never* have met a man properly before.

To her bemusement, the sky had started to grow lighter in the east. How could the night have passed already?

She put her knife back in her belt and quietly picked up her pack. She was about to steal away when the man stirred, and his eyes flickered open. Imogen took a few hasty steps back and watched apprehensively as he struggled awake. He coughed and rolled over onto his side to face her, grunting in pain.

Imogen took another few steps back. "Don't come after me. I'll kill you."

His weary grey eyes fixed on hers and he grimaced in pain. "I was sent to find you."

"I don't even know who you are. Who could have sent you?"

"Your mother."

IX

Imogen ran a hand through her hair, unable to find any words. "I don't know you," she repeated at last. "I'm leaving. Don't try to follow me."

Her courage rose as she observed his weakened condition. The man was clearly in no fit state to pursue her, and if he did then she'd put an end to him. He looked pathetic in the pale dawn light, a husk of a creature.

"Anyway, I don't have a mother," she heard herself say, almost as if she wanted him to say otherwise.

"You most certainly do."

Imogen gave him a quizzical look and pulled her cloak about herself.

"Your name is Imogen. You were taken to the Faering when you were ten. You remember that much, yes?"

She nodded warily.

"Anything from before that time?"

"No."

He looked strangely relieved. "Just as well. The Faering was meant to be a safe place for you, somewhere your enemies wouldn't think to look." He slowly sat up and watched as Imogen's hand stole to her hunting knife once again. "I'll bet you're good with that."

"Good enough. How could you have known I'd be here?"

He managed a weak smile. "That will take a while to explain. In the meantime, can I ask that you *not* disembowel me with that knife?"

Imogen frowned. "I had thought a quick strike through the heart would be a better death," she said finally, and the man laughed weakly until a painful spasm stopped him. Imogen scowled, wondering why he had found the idea so amusing. "Disembowelment would be immensely painful. You would linger pointlessly in the dirt, and take a long time to die," she said by way of explanation.

He got unsteadily to his feet, grimacing, and extended a grubby hand. "My name is Arc Thendrin."

Imogen stared suspiciously at his hand until he withdrew it. "Are you ill?" she asked. "You collapsed last night. I could have killed you."

"Yes. Thank you for not killing me, Imogen."

She had no idea what to make of that.

"Well, I have much to tell you. Would you care for some breakfast?"

Imogen's stomach rumbled loudly in answer. "Maybe," she admitted.

Arc limped slowly back towards the tower, and Imogen followed cautiously. They walked around the ancient rubble to a corner between two walls where a backpack lay near a makeshift stove made from a metal grid placed over two piles of rocks. Kindling had been placed underneath, which Arc lit with some firepowder.

He sat and gestured for her to do the same. Imogen tried to make herself comfortable and watched as he took some wrapped meat- salted pig, she noted as she swallowed down the saliva that had flooded her mouth- and placed it over the fire. The meat hissed on the grid and Imogen's stomach growled again as her companion waited awhile and then turned the cuts to cook on the other side.

"Maybe it's better if you ask, and I answer you if I can," he said presently. "There are some things I can't tell you. But *she* might."

"All right. Start with what you said before. Why would you think I wasn't alone?"

"I just wanted to make sure."

Imogen felt certain he was lying but said nothing.

"Also, the women of the Lower Faering have ways of finding and bringing back those who... stray from the path, shall we say."

"I didn't stray from any path. I wanted to leave, so I left. That's all." Her own lie fell easily from her mouth, and she stared boldly at him.

"I suspect it's much the same to them."

"Do you think they'll come after me?"

"That," he remarked, "depends very much on how determined they are to find you. What do *you* think, Imogen?"

The girl shrugged and looked away.

"I set out from the town of Waters Green by the Greatwater when your mother told me that something had happened. She has... a sixth sense of sorts. She can explain it somewhat better than I can. It's taken me a week to get here."

"You mean she..." Imogen paused uncertainly. "Does she know *what* happened?"

"If she does, then she didn't see fit to tell me." Arc gave her a thoughtful look. "I'm sure the two of you can discuss it when you're reunited." He returned his attention to the grilled meat, which was almost done.

Imogen's unease grew. "My *mother*." She murmured the word. It felt and sounded odd to her. She couldn't recall ever having used the word before, although she had wondered about her past many times over the last seven years. "I don't remember anything about her. I don't even have a picture in my head of what she looks like. I can't recall anything before my journey to the Faering, and only a little about the journey."

"I know. She told me you wouldn't."

"What about *you*? Are you my father?"

His smile seemed oddly sad. "Me? I'm no one's father, Imogen."

When she ate the saltmeat and bread, Imogen's taste buds tingled so intensely it almost hurt. The meat was delicious, and the bread became a little softer and tasted better when it absorbed the juices.

Questions chased one another through her mind. Might the mysterious woman who gave her to the women of Greenwood have been paid by her mother? Did Arc know anything about her? She almost asked but resolved not to. The more she tried to find out about a past she couldn't remember, the more she might inadvertently reveal about herself.

And perhaps Arc didn't know as much about her as he made out.

"What are you?" she asked after a while. "I mean, are you a sellsword, or a tracker? A bounty hunter?"

In no hurry to answer, Arc finished his breakfast first and wiped his mouth with the sleeve of his cloak. "None of those things. I studied and trained with the Protectorate, in the city of Fort Cailan."

"You're a *Protector*?" Imogen had heard much about the Protectorate. From their stronghold in the far southern land of Anphay, they sought to defend Theya from outworlders, demonic creatures from other planes of existence that occasionally found their way into the world through means that no one properly understood.

The Protectorate governed Anphay and could also claim allies in much of Saanu and Wisteren, but in Gharaan, where the Church's power was greatest, they were viewed with open hostility. A widespread belief held that the Protectors were themselves demonic in nature, although the women of the Lower Faering had pointed out that the Church reckoned almost anything that didn't fit their ideology was demonic.

Wasn't Waters Green in Gharaan, though? Why would he have been there, with her mother?

As Arc began tidying his makeshift camp, Imogen tried to recall why the Church reviled the Protectorate so much. Finally, she remembered something from a long-ago lesson.

When they destroyed an outworlder, Protectors absorbed a small part of their enemy- an essence- into themselves. It was, apparently, the only way to be sure of their destruction, imprisoning a faint ghost or memory of that being with the Protector's body and mind as the prison. But the Protector had no choice in the matter. It had something to do with the swords they carried.

Imogen found herself thinking aloud. "Does it... is it... dangerous?"

He glanced at her. "Is what dangerous, Imogen?"

"Living with the ghosts of demons inside you," she said bluntly, not sure how else to describe it.

Then, when he failed to reply but instead merely stared back at her as if he hadn't heard- or worse, as if *something else* had heard- Imogen felt a moment of irrational but palpable fear, a cold reminder that her time alive was a short breath amidst eons and could be made shorter yet.

Arc slung his backpack over his shoulder. "Are you coming?"

"Or else what? You drag me all the way to the Greatwater?"

The Protector smiled thinly, then turned and limped away. Imogen watched his bedraggled shape and uncertain walk and wondered why, a moment ago, she had felt afraid of him.

But then, without having made a conscious decision either way, she followed. Arc must have heard her, but he said nothing, nor did he turn around.

X

Over the next few days as they headed south across the dismal landscape, Imogen's nervousness grew. Arc knew she hadn't told him everything about her leaving the Faering. She could see the mistrust in his eyes, not that he said anything on the matter.

No one could ever find out, Imogen decided. Ever.

Although wouldn't news of Shaya's demise eventually spread beyond the Lower Faering?

"One thing you must never do," Arc told her as they rested two evenings later in the moon-shadow of a rock pile, "is mention the Protectorate, or that I am a Protector, to anyone. Except your mother, who already knows."

"I wouldn't think to. Not in Gharaan."

"Good." Arc laid out his cloak for resting on. "Waters Green lies on the far shore of the Greatwater, near the foothills of the Spine. We'll go south over Hearts Crossing and walk along the south side of the river for a few days."

"Does she look like me?"

"Your mother? Yes. Her hair is a little shorter, but the colour is the same. You have the same green eyes as her." Arc's voice had grown softer. He gave her an apprehensive look. "Are you beginning to remember?"

Imogen shrugged. "I'm not sure. I just have a picture of her in my head now. That's all it is. A picture. I don't know if it's true or not."

"The spell begins to break," Arc said ominously.

The Protector's behaviour grew odd at times, especially when they rested each evening. He would berate himself and even struck the side of his head hard with the palm of his hand twice. Sometimes he whispered words that Imogen couldn't quite make out.

One evening, just after dusk he quietly counted the stars over and over, frustrated every time he lost track.

That same evening, he fell asleep abruptly after they ate their meal, then woke up sobbing a short while later, seemingly oblivious to Imogen staring at him.

She said nothing. What was there to say? She was no stranger to bad dreams.

Arc turned away, revealing nothing of whatever terror gripped him.

As they rested on the fourth day of their journey together, Imogen and Arc sat in the sun-shadow of a crumbling sandstone wall. A light breeze stirred the dust, blowing it this way and that across the faded track.

"What happened here?" Imogen asked.

The Protector gave her an odd look. "What do you mean?"

She gestured to the surrounding desert, the scattered ruins of distant buildings and a deep rift in the ground nearby. They had been forced to take a long detour around two of those already. "All of this. The Barrens. Why would land so close to the Faering be so... *dead*, when the Faering itself is so full of life? I've heard stories about a battle of great magics that was fought, many centuries ago, when this land was called Caian."

"Yes. That's why it's like this. Dead, as you so eloquently put it. Eventually, the corruption seeped through everything here. Nothing could stop it. Over time, the Barrens became what you see now. Barren."

"Who fought this battle?"

"That depends on which history books you read. As you can imagine, no one wants the blame." His eyes held a faraway look. "It should be a useful lesson, this desert- about our impermanence, our precarious place in a finely balanced world. But people prefer not to learn."

XI

The Protector found that the faint but persistent shades of long vanquished outworlders were especially agitated that night. They could not communicate and were not even alive in a way that anyone understood, but Imogen's presence had stirred them into a state of fervour- or whatever substituted for that, given that they were only shadows, imprints of what they had once been.

Arc had not known what manner of demons they were when he vanquished them many years ago. He hadn't known or cared what realm they had torn their way through from, focused only on their annihilation. He barely remembered what they looked like, other than blurs of savage darkness.

But these shades were proof that some things were a paradox, living on- or at least, lingering faintly- even after their destruction.

The Protectorate believed that the greater part of outworlders was sent to the Great Burning, that desolate afterworld with neither beginning nor end, even as a smaller part of the demon- the imprint or *faintness* as some called it- lingered in the minds of those who slew them. The Protectorate believed so mainly because many of the *faer* races did, and Anphayans shared many *faer* beliefs. A few of their more overt customs persisted even now in the more far-flung corners of Anphay. Bloodletting rituals still occurred in Westport and Witherport during the dim winter months when the sun barely rose at all. The River Nights, they were called, and the rivers were not made of water.

Tonight, the faintness was not so faint.

It stirred and roiled in Arc's head, and he had no recourse to any way of stilling it. He dared not use his remaining quickdust tonight and leave nothing for the remaining journey.

He lay in silence and fancied that a translation of the shades' thoughts whispered through his inner darkness.

It runs in her. She meets the ocean, becomes the ocean.

To taste it! To dream of those places. She has roots in worlds.

Can she see us? Does she know us?

Do we know her?

The blood, at least, is known.

Arc tolerated the whispers and the nonsense for hours. Somehow the shadows of dead demons reacted to the wild magic that ran through Imogen's blood, a power that Alianne herself had said was considerably more potent than her own. Even Arc sensed a violent darkness to her.

I'm afraid of Imogen as much as for *her,* Alianne had confessed before he left. *But she's my only flesh and blood. It's time for her to be at my side again. Anywhere else is too dangerous, now.*

How much would you forgive her? he had asked, immediately wishing he hadn't.

Anything, to my shame, Alianne had admitted.

Pensively he glanced across at Imogen's sleeping form, but that made the mutterings of his ghostly inhabitants faster and more urgent than ever. Finally, he turned on his side, directly away from the object of their interest, and focused on the visible constellations.

Their babble dropped to a murmur. The outworlder shadows had never liked the stars for some reason.

Arc wondered if that might be because there were no stars in the Great Burning.

The landscape began to change as Imogen and Arc continued south. After three more days, just when Imogen decided she could no longer bear this dreary, dusty land, it slowly petered out into rough scrub which in turn gave way to open plain over the next day. The land became steadily greener, and soon they walked through pasture and past secluded woodlands. They had, Imogen realised, crossed an unmarked border into Gharaan.

"Where are you from?" she asked when they rested later to eat.

"Far away." Arc made a vague gesture towards the south. "A village in the south-west of Anphay. Not somewhere you or anyone else has heard of."

"I haven't been back in many years," he added. "Nothing to go back to. Cold place, dark winters, little to do but get into trouble."

"So where do you live now, when you're not travelling?"

"Wherever your mother and I agree we should go next." He gave her a considering look. "This sudden interest in me is very flattering, Imogen."

"I'm just making conversation," she said bluntly.

"Keep working on that." Arc finished the last of his luncheon, stood up, slung his pack over his shoulder and set off. Imogen hurried after him, wondering why whenever she asked the man a question about himself, his answer seemed only to create more questions.

With the failing of the light, clouds from the distant Spine mountains approached from the south, bringing rain. The down-pour soon grew heavy, and they took shelter in a copse of birch and aspen.

"We'll wait until the morning. It'll be too dark to continue even if the rain eases," Arc said as they made themselves as comfortable as possible.

Imogen nodded tiredly. After a short while she slumped slowly to one side so her head rested on his shoulder. "Would that I could sleep so easily," Arc remarked quietly a while later as he listened to her steady breaths.

"Hmm," Imogen murmured in her sleep.

Arc listened to the sound of the rain in the canopy above. He let his thoughts drift. As often happened, they gravitated towards the peculiarity of his ongoing duty- defending the last surviving women of the Omerian bloodline.

What made him special? Nothing. Ceiran of Witherport, leader of the Protectorate, had assigned the mission to him because he had no one else to assign it to. Arc should not have attained the status of Protector- he had not passed his training, but Ceiran had kept him anyway, and given him his rank. Arc owed him, and he had been repaying the First Protector for the last seven years in the form of this task.

A mission that ran contrary to everything the Protectorate stood for. Were it to be discovered, the entire matter would be viewed as treachery.

Arc had always been an outsider, grateful for the support Ceiran had initially offered during his difficult initiation. So grateful, per-haps, that he hadn't guessed a price would need to be paid. Inevita-bly, he became caught in a web from which escape was impossible. Ceiran emmeshed Arc in matters that would have meant a swift death sentence at the hands of the Protectorate's Grand Assembly, if they found out what he was doing.

In short, he had taken Arc under his wing and into his hell.

The First Protector had not expressly forbidden Arc and Alianne from complicating an already dangerous relationship, but Arc often wondered if Ceiran knew they had become lovers not long after meeting. It was likely. What *didn't* the man know?

And yet he had kept Arc immersed in this treacherous duty, for his own reasons.

Sometime during the small hours of the night, The Protector woke the girl up so she could keep watch and fell asleep. It was a risk he must take, until they reached Alianne.

"You begged forgiveness in your sleep," Imogen commented when he woke sometime after dawn. "Who needs to forgive you?"

They hadn't walked far the following morning before the land sloped gradually downwards towards the Greatwater- a vast, wide river across which many bridges had been built, some narrow and precarious, others wide and grand with tall arches. Small settlements huddled on both sides of the water, and beyond the far shore, the land swiftly rose into craggy mountainsides where villages and some lone homesteads nestled against the lower slopes. Imogen's gaze did not have to wander far before she noticed forbidding snow-capped peaks that sheltered deep, shadowy chasms.

Arc pointed towards the water. "We'll cross soon. Are you tired?"

"No. I could walk forever if I had to."

She felt ready to drop.

They continued their gradual descent into the wide river valley. The sky remained gloomy, and a few spots of rain fell. Boats of many shapes and sizes dotted the vast river, some navigating the breadth of the water to ferry people or goods while others headed upstream or downstream. Most carried cargo but one appeared to be a passenger vessel, heading slowly up the river with a hundred or more people visible on its two main decks and no doubt more inside.

As Arc and Imogen drew near to the settlements along the riverbank it became obvious just how busy these places were. Imogen found the sheer number of people and the scale of activity almost overwhelming. She remembered almost nothing of towns and crowds and merely looking at so many people made her feel nauseous.

Imogen followed Arc as he threaded his way between groups of travellers, trader stalls and wagons loading or offloading crates to be sent on boats or taken to locations on the near side of the river. Finally, they reached a port area for smaller vessels. Arc spoke quietly with a man who appeared to be overseeing proceedings, and something small and shiny passed between them. Imogen guessed it was a coin, perhaps like those the women of Greenwood sometimes used when traders came to the village.

They headed for a sailing vessel moored next to the quayside. People queued to make their cautious way along a rope bridge from the quayside onto the boat, clutching at the sides as it swayed. "Have you been on a boat before?" Arc asked.

"No. Maybe. I don't know." Imogen glanced at the water, but only for a moment. "I can swim. I've swam in rivers and lakes."

"Let's hope you don't need to prove it." Arc set off along the rope bridge when it came to their turn, and Imogen followed, holding on even more tightly.

XII

As the boat negotiated the width of the Greatwater, Arc wrestled with troubling questions.

A whisper, not even a thought, flitted across his mind like a shadow, a familiar stain. One of the outworlders had stirred- if the mental imprint of a dead beast could stir. Like the others, it sensed the presence of Imogen's wild, unfulfilled magic and reacted to it, blind and unknowing but still possessed of a certain primitive thirst. This was not unexpected, after the last several days of cacophony in his head.

With Imogen distracted by the passing scenery, Arc closed his eyes and lightly touched the hilt of his sword- a blade forged in the

White Fire, the ancient gift to Anphay from the *faer*, given longer ago than most Theyan realms had been in existence. All Protectors' blades were born in that mystical heat. All reacted to the presence of outworlders. If any lurked nearby, he would soon know.

Even in his younger days, there had been three other occasions where he had survived only because of another Protector's intervention. Better if he never saw an outworlder again, for even a lone one would easily best him now. His wits remained sharp- when he wasn't under the quickdust- but physically he was long past his peak.

In any case, the main danger to Alianne was other Protectors, not outworlders.

It was, after all, a sect within the Protectorate that had, twelve years ago, tried to assassinate both mother and daughter.

He had met Alianne only days after she had Imogen sent away. Ceiran had arranged for a woman with substantial powers to take Imogen to the Faering and do whatever was needed to fade the girl's memory of the traumatic separation from her mother. *Dark days they were,* he thought. Alianne had not been afforded the luxury of forgetting.

And seven years later...

Alianne had sensed that something had happened to Imogen- some momentous change that meant she would leave the Faering. Many Omerians down the ages had harboured a powerful ability to tell if something happened to their children, wherever they might be in the world, so Arc had been troubled but not entirely surprised. Alianne hadn't known which way Imogen would go, of course- but she reckoned her daughter would choose to come towards Gharaan, and she had been right. It was the safest direction, after all.

For their safety Arc and Alianne seldom travelled together unless they were moving from one town to another, so Alianne had reluctantly asked Arc to make the journey alone. As he hastened north towards the Barrens, Arc doubted Alianne would be anywhere near prepared for Imogen's return. At best, their reunion would be complicated, but it could easily be far worse.

However, something else worried him far more and had done since the night he found Imogen.

Why had the shades reacted so strongly as to make him pass out when he encountered her? That troubled him more than anything else. No matter the power of the Omerian blood, she wasn't an outworlder.

It made no sense.

He turned to Imogen as the boat's captain brought the vessel carefully alongside the far shore and the passengers prepared to disembark. "Are you ready?"

The girl turned and gave him a haughty look, picked up her pack and slung it over her shoulder. "How much further?"

"Waters Green is a couple of days' walk from here. I did tell you."

"Maybe you should find us a couple of horses. I can ride."

Arc shook his head. "I don't know how much silver you think I have, Imogen, but it isn't enough to buy *half* a horse, let alone two. If I can walk the distance, you certainly can."

They left the waterside and joined a track that followed the river east. The path ascended gradually until they 1were considerably higher than the Greatwater's placid flow. Arc needed to rest a few times during the afternoon, although Imogen barely broke sweat. At one point she stood with hands on hips and watched him as he sat on a rocky outcrop to get his breath back. "Why *you*?" she wondered aloud.

Arc gave a wry smile as he stared down into the valley. "No one else was available."

As the afternoon began to darken, they came to a place where tall stones stood in circles above and below the level of the path and cast long, thin shadows in the late sun. Some of these monoliths stood as high as two men. Imogen stopped and observed the scene as if she saw something that Arc couldn't. "I don't like this place," she declared.

Arc nodded. "No one likes this place."

"What is it?"

"Its name is Manlin Har. The stones mark places of burial from long-ago millennia. Some say the place is haunted, but the way east cuts through it and has for centuries, so..." He shrugged. "There was always a road. Even back then."

Imogen's intense stare did not waver. "Who placed them here?"

Her behaviour had started to set Arc on edge. "Let's go. It's getting dark. There's a village with an inn not far ahead. With luck we can eat and rest there for the night."

As she looked at him Arc saw something dark move across her right eye and then her left, like a tiny black flame. For a moment, he genuinely feared for his life. His right hand strayed to the pommel of his sword, but his companion appeared not to notice.

"Good. I'm hungry," Imogen said at last, and strode past him along the path.

XIII

That evening, Imogen lay in a bed for the first time since fleeing Greenwood. As she waited for sleep, she was startled to find she could recall fragments of her journey to the Faering seven years ago-episodes other than the last few conversations with her companion.

Shadows leapt all around, but worse than that, they were inside her. Everything had grown dark. She had begun to change into something else, something that had to do with her blood, her family, and a dreadful secret that they all knew about, but no one dared speak of.

Somehow it was worse for her than anyone before.

She cried out, or tried to, but she no longer had a voice.

A hand reached out, the last light in the world. Imogen seized it and held fast, as if by letting go she might drown. "Have hope," came a whisper through the gloom. But Imogen's fear had taken a complete hold, and darkness filled every part of her.

Then, a blinding, savage light cut through it, and agony so intense that Imogen's voice suddenly returned, and she screamed.

Her eyes flickered open, and she saw the face of a grey-eyed, dark-haired woman looming over her. "Uelene," she whispered as the pain and the light dissipated.

Uelene was not old, but her eyes seemed ancient.

"What am I?" Imogen whispered, and Uelene's look changed to something else- sympathy? "You're special. Your mother told you so, didn't she?"

"Yes. She did," Imogen recalled.

"Your power can feed on fear and become a dark thing, full of despair and hatred- or it can nurture the love that you feel and amplify those feelings- and then it becomes a true wonder."

"But why..." Ten-year-old Imogen struggled to understand. "Why would it do that to me? I was being eaten from the inside out... no, it was worse than that, I became something else, something terrible!"

"It fed on your fears." Uelene squeezed her hand gently. "Your sadness and anger at being parted from your mother. Your fear of travelling through strange places with someone you barely know. The magic feasts on those things. It becomes stronger, but not in a good way."

"What can I do about it?" Imogen asked in a small voice.

Uelene smiled sadly. "Only try not to let those bad feelings overwhelm you. I will help. By the time we get to where we're going, it will all be locked away."

"Will I ever see her again?"

"I won't lie to you, Imogen. Maybe you will, maybe you won't. It's not for me to say. I have no visions of the future, nor do I want any." Uelene picked up her backpack and slung it over her shoulder. *"We've a way to go today, and then we'll rest in a town overlooking the Greatwater tonight."*

"Will I get a proper bed?" Imogen suddenly felt more hopeful.

Uelene's laughter made her smile. "Yes, my love. You'll get a proper bed."

"A proper bed," Imogen murmured, touching both sides of the soft mattress. She shivered, sensing that something inexplicable had gone full circle, and yet it was only a circle of events inside something greater, more complex.

Now she remembered that day clearly. Soft rain fell. The air held the warmth of late summer. The Greatwater stretched away west before them, snaking its way from Saanu. Eventually, their path upriver would take them through wild lands, towards the Faering.

And there she had stayed for seven years. "Part of me was locked away," Imogen told herself. "But it found me again."

She fell asleep imagining ripples made by raindrops in a deep, black-watered lake.

The following morning, Arc and Imogen breakfasted at the inn and set off along the village's single, dusty track with the sun newly risen and a cool breeze at their backs. Imogen had little to say, and Arc spent much of the day lost in his own worries.

The Protector could barely hide his relief when he saw Waters Green in the distance just as the light began to fail. Despite the chill in the air, he had begun to sweat, and several times during the day a scratchy discomfort had washed over him.

He had taken his last pinch of quickdust the other night. But he would buy some tonight. He deserved that much.

"Is that Waters Green?" Imogen asked.

"It is. Hurry and we'll get there before dark. Wear the hood of your robe up."

"Why?"

"Just do it."

Dusk had fallen when they finally arrived at the town gates. They headed along one of the main thoroughfares towards the Gate and Star Inn where Arc and Alianne were staying, stopping by a fountain in the central town square to drink some water. Then they pressed on into the western quarter and up a cobbled hill to the inn, hurrying through the fading light. The Protector had quickened his step almost without realising.

Imogen, meanwhile, drank in the sights and sounds calmly, although her wide eyes and silence said as much as any words could.

Although not especially busy, the bar room of the tavern was heavy with smoke so acrid and pungent it made their eyes sting. Imogen hurried after Arc towards a door at the rear, and the bartender looked up from his mopping and tidying to give them a distracted glance as they walked past. Imogen had the good sense to keep her hood pulled well over her head and looked neither left nor right as she followed the Protector through the doorway and up a creaking flight of wooden stairs beyond. She had fallen completely silent. Arc tried to think of words that might help but couldn't.

Get it over with, he told himself. *Always best in situations like this.*

The Gate and Star was not the cleanest establishment in the town, but they hadn't the funds for one of the better taverns in the South Hill area. The walls and stairs here were sticky with grease and an odour made of many unpalatable smells- cooking fats, smokeweed and sweat chief amongst them- hung in the gloomy air. Arc decided that when his allowance arrived, he would try to find them somewhere better. It didn't need to be palatial, but neither he nor Alianne slept well listening to the scurrying of rats.

He knocked on a door halfway along the gloomy landing- first once, then a pause, then three times, then a pause, and finally twice- a sequence he and Alianne had agreed longer ago than he could remember. After a short while bolts were drawn back on the other side. Arc opened the door and stepped through followed by an increasingly hesitant Imogen.

The room into which they stepped was almost completely dark, but its occupant lit a couple of lanterns as Arc softly closed the door behind them and bolted it again. To his surprise, Imogen's hand clutched his own as soon as she saw her mother.

Alianne's blonde hair cascaded past her shoulders as she regarded them by the flickering lamplight. Arc was shocked to see how frightened she looked.

"Imogen," she murmured finally. "I have so much to tell you. And so much to explain."

The girl appeared to be lost for words. Her grip on Arc's hand tightened, until she realised what she had done and quickly let go.

"Imogen, this is your mother." Arc spoke softly, almost reverently. "Queen Alianne of Asqabal."

XIV

Queen..." Imogen stared wide-eyed at Arc. Then she looked into her mother's green eyes. They looked so much like her own. Ought she feel something? In this moment, she simply felt numb. She couldn't remember her properly, even now that she could see her mother's face.

Looking upon Alianne was not unlike looking into a mirror that showed an older version of herself. The candlelight made her mother look almost soft, gentle- yet a hardness, a pain lurked in her eyes.

"So." Alianne's voice shook slightly. "How much do you remember?"

"Some things," Imogen said uncomfortably. "A little more only last night. But I still barely remember you. And I don't know *anything* about you being... I mean... that means I..." She shook her head in bewilderment.

"I was told that the effects of the spell would eventually fall away. You'll recall everything in time. Some of it will be painful." Alianne appeared lost for words for a moment. "Look at you," she said at last, her voice breaking. "You were a little girl, and now you're all but a grown woman."

Imogen shrugged, embarrassed. What could she say to that?

"I need to explain why you were sent away. I wish beyond anything that I could have kept you with me, but the Protectorate were closing in on us. I did what I could to give you the best chance of survival."

"They didn't find you."

"No, by nothing more than luck. But I couldn't take that risk with you. I had to send you away. Do you understand?"

"You sent a *Protector* to find me."

"And I will try to explain that too. The Protectorate has long been an enemy of our family, Imogen, with a couple of notable exceptions. Many amongst them say we should be erased from the world."

"Why? What have we done to them?"

Alianne's smile was wintry. "You and I? Nothing. But our ancestors fought them many times over the centuries when they tried to bring ruin to our land. Our family, on the maternal side, has a powerful magic in its blood. Occasionally it runs wild. The Protectorate, who value order above all else, think of us as little better than outworlders, demons from the void."

A fleeting image flashed through Imogen's mind, of something dark and shapeless circling through the woods, of her own self seeing through its eyes even as she sat in Shaya's house.

She had been invited in.

That was Shaya's undoing, came a whisper from somewhere.

She wanted to ask: *Is it a magic that kills?*

"It enabled some of our ancestors to become great, even legendary, kings and queens of Asqabal. But the same blood-gift causes mayhem whenever it manifests in someone of weak will and a malleable nature. This has meant poor relations with Anphay, where the Protectorate rule, but also Wisteren and the western regions of Saanu, where the *faer* are strong. The *faer* are no friends of ours either, for much the same reason. Our gift comes not from the world itself, as theirs does, but from..." Alianne paused. A shadow seemed to cross her face. "I'll explain it to you as best I can, but it will take time. And you won't like what you hear."

Imogen thought for a moment. "I don't understand. If the *faer* are our enemies, why send me to their land?"

"Where better to hide you than in plain sight, in a place where we would never dare go? The cloaking spell created by Uelene hid your nature, so I took a calculated risk. If they discovered your nature and denied you passage into the Faering..." Alianne shrugged wearily. "Uelene had been instructed to take you elsewhere if that happened."

"A calculated risk." Imogen uttered the phrase slowly. "With my *life.*"

"I expect you remember something of her..."

"Yes. Where is she now? I would like to see her."

"I have no idea where she went, Imogen. She returned only to give me the name of the village that took you in, and I neither saw nor heard from her again."

Alianne continued quietly, "You and I have lived as fugitives, one way or another, for twelve years- since the night when Protectorate assassins, likely aided by treacherous forces within the palace in Char, attacked us in our home. We fled and have been in hiding since then. The Court of the Sentai, headed by the Court Leader and the Chancellor, have ruled Asqabal in my absence."

Imogen sat in the nearest chair, her thoughts whirling so much that Alianne's words barely registered. "You made me forget who I was!"

"Yes. You had to forget the life you had, until the time was right for you to remember. If the women of the Faering decided to interrogate you, they would discover nothing. And what could you possibly run back to, if you remembered nothing of the life you'd left?"

Imogen could only stare in astonishment.

"Days ago, I felt a disturbance- a sixth sense, some would call it- making me certain that something important had happened to you. I knew there and then that you'd left the Faering. But *why*?"

"There's nothing to tell." Imogen knew immediately that her tone was too guarded, and she looked away.

"You always were a poor liar, Imogen." Alianne's voice became quieter, and she took a few tentative steps towards her daughter. "Whatever it is, you can tell me. There is nothing I won't forgive. But I must know what happened."

Imogen willed herself to look boldly back at her. "If you must know, I decided I was old enough to make my own way in the world. I'd put up with their backward ways, their rules, for long enough. I'd wanted to leave for months. I never felt as if I belonged there-

and now I know why. I decided to come this way- into Gharaan. But then I met Arc, in the Barrens, and he said you'd sent him to find me."

"The women of the Faering don't allow those invited to live in their communities, those who have spent years amongst them, to leave without so much as an explanation or an excuse."

"I didn't tell them I was leaving."

Alianne and Arc exchanged glances, and Arc gave a small, grim shake of the head. Imogen desperately tried to change the subject. "What do you have planned for me?" she blurted out. "Now that I'm here?"

For a fleeting moment Alianne looked taken aback. "None of this was planned, Imogen. We will look after you..."

"I don't need *looking after*. Your chance to do that has gone. I don't know you. I can't even speak more than a few words of Asqabalese. I only recall fragments that don't make sense. I remember *Uelene* better than I remember you."

Alianne flinched at that. "Well, it's the truth," Imogen added uncomfortably, "and I never asked for this."

Silence filled the room for a short while. "I am not going to argue with you," Alianne said finally. "Not tonight, when you've just come back to me. But I *will* do whatever it takes to keep you safe."

"I can do that myself. And if I misspoke, it's because I have no idea what else to say. Did you expect me to rush back into your arms like a little girl?"

"Hardly," Alianne said quietly.

"Why are you still hiding? Why haven't you returned to reclaim the throne?"

"This anonymous existence is safer. Enemies are everywhere even in the city of Char. Agents of the Protectorate, and many of the more self-serving lords and ladies in the Court of the Sentai. Things have changed since we left."

To Imogen's surprise, Alianne turned to Arc. "You can go now." Imogen noticed a strange expression in her mother's eyes- displeasure or disgust? Anger?

"Are you sure?" Arc looked pensively at Imogen.

"Yes. Go."

"Well," Alianne said a little later as Arc's footfall on the creaking stairs faded into silence. "Where do we even begin?"

XV

Ichaan pressed himself against the smooth granite tiles in a gesture of subservience. Bone and flesh readjusted itself as needed until he lay almost flat against the surface- his subtle way of expressing his power even as he obeyed protocol. The unyielding chill met the natural heat of his *xyrral* form implacably, a barrier beyond even him.

The Sentai Court Leader, Emar Naii, stood as near as he dared to the dark stone and metal throne. Asqabal's ancient seat of power could not be so much as touched by anyone without Omerian blood flowing in their veins. Over the dozen years of corruption and incompetence since the disappearance of the Queen and her daughter, a few of the Sentai lords had nurtured the persuasive idea that they might overcome the implacable, terrible power of the throne, and had, apparently with the aid of men and women who claimed to be sorcerers, tried to sit upon it. In doing so and surviving, they would make themselves valid and absolute ruler of the realm, or at least a contestant for that title. In their greed they put aside the inconvenient fact that Asqabalese history was littered with failed attempts to do the same. Ichaan knew his history and had learned the story of Asqabal's royal bloodline- and the pretenders who had perished attempting to disrupt it.

If the rumours were to be believed, the most recent fools had each turned to fine ash. It would have been some unfortunate servant's fate to brush the area clear of that perfect deconstruction each time. Ichaan marvelled at the utter lack of logic that compelled landed lords and ladies to repeat that mistake, as if they had convinced themselves they were somehow different, better than their peers, able to withstand the violent power of the throne.

Even Ichaan found himself drawn to it whenever he happened to be nearby. Granite and mica twisted and ran in patterns interspersed with untreated black iron that never rusted. Great barbs of stone and metal sprang from this impossible chaos, at the places where hands might rest, and likewise where shoulders might lean back.

This was not a seat of any comfort, nor was it designed to be.

Ichaan permitted himself a secret smile as his face pressed against the cold stone. Sometimes, especially in the small nuances, the Sentai were entirely predictable. Their lust for power could not be entirely sated, and as with all privileged human men and women, greed blindsided them.

"Rise," Emar commanded him.

The *xyrral* smoothly obeyed. His arms shortened a little and his legs, tucked beneath him, sank a little way through his humanlike torso. Ichaan let out the faintest sigh of pleasure at the subtle change. If Emar heard him then he chose to ignore the sound. Like all the landed lords and ladies of Asqabal, he could not sense shapechanging of such subtlety, an ability that less than one tenth of the *xyrral* possessed.

His gaze shifted to the two guards standing in the shadows further back in the room- effectively the Sentai lord's protectors. Asqabal's self-appointed custodians did not trust their *xyrral* partners-why would they? And yet they used them and employed them for numerous reasons. The *xyrral* were their commodity, Ichaan reminded himself, and had been for too long.

But it would not always be so.

These two wore the grey and blue uniforms of the Towerblades, the special regiment of guardsmen whose role had once been the defence of the Queen and her family. They had failed abjectly in that when Protectorate assassins attacked on that bloody day twelve years ago. The Towerblades had never truly shrugged off the taint of shame.

And yet the Sentai kept them even now, along with most other traditions from the Omerian era.

"We have a matter of some urgency," Emar told him, aged hands holding either side of his robe. "One that requires great speed."

"You need me to fly somewhere?" That much was obvious.

"Yes. We also require the utmost secrecy to be maintained."

"Naturally." When had they not?

"Let me come straight to the point. After all these years, we may have found a way to locate our Queen at last."

Ichaan blinked in surprise. He hadn't thought the Sentai lords were even that concerned about looking for their Queen anymore, too beaten down by their own struggle to govern, and mired in corruption of their own making.

Emar tossed something to the *xyrral.* Ichaan caught it neatly. It was a necklace, set with a single black stone, and he immediately identified it as nightglass. A mineral not often used in jewellery, because of its unstable nature, but the Omerians had worn nightglass items for centuries.

"That necklace belonged to her," Emar told him. "It was left here along with most of her other belongings. It has been locked away in the Observatory along with other selected items, and monitored regularly in case it ever..." The old man appeared to struggle for words momentarily. "In case it ever woke up. You'll notice that it now has a faint tremor. Such items act like magnets. Go in the direction that produces the greatest disturbance, and sooner or later you will find her- wherever she may be in the world."

Ichaan cautiously studied the necklace. The nightglass made it as heavy as a fist-sized rock. It shivered faintly in his hand. He wondered why anyone would wear such a thing.

"I believe that to Her Majesty, it's as light as air," Emar said with a faint smile.

The *xyrral* traced a finger over the nightglass, wondering how safe this object was. "What if, when I find her, the Queen doesn't wish to return?"

Emar gave him a shocked look. "Why would she *not* wish to?"

Ichaan decided to ask a different question. "Supposing she is being held captive?"

The Sentai Court Leader scowled. "You creatures are masters at solving problems, are you not? Find a way to bring her back, *unharmed*. You will be handsomely rewarded. Your father will hear of your success as soon as possible."

"I am thankful for your generosity, Lord." Ichaan had no desire for worldly trappings such as wealth, property, nor the sort of power that humans craved. The promise of a *handsome reward*- which to humans, always meant money- failed to motivate him. His needs were more primal- more *basic,* some might have said, although his senses were deeper, wider, and more attuned to the natural forces of this world than those of any human.

He had never understood their universal need to be surrounded by *things.* Provided that it didn't upset the Sentai or cause disruption, Ichaan and his sister were permitted to do as they wished in the city of Char and throughout the wider land of Asqabal. Neither of them wanted anything else from the Sentai- except, of course, their leave to remain in Theya and never have to return to burning, condemned Ilentra.

Only their father could demand their return, and he had no cause to.

Not yet anyway.

"Go now," Emar said, "and return with her."

Darkness had already fallen. Ichaan, wishing to quickly contemplate the task ahead, sat unseen in the shadowed corner of a fortress rooftop- he enjoyed exploring the high ramparts of Char- where a most unlikely notion occurred to him.

For the first time in his life, he considered keeping a secret from his sister.

Did the Sentai care if she accompanied him or not? Perhaps they thought her too volatile for such an important task. After all, they hadn't summoned her. And Ishiya wouldn't even know that he had gone. She simply wouldn't be able to find him.

Why hadn't the idea occurred to him before now? They had no sworn familial allegiance to each other after all, only to their father as head of the family clan- not that much of their family remained now. They did not love each other in the way that some human brethren apparently did- they had no use for the human concept and struggled to understand it. Their mutual attraction was compulsive, violent, bestial.

Ichaan found himself warming to the idea of hunting alone. Besides, this hunt was different. His quarry was the Queen herself, and she was to be protected and brought safely home.

Ishiya would not be a good companion in such circumstances. She could become a distraction that might even result in his failure- and he could not fail the Sentai. He must perform the role of perfect servant. Their father had agreed this with the Queen herself, more than twenty Theyan years ago when he and Ishiya, both still very young, were brought here. Ihar had since ensured that the arrangement continued even after the Queen's disappearance.

The *xyrral* stretched languidly, removed his clothing, and allowed himself to slowly transform into his natural form as he lurked in shadow. His fingers extended and needle-sharp claws emerged. His musculature grew sharper and more defined. His eyes became larger and darkened to black, reflecting the dim stars and glow of the city lights. His joints became more angular, his jaw more pointed. Long, needle-like teeth pushed their way into view. The transformation was always a kind of relief. He could only bear the soft human physique for so long. It lacked the ability to hunt effectively.

And it certainly could not fly.

Ichaan's claws scratched agitatedly against the moss-crusted slate-work, making white lines. His stomach groaned, and his tongue licked against rows of sharp teeth. His hunger had grown through the day and would become unbearable if it remained unsated.

He would eat first, and then he would leave the city.

A while later he squatted in an unlit alleyway deep within the warrens of Char's poor quarter, methodically picking his way through the meat of a vagrant who had been drunk and half asleep, propped up against the wall of a nearby building. Ishiya would have woken her up and ensured that the woman's last moments were filled with undiluted horror, but Ichaan wanted only to feed. He had torn out the creature's windpipe and drunk the salty warm blood that gushed forth, his appetiser of soup for the feast to follow. He removed the woman's clothing and savaged her soft flesh. She was, he observed, uncommonly fat for a street scavenger. Ichaan guessed that she had not spent long in her homeless state.

He ripped and chewed the meat down to the bone, casting aside only the entrails- he had no love for those, having learned that in humans they were often riddled with disease.

Sated at last, he left the ruined carcass for the rats and foxes.

He wouldn't tell Ishiya about his task. Why would she want to help him find someone they had to *protect* rather than kill?

It would bore her, Queen or not.

But even with the decision made, a strange unease stayed with him.

XVI

Two days later, Ichaan sat on a large boulder near the top of a hill in the north-facing Spine, watching the moonlit land below as he feasted on warm horsemeat. He had drawn near enough to Waters Green to see its multitude of shapes and lights from his vantage point, and the nightglass necklace now shuddered violently. The tremors dissipated whenever he put greater distance between himself and the town, no matter the direction. Queen Alianne was somewhere in that place.

But his thoughts were not of his quarry.

Had he made a terrible misjudgement?

What would Ishiya do if she found him? Ichaan couldn't say. No one, not even he, could second-guess his sister's actions.

Would she forgive him? Perhaps, when her rage was spent.

Perhaps not.

He recalled their brutal initiation at the hands of their father. At a young age, Ichaan and Ishiya had been taken to fight each other many times in the distant Pits of Ouan, far beyond their home settlement. Their father had watched with evident satisfaction, pleasuring himself as his offspring tore and bit at each other. The victor of each fight would then be made to watch as their father unleashed the full force of his lust on the loser.

Ichaan finished his meal and sighed. His breath, warm with the tang of fresh butchery, drifted into the still evening air. *I miss you,* he silently told her, *but this task was never yours.*

He imagined her angrily pointing out that his loyalties had become muddied, that he cared more about doing the work of the Sentai than the advancement of the *xyrral* race. The possibility that such an accusation might hold some truth discomforted him. He did not live to serve- far from it- but if he displeased the Sentai their father would hear about it, and swiftly. The same applied to Ishiya. What would Ihar think if their relationship with the powers of Asqabal was compromised? He and others within the Iron Circle had spent painstaking decades cultivating that relationship, with the aim of gradually increasing the number of *xyrral* allowed to stay permanently in Asqabal.

Paths had been created between Theya and Ilentra through which- using considerable energy kept in control by gifted sorcerers at either end- beings might pass back and forth. He and Ishiya had made that journey once, although they remembered nothing of it. Apparently, no one ever did. Only a small number passed through, and only occasionally. The allowance was the result of an agreement involving gold or other metals deemed precious by the Sentai, provided by the *xyrral.* Neither the Sentai's sorcerers nor the *xyrral* astromancers on the other side of the gateway possessed the power to allow more than that- but it was nevertheless an impressive work of magical power on a scale he could never have imagined, had he not seen it for himself.

As Ichaan contemplated the backcloth of stellar points across the sky he wondered with some trepidation when he might encounter their father again. He and Ishiya had reported to him their failure to locate the *artar* in the Faering. To their surprise, Ihar had reacted calmly, although he had left for Ilentra the next day. "Heads will roll," Ishiya had forecasted.

Ichaan turned his attention back to the Queen's necklace. He would rather not have this unstable item in his possession. One moment it radiated such savage cold that frost would form on its surface. The next, it would become almost too hot to hold. All the while, the tremors coming from within the nightglass stone became stronger, as if the object knew that he was sitting here distracted rather than reuniting it with its owner.

He would be eager to relinquish it when he found Queen Alianne. No doubt the nightglass would go to sleep at her touch.

Ichaan finished his meal and wiped blood from around his mouth. Reluctantly he settled back into his humanlike form and dressed in the clothes he had brought. One day, he promised himself, his kind would never need to hide their true selves again. Theya would be theirs. Ihar had sworn as much- and whatever his father wanted, he found a way to get, sooner or later.

Ichaan set off down the hill towards the city's inviting lights.

Waters Green was not a garrison town, and Ichaan, who now appeared to be a young, average-looking man, was allowed through the town gates by the night guard with barely a look, much less an inspection.

Few people were about in the fading light. Trade was done for the day although the taverns had not yet filled out. The *xyrral* allowed himself a moment to rest and idly watch the comings and goings of human men and women intent on whatever trivial business occupied their little minds.

He had a thirst on him, so he went to a tavern called *The Sleeper and the Sword* and purchased a small flagon of water, which was enough to earn him a suspicious look from the bartender. The *xyrral* constitution did not react well to the alcohol that tainted so many human-made concoctions, and Ichaan disliked the idea of ingesting anything that might dull his wits even the tiniest amount.

He sat at the back of the tavern and sipped at his water. But no sooner had he settled down than he sensed a familiar presence at a table to his left- one that only now revealed itself.

Ishiya smiled as he turned slowly to look at her. The expression was both amused and predatory, and Ichaan felt a prickle of unease. His sister could be unpredictable. If she fought him here and now, perhaps even reverting to her natural form in so doing, she would not only sabotage his task, but the resulting chaos and terror would result in them both being sent back to Ilentra.

He never wanted to set foot in that hell-gone world again.

"Sweet brother," she murmured, in the common Theyan language. Ichaan's skin crawled, and his heart leapt at the sound of her voice. "What are we to do now? Should we talk, perhaps? You *do* have something to tell me, don't you?"

He forced a smile. "Not here. Somewhere dark and quiet."

Ichaan got up, allowed himself a last sip of water and walked out of the tavern, closely followed by his sister. No one paid them any attention. Outside, he looked around and finally chose an alleyway across the street and down the hill a little way. "Perfect," he heard Ishiya murmur from close behind as they crossed the road.

He had expected violence as soon as they walked into the deep shadows of the alleyway, but Ishiya waited until they were twenty paces from the flickering torchlights of the main thoroughfare. Uttering a hiss of rage, his sister jumped on him, bit at his ear and made deep gouges in his arm, her sharp nails easily penetrating the fabric of his shirt and the skin beneath. She at least had the good sense not to draw attention by screaming, and he in turn knew to suffer his punishment in silence.

He threw her over his shoulder to the ground. She scrambled to her feet, and they stared at each other before swiftly removing their clothes. "Each night, as I drew closer," Ishiya whispered, "all my thoughts were of you, and what I would do to you. Did you think you could hide your activities from me?"

"Never," he lied. Then he added truthfully, "I missed you. But this task is not yours."

"Your deceit was mistaken. You need to be reminded where your loyalties should lie."

"Am I to be punished?" His heart pounded in anticipation.

"Yes," she said, "but I will lie with you afterwards."

She threw herself at him, and in mid-air she partly changed to her natural form, claws extending like needles. The savagery of her assault surprised him, and Ichaan resisted the urge to scream as she ripped at his skin, drawing blood, and cutting down to the bone. Her jaws snapped at his arm. He looked into her jet-black eyes, and she snarled, baring a multitude of razor-sharp teeth as she bit deeply into his flesh.

The two *xyrral* tortured and mutilated each other in near silence, until the alleyway stank with the harsh tang of their blood. Such was Ichaan's pain that his vision blurred, and the distant light of the unknowing town became a faint smear.

Finally, he ceased his offence and knelt on the ground. Throughout their lives they had shared this silent signal of submission, to show the other that victory was theirs.

Ishiya pushed him so he lay on his back, then lay on top of him, breathless. She uttered a low, bestial growl as his phallus swelled beneath her. She shifted her position and allowed him to slide into her welcoming darkness. Ichaan groaned as she licked blood from his chest. Some of it was his, but not all. "If only Father could see us now," she murmured.

Delirious with the ecstasy of pain, Ichaan could hold himself back no longer, and spat the thick, viscous carrier of his seed into his sister's womb. Ishiya sighed and leaned closer to kiss him. Ichaan breathed in the familiar scent of blood and sweat. "We have a Queen to find," he said quietly, as Ishiya allowed him to slip out of her. "We'll celebrate together once we're back in Char."

But he found an unfathomable expression in her eyes. "What is it?" he whispered. But his sister merely shook her head, and then Ichaan saw something that utterly confounded him.

A tear escaped from one of Ishiya's eyes and rolled slowly down her cheek.

A *tear*.

In that moment, Ichaan finally realised the magnitude of what he had done, the devastation she felt at his deliberate treachery. He felt a desperate urge to plea for mercy, forgiveness. But those things were not part of his instinct. They were traits he had learned about from spending time with humans.

"We will never hunt together again," Ishiya said brokenly.

She lunged at his throat.

Ishiya watched as the last of her brother's lifeblood leaked away into the damp dirt. His body slowly reverted to its natural form, but then became shrivelled and fragmented. In a short while, nothing remained of him but bones, and finally- as she waited in the gloom- even they crumbled to dark dust. Thus ended the lives of all *xyrral* who perished in Theya, and no one knew why. They lived for a century or more, but then they winked out of existence in an instant, leaving nothing that the wind couldn't carry away.

"Farewell, brother," Ishiya whispered to the space where he had lain.

The *xyrral* cleaned herself using Ichaan's shirt, then threw it to one side. She dressed, and carefully picked up the weighty nightglass necklace. It had grown hot and trembled violently at her touch.

Ishiya walked away through the thick shadows, towards the faint sounds and dim lights of human civilisation- and the Queen of Asqabal.

XVII

Arc headed swiftly along the wide paved streets of Waters Green's northern quarter, past tall houses and through parks and squares, then he hurried on into an area known as the Burnings. This part of Waters Green was not burned- no one knew quite where the name originated- but it was a poor, crime-ridden place with an unsavoury reputation stemming from the illicit trade in substances outlawed by the Gharaanian government. Such things were considered un-befitting of God-fearing Gharaanian citizens- but in areas such as this, far from Toran's pious eye, they were still smoked, swallowed, or otherwise consumed.

The Burnings' reputation also owed much to the scourge of de-pravity in the area. It was said that whatever a man desired, he could find in the Burnings and usually at a reasonable price. Many had entered these grim warrens for a prostitute, some out of curiosity as much as physical need, but returned often enough to be drawn down a much darker path, sometimes even of torture and murder.

Arc had no interest in prostitutes. He had eyes only for Alianne. But he sought to bend reality enough to live through it, because even Alianne's love was not enough to chase the darkness from his life.

Quickdust was the only way he had found of achieving this, and even then, the shadows on the periphery of his existence soon crept back, gathering like crows at a field's edge. Arc's father had suffered something similar for many years before he finally went out into the snow one night, distraught. A deersman had found his frozen body the next morning, deep in the woods. He had slit his own throat. "You can beat the black dog and send him away for a while," Arrin Thendrin had once said- then, with a knowing smile, "But he knows your scent, and he'll come back for you again and again."

That black dog had been too persistent for Arrin.

I shouldn't need it, Arc had berated himself over the years, more times than he could count. *I'm better than that.*

And yet he came back to that hellish herb, time and again.

The dried and powdered root of the blackwood plant, quickdust had several powerful effects- and some side-effects that were almost as potent. It produced, in the short term, intense euphoria and confidence. Fears and worries melted away. Arc craved contentment and a life free of fear more than anything, but he had only known something like it under the influence of quickdust- a bright, sharp illusion that faded too soon.

The powder's side-effects usually manifested in the small hours of the night. Arc would wake from a powerful nightmare, sweating profusely and screaming nonsense. Often, he scratched himself enough to bleed. Occasionally he lost control of his bowels and defecated in his smallclothes. Arc was humiliated by Alianne's weary tolerance more than he would have been had she railed at him in disgust.

A few times, the quickdust had been a bad batch- *demondust* it was called, by those unfortunate enough to be caught out that way- and Arc had spent the best part of three days caught in a waking nightmare where he couldn't tell if he was awake or asleep, nor if the monstrosities that appeared were real or imaginary. He became convinced that a wound received during one such extended horror had been inflicted by a monster from some other realm- an outworlder, but one that *he* had temporarily brought into being through his nightmare. He would even fear that one of those vanquished outworlders had become something more than a disembodied voice.

The fact that he had fought such beings made that hell even more plausible.

Alianne looked after him and kept him under lock and key on those mercifully rare occasions, the two of them hiding in whatever low-down hovel or guesthouse room they occupied at the time. Sometimes she would stuff his mouth with rags to muffle his shouts and screams. Once he recovered, after the relief had passed, she would tell him in no uncertain terms how much she hated the quickdust. He hated it too, in those remorseful moments, and he swore never to touch it again.

He meant it, every time. She said she believed him, but he saw the sadness and resignation in her eyes.

Despite the horrors and the humiliation, sooner or later Arc would convince himself that quickdust remained a risk worth taking, because nothing else could create the way it made him feel. Often penniless, always friendless, he had found life before he met Alianne a landscape with nothing on the horizon, and yet the quickdust had ensnared him *after* they met. Arc had never understood that. Perhaps he had thought to celebrate their union one night, and instead of a few merry ales he had taken a darker road.

He couldn't properly remember. Wasn't that always the way with life's bad steps?

Whatever the truth, the times between quickdust sessions often grew unbearable, worsened by the exhaustion of expecting enemies around every corner. He could think only of his next meeting with the black powder. Even over the last seven years as Alianne's companion, the gnawing hunger for something better than this existence, assuaged only by the mountains and troughs of quick-dust's manipulation, had never left.

No matter the complication of quickdust, Arc knew that as his feelings for Alianne swiftly developed, he should have extricated himself from the situation of his own accord. He should have sent a message back to the First Protector and asked to be removed from the mission. Protectors could never allow feelings for those they protected or worked for to cloud their judgement. And yet Ceiran, who must have learned about their relationship early on, did nothing about it.

Should have. A phrase that echoed down Arc's entire life.

We must go to Asqabal, and to the Great Burning with your enemies, he had urged Alianne several times, frustrated by the inertia of their existence. *Those who wish you harm are everywhere, not just in Char. Take back the seat of your power. Those who remain loyal will rally to you.*

But she wouldn't. Maybe she no longer wanted to.

Maybe she no longer knew *how* to.

He reached the bottom of Seepwood Hill and headed along a narrow little street with no name other than "south-west at the bottom". Deeper into the Burnings, the passages grew ever more squalid, and he had to tread carefully around heaps of excrement, crippled madmen, and dark holes where the surface had collapsed into the unstable earth. A cold mist had crept up from the river, but Arc didn't need to hesitate to check his directions. To his shame, he knew the Burnings better than anyone who didn't live here.

He arrived at a low, nameless tavern. Ignoring the dull stares of the men in the dimly lit tap room he walked through the pungent haze of blue-tinged pipeweed smoke and past the bar to a narrow, damp passageway that led to the rear rooms- the *business* area. The sullen bartender glanced up but offered neither a challenge nor a greeting.

The Protector hurried along the passageway and past the many doors in the walls. He tried not to listen to the various sounds of torture, fornication and sometimes acts he couldn't identify by sound. From behind one door, pitiful sobbing could be heard, together with a rough panting and growling.

At the end of the corridor stood a half-open door, which led into a dirty, refuse-strewn room. This stale-smelling den served as an office for Ghelyn, the man who owned the establishment.

Ghelyn smiled as he looked up. Arc observed with distaste that the man's lips always looked freshly moistened. "I've missed you, Anphayan," he remarked, sunken dark-rimmed eyes peering cautiously. "What will it be this evening? A silverweight? Two?"

"One," Arc said, with some effort. He wanted to be in control of himself tomorrow morning. With Imogen returned, Alianne might decide they needed to go somewhere else in a hurry. He could buy another tomorrow, time permitting, and didn't trust himself not to consume two silverweights if he bought them both now.

"Are you sure? My favourite heathen southerner isn't normally a man for half measures." The fat lips curved upwards a little.

"One, I said." Arc gritted his teeth in frustration.

Ghelyn busied himself weighing quickdust from a glass jar on an intricate pair of scales, before adding it to the leather pouch Arc had provided. "You're an odd fellow, aren't you?" he remarked as Arc paid him.

"Compared to the lowlife you entertain here?" Arc could not hide his amusement.

Undeterred, Ghelyn continued, "What sort of thing interests you? Every man has his needs. What do *you* desire? Beyond the dust, I mean. I can help you. Don't be coy."

"We've had this conversation before." Arc swallowed. His mouth already watered almost uncontrollably as he squeezed the leather pouch.

"I'm interested in serving you, my friend. How young or old do you like your ladies? We have all ages here."

"I haven't really thought about it."

"*Oh.* Maybe you prefer men." Ghelyn grinned broadly.

Arc stood up and carefully placed the leather pouch in an unpickable pocket inside his trousers. "I don't prefer men, but if I did, I wouldn't come here to satisfy myself."

Ghelyn scowled and waved him away, his good humour evaporating.

Arc left the Burnings with haste. The river mist had grown thick. At this cold time of year, these conditions were not uncommon near the Greatwater, and Waters Green, like the other towns and villages nearby, often lay obscured through the nights and into the early hours of the morning. But the mist lay especially dense tonight.

He stopped abruptly.

Arc's hand seized the pommel of his sword. He stood still, certain that he had sensed an outworlder nearby. Perhaps somewhere in the town, perhaps the other side of the river or even up in the shadows of the Spine. He couldn't be sure. "Gods, not now," he mumbled. "Never again," he added a moment later. "I'm done with you."

The sensation swiftly faded, and he waited awhile, then breathed a long sigh of relief. Whatever it was, Arc told himself, it had gone now. Maybe he'd imagined it.

Sometime later, he stopped at a corner between a wide thoroughfare and a winding, pothole-ridden street that wound up Back Hill, and realised he'd taken a wrong turn. He retraced his steps to what he thought was the previous junction but that led to another unfamiliar road. Arc leaned against the wall of a tall storehouse on the corner and peered at the sooty, smeared-out light of lanterns across the street and the faint silhouettes of buildings, among them a church with a tall spire. A lantern flickered almost above him also, adorned with thick spiderwebs that glimmered in the misty light.

Arc's hand touched the pouch where he had placed the quick-dust. That same hand began to shake madly. Mist and sweat prickled his brow.

Just a little, he thought.

After all, in these conditions, why wander around only to become more lost? Surely it made sense to sit for a while, maybe have a little quickdust- not too much, of course- and find his way back later under clearer skies?

Besides, Alianne would value some time with her daughter tonight.

"It makes sense," Arc murmured. "I did well, didn't I? I brought her back to you. I deserve a little reward." He had already opened the pouch.

As the renegade Protector leaned against the cold brick wall, he stared ahead, no longer observing, no longer even thinking for himself.

XVIII

"You and I are the last of our family," Alianne began. "Your father, Selurin, died when you were not even a year old. I have no sisters or brothers, and neither do you. So, we are the last of our kind. But *you* are the future, Imogen. Maybe one day the throne of Asqabal will be yours. If the situation changes."

Imogen almost asked how much it would need to change.

"The Protectorate have worked against our family for centuries. Twelve years ago, when you were five, they sent assassins into the palace in Char- men and women who were bought by the Protectorate and attempted to murder us. Most masqueraded as servants, or men and women of the Towerblades, our personal regiment. That was when you and I had to leave our lives behind. Helped by those loyal to us, we were given passage out of Char and eventually out of Asqabal altogether. We did our best to stay hidden, and we never remained in one place for too long, over the next five years. But even with the help of Ceiran, the First Protector who went against the Protectorate's Grand Assembly, it became obvious that I couldn't keep you safe indefinitely."

"So, you sent me away."

"To a place where no one would think to look. Ceiran sent Uelene to us. She had a powerful kind of magic that works on the mind. During your journey to the Faering, she weaved a spell that would make you forget everything that had happened to you."

"But now I'm beginning to remember," Imogen said softly. "It's like slowly waking up."

"Soon after, Ceiran sent Arc to help me keep a few steps ahead of the Protectorate. Often, we've stayed in Gharaan. The Protectorate have no allies here and no hold over the powers of this land. For us, it's as safe as anywhere else."

"You sleep with him."

The response appeared to surprise Alianne. "Yes. But tonight, Arc has certain... other needs." For a moment genuine venom entered her voice. "Something called quickdust, which I hope you never take. Quickdust is his other woman, you might say."

Alianne continued to talk about their ancestors. Some sounded heroic, others villainous. The tales whirled through Imogen's head-stories of the dynasty that had ruled Asqabal for so many centuries. Her mother's words filled Imogen with wonder as she spoke of figures such as Queen Olnya the Visionary, Empress Kailene who waged war on eastern Gharaan, and the Two-Faced Queen, Eshaan, adored by some and loathed by others.

Imogen couldn't help but feel there was something else, something important that Alianne hadn't yet told her and was perhaps afraid to. She wanted to ask about it, but she could barely keep her eyes open. Eventually, Alianne gestured to a mattress across the room where she had placed a couple of blankets earlier. "We can talk more tomorrow," she said. "You need to sleep." Abruptly her mother leaned forward and hugged her close. Imogen froze, arms rigid at her sides, bewildered at the strange feeling of panic the intimacy caused. Her heart raced, and she felt suddenly far warmer than a moment ago.

"Will you forgive me?" Alianne put her hands on Imogen's shoulders and looked searchingly at her. "*Can* you?"

"Yes. Of course." Imogen had no idea what else to say. She hadn't even been thinking of forgiveness. She looked away, uncomfortable. "I'm so tired."

Alianne smiled. "Sleep now. Tomorrow, we'll talk about the future."

Imogen went to lie down and gazed drowsily up at the ceiling and the wooden beams that spanned the chamber. The ancient, warped wood was riddled with small holes, and she wondered how it hadn't already crumbled away. In places the cobwebs clustered so thickly that she couldn't see beyond them. Did her mother and Arc always live in places like this?

She watched the shadows and faint flickers of light dancing upon the walls. But soon her eyes closed, and she drifted off into a deep slumber.

Imogen woke suddenly.

But she no longer lay on the mattress in the corner.

She stood over Alianne's sleeping form.

A spiteful voice whispered in her head, bitter with all the feelings of betrayal and anger she had stored away, a violence of emotion that shocked her with its intensity.

Look at her, the mother who abandoned you, it sneered. *The mother who sent you away when she should have protected you.*

You're so much stronger than her. After all her failures, does she even deserve to live?

Then Alianne's eyes flickered open, settled on Imogen, and widened in terror.

Alianne shrank back in fear as Imogen tried to speak. But no words would come out.

She looked down and saw a knife in her hand.

I almost killed her, Imogen realised numbly.

She backed away as Alianne stared in terror.

Imogen grabbed her pack and robe and made for the door. "No!" Alianne pleaded, and when Imogen looked back her mother was stumbling desperately towards her. An invisible force swept from inside Imogen, slammed into Alianne, and threw her back against the wall. As she heard the impact an exhilaration swept through Imogen, an excitement she had never felt before.

Again, a voice whispered. *Did you hear the sound she made? Do it again!*

Imogen gestured, willing Alianne to rise. Then she made a sudden movement with her hand and something invisible struck the side of Alianne's head, first on the left and then the right.

Again.

She didn't know when she finally stopped, but Alianne would no longer respond to her silent demands. She lay battered and unmoving on the floor, glistening wetly.

Imogen stared in horror. "No," she whispered. "No!"

She ran to the door and threw the bolts, already sobbing.

Moments later she had rushed downstairs and fled into the night.

Imogen had no idea where she would go, knowing only that she must make herself impossible to find. She ran from street to street, choosing directions at random.

Her life had led up to moments like this, over and again.

She had fled her home in the palace in Char.

Then she had fled her refuge in the Faering.

Now, she ran from her mother.

None of it made any sense, and yet in an awful way Imogen knew she was trying to outrun *herself*.

What am I?

That terrible question would not let her be, and the only hint of an answer lay in her merciless reflection- a cruel stare riven with madness.

XIX

Imogen leaned against the wall of an unlit passageway and tried to swallow down the panic that threatened to take control as she breathed in the cold, foul air. Her legs ached. Soon she would need to find somewhere to rest. But she dared not let her guard down anywhere outside. The mist had grown thicker than ever, and she had no idea where in the town she might be.

She looked back, suddenly certain that someone approached. But no one emerged from out of the murk. Sounds behaved oddly here where the buildings sometimes almost touched one another across the narrow, winding passages. She even imagined for a moment that she could hear her mother's voice.

Imogen negotiated the moist cobbles and chose the left turn at the next junction of alleyways, taking care to avoid potholes and cracks in the ground. Every now and then faint shouts or laughs issued from behind one or other of the dimly lit windows of houses nearby. The mist and occasional drizzle had dampened her clothes, and the stench from the gutters almost made her retch. Perhaps because she paid insufficient attention to objects in front of her, she stumbled on a loose cobblestone and just about managed not to fall.

The vague shapes of buildings materialised out of the gloom and then faded. The only light nearby came from a gas-lamp at each end of the short passageway she now found herself in, and a nearby guesthouse, where a flickering light glowed behind one of the ground-floor windows. A makeshift sign, written in clumsy, poorly spelled Theyan, proclaimed that rooms were available.

No, she told herself as she stood near the door. *Arc may have returned to the inn. He would look for me in places like this.*

Of course, she had no idea where the Protector might look for her, or even if he would look at all. But if she were him, she would want revenge, Imogen decided.

She leaned against the wall and bowed her head, exhausted.

Finally, she continued along the passageway until it joined a narrow, winding road that drew close to the river.

Might the river boats still travel up and down the Greatwater at this time? Imogen reckoned that was unlikely in these conditions. Maybe if she begged someone, they might take pity on her and take her downriver, no matter that she had no money.

No, she decided miserably. That wasn't at all likely.

I must get away, she told herself frantically.

But then someone stepped from the shadows.

She appeared to be a young woman with long brown hair, dressed in simple travelling clothes. But Imogen looked at her and knew immediately that she was something altogether different. This creature radiated danger- and yet she was familiar.

As their eyes met, Imogen saw momentary confusion. The stranger muttered something in a language Imogen couldn't understand. "Princess Imogen," she added. She took a necklace with a large black gemstone from her pocket, then shook her head before returning her attention to Imogen. "Where is your mother?"

Imogen stared in shock. "That's..." She blinked, shivering as a sudden memory bloomed. "That's *my* necklace!"

The woman frowned. "*Your...*" Then she stopped. "Where is your mother?" she repeated.

Imogen swallowed and thought quickly. "I... I haven't seen her for seven years. She sent me away. Who are you?"

"Where did she send you? Here?"

"No. The Faering." The words spilled out before she could stop them. Her eyes fixed on the necklace again, drawn to the dark stone. "That's mine," she whispered. "That's *my* necklace. From when I was little. How could..."

The woman passed her the necklace, which was trembling violently. As Imogen's hand wrapped around it, she felt a curious shudder and then the stone became cold and still.

"Well." The woman shook her head, a faint smile upon her lips for a moment. "It appears the Sentai got at least one thing wrong."

Her new companion looked thoughtfully at her, and Imogen found she could no longer meet that dark, searching gaze. "So, you have no idea where your mother the Queen might be?"

Imogen shook her head and looked pointedly away into the mist-obscured night. She felt simultaneously afraid and exhilarated.

"My name is Ishiya. I am a servant of the Sentai, and of course, I also serve the throne of Asqabal. I have been looking for your mother. Of course, I expected to find you with her." Ishiya paused. "Do you remember me? I remember *you*. Your Highness." She gave a little bow but showed no hint of subservience.

"I... I'm not sure. I think so." Imogen glanced tentatively back and found herself transfixed by Ishiya's eyes, now almost as black as the gemstone in her necklace. Another memory materialised as she touched it. The gem was nightglass, an unstable and even dangerous substance which only her family could properly tame.

"You were very young. We barely exchanged a word. It was not my place to talk to you."

Imogen tried to respond, but exhaustion and the numbing chill of the night air had sapped her ability to think properly. "Can you... will you take me there? To Char?" she managed to ask eventually.

Ishiya's smile was frightening. "That, your Highness, is now my task."

For one wild moment, Ishiya considered taking on her natural form and flying back to Char with Imogen on her back, but the idea was fraught with danger. In her bewildered state, the Princess was not ready to see the *xyrral's* true form. Even if she did recover her wits sufficiently, Imogen might slip and fall as they flew. Maybe Ishiya could save her before she hit the ground, maybe not. Either way, she could not risk spoiling this prize and incurring the wrath of the Sentai, not to mention her father.

She had enough money for a horse and a thick cloak for Imogen to wrap herself in and bought both soon after first light. Then they left through the west gate.

Ishiya stole a quick look at Imogen's nightglass necklace, now around the girl's neck. She saw something opaque and almost shapeless, like grey smoke, inside the gemstone. Whatever it was, it had appeared only after Imogen put the necklace on.

And where was the Queen? Ostensibly, she could be anywhere in the world, but Ishiya reckoned Imogen knew something about her mother and was hiding it. Alianne might well be somewhere nearby. And yet Ishiya's instincts made her put that matter aside. Imogen was young and pliable. It might be possible to influence her in a way that could benefit the *xyrral*. Certainly, the Princess could do with an ally in the Palace.

As things stood, she could benefit hugely by safely delivering Imogen back to the seat of Omerian power. It was her duty, after all, but could mean much more, Ishiya reminded herself.

Princess Imogen, a Queen in waiting. And she *would* be crowned, not least because the people of Asqabal were unhappy and restless, the Sentai court and Chancellor had ruled poorly, and the happy diversion caused by the coronation of a new Queen would be a tactic even those fools couldn't miss.

See, Ichaan- I'm thinking ahead and planning, she thought, but the thought stirred pain and anger inside her. He was gone forever now, and that was her fault as much as his.

Imogen's arms were warm around her as they rode. From the moment she had set eyes upon the Princess, Ishiya had sensed in her a distinct, roiling magical force, a nature that was familiar in a way she couldn't describe. Soft, weak creatures that humans were, their kind were usually nothing but playthings or meat. But Ishiya had found herself drawn to the rare creature that was Princess Imogen of Asqabal from the day they were introduced, more than thirteen years ago- although the Princess would have been likely too young to remember that brief meeting.

I am a moth to her flame, Ishiya thought, and that notion exhilarated her beyond anything she could imagine.

Of course, Court Leader Emar Naii and Chancellor Bhal might at first be less than satisfied that the nightglass necklace had taken her not to the Queen but to the Queen's daughter. However, they knew little about the peculiarities of nightglass. The substance was linked to the Omerians in ways that no one truly understood. They wouldn't have known that the necklace belonged not to Alianne but to Imogen.

Ishiya's mind raced as she turned ideas and possibilities over in her head. The Sentai would think Imogen, callow and inexperienced, could make a pliable monarch behind whom they might consolidate their power. But she, Ishiya, would quietly counsel against them, and become a valued advisor to Imogen if she could. After all, the power to allow more *xyrral* to come to Theya would rest with the new Queen, as it had done for centuries.

And *that* meant more of her people could escape the ruins of Ilentra and live fruitful lives in Theya's bountiful hunting ground.

Alianne might return sometime after Imogen's coronation, if she still lived. But, awkwardness aside, it would be too late for her to make her own claim, if she even hoped to.

The beginnings of a plan began to percolate through Ishiya's mind- a plan that perhaps even her father would be proud of.

"I think I remember you now," Imogen said, leaning forward to speak in her ear.

Ishiya couldn't resist a quick smile to herself. "I'm glad you remember me," she called back.

As they rode, she recalled another thing Imogen had mentioned. "You told me your mother sent you away to the Faering. Why?"

"She said it was the last place our enemies in the Protectorate would look."

Ishiya doubted the logic of that argument but didn't pursue the matter further. How Imogen's nature had been kept shrouded from not only the witch-hags but the *faer*, would be an interesting topic for another day.

"We will be close companions for some time," Ishiya remarked as they rested a little later in the emerging light of morning.

The Princess gave her a look that Ishiya couldn't work out. Did Imogen, in her undoubted arrogance, think that she might somehow get the better of a *xyrral* huntress, if she had to?

Well, if she decided to flee at any point, perhaps Ishiya would allow her to get away- within reason. She might even let the Princess think she had put enough distance between them to have escaped properly. But Imogen had a unique scent. Ishiya would come for her, over land and water, through the dark thickets of the wooded land, across the open fields and the high mountains and even the rotten arteries of foul cities, if she had to. The thrill of the chase had always excited her.

The *xyrral* shook herself free of those errant, wild thoughts. Imogen had shown no desire to run away- quite the opposite. In any case, Ishiya knew she could not take any chances with her charge. She formed part of a much wider strategy, as her father would harshly remind her. She, Ishiya, must remain a faithful servant, and do whatever necessary to ensure the eventual rescue of her people, and their delivery into the world promised to them a century ago, when the slow but inevitable death of Ilentra became known beyond reasonable doubt.

Ishiya sighed. If only Imogen were hers.

But even she, lucky enough to have escaped Ilentran hell, could not have everything she desired in life.

XX

Anwynne's sleep had been troubled since Merrilin's departure, but in the days after the discovery of Shaya's mutilated body it had grown even worse. As the first light of day brought her bedchamber into view, she rose and dressed and gazed through the window and into the woods, anxious. Why hadn't Merrilin let her come along? The Elder hadn't expressly forbidden it. Hadn't they agreed some time ago to face all their challenges together?

Maybe a walk through the grey quiet of dawn to her secret place would help calm her. She hoped.

Within a short while Anwynne had left Greenwood and headed south-west along a small path. This route was seldom used by anyone other than herself, for it led nowhere in particular. After a while, she turned off onto a different, more overgrown path, where she had to pick her way past thick curls of bramble and fading, browned bracken still tall from the summer. As she brushed foliage from the dark ringlets of her hair, a deer looked up from her early breakfast and gazed warily at the interloper in her midst before trotting some distance away.

Anwynne followed the path on its gentle downward slope into a valley known as the Silver Trail- so named because of the many and graceful silver larches that grew here, although no proper trail cut through the valley, only a minor river.

At the base of the valley, the river ran south to join the Greatwater after many further miles- not that the Greatwater was so great this far west. Recent dry days further upriver had reduced the Silver Trail River to a slow-moving stream. Anwynne walked alongside the brook for several hundred paces until she reached an area where the rocky bank on the east side became taller but the slope less extreme. She clambered up the incline to a small cave in the cliff, far above the water level.

Anwynne had come to this place many times before, sometimes to think and meditate but mainly because she had stored something here that could not be safely kept in Greenwood. She had no choice but to keep it a secret, even from Merrilin. Perhaps *especially* from Merrilin- for she couldn't bear the thought of harm coming to the woman she loved.

Anwynne's heart quickened as she crawled into the musty interior of the cave, not only simply from exertion but because of what lay hidden in the earthy darkness.

At the back of the cave, where the ceiling was high enough for her to sit or kneel more comfortably, Anwynne moved a group of rocks to reveal a dusty brown cloth bag into which she placed her hand.

A moment later, Anwynne held an irregularly shaped, softly glowing blue stone. The light pulsed slowly and followed no pattern or rhythm she could detect. For a long time, she gazed at the strange, unknowable magic of the object in her hand, everything around her forgotten.

"I know that one day I must use you for something," Anwynne said softly after a while. How much time had passed? She couldn't be certain. "But I don't know what it is or how I find out."

She had long feared that someone would discover this cave and the stone she had hidden here. But there was surely no one within miles. The nearest settlement was Greenwood, a good half-morning's trek away. It would be time for luncheon when she arrived back, not that she had much appetite.

Anwynne had inherited the stone from her grandfather two years ago, just before she finally made the decision to leave her parents' home in the Saanuese capital of Isaan. Back then, it hadn't glowed. It had looked entirely unremarkable, causing her to question why something so mundane had been passed down to her. No one had any knowledge of the stone, and as the man himself had passed on it remained a mystery.

The inheritance had not been on her mind much back then. Anwynne had set her heart on an apprenticeship in the Faering, something about which her mother and father had long shown mixed feelings.

"Don't you want to settle down with a young man?" her mother had pleaded more times than Anwynne could count, and no matter how often the girl patiently explained that she had no interest in settling down- at least, not with a man. Oblivious to what Anwynne had thought was a suitably heavy hint, her mother had continued prattling on about marriage and how, if she married into enough money, she would have plenty of time for the studies that she valued so dearly. "And then you'll never have to leave Isaan!"

That exclamation alone had been enough to make her want to leave.

Anwynne had taken only a few possessions when she left home, including the stone given by her grandfather. The women of the Lower Faering settlements took a dim view of apprentices who arrived with much luggage in attendance- carrying too much of their past lives with them, they thought. Anwynne had always kept the stone close- a peculiar written instruction from her grandfather told her she must guard it closely- but soon she grew worried that it would come to the attention of the other women in Greenwood, and that no good could possibly come of such a discovery. The stone's nature remained a mystery and had proved itself subtle. The inspections of the Elder and her advisors, who rigorously went through the belongings of any girl or woman seeking to join their community, revealed nothing.

But the stone had begun to glow faintly at times when Anwynne held it, as if some primal force stirred within. So, one day Anwynne took her heirloom to this remote part of the Lower Faering where no one had reason to venture, looking for a place where it could be safely kept. She didn't trust any of the women in Greenwood to look after it and feared that sooner or later they might discover that the stone was more than it appeared to be.

In hindsight, she ought never to have left it out of her sight, but that would only have been possible if she turned down the chance to go to the Lower Faering, and her ambition to study and learn the natural arts was not one she could put aside. The situation had complicated everything.

But nothing could be done about that now.

Anwynne sighed. Even though she trusted Merrilin in almost all matters, she couldn't burden her with the knowledge of this mysterious object. Something told her it would be dangerous for Merrilin to become involved.

"I would tell you if I could," Anwynne said sadly, tracing a finger over the rough, craggy surface of the rock. "I *want* to share everything. But some things cannot be shared."

Sometime later, she placed the stone back in its bag and was about to hide it under the rocks again when something made her pause.

For some inexplicable reason, Anwynne felt certain that she couldn't leave it here again, no matter the dangers of bringing it back to Greenwood.

She must take the stone with her, no matter what.

Anwynne placed the stone in the deep pocket of her cloak, and carefully made her way down the slope to the stream. As she walked back to where the path led up the side of the quiet valley a cold certainty washed through her. Nothing would be the same from now on. Something would happen.

She had ascended to the top of the Silver Trail's eastern side and was resting on a mossy boulder alongside the path when the stone suddenly grew hot and caused her robe to first smoulder and then burst into flames as she cast it off in a panic. The stone tumbled from her pocket onto the path where it glowed brightly, causing the soft, damp ground beneath to hiss and scorch. Blue light reflected in the nearby foliage as Anwynne stamped out the flames licking at her robe.

The fire had ruined half the garment, but the morning was chilly and eventually she put it on anyway. At long last, as the heat of the stone faded, Anwynne dared to touch its surface.

To her dismay, it crumbled to dust.

Anwynne stared in disbelief. "That's impossible!" She tried to gather up the dust, but as she did, a stabbing pain cut through her hands. When she looked, she saw that the tiny fragments of the stone were sinking into her hands like fragments of glass. She tried to brush them away but it was too late. Somehow, the remains of the stone had found their way through the skin of her hands and into her flesh.

Fearfully she pressed on along the path. As soon as she got back to Greenwood, she would arrange to see the healer.

After another mile's walk the acrid odour of smoke came on the breeze. Then, as she reached a high area where the land to the east could be seen for a greater distance, Anwynne espied many plumes of thick dark smoke rising above the treeline.

From the direction of Greenwood.

"No!" Anwynne whispered. "What's happened?"

She hurried on along the path, running where she could.

Even before she reached the settlement, Anwynne felt the heat of fire and struggled to breathe amidst the thickening smoke. Tall orange flames licked against buildings and a continuous loud crackle filled the air. When she reached the point where the path emerged into Greenwood, Anwynne fell to her knees, transfixed, horrified by the scene.

Barely a dwelling or storehouse remained untouched by the fire that raged throughout the settlement. The flames roared, climbing into the sky, and she had to retreat, beaten back by the fierce heat.

No shouts or screams could be heard, no evidence that anyone here remained alive.

III - A Long Night of the Soul

I

Keren Sedgewick shivered and pulled his oilskin robe more tightly about his slight frame as he took in the sight of Hopesfall, a miserable town of slate-roofed houses, muddy boneyards, and drab grey shrines to violent Gods in the remote north-western corner of Anphay.

A town that was at least aptly named.

The sleet that angled in, driven by the bitter sea wind out of the west, cut through every layer of clothing he wore. A man of Wisteren, born north of the Farwater, Keren's life had been spent in far balmier conditions that altered only in subtle ways through the year. Snow, which he had already encountered briefly during his journey, was a marvel seen only on the heights of the great Firemount volcano, but sleet was somehow worse. It chilled him to the core without transforming the surrounding world.

His back ached, exhaustion had almost crippled him, and a deep hunger gnawed away at his insides. During the last month spent riding through the remote west of Saanu, he had eaten fish more times than he had thought possible. That was not all the west Saanuese ate, of course, but it seemed like it.

"Thank you, Father," he said, bitterly.

His father Shyam, the Earthkeeper of Mirrordeep, had sent him on this long and increasingly cold journey. The Earthkeeper's son knew only that he was here to meet with Errik Laaste, a retired soldier who, according to Keren's father, had fought in the Anphayan army and as a High Guard in the Protectorate. Shyam appeared to hold this man in oddly high regard. Friendships sometimes formed between people with ostensibly nothing in common, Keren supposed.

The Earthkeeper's son wondered if he might learn the reason for such mutual admiration, over the next few days.

Errik's grim, wood-and-roundstone fortress stood no more than two hundred paces from the clifftop. It matched the miserably cold day to perfection. Not all the window spaces were filled with glass. The roofs were riddled with holes, and one of the tower spires had come crashing down at some point, loosening other parts of the infrastructure during its descent. Another leaned precariously to one side as if desperate to join it.

Maybe Errik had no money for repairs to be carried out and had asked his friend Shyam to help keep his home from falling. But nothing as banal as repair work had been mentioned by Keren's father. Besides, why ask for help from someone in a distant foreign land, no matter their friendship?

Keren hoped the reason behind his journey was not trivial. His ride from Mirrordeep had taken a month and a half, and the return journey would likely take just as long. That would be three months away from his father, and his sister Lyrith, although it had been longer than that since he'd last seen her. Lyrith was a General in the Wisterene army, which had lately become involved in skirmishes with Hyliosen where the foothills of the Blood Peaks fell towards the waters of Traitor's Channel. The crazed warlords of Ai Salar had urged attacks on the border, following an apparent order from their God, repeated by one of the gibbering *shahena,* the shamen of the tribes.

Unpredictability was the one predictable thing about their ancient enemies.

I miss you, Lyrith, he thought with an inward sigh. They were entirely unlike- she was blunt, direct, and impatient, whereas he always thought before he acted. Lyrith would say he seldom acted at all. She commanded respect. People naturally followed her. To Keren, that elusive skill may as well have been sorcery.

But he had always looked up to his big sister. When they were children, she had protected and defended him, sometimes with ferocity- and not always when wanted.

Keren dismounted painfully and waited with his horse by the entrance gate, wiping his dark brown hair from in front of his face. The lone guard beckoned him forward and said something in Anphayan, then spoke in broad, heavily accented Theyan when the Wisterene shrugged apologetically. "From Wisteren?"

"Yes." Keren's light brown skin and slight build immediately marked him as such- and perhaps even the hints of *faer* blood- eyes too green for some people's liking and an unconscious grace, though that was barely in evidence after so many days spent riding.

Not for the first time, he gave thanks to the Spirits of Old Theya that his journey had taken him through lands where little prejudice towards mixed ancestry existed. "I have come from Mirrordeep, to meet Errik Laaste."

The guard peered uncertainly through the gloom. "Syam?"

"*Shyam*," Keren corrected him, a little more sharply than he intended. Exhaustion had made him irritable. Would he be offered lodging and supper, or must he find somewhere in the town? His stomach growled so loudly that he heard it above the wind and the patter of sleet. "Shyam could not come, so he sent me instead. I am Keren, his son."

This earned him only a blank look, and Keren wondered dismally if he had confused the poor man further. Finally, the guard waved Keren through into the courtyard, the earthy ground of which had started to turn to mud. Keren eased his horse gently over to the stable on the far side and left him there with a shivering boy who emerged from a small hut nearby. "He'll be hungry," the Wisterene said, patting his tired horse, and the young groom nodded glumly as if he too had not eaten all day.

Ushered by the guardsman, Keren headed through the archway into the fortress proper, limping after his time in the saddle.

Another man waited in the gloomy, low-ceilinged hall beyond. The two conversed briefly in Anphayan, and the second guard left through one of the doorways in the far side of the hall. "Wait here," his comrade said brusquely to Keren, and then he hurried back across the courtyard to his post, boots squelching in the mud. Keren looked around the sparsely furnished room, wishing it at least had a chair he could sink into.

After some time, another door opened and a portly, middle-aged woman in plain grey clothes arrived, bearing a lantern. The light had worsened outside. "Keren," she said and gave a somewhat forced smile. "Welcome. You must be tired and hungry after your long journey."

"I'm grateful for whatever you can provide," Keren agreed, relieved.

"I'll arrange for a room to be made ready. In the meantime, come to the hall to eat. Errik will see you in the morning."

That's just as well, the Earthkeeper's son almost remarked, doubting that he could stay awake for much longer anyway.

She led him to a large, draughty hall where the last light of the day seeped through iron-crossed windows. Paintings hung on gloomy walls, their subject matter mostly obscured by shadow.

His guide left him seated alone at a long wooden table with the promise of food to come soon, and sometime later a young girl with blonde pigtails arrived, all doubt and nervousness as she bore a lantern in one hand and a tray in the other. The tray held a small loaf of dark bread, a flagon of watered wine, some ham and cheese and a quarter of dense fruit cake. It was more than Keren had expected after seeing the inside of this place, and he smiled gratefully.

The girl set the food carefully down on the table and crossed to the hearth to light some kindling under the logs. "Is the food acceptable, m'lord?" she asked, in surprisingly good Theyan.

"More than acceptable. Thank you. But I'm no lord."

"Oh." She waited to make sure the fire had caught, then smiled and left.

The cake was a little dry, but the ham, cheese and bread were all fresh- although Keren would have swiftly consumed far worse offerings this evening- and the watered wine pleasant enough. After eating, he stood near the fire and listened to the crackle of flames and patter of sleet on the windows. At least he was inside, with food in his belly.

His clothes had almost dried when the woman who had met him earlier arrived to escort him to his room. They ascended in silence up two flights of stairs to a room whose door she unlocked with one of her many large iron keys. The light of the extra lantern which she left with Keren revealed a small but clean bed, a table at the near end, and an unlit hearth in the opposite wall.

"Sleep well," she said, and headed downstairs.

II

Bright morning light shone through the window. Keren woke, stretched, and found that after a good night's sleep his mood had improved, no matter that his back still ached and his legs required considerable stretching before he could stand properly. He wondered if a bath might be possible. Other than a quick splash in chilly country streams he hadn't washed properly for over a week.

Keren was hungry enough to eat a substantial breakfast, provided for him in the hall where he had eaten the previous evening. As he feasted on cold meats, smoked fish, and some plump, dark berries, he wondered if he might be permitted to take some supplies with him when he began his return journey. Afterwards, a bath of hot water was provided in a wood-panelled bathing room, and he dressed in his spare set of clothes which he had last cleaned in a river somewhere in the West Saanuese hinterlands.

Once he had made himself presentable, a servant took him to a different part of the fortress, along dismal corridors lined with faded paintings and rusting suits of ancient armour. At last, he was shown into a large chamber where a wide window looked out east over the grounds.

A gaunt man with thinning grey hair rose from his chair to greet him.

"Keren. Shyam's son." Errik gave him a searching look as he clasped Keren's hand. "My thanks for coming all this way. I expect it wasn't the easiest journey."

"I'm glad to have arrived," Keren politely replied as Errik waved him to one of the chairs near the hearth before sitting back down. "My father said the two of you met while studying at a guild in the city of Aun, in East Saanu."

"That's correct. It was a long time ago. I don't suppose he's had cause to mention me much."

"Truthfully, he never mentioned you, until he asked me to make the journey here."

Errik sat back in his chair and steepled his hands. "Your father told me five years ago that one day you would come to me. And here you are."

"Five *years* ago? I don't understand. How would he..." Suddenly, Keren *did* understand. Shyam had the gift of foretelling. That rare ability to sometimes glimpse fragments of the future was one of the reasons the Elders of Wisteren- both human and *faer*- had appointed him as Earthkeeper. Although the foresight could be fickle and wayward, nevertheless it had important uses, allowing the prediction of meteorological and geological events, and even the subtle ways in which the past pulled at the strings of the future. Shyam Sedgewick had a deep sense for events affecting the natural order of things.

"Ought I... pass a message to my father? I would be happy to do so."

"A message? No." Errik smiled. "In fact, *he* has a message for *you*."

The castellan walked to a desk on the other side of the room. He unlocked a drawer and took a scroll from inside. When Errik passed it to him, Keren's eyes immediately fell upon the Sedgewick family's unique insignia. Only his father or Lyrith could have sealed this scroll. "He gave you this?"

"Yes, Keren- five years ago, when I last saw him. I think he knew that one day he would send you to me. And here you are, as foretold."

"Here I am," Keren echoed softly. The sigil gleamed faintly in the light from the window. Below it, in a small decorative script, were the words *For Keren only.*

"Are you going to open it?"

"Should I?" The Earthkeeper's son traced a finger over the insignia, and a flicker of fear passed through him for no reason he could understand.

"Of course. He gave me only one instruction - that I pass that scroll to you when you came to me and ensure that you open and read it. You *alone*, I should add."

Errik sat back in his chair and waited, looking towards the east-facing window as Keren broke the seal and unfolded the scroll, then held it so only he could read its contents.

He immediately recognised his father's painstaking, deliberate script.

Keren, when you read this, I ask one thing of you above all else. Do not, under any circumstances, reveal any part of this message to anyone, even Errik of Hopesfall.

Memorise the contents of this message, and then destroy the scroll. Cast it into the flames of the nearest hearth or hold it to a candle- ensure its destruction as soon as you possibly can, and do not- DO NOT- reveal anything of what I will now tell you.

You must find your way to a distant place- yes, even further from home than Hopesfall. Far to the south and east, beyond the edge of Anphay and near the Frostwastes, lies Blood Bear Island. Likely you will remember the name from maps you memorised during your schooling, although you will have had no occasion to think of this place until now.

On this island stands a mountain known as Black Peak, the tall-est point. Directly to the south is a smaller mountain, distinctive by virtue of its conical shape and sharp summit- a volcano, which has not erupted for many centuries. The Anphayan mapmakers know it simply as the Cone. It is to this mountain that you must go- specifically, its southern face.

Here, in a few places the rock forms red-coloured lines that snake up and down the otherwise dark slope of rocks formed from ancient lava flows. The colour is formed from a mineral present on the island.

One such line is wider and longer than the others. Follow this line up the slope, until you reach its end. Here, you will find the entrance to a small fissure in the surface. Inside that you will find- I hope beyond hope- a single object with which you must return to Mirrordeep.

I cannot describe it to you because I have no idea what it will look like. But you MUST take it and return home with all haste.

Given your good sense in financial matters, you should already have some money left from the amount I gave you. But this will not be enough, and I could borrow no more from the treasury without arousing suspicion. Ask Errik for further funds, as well as companions for your journey- Anphayan men who know the land and whose help you will need. You must enlist others when you sail the Southern Sea to the island.

Errik does not, and must not, know the details of your onward journey.

May all the Great Spirits of Theya give you luck and deliver you back to me.

The message ended with Shyam's distinctive, flamboyant signature- a sharp contrast to the reserved man to whom it belonged.

Still reeling with shock, Keren read the entire message again to commit it properly to memory. Then he rolled the scroll up and cast it into the fire. He watched it swiftly burn away, then sank into his chair.

Why would his father have asked this of him- a task that had no given reason, a journey to a place near the end of the known world, to find and bring back something that his father hadn't even described? Something that he apparently *couldn't* describe?

Gifted with the Foretelling, Shyam had an acute sense of cause and effect. No one took their duties more seriously than the

Earthkeeper of Mirrordeep. Whatever he had set in motion, had been done with good reason, Keren reminded himself.

The Earthkeeper's son put his head in his hands. The idea of heading into the dismal far south of Anphay and beyond, after what had already been the longest journey of his life, filled him with despair. For a moment he even considered heading back home, no matter the reception he might receive.

Errik spoke up quietly. "I know your father well, Keren. He is a man of great honour and purpose. The best intent lies behind everything he does. Many years ago, he saved my life. I will never forget that."

Keren nodded tiredly. Maybe he would ask about that if he ever found his way back home.

"I will need funds," he said at last. He thought quickly, wondering how many companions he should have for an onward journey. Two, perhaps? Would that be enough? He had no idea. "And two of your guardsmen, if you can spare them. I must go as soon as possible. Will you help?" *Can you afford to help?* he silently echoed.

Errik blinked in surprise, but quickly nodded. "I will."

Matters proceeded swiftly. Errik arranged for the coinmaster to give him a further thirty gold Theyan suns and the same in silver. Provisions from the kitchens were wrapped and provided, as Keren had hoped. As he waited in the inner courtyard for his horse later that morning, two of Errik's guardsmen approached, bearing saddle bags for their own horses. Both wore scrappy leather armour which had seen better days.

"Keren," the taller and leaner of the two called out, brushing untidy blond hair from in front of his face as they wandered up to him. "My name is Larnus. This is Tomas. We're to accompany you for as long as needed. Where are we headed?"

"South."

"South *where?*"

"I'll tell you when we're on the road." The stable hands were too near for Keren's liking, and a few other servants frowned in his direction as they passed by on their morning errands. "That's the way it is, I'm afraid."

By the time they were ready to ride, the early morning clouds had disappeared. Low, wintry sunlight cut across the low hills to the east and the flat grasslands to the south as the three men rode away from Hopesfall.

Errik watched from the window of his morning room, lost in thought but not sure what he was thinking, as the two guardsmen and the Wisterene became specks in the distance.

Well, it was done now- not that he knew exactly *what* had been done.

Errik turned as the slightly built, dark-haired man from Urath Hai entered. He didn't truly believe the man was from Urath Hai or anywhere else in Asqabal for that matter. He had never been able to place the man's accent, but neither had he asked about his origins. After all, Mallik- if that was truly his name- had invested in the castle and the surrounding land, sufficiently for Errik to keep his ancestral home, even if the money hadn't been quite enough to repair the place completely. Without those funds, he would have needed to sell everything, not that it would have raised much.

Aside from his interest in Shyam's scroll, Mallik had revealed very little and asked for nothing in the last five years except Errik's silence in all matters relating to that message.

"So," Mallik said quietly, "your work for me is at an end."

Mallik had come to him only a few weeks after Shyam gave Errik the scroll five years ago. Somehow, with the help of a considerable sum of gold, he had convinced Errik to let him see its contents. He possessed a certain sorcerous talent, enough to melt away the protective magic around the message- clearly without Shyam ever finding out. He had studied the contents and resealed the scroll. Then Mallik had gone away, occasionally making an appearance to remind Errik of his existence or to make another donation towards the upkeep of the castle.

In return, Errik needed only to let fly the bird that Mallik had given him- a curious, dark mess of a creature that never uttered a sound- as soon as Keren or anyone else sent by Shyam arrived in Hopesfall.

Months passed. Years passed. His mysterious benefactor appeared less often as time went on, and Errik had almost forgotten about the scroll locked away in his safe when Shyam's son finally arrived at the gates of his keep and the bird was set free.

"You never explained why you couldn't have simply retrieved this thing five years ago," Errik noted.

"It would not have been there five years ago, nor at any time until now- or, more specifically, *soon*." Mallik's smile did not reach his eyes, which remained as coldly distant as ever. "The *arterrim* occupy specific times and places. They are not always where they were originally placed. Much of the time, they are nowhere at all."

"I don't understand."

Mallik gave him a contemptuous look. "You are not equipped to *understand*. But I pay great attention to the actions of men such as Shyam Sedgewick. No matter that he likely doesn't know *how* he arrived at his conclusion. If he strongly believes that one of the *arterrim* will appear in that place, around the time his son arrives on the island- then we must be there too."

"*We?*" Errik summoned reserves of courage from somewhere. "No. I'm not going there. I wouldn't be of much use to you at my..."

"I didn't mean *you*." Mallik shook his head. "I wouldn't expect an old man to embark on such a voyage. Rest assured, Errik of Hopesfall, your usefulness to me is at an end."

Errik did not like the sound of that. "You have my final payment with you, I trust."

Mallik laughed softly. "Your final payment? Of course." He took a cloth bag from the inner pocket of his robe and tossed it onto the table. "Here. Try not to spend it all at once."

Errik cautiously opened the bag and looked inside. He reckoned the bag contained at least fifty suns.

Something about the look of the coins perturbed him, and Errik thought of Keren on his long ride through the Anphayan hinterland with Tomas and Larnus- helped on his way, heavy with Hopesfall gold, but perhaps condemned. "What will..." He paused, uncomfortable. "What will happen to Keren and my men?"

"What happens to anyone caught up in this matter is no longer your concern. Enjoy your wealth, Errik of Hopesfall." Mallik gestured to Errik's midriff. "You may want to get that wound seen to."

"Wound...?" Errik's vision swayed for a moment. He looked down and saw that his shirt was soaked with blood. His stomach had been cut open, and yet he felt no pain. "How..."

Mallik gave a mocking bow as Errik's legs gave way and his awareness began to fade. Blood seeped between his fingers as he clutched at his stomach.

The castellan's last thought was that he had been entirely wrong about life. He had reckoned to quietly accrue rewards without needing to do anything too unpleasant, and in return he would be left to lead a comfortably quiet, unremarkable life.

It hadn't turned out that way at all.

III

Snow swirled through the darkness. Keren stared through the window of the stone hut at the edge of the vast Dankwood forest, watching the gentle cascade. They had passed more than a dozen such buildings dotted about the bleak landscape over the last few days. They were simple structures, but sturdy.

Errik's men had inexplicably grown more cheerful as the weather worsened. They issued Keren with almost continuous advice on how to survive Anphayan winters, no matter that he firmly intended for this to be the first and last one he suffered. "Keeping out of the wind is the most important thing," Larnus had told him. "The chill, that we can deal with, but the wind makes it many times worse. These *bothra-* the huts like this one- they are not much to look at, but they save many lives."

Keren had never closely examined the tiny, fascinating crystals from which snow was made, until his journey through the south of Saanu some days ago. His father had described it to him once when Keren was a child and had drawn intricate shapes of snow crystals which he had apparently committed to memory, but even the Earthkeeper's vivid description and enthusiastic artwork failed to do it justice.

The two Anphayan men derived much amusement from Keren's continued wonderment. "Imagine if we were as excited by your desert sand," Tomas remarked.

"Wisteren isn't a desert," Keren corrected him. "Far from it. You're thinking of Hylios."

"Speaking of far places," Larnus said, "What will you be doing in Sun's End? Do we go anywhere else afterwards?"

Keren recalled Larnus mentioning that they were to accompany him for as long as needed. Had Errik really said that? The truth might test their resolve, but now they were far from Hopesfall he told them anyway. "Blood Bear Island."

The two men exchanged glances. "Errik did not mention this," Tomas said at last.

"He didn't know. And for now, it's important that no one else does. When we obtain a ship and crew, we tell those who need to know."

"Why would any sane man go there?" Tomas demanded, and Keren gave them the story he had prepared over the last few days- that he was a student of the natural world and needed to collect samples of rocks and plants from the island. He reckoned he knew enough on the subject to make his explanation plausible.

Tomas remained unimpressed. "You could have gone in the summer."

Keren had a ready answer for that. "Conditions are not right in the summer."

"Too much rain?"

"Exactly. I wouldn't be able to study and collect the specimens I need," the Wisterene agreed. The lies came easily.

"You won't like blizzards," Larnus warned him with a mischievous look in his eyes.

"You won't *survive* a blizzard." Tomas' sense of humour was even darker. "Where did you buy that cloak?"

"Somewhere in Saanu. I don't remember which town. Why?"

"You'll need something a lot thicker where we're going." The Anphayan shook his head reproachfully.

Neither of his companions had ever been as far south as Sun's End, let alone sailed the Southern Sea. Both admitted they had never set foot on a ship, and when they contemplated the voyage, their mood grew pensive. "It will be winter proper when we're there," Tomas remarked. "Won't be much daylight."

Keren couldn't help but wonder what kind of dark, cold hell Blood Bear Island would turn out to be.

Later that evening, they shared some of the clear, harsh spirit the Anphayans called *vakushla*. The taste of this unfamiliar concoction was grim- certainly compared to the honeyed wines he enjoyed at home- but Keren was glad of the warmth it provided once the foulness had worn off. Larnus and Tomas swallowed it quickly rather than allow the *vakushla* to linger long on the palette and advised him to do the same. "It's not for savouring," Larnus told him unnecessarily when he handed Keren the bottle the second time.

Keren sniffed at the drink. "It smells like the alcohol physicians use."

"Then it must be good for you," Larnus reasoned.

The snow eased off later that evening, and Keren ventured out to relieve himself. Afterwards he stood and observed the now-clear sky. He knew the names of the major stars and the constellations they formed, but their positions were a little different to those they occupied in Wisteren.

The sheer magnitude of the night canopy reminded him of the task ahead, incomprehensibly huge, impossible to understand. "I don't know what I'm doing," he muttered.

"You sure you're not a Protector?" Larnus laughed from behind him.

Keren flinched and looked back. He hadn't heard the other man leave the hut. "A Protector?" he repeated.

Larnus wandered over and unbuttoned his trousers to piss. "They are *famous* for talking to themselves," he remarked as steam rose from the snow. "Mind you, maybe it's not themselves they talk to. Some say the fragments of demons they've killed stay inside their heads. Doesn't seem fair, does it? Like being bitten by a dead wolf. Takes an odd sort of man to be one of them. Or woman."

Keren found himself flustered by the Anphayan's presence. He knew why, of course, and Larnus relieving himself next to him didn't help. He half-turned to go back in, but Larnus suddenly asked, "You have anyone? Back home?"

"Have anyone?"

"I mean, like a wife, or betrothed- or whatever name you have for that sort of thing in Wisteren. Do you have a woman?"

Keren took a gulp of the chilly night air. He suddenly felt the need for more *vakushla,* although his head had started to spin a little. "No." He saw an intent look in the Anphayan man's eyes, and he realised what Larnus was trying to say. A strange feeling of exhilaration swept through him.

"A man?"

"I did. But not now. It..." Keren struggled for words. "It wasn't important."

Larnus finally finished urinating and buttoned his trousers, then gave Keren an altogether different look, his earlier wariness now entirely gone. "I did too, a few years ago. No one now. People come and go. That's life."

Keren inhaled deeply. His pulse thumped in his ears, a sudden drumbeat. He had no idea what to say.

When the Wisterene went back to the hut and paused in the doorway to look back, his companion was still staring across the snowbound plain.

The companions continued to skirt the close gloom of the Dankwood the following day as they headed south towards Aaler. The conifers huddled together, a thick darkness between them. Keren thought the Dankwood an entirely miserable, soulless place and felt a shiver of unease as he glanced towards the vast forest, imagining it full of unpleasant secrets.

They stopped for the evening at a village with one large inn where they ate and drank only a little before sleeping. Only the following morning did Keren realise how tired he was. He had once hoped he might grow used to riding after the last few months, but no more.

The three men breakfasted in the front guest room on thin-cut strips of smoked venison and fresh bread, washed down with goat's milk heated over the fire. The smell of pine mingled with the aroma of the food as they ate, and outside the sun came up and lit the fallen snow as if it were glass. "Good weather for good progress," Tomas remarked, but then- perhaps simply because he was Tomas- he added glumly, "It won't last."

By midday, as they rode along the wide fence-bordered track, the coast and Western Ocean had emerged in the distance, and soon afterwards the town and harbour of Aaler, made almost exclusively of low, squat buildings that lay huddled around the curve of the bay. Keren's face had become numb and the cold cut through his gloves and even his cloak. The breath of men and horses steamed in the frosty air.

"How long until we reach Sun's End?" Keren wanted to know.

"Maybe a week," Larnus estimated. "Two, if the weather is bad." He glanced across and shook his head. "I never imagined anyone could be so desperate to reach that place."

"Never mind an island near the end of the world," Tomas added.

IV

The weather remained mercifully calm for the remainder of their journey, and the companions sheltered each night either in one of the ubiquitous *bothra* that dotted the Anphayan hinterland, or in a guest house or tavern room whenever one could be found. By day, they kept to well-trodden, wide tracks for the horses' sake. The snow, where it had fallen, was not deep enough to cause problems.

At last, they reached the crest of a low hill beyond which the land sloped away towards the coast. "Welcome to Sun's End," Larnus remarked.

The town looked every bit as dismal as Keren had expected. He took in the view of low, ugly huts and storehouses, muddy tracks, and a refuse pile near the western edge of the settlement, which had been set on fire. Thick black smoke billowed into the bright morning sky. Out in the harbour, four large sailing ships lay at anchor.

"Ugly place." Larnus grimaced in distaste. "I heard that sometimes the air is thick with the stench of whale flesh." He turned to Tomas. "Do they have any decent taverns in this place? They better had."

Tomas shrugged. "Decent may be hard to come by. But a roof is a roof. There'll be food of some sort. Do you like fish, Keren?"

The Wisterene did not want to think about fish.

Near the middle of the town, they found a large, ramshackle inn called The Anchor. The pine interior held an odour of pipeweed along with something sour and almost vinegary, which Keren couldn't identify. When he bought their accommodation- a room was available for each of them, and the cost was less than expected- Tomas recommended that they hold their rooms for at least three nights. "Reckon it will take that long to negotiate the cost of the journey, if that's possible."

Keren reminded himself that every man had his price. He just needed to find out how much was enough to sway one of the ships' captains. Sun's End did not have the look of a wealthy place. Hopefully, the gold would be more than enough.

If not, he would be heading home.

The three men relaxed and drank that night. Much later, they retired to their rooms, taking candles to light the way up the narrow, uncertain staircase and along a landing whose floor creaked alarmingly. "How does this place stay up?" Tomas slurred as he stumbled through his doorway.

"How do *you* stay up?" Larnus retorted with a laugh.

Keren found his way into his room, closed the door, and set his candle on the wooden table. He went to the hearth to stir the embers into some sort of life, and was still staring at the glowing remnants, wondering whether to add a few logs from the pile, when he heard a soft knock at the door.

He opened the door a little to find Larnus leaning against the doorway. "Need some company? I'll not be offended if you say no." He held up an almost-full bottle of black liquid. "I bought this earlier. You want to try some?"

"I don't remember you doing that."

"It's *vakushla,* but different. The black one *is* for savouring."

"You'd better come in," Keren murmured. "Where's Tomas?"

"Never mind Tomas. He'll sleep through to the morning."

Keren went to stoke the fire up and added a few more logs. Larnus sat next to him and passed the bottle, and Keren took a cautious sip. His eyes widened as the taste caught him entirely by surprise. The black *vakushla* was slightly sweet and smooth as velvet.

The Wisterene smiled, and when he felt an arm around his shoulder and a hand in his hair, then a kiss on the back of his neck, he closed his eyes and sank into the moment.

For a while, he forgot everything else.

Keren woke into almost complete darkness, on the goose-feather mattress. He was naked under a thick blanket. The air felt cold on his face, and the fire had all but gone out. As his eyes gradually adjusted to the deep gloom, he sat up and saw that Larnus had gone.

All manner of thoughts cut through the small-hours fog in his head. He lay back, wrapped the blanket more tightly about himself and stared up at the dusty beams and the cracks in the ceiling.

Had something important happened? It felt like it had.

Listen to yourself, he thought. Lyrith had warned that he became attached too quickly and sometimes too desperately- in love with the idea of being in love, she called it, blaming some of the books he read in the Summer Library. Perhaps she was right. Lyrith rarely spared anyone the truth, no matter how it might be received.

Keren could recall everything he and Larnus had *done-* he remembered almost weeping, confounded by the man's gentleness- but nothing that they'd said.

Had they spoken at all? Keren wished he could remember.

He found his clothes scattered all over the floor. After dressing, he opened the shutters of the little window on the other side of the room. In the blue half-light of the early morning the odd, misaligned shapes of houses and huts spread out almost as far as he could see. Vivid and varied colours painted many of these dwellings, but in the quiet gloom he could not make out those features properly. Sun's End appeared sullen and brooding. This was not a friendly place, even for his Anphayan companions.

The Earthkeeper's son watched the light strengthen, allowing his thoughts to drift back and forth. More than once, he considered going to find Larnus. Why had he gone back to his room last night? Maybe an uncomfortable silence would rise between them. Might Larnus be embarrassed, even regretful? They had both had much to drink, Keren reminded himself. Before, and maybe after.

The deeply contented glow he had felt after waking began to ebb away.

Sometime later, near full light, he heard a door open and close. Footsteps passed by his door and faded on the creaking wooden stairs.

Keren took a deep breath, picked up his pack and left.

After a breakfast of fried fish, bread and saltmeat the three men headed down to the local authority office, which Keren's companions reckoned was the best place to get the information they needed. The office turned out to be a single-roomed shack with a desk, chair and shelves holding a few pots and jars along with supplies such as rope and fishing weights. The hut stank of rust and mildew.

"We need a ship and crew to sail to Blood Bear Island," Keren told the clerk, a young man with ragged stubble and blond hair, who sat miserably in his grimy fur cloak. "If you can give me the name and whereabouts of a ship's captain who might agree a price…"

But the clerk was already shaking his head. "No. It will be winter soon. Why do you want to go *there*?"

"I study the natural arts. Creatures, plant life. Rocks."

The young clerk gave him a blank look.

"It hasn't been properly explored," Keren continued patiently. "Any knowledge I gain will be useful in my further studies."

The youth frowned. "I think you should go back to where you came from."

Keren ignored the advice. "Four large sailing vessels are at anchor in the harbour. Whose are they?"

"I don't have that information. You need to speak with Jan the harbourmaster." The clerk had become restless, perhaps having decided he ought not to be speaking with them at all. He peered behind them to the doorway as if a supervisor might return to berate him.

"Where would we find him?"

"Likely the Bay Tavern on the west side of town. I think it has opened now." The clerk grimaced. "Best go there soon. He likes a drink and won't be much use later. And he doesn't speak Theyan."

They found the Bay Tavern easily, and Jan the harbourmaster was almost as easy to find- the barkeeper pointed to him when Tomas enquired. Jan was a giant of a man, with a long, thick beard and an over-abundance of jewellery on his fingers and around his neck, as if he had plundered a treasure trove and decided to wear most of it. Four empty tankards stood on his table already. He fixed the newcomers with a yellow-eyed stare as they approached, then folded his tree-trunk arms defensively when Tomas began to talk to him in Anphayan. The man's eyes swivelled from Tomas to Larnus and then narrowed suspiciously when they settled on Keren.

Finally, he spoke, in a low, phlegmy voice, interrupting his monologue with a hacking cough. Then he got up and lumbered over to the bar, and Tomas turned to Keren with a shrug. "He said no ships set sail from Sun's End, or anywhere south or west of here, until the spring. Only fishing vessels that head into the bay and back."

Keren shook his head. "No. That can't be right."

Tomas gave him a look that was half amused, half frustrated. "He may be a drunk, Keren, but I'd believe him in this."

"Ask him where we can find the captains of the ships in the harbour. Then we can go to speak with them."

Tomas shrugged wearily and followed Jan, who had already procured another large tankard of ale and was leaning on the bar. One giant hand clutched possessively at his drink. Keren watched pensively as Tomas and Jan talked.

"He says only one of those ships is seaworthy enough to go as far as Blood Bear Island and back," Tomas said when he returned. "The ship with the grey sails, furthest east in the harbour. Its name is Fairwind, and it belongs to a man called Ishan Rhel. He has sailed across the Southern Sea before, although not at this time of year."

"Then let's talk with him," Keren said immediately.

"He's on the ship now. But Jan said he returned last week and doesn't intend to sail again."

"*Ever* again?" Keren wondered bleakly why events were stacking up against them.

"He announced his retirement three days ago. I hope you're willing to pay a small fortune for your journey."

V

Captain Rhel gave them a look that could have indicated anything or nothing, and sat back, methodically filling his pipe with an especially dark, coarse smoking weed. The faintly acrid odour reminded Keren of damp, burned wood. "If I were you," Rhel remarked at last, scratching at his unruly, grey-flecked beard, "I would come back in the summer. I won't be here, but others will take you for the right price."

"You're not the first to say that. But this is the best season for my studies," Keren told him.

"Study something else." The chair creaked alarmingly as the captain shifted his position.

"I hear you've sailed across the Southern Sea before."

"So why would I want to do it again?" Rhel laughed. "I intend to spend the dark months drinking and sleeping. A month from now, there'll be no daylight worth getting out of bed for. I'll sell my ship and buy myself a little house somewhere in the north."

One of his men sitting across the galley added something in Anphayan, and the whole group laughed. Even Rhel smiled a little.

"I'll make it worth your while."

"Will you? Show me what you have then, so we can both be disappointed."

Keren untied the pouches containing his gold, and cautiously allowed the ship's captain to see inside them. Tomas and Larnus stood ready on either side in case he attempted to seize the bag, but Rhel simply looked and sat back, carefully expressionless.

"There are fifty gold Theyan suns here," Keren quietly informed him, and heard his companions draw a sharp intake of breath behind him.

"Enough to buy a small manor in Fort Cailan," Tomas remarked. "Better weather there. Fewer cutthroats walking the streets."

"Careful, now. I've employed some of those cutthroats from time to time." Rhel tapped his dirty fingers on the pine table as an ill-tempered mutter rose amongst his men.

The ship's captain lit his pipe. Blowing a cloud of blue-grey smoke up towards the rafters, he remarked, "Why are you so desperate to reach that Gods-forsaken place?"

"There are mineral deposits, plants and certain other natural curiosities I must study," Keren told him.

"And these *natural curiosities* cannot wait until the spring?"

"No. They're dependent on the winter environment."

Rhel's eyes strayed to the pouch again. "I'm not sure you've made me a good enough offer," he sighed. "How much more do you have?"

"This is all..."

"Don't take me for a fool, Wisterene. How much more do you have?"

"Only enough for the journey home afterwards. Another ten in gold, no more than that. Some silver..."

"Never mind the silver. Let's agree sixty gold suns." He motioned for Keren to spill the coins from the bag, and the companions watched as he counted them. "Show me your other ten," Rhel demanded, and Keren took the others from his various trouser and shirt pockets.

"Good." Rhel almost looked satisfied. "I will take forty now. It will be stored by the town authorities, in the vaults. You will submit the remainder to me when we return before you disembark. Apart from the crew and provisions, I must pay for an iceguide who will journey with you to the island. Unless you want to set foot there and be dead within a day."

"Iceguide?"

"His name is Senning. He's spent time on Barren Isle and knows how to survive in the similar conditions you'll find on Blood Bear Island." The captain extended a scarred hand. "Are we agreed?"

Keren shook his hand, bewildered at how quickly matters had changed. "We are."

Rhel moved forty of the gold coins into a separate cloth bag, then turned to the sailsmen who lingered nearby. "We leave in two days, at dawn. These three are now under my personal protection. Anyone seeing fit to harm or steal from them will be meat for the sharks. When we return, you will all be paid handsomely." He gestured to two of the larger men, continuing to speak in Theyan for Keren's benefit. "Torim, Dayn- you'll come with us to the town hall and bear witness to the coin deposit. The rest of you know what to do. Make good the Fairwind for one more voyage."

Keren and his companions had little to do but wait over the next couple of days as the ship was made ready and paperwork drawn up by the town authorities to confirm the agreement. When Keren wandered by the harbour, he saw stocks of food and other supplies being loaded, and repairs being made to the vessel. He couldn't stand and watch for long with the icy, damp breeze issuing from the south-west.

It would be even worse on the open sea, he reminded himself.

He met the iceguide Senning on the second day of preparations. A lean but muscular man with numerous scars and pockmarks on his wind-reddened countenance, Senning greeted Keren with nothing more than a frown and remarked, "You do not look like a man who travels to dangerous places."

"I could do without the danger," Keren admitted.

"Do you know how the island got its name?"

"Because of the bears that live there?"

"*Blood* bears. No one knows more than a little about them. They are not natural."

"Not *natural*?"

"You have bears in Wisteren?"

"Yes, in the hilly woodlands near the border with Saanu."

"And they are fast and strong- but they are only creatures, going about whatever business creatures have. You leave them alone, they leave *you* alone most of the time. In the far south-west of Anphay there are large white bears. They can be savage when they have a hunger on them, or if it's a mother with cubs to defend. It takes a team of spearsmen to put one of them down. But the blood bears are different. They have a..." Senning pondered. "A *rage* inside."

"When did you encounter them?"

The iceguide laughed. "Me? I have never encountered any such creature. How do you think I am here now? Two expeditions have gone to the Frostwastes. Half the men who went did not come back. Those who did, spoke fearfully of the blood bears. I listened to their testimonies. These were hard men, not given to fright. Most never went out to sea again after. It was as if their encounters... *took* something from them. Like I said, Wisterene- they are unnatural."

"Rhel said you lived on Barren Isle. Don't the bears find their way over there when the sea freezes?"

"The sea never freezes across the distance between the Frostwastes and Barren Isle. Blood Bear Island lies much closer to the coast of the Frostwastes, and in the depths of winter, the bears are known to cross to it." Senning gave him a slightly contemptuous look. "You need not worry. They can swim, but they never swim near to the island. The currents are too strong. They come only when the sea ice forms, and that is more than two months away. I have studied all the maps and reports from Blood Bear Island." He grinned humourlessly. "It didn't take long."

Keren gazed into the distant south. No land could be seen in that direction- even the coast of the Frostwastes was too far away. "What lies even further away, beyond the Frostwastes?"

The iceguide gave him an odd look. "I don't know. That's a question for the Gods, Keren. Never ending darkness, maybe."

On the morning of the day before their voyage, Rhel and two of his men were at the harbour checking goods before they were carried onboard, helped by Tomas, Larnus and Keren. The wind had died down and the sun came out for a while, and Keren felt a rare dash of optimism. Somehow, he had got this far, and soon they would be setting off for the island. Maybe everything would work out.

Around midday a small two-horse carriage approached on the north-eastern road and stopped a few hundred paces away before the point where the road deteriorated into a morass of mud and slush. A tall, dark-haired figure emerged from the interior and walked towards them. He wore light leather armour under a pristine grey cloak. Polished boots made a steady sound as he approached, skirting carefully around deep puddles and potholes.

When the man reached them, he showed a star symbol on a pendant around his neck, which further identified him as a Protector.

Without any preamble he addressed Keren in brisk, immaculate Theyan. "You must be Keren Sedgewick of Wisteren."

"I am," Keren replied. His stomach tightened with unease. How could the Protectorate know who he was, and why were they interested enough in him to send one of their own here?

"I believe you're due to sail to Blood Bear Island."

"I am a student of the natural arts and..."

"And I am Protector Darien White. I have been sent here to accompany you."

"You've come a long way," Rhel remarked sardonically, "given that at least two of your comrades are already stationed here in the town. I'm sure we could have found a berth for one of them if they'd asked."

Darien gave him a dismissive look. "They have their own, unrelated duties."

"So, our Wisterene guest has his own Protector." Rhel turned his unsmiling gaze to Keren. "Friends in high places?"

Darien's expression did not change as he handed a rolled and tied paper to Rhel. "Can you read, Captain?"

"I read well enough." Rhel gave him a dangerous look.

"Then study this. It gives me the right, as decreed by First Protector Ferrim, to travel with you. Read at your leisure and keep. I have my own copy."

Rhel untied the paper and slowly read its contents. "Seems in order," he said at last, displeased. Then his expression changed. "First Protector *Ferrim*?"

"Yes." Darien smiled thinly. "I forget that news takes time to reach places like this. Our previous leader was relieved of his duties a two weeks ago, by order of the Grand Assembly."

Rhel looked thoughtfully at him, then shrugged. "Whoever's in charge matters little here. We're only remembered when Fort

Cailan's stock of fish runs low. Welcome aboard, Protector. I do hope you enjoy the voyage."

Keren looked out across the harbour towards the huddled rows of houses and huts that straddled the coast- a town that looked like it was shivering. He remembered his father once pointing out that the loose alliance of the western lands' people- including the *faer*- meant a lot less than it had. This implied that even supposed allies might be less than trustworthy. Protectors were certainly included in that estimation.

The Protectorate valued order and sense, and especially knowledge. Perhaps they had known of his journey for some time already. Had one of their eyes-and-ears been working as a servant in Errik's fortress in Hopesfall? Even so, how could they have known his eventual destination?

He flinched as Darien clapped him on the shoulder. The Protector flashed a warm smile when Keren reluctantly looked at him. "My mission is to help you find and document everything you need to on the island. Maybe I'll even learn a thing or two about these plants and rocks that interest you so."

Keren smiled wanly but could find nothing to say.

The Fairwind left harbour the following morning. A breeze from the west bore them along under gloomy skies. Even in the relative calm, Keren soon found the constant movement of the ship unsettling, and over the next few days as the wind increased and conditions became choppier in the open sea, he was overcome by unbearable nausea, disorientation, and poor balance made worse by slippery decks and steps.

Dark clouds scudded across the sky, pushed from the remote western Frostwastes. Keren soon learned to look away from the ever-oscillating horizon, and to keep a firm grip on the rails wherever possible, but several times each day he would vomit up much of what he'd eaten. He made sure to drink his ration of purified water, and ale from the barrels stocked on the ship, although nothing entirely cleansed his mouth of the acrid taste.

After a few days the seasickness abated enough for him to keep down the cold breakfasts of saltfish and crackers, and the luncheons of seal meat, thin broth, and dried fruit, but he continued to sleep poorly and never felt anything less than unsteady when he moved around the ship.

Larnus and Tomas coped only a little better with the season's ungentle seas, but Keren, as a foreigner, found himself subjected to ridicule every time he stumbled past a group of sailsmen, or worse, slipped on the deck.

Captain Rhel remained a brooding presence, often poring over maps of the Southern Sea as if he hadn't sailed it before. More than once he voiced his concern that Blood Bear Island's rugged coastline had no natural harbour and presented a danger to any vessel that drew too close. "No harbour, no beach," he ominously reminded Keren on the fourth day of the voyage. "Not many places where even a rowing boat might safely reach shore. But that's the only way you're reaching the island. We'll drop anchor before we get too near the barnacled rocks that hide under the shallow waters. If we sink, we all die." He pointed his smoke-pipe accusingly. "And I'm not dying for *you*, Wisterene. Not with your gold waiting for me back home."

"So, we row to shore?" Keren did not like the sound of that.

"*You* and your two men along with the iceguide row to shore. I expect your new friend the Protector will want to join you too. He seems *very* keen on helping you."

He does, Keren silently agreed.

"Meantime, we wait at anchor. I'll give you six days to come back. After that, we leave, with or without you. There's talk of an early storm this winter and I don't wish to be caught in it."

Keren began to protest- from the maps he had already seen, the island extended about a hundred miles from west to east, and he might need more time. Then he saw Rhel's forbidding expression.

"There are one or two places in the west bay where you might land the boat without smashing it to splinters," the captain added, as if in dark encouragement. "Here. Look." He pointed to the shape of the island on his map, although it lacked any details that might help. "But it depends on conditions. Are you a lucky man?"

Rhel gave him a long stare. By the lamplight in the low-ceilinged cabin his face looked sallow and unhealthy, carved with lines of worry, and worn by the cold, salty air. He looked almost as if he might be carved from rotting wood.

Then the ship emitted a dolorous groan, and Keren gripped the edge of the table. The reaction did not go unnoticed by the captain. "You sure you don't want to go and lie down, Wisterene?" Rhel's laugh turned into a wet cough and he turned to spit in a bucket by his chair.

"Senning will lead you as well as anyone can," he added when he finally recovered. "But if you or your men are stupid enough to not pay attention and get yourselves hurt..." The captain shrugged. "Best you don't. It would be a lonely place to die."

Keren knew it wouldn't be long until Darien sought him out, and so it proved to be, later that day.

"Found your sea legs yet?"

"I don't think I'll ever grow sea legs," Keren remarked ruefully.

"Where in Wisteren are you from?" The Protector's sharp-eyed look betrayed his casual tone. "I know my accents well, but I couldn't quite place yours. Somewhere in the north-west of the land, I'm guessing."

"Very good." Keren smiled as disarmingly as he could while meeting the man's gaze. Likely Darien already knew where he was from and perhaps his familial connections. Nothing could be gained from being evasive. "Mirrordeep," he added. "My father is the Earthkeeper there."

"Earthkeeper." Darien looked impressed. "A sorcerer of weather, yes? Keeping the elements and natural forces in harmony?"

"Only Theya herself keeps natural forces in harmony- no man or woman has that power," Keren couldn't help but correct him. "The work of earthkeepers is less exciting than you may think. They measure and observe things to do with the weather and natural events, and they influence such things positively where they can, in small ways. There's a lot less sorcery than you would expect, and a lot more diligent monitoring."

"And he sent you to Blood Bear Island? What could you possibly have done to deserve that?"

Keren laughed good-naturedly. "I'm to collect samples of certain rocks, along with some plants that only grow on that island. They're of no financial value but they are of great interest to my father. And to myself, for I hope to follow in his footsteps."

"They must be of great interest indeed." Darien cast his gaze around the ship and nodded. "Not cheap at all, a fully equipped sailing vessel and crew." He laughed. "You should have come here in the summer, Keren. It might have cost you less."

"I keep hearing that advice."

"It might also have meant a journey with more reputable sorts than this gang of goldthirsty renegades. If such exist in Sun's End."

Keren looked nervously around to ensure no one had overheard Darien's blithe insult.

"I'll be honest with you- I don't enjoy these conditions any more than you do," the Protector confessed. "The climate is a little less miserable in Fort Cailan."

"Is that where you're from?"

The Protector nodded. "Maybe I was sent on this voyage to be toughened up."

Perhaps, Keren thought. *But I don't think so.* He had already decided there was more to Darien White than met the eye, and the man's self-deprecating demeanour was not, Keren reasoned, something to be expected from an appointed defender of the world.

"How did the Protectorate learn of this voyage?" he asked. "It seems odd that you would be assigned to help a man from Wisteren collect plant and rock specimens."

Darien shrugged. "I don't get to make decisions, Keren. I only get to obey orders."

Silence fell between them. Keren listened to the churn of the sea and the whistling of the wind in the sails.

"Well, I'm going to see if they have such a thing as breakfast this morning," Darien remarked at last. He half-turned and then paused. "Be sure to remember, Keren- if you need help with anything, let me know." He added in a low voice, "These seafarers hold scant regard for the law. And given that their captain has legally bound himself and his men to your safe voyage, it is my duty to ensure that the law and agreement are upheld."

Keren wasn't at all sure that it was- he doubted that any such legal agreement even existed, despite the paperwork drawn up by the authorities in Sun's End- but thanked him anyway.

He watched the Protector negotiate his way along the deck towards the stairs that led down to the galley and felt the knot of unease inside him tighten.

"When this is over, I want us to stay together," Keren told Larnus that evening. They lay under three layers of blankets, warmed also by each other's heat. A rare feeling of contentment had emboldened Keren, yet he wondered fearfully what the other man would say in reply.

"Where?" Larnus traced a finger along his cheek.

"Anywhere." Keren reconsidered. "No. Somewhere warm."

"I've never been to Wisteren. Never been anywhere near."

"Would you like to?"

"With you, yes. What would your family think of me- this pale ruffian?"

Keren studied his lover for a moment, a faint smile on his face. "They would like you. Those who matter. My father. And my sister, Lyrith."

"They... know about you?" Larnus seemed uncomfortable with the question.

"Yes. And have done for many years."

The Anphayan grimaced. "Would that I had a family like yours."

They said nothing for a while, listening to the creak and groan of the ship, lost in thoughts of other people and other places. The lanterns flickered and cast dancing shadows on the low ceiling.

"We need to look out for one another- you and I, and Tomas," Larnus told him eventually. "I don't trust any of these sailsmen, and certainly not the captain."

"I spoke with the Protector earlier. He said much the same thing, in his own way. He invited me to seek his help if I needed it."

"And he's another not to be trusted." Larnus sat up, swung his legs over the side of the bed, and began putting his clothes on.

"You're going?" Keren asked.

"Best I do. Tongues will wag and rumours spread if I spend the night here."

"Let them," Keren muttered.

"No. We can't let them. They already find it suspicious that a Wisterene has come all the way to this part of the world. They likely think you're half-*faer*."

"I do have *faer* blood," Keren admitted. "On my mother's side. My maternal great-grandmother was of the *flammar* on Firemount."

Larnus grinned in the gloom. "I don't know what or where that is, but I knew you had something exotic about you."

Keren couldn't help but laugh.

"I'm glad for this," Larnus added a moment later. "Glad the gods sent you to me. We're likely all going to die on that island, only now it doesn't matter so much."

The Earthkeeper's son was puzzled by that fatalistic idea. Maybe they would and maybe they wouldn't, but since he'd met Larnus he felt *more* determined to survive, more determined to fight his way to a future the two of them could share.

"We won't," he said. "When this is done, we'll go to Mirrordeep."

"I would like that." Larnus leaned over, kissed him, and left.

Nonetheless, fears of all the things that could ruin that distant future began to manifest in Keren's thoughts. After a while he fell asleep, and dreamed of lying in a field on the lower slopes of Firemount, staring up at a perfect blue sky as red flowers bloomed everywhere in the warmth. Far away, on the other side of the world, black clouds gathered, and a mournful wind sighed over an icy, dead landscape.

Keren turned away from it, but the storm whispered insistently to him.

You can't deny me. You're mine, and you'll die in my domain.

VI

Senning had much to tell Keren and his companions about the conditions on Blood Bear Island, the following morning.

"The wind can be cold enough to kill- so we must shelter wherever we can, away from that prevailing west wind. We may find shelter in caves or behind stone formations. The ground is split in places with deep rifts. You fall into one, you're gone. Understand?"

"Can the mountains be climbed without rope?" Keren asked.

"If you're careful, yes. There is loose scree, and no paths, so any climb should be done when the light is at its best- and we won't have much daylight. The afternoon grows dark quickly." Senning frowned. "You want to *climb* the mountains?"

"I may need to go up the slope of one of them a little way. The one called the Cone. It lies to the south of Black Peak."

The iceguide's lips twisted in a half-smile. "I know the one. The Gharaanians also mapped that part of the island, some years ago. They call it Hellspike."

"Hellspike."

Senning shrugged. "To them, everything must have something to do with hell, or heaven. Usually hell. The afterlife rules their worldly lives."

"Has anyone climbed it?"

"To the top? I doubt it." Senning gave him an incredulous look. "Why would they?"

They were spared rough seas over the next few days. The waters through which they sailed were never less than choppy, but no storms came their way. Even so, Keren still could not stomach much of the food the sailsmen ate, but he managed to get through each day without succumbing to the *bleakness* as Larnus had called it. They both felt that dismal, yawning chasm in their heads throughout their waking hours- a faint yet persistent despair alleviated only when they were together alone, or asleep. But they managed to keep it at bay, simply by talking about it.

"I have never known anything like this before," Keren confessed one day as they stood on deck looking out over a grey scene of low, dark cloud and the gloomy, churning sea. "The misery of this watery prison."

"I've known something like it, but not quite this way."

Keren shook his head. "I've enjoyed privileges that most can only dream of. I had everything I wanted as a child. Perhaps too much. I am not cut out for this, Larnus."

"We are the sum of the things we do," the Anphayan mused. "And there are always choices."

Keren wondered what he himself had done of note, other than throw himself headlong into the jaws of madness.

Four days later they came within sight of Blood Bear Island. The sailsman in the crow's nest made the call, and soon afterwards the land became visible from the deck. The five men who would be rowing to the island gathered to watch pensively near the prow as dark, jagged cliffs rose awkwardly from the water, slowly gaining in definition as the ship drew near. Mid-morning approached, and for once the near continual cloud cover had lifted and harsh sunlight danced upon the water. Somehow that served to make Blood Bear Island darker than it ought to be, like a hellish black maw rising from the waves.

Just before noon, Rhel ordered the anchor to be dropped and told them, "This is as near as we go. We'll lower the rowboat." He looked towards the island. "Pretty, isn't she?"

Keren tried to estimate their distance from the rocky shore. He thought perhaps a mile still separated them from land. "Is six days enough?" he muttered, half to himself.

"Your problem," Rhel said.

The descent by rope-ladder to the rowing boat was perilous, even though the sea had become calmer. Keren managed it well enough but found that panic truly set in once he settled himself in the boat and felt the full swell of the ocean bear him up and down as if he were as light as a stick-doll, able to crush him under its watery weight at any moment.

He had been a good swimmer from a young age. But now he was at the mercy of something so vast he became numb with fear. He gripped the side of the boat with a shaking hand and almost shouted out when a wave cast the vessel against the side of the ship with a resounding thump.

Keren looked up and saw Rhel staring down at them from the deck, along with five of the sailsmen. The captain, his expression unreadable, filled his smoking pipe. The sailsmen threw down a few predictable taunts and joked amongst themselves, but their mood seemed more subdued than usual.

Once their packs of provisions and walking gear were in the boat with them, the companions took the oars and with much effort began to row towards the dark shape of the island. Keren managed to row without making a fool of himself, although his hands slipped so many times that he feared losing the oars overboard.

For a long time, although they left the vicinity of the ship, they appeared to be getting only a little nearer to the island. The five men were soon dampened and chilled by the spray, as they strained to take the boat towards the shore.

The sun had swung towards the south by the time they arrived at a short stretch of shingle beach. Keren saw a seal a short distance away, large and ponderous, its dark eyes full of curiosity as the be-draggled, shivering invaders struggled to land their boat.

Beyond the beach, tufts of grass and other vegetation occupied a steep valley between two sections of cliff, which might provide a way to ascend without too much difficulty. The barrier before them was a patchwork of faded green where vegetation grew, next to the dark greys and blacks of bare stone. Snow had gathered in crevices where sunlight likely never reached. Clusters of seabird nests clung to the less accessible precipices either side of the central route, and the area echoed with the harsh cries of their owners as they wheeled on the breeze or darted over the churning sea in search of fish. A black-headed gull standing on a barnacle-crusted rock fixed Keren with a cruel stare as he surveyed the cliff and tried to work out a safe route to the top. The undertow sucked at the gravel where the land met the sea and made a loud rattle that contrasted with the continuous roar and crash of the ocean.

The men hauled the boat up above the high waterline and sat on the smooth boulders to recover. The faint grey silhouette of the ship made a ghostly shimmer on the horizon. "Let's hope they wait the six days," Tomas remarked, and Senning laughed. "If they don't, you'd best work out how to make yourself a good sealskin coat and get yourself a taste for birds' eggs."

They made a slow, careful ascent of the cliff valley in the early afternoon light. By the time they reached the top, the sun had started to sink towards the horizon. The scene before them was one of bleak desolation. Shale rock lay exposed across much of the landscape, grey and severe. The only plants that grew were short and tough, grasses or small shrubs shivering in the icy wind. Patches of snow lay here and there. The ground undulated in places, descending into shallow valleys, or rising to form dismal, dark hills. In the far south-east, south of another, larger mountain, stood a sharp peak. "That's the Cone?" Keren asked Senning.

The iceguide scratched at his beard and nodded. "That's it. We're about two days away. Rhel gave us six days to return. I hope that's enough for you to gather whatever you need. If not..." He shrugged laconically. "I guess he won't mind if you stay here. Me, I'd like to get back."

Senning slung his pack over his shoulder and began the long walk across the sparse, rocky moorland. "Watch out for the chasms," he called back.

They walked for what remained of the afternoon. At one point, Senning stopped to unfurl a map, which he pinned down with three rocks before peering intently at it. The outline of the island was shown, along with some of the taller mountains and a couple of inland lakes. But Keren's attention was drawn to seven symbols in a dark, blocky script that he hadn't seen anything like before. "What are those?"

"This map is from the Protectorate. The symbols..."

"It's not one that I've seen before," Darien commented.

"Very few have," Senning said bluntly. "I was given this map years ago."

"Who gave it to you? Were you a Protector once?"

Senning pointedly ignored Darien's questions. "The symbols mark..." He frowned, either trying either to recall what he'd been told or perhaps translate the phrase into Theyan. "Weak areas."

"Perhaps the mapmakers meant places where the ground underfoot is unsafe," Keren suggested.

Senning shrugged. "Maybe. But I think they meant locations where things are... not as they should be."

"Have you been here before?" Darien persisted. "You must have professed some interest in this island, if an officer of the Protectorate saw fit to give you this map."

Senning gave him a long look. "If we survive the days ahead, you may find the transaction in the archives in Fort Cailan. Some notes will accompany it. No, Protector. I have not been here before."

"Well, if we know where these... weak areas are, we can avoid them," Larnus said.

The iceguide smiled. "I like your enthusiasm. But this is an old map, and things change."

The pathless ground required the companions to pay constant attention to where their feet landed. At one point, Senning, who happened to be walking next to Keren, grabbed the Wisterene's arm and pointed wordlessly to a deep crack in the ground that Keren hadn't noticed. He might have stepped into it had the iceguide not stopped him. Surrounded by tufts of the long, hardy grass that grew expansively here, the schism ran jaggedly north to south. Keren peered into the pitch darkness but saw nothing.

The two of them walked around to where the gap was only a foot's width across and stepped over to join Tomas and Larnus who had crossed at the narrow point. "How deep do you suppose it is?" Keren wondered aloud.

"Deep enough to kill you when you hit the bottom," Senning said. "What more is there to know?"

They discovered a cave in the side of a rocky valley soon afterwards, and Senning suggested they rest for the night. The sky had grown dark quickly, and a few flurries of snow spiralled down from the low grey cloud. The faint calls of seabirds pierced the dusk and the continuous wind sighed around the rocks as the men huddled in the cave.

They had brought some well-wrapped firepowder and small kindling from stores on the ship. Soon a small, smokeless fire burned, and the exhausted companions arranged themselves around it as best they could. Little was said at first, but Tomas brought out a bottle of *vakushla* to share, and their mood improved a little as the evening wore on.

"How long do you need at the Cone?" Senning asked Keren later.

"I don't know. As long as it takes to gather what I need."

"Remember what I said," Senning warned him. "I'm going back before Rhel decides to turn the ship around. No matter what."

As soon as it grew light enough to see the way ahead the following morning, the companions pressed on through the interior of the island. The flat land they now crossed was covered in hardy heathers and grass, and partly frozen lakes glimmered faintly in the poor light. Now and again the sun's disc appeared from behind the clouds, but it offered no warmth.

They reached the Cone around the middle of the afternoon. Senning reluctantly decided to seek shelter for the evening, given the failing light. "You don't stumble around a place like this in the dark."

The morning after, the men wasted no time in navigating their way to the southern face of the great mountain, which they reached with the pale sun still climbing in the sky.

Keren looked up at the vast slope and recalled his father's description of what he needed to find. *In places the rock forms red-coloured lines that snake up and down the rocks formed from ancient lava flows. The colour is formed from a mineral.*

"What else did he say?" Keren muttered distractedly.

The other men exchanged blank looks.

One line is wider and longer than the others. You must follow this line upwards, until at last you reach the place where it ends.

"And then..."

If you remove enough loose rocks, you will find the entrance to a small fissure in the surface.

"Is this the right place?" Darien asked.

"We're in the right area," Keren confirmed. "But this is a big mountain. We need to walk around this southern face. Look for an especially wide red line leading up the slope."

"Well, it's a good day for it," Larnus said brightly. "Not a cloud in the sky."

Tomas grimaced. "Now you've cursed us."

They had walked for a mile or so and were resting when Senning remarked to Keren, "You said that you're a student of the natural arts. Flowers, plants, rocks... isn't that so?"

"That's right."

"Interesting. We have passed by several clusters of small blue flowers that grow only on this island in the months just before winter. I was surprised to see you had no interest in them. Look. There are more here." Senning gestured to a group of delicate, sky-blue flowers sheltering from the west wind behind a boulder. He gave Keren an intense look. "Their name escapes me now, but I'm sure *you* must know."

Keren looked away and up the slope, grimly fighting down his panic. He had no idea what to say and feared that Senning knew their name perfectly well.

It was then that he saw a wide streak of red through the rocks a little further along. He shielded his eyes and walked nearer. As he had hoped, the line stretched up the slope. In a few places it couldn't be seen at all, but then it started again further up.

"This it?" Tomas had followed him and prodded the nearest rock with his boot.

Keren nodded. "I need to go the rest of the way on my own." He peered up the slope, trying to map a way in his head as his other companions joined him.

"Why?" Darien asked, entirely unconvinced, but the Earth-keeper's son chose not to reply. He had no adequate answer.

"I'll be back as soon as I can," he said.

Then he set off up the rocky slope, his long shadow climbing alongside him.

Keren clambered as surefootedly as he could, keeping an even pace. He rested briefly a little later and looked down at the tiny forms of his companions. Then he pressed on, each breath frosting in the bright sunlight.

The red vein ended at a fissure in a rock face further up. He stopped to gather his breath and saw that the sun had already begun to sink westwards. How had so much time passed?

As he drew gradually closer, a loud crack of thunder boomed and rolled through the sky, startling Keren so much that he almost lost his footing. A stone tumbled down the slope a little way, taking two smaller ones with it. Keren peered up into the sky but saw no clouds. Had he imagined the sound?

He thought someone called out, although his companions were so distant now, he could barely make them out at all. Their voices could not carry up here.

Everything became blurred. The air fizzed with power, becoming strangely warm one moment before reverting to the previous icy temperature, as if the natural laws were breaking down. Something was affecting his body. His heart rate quickened, slowed, and quickened again in a matter of moments, alarmingly irregular. He heard the urgent sound of his breaths even above the strong breeze.

What if this was one of the *weak places* on Senning's map?

Did his father also know about them?

Keren clambered carefully up to where the rock split and glimpsed a dim glow inside. "Is that it?" he muttered.

Without thinking, he reached towards it and with an effort willed himself to stop.

Touching it could kill him. But he had no plan of action, only his instincts.

This was what he had come here for, he reminded himself. This was what Shyam had told him to find and take. Wasn't it?

He reached into the darkness and his hand touched something in the chasm. It reacted immediately and violently to his touch, seizing his hand. Keren feared he would be pulled through into that inner darkness, ripped to shreds as a hidden inhabitant tore the flesh from his bones.

When his panic cleared and he found himself still crouching on the slope, Keren withdrew his hand and stared at the object it held- a rough-hewn, green crystalline rock. It didn't glow from within. The stone merely glittered in the afternoon sunlight and looked entirely ordinary.

This is it, he realised numbly, but at the same time he felt oddly deflated and wondered what the importance or purpose of this object could be. *A rock,* he thought, as exhaustion sank through his shaking body. Valuable, perhaps, but only a rock.

He had been sent to the far reaches of the world for this?

Then intense pain, like a thousand pinpricks, stabbed through his hand as if the rock was pushing razor-sharp needles into his skin. Keren cried out and tried to drop it, but the stone was becoming *smaller,* slowly diminishing as if it was dissolving into his hand.

The Earthkeeper's son watched in agonised disbelief until the stone had disappeared entirely. As it vanished, so did the pain.

"What just happened?" he whispered.

A faint, continuous cracking noise sounded somewhere in the distance. Keren had no idea what it might be, but as he looked up and listened, the air became almost perfectly still.

He made his way down the slope.

When Keren reached his companions, Senning had a spyglass raised to his eye, and looked south towards the distant coast. Finally, he returned it to his pack. His face looked ashen, and he muttered something in Anphayan, running a hand through his thinning hair.

"What is it?" Keren asked.

"What *is* it?!" Senning exclaimed, and he laughed weakly. "The sea to the south has frozen. The Strait of Frost has *frozen over*, and in short order the bears will be here."

He shot Keren a bleak look. "We heard a vast sound in the sky. We saw a *light* around you, brighter than the sun! Whatever sorcery you stirred up there, you should have let it be. You've condemned us all, Keren."

IV - The Inner Scream

I

Anna had never known that state of bliss the faithful claimed to experience when they prayed.

She thought only of the prayer's mechanical recitation, the words committed to memory. Long ago Anna had absorbed the harsh lesson that prayers must be memorised to perfection. On the rare occasions when she made a mistake, her grandmother would hit her hard enough to draw blood. Little more than skin and bone, the old woman was nevertheless surprisingly strong and possessed a temper that could flare at the slightest transgression. Not that she needed to shout much- no, Saian was a creature of malice and cruelty and focused her energies on hurting.

Anna couldn't even be sure she knew what joy was. Did the faithful truly know the bliss they purported to feel? The priests, the prayer leaders, perhaps the simple-living Devotees who meditated, gave charity, and spread God's word in far-flung places? The Cardinals, even? Or were they all simply fooling themselves and one another for the sake of doctrine?

Maybe joy was nothing more than one of those fleeting moments when she would almost smile- if warm sunlight touched her skin, or if she discovered something exciting in a book. Points in her existence when, just for a quiet breath or two, the misery of life could be forgotten.

"I have dedicated my life to your protection," Saian would complain- or words to the same effect- each time Anna committed even a minor transgression. "Protection of your *soul*. You'd better start recalling your prayers a little better, you errant little chit. *He* sees and hears everything."

Then came the mantra, to reinforce those words. She would make Anna repeat after her, "God loves those who dedicate their lives to Him. God will punish the unbelievers, the faithless. He will destroy the demons, and those who do their bidding."

If God is love, then why is Saian so full of hate? Anna would sometimes ask herself.

Nothing she did could ever be good enough for her grandmother, and presumably it wasn't good enough for God either, but Anna had at least now managed to memorise her prayers to perfection. Saian would still complain that she lacked enthusiasm, but this was seldom enough to earn her a beating.

Father Michal, a priest who sometimes visited their good-sized but ramshackle house in lower Toran, appeared to be a friend of Saian's. They certainly shared a liking for violence. Sometimes he would suggest that Anna could do with a thrashing and had even offered to beat her himself. "I don't like the way she looks at us," he would say, although Anna always did her best to look neither at him nor her grandmother unless directed to. Saian would reply disinterestedly, "Anna has always borne a sour disposition. If I thought one of your beatings would improve her, I'd have asked you already."

Anna always took care to maintain a neutral expression in Michal's presence, and hoped she attracted no more than fleeting attention. His eyes held a strange emptiness, and Anna feared that more than almost anything else.

Saian, for her part, strove to make Anna even more frightened of the man- as if by doing so she could extract ever greater obedience from her grand-daughter. "Did I tell you what happened to Michal's niece?" she would ask occasionally. Something in her voice- not to mention the glint of excitement in her eyes- made it clear that Saian would relish telling the story.

"No, Grandmother," she would say each time.

"Do you *want* to know?" The semblance of hope in that question always sent a shiver through her spine.

Anna would shake her head and promise to be good. She could imagine perfectly well the horrific fate of Michal's niece- perhaps an *errant little chit* who could have been a friend of hers, in another, luckier life for them both.

Aside from those grim days when she wished only to curl up in a corner and never wake up, Anna had only ever wanted to live without fear, and to learn. She had no idea what might happen to her and how she would survive when her grandmother finally died. Where would she go? She was fourteen, two years short of her majority by Gharaanian law, so if Saian dropped dead tomorrow Anna's fate would be decided by those who made and kept the laws in the city of Toran- or more likely the Church, which held considerable influence over the Lords' Council in the Palace.

Anna feared that she might be sent to a Church-run orphanage, no matter that she was almost too old for such places. An orphanage would, though she could scarcely imagine it, be an even worse fate than that she now suffered.

Anyway, Saian would surely live for many more years yet. Anna resigned herself to waiting out the next two years and then working out what to do.

Her parents- dedicated members of the Church by all accounts- had died when she was three years old, leaving her in the care of her father's mother. Saian had never hidden her displeasure at having to look after Anna. "I made a promise to your father," she would say occasionally, followed by an especially pious "I honour my promises in the sight of God."

Anna had never learned the circumstances of their deaths, and Saian said little about them on the rare occasions that Anna dared bring the subject up. "We have many enemies," was the most she would say. "There are demons, and then there are the Godless eaters of demons. *They* are *possessed*." She meant the mysterious, grey-robed Protectors of Anphay. No one in Toran- and presumably the whole of Gharaan- seemed to have anything good to say about them. The Protectorate, which held power in Anphay, did not subscribe to the teachings of God. The Anphayans had many gods, apparently-those who worshipped anything at all. In the eyes of the Church, the act of worshipping many gods, or none, was enough to shut you out of Heaven and condemn you to the unending horror of the Abyss, or the Abyssal Plains. Or Hell, or the Eternal Fire. Many versions existed of the fearful netherworld where the insufficiently faithful were sent.

Perhaps a different one for each sinner.

"Did the Protectors kill them?" she had asked, years ago.

Saian's response was entirely unsatisfactory. "Possibly. The Church authorities are still investigating."

After all this time? Anna had thought.

She knew a little about the Protectorate from her reading at the local library but didn't dare talk to Saian about it. Her grandmother would immediately suspect her of showing far too much interest in the subject, at the expense of living a Godly life in the shadow of the Church.

Almost everyone and everything that did not fall under the Church's jurisdiction had to do with demons, in Saian's estimation. The mythical *faer* creatures were the worst of these, except that sometimes outworlders- fearsome creatures that occasionally forced their way into the world from some other realm- were the worst. Anna imagined the *faer* as walking nightmares that roamed the distant land of Wisteren, the Faering, and perhaps western Saanu. But they had no power in Gharaan, Saian assured her, because Gharaan was a God-fearing land and its people lived in His Light. "Have you ever seen such a creature?" she would sometimes ask, knowing full well that Anna hadn't.

"No, Grandmother."

"And you *won't.* Not here. We chased out the darkness centuries ago."

"What about outworlders?" Anna had once asked.

"Demons from Hell, come to snatch unrepentant sinners and pull them into eternal damnation," was her grandmother's resolutely cheerless response.

"The Protectors slay them," Anna had dared to point out.

Saian had spat venomously into the pot she kept for that purpose. "They call themselves *Protectors*- but such creatures cannot be killed. They can only be overcome by God- and the Protectorate exists in denial of His Light. Those men and women are nothing more than husks, doing the bidding of the demons that hide inside them. They may as well *lay* with them as try to destroy them."

On some days, when a black mood took her, Anna wished for a demon to force its way through from Hell into their house, tear the old woman apart with its claws and return to its distant lair to feast on the still-quivering pieces of flesh. Occasionally, she even dared pray for that to happen.

God hadn't listened to her yet. Then again, he hadn't punished her for praying for such a terrible thing, either.

Sensibly the girl would remind herself that much as she hated the sour old woman, without Saian she would be destined for life in the maze of Toran's stinking alleyways, if she wasn't sent away to an orphanage. Her grandmother would throw her out if she had to- a promise to her dead son was one thing but Saian's sense of duty to the Church was far stronger.

The area where they lived was poor and crime-riddled, sanitation almost non-existent, the house afflicted with wet mould and miserable draughts. Anna's many chores included the general upkeep of the property and errands such as shopping at the market, on the days when Saian professed to be too tired. "I'm too old for such things," the old woman would complain, although the next day she would clearly show that she wasn't.

Saian and her few friends- if they could be called friends, for they never appeared to find much pleasure in one another's company- clung determinedly to their ways and worshipped at their cramped little prayer-house, a grim building of grey bricks four streets away on the corner of Bakers Road and Cobble Hill. Because only several folk gathered there, the Lords' Council in the Palace had declared that the prayer-house would be knocked down. "Doubtless they'll build a *tavern* or a *whorehouse* in its place," Saian had sneered. But so far, they had stayed their hand, no doubt discouraged by a cautionary word from the Church.

Besides, more urgent problems plagued Toran than buildings that might or might not need to be knocked down.

Only three months past her fourteenth birthday, Anna was nevertheless well-read and knew her history well, reading being one of the few joys her grandmother hadn't expressly forbidden. Other than religious texts Saian kept few books in the house, but a library open to all the people of Toran stood not far from the food market down in East Square, and Anna sometimes allowed herself time to read there for a little while. Ironically, it was Saian who had taught her to read, in order that she might recite from the holy books and scriptures. But Anna had developed a far stronger thirst for written words than her grandmother suspected.

Unwittingly, Saian had helped Anna become a free thinker. Books had not changed her situation, but they had unlocked her imagination and shown what the world *could* be.

If her luck ever changed.

In the back wall of Saian's cellar stood a hidden door. Its existence was better known than the old woman thought, for Anna, in a rare moment of courage, had crept part of the way down the cellar stairs two years ago, curious for no reason she could explain, and watched her grandmother press a section of wall until it slid back and sideways. It revealed a dark opening that led to some other place.

That the movement happened without a sound was evidence enough for Anna to conclude that magic had been used to create it and keep the doorway silent.

Witnessing this curiosity had been a quiet revelation. Saian had long lectured her about the *demonic* nature of sorcery. The old woman insisted that the *only* magic not innately evil was that which manifested in the miracles of God. Anna had no magic of her own- few people did, and in Gharaan anyone with such a talent kept it to themselves if they had any sense. But she knew this hidden door was no miracle. Likely it had been built by someone with magical abilities, long ago. Perhaps even Saian, although if her grandmother had such a talent then she kept it well hidden.

And there was the God-fearing old woman, wilfully touching and manipulating such an object. Anna was an intelligent girl, and the hypocrisy was not lost on her. She knew what the Church authorities would think of Saian's meddling with forbidden forces.

Something only a demon-lover would do, she had thought at the time, mimicking Saian's spiteful voice.

Often over the last two years she had thought about the opening in the wall and what might lie beyond it. Why would her grandmother go in there? What had she hidden?

For a long time, fear of discovery had stopped her from investigating. Saian's more ferocious punishments were truly terrifying. On some occasions her grandmother had ordered her to remove her clothes and then beat her backside so fiercely with her belt that Anna hadn't been able to sit down for days. Even now she recalled the old woman's look of satisfaction as Anna was forced to eat her meagre dinner standing up at the kitchen table.

As the months passed, Anna thought about the cellar more often rather than less, and now she was a little taller and perhaps as strong as her grandmother, she began to entertain the idea of going down to the cellar and trying to open the door.

A dangerous notion, but persuasive.

Finally, one day when Saian had decided to go shopping and meet with a few of her Church acquaintances afterwards, Anna made the decision to head down to the cellar. She lit a lantern and made her way cautiously down the stairs. Even though her grandmother wasn't in the house, she winced from habit every time she made a sound.

The door opened readily when Anna pressed her hand against the wall. She took a deep breath and stepped into the space beyond, holding the lantern in front of her.

Dusty old boxes piled against the walls met her cautious gaze. Some were open and filled with junk. Pots and vases, faded and yellowing papers, and mildew-spotted books whose covers and spines had fallen apart, all revealed themselves reluctantly in the faint light. *Junk,* Anna thought, disappointed.

But then, as she stepped further in, the light revealed something at the back of this cobweb-festooned room. A sword lay on a table, still in its scabbard and partly wrapped in a once-white cloth.

Anna stopped transfixed when her eyes fell upon this weapon. The design on the hilt was of a red arm and black wing curved around each other, and a single blood-red ruby glittered in the middle of the pommel.

"Oh," the girl whispered, and she had to stop herself from walking over to seize the sword. It looked like a relic someone in an old story might find. She had read about ancient artefacts in the library, and some of the fables attached to them.

What would such a thing be doing here, hidden away in the annexed cellar room of an old woman?

Fearful that Saian would return early and find her down here- and worse than that, lock her away in this dark place for the rest of her life- Anna backed out of the secret room, rubbing away the footsteps she had made in the dust.

Shaking, she headed back upstairs.

Dangerous, irrational thoughts plagued her, and they would not be put aside.

I'm old enough and strong enough to hold that sword.

It doesn't belong to her.

Maybe it belongs to me.

That evening she glanced across the dinner table at her grandmother, who was engrossed in a copy of *The Divine Path,* a dreary lecture on the benefits of a life lived without sin. Anna reckoned Saian had read this book so many times she couldn't possibly learn anything more from it.

Questions with no easy answers crept into her head. Why did her grandmother have a sword hidden away in her cellar? The old woman never used any weapon other than her own hands, a belt, or occasionally a stick.

Had it belonged to Anna's father, or possibly her mother?

The idea must have given vent to outward expression, for Saian looked up from her battered old book and scowled. "Why are you fidgeting, girl?"

"I'm not, Grandmother," Anna said, and quickly added, "I don't mean to."

"Wash the pots up," Saian said absently. She had already resumed her reading.

The following morning, Saian went out to the market again, where Anna knew she would spend most of the day. Today was Coinsday which meant a bigger market than usual, and some of the folk her grandmother knew from the Church would be there.

Inevitably Anna's thoughts were drawn to the sword.

She lit a lantern and went down to the cellar. She resolved not to spend long down there, knowing what sort of trouble she would find herself in if Saian caught her.

Anna walked into the concealed antechamber. As before, the sword lay on the table, partly wrapped in its grubby cloth. Everything was exactly as she had left it.

Something about the weapon transfixed her. Anna moved the cloth aside, gently pulled the blade free of its scabbard, and finally touched the hilt.

It felt *warm*, as if she had grasped it already.

Carefully she picked up the sword and gripped the hilt with both hands, marvelling at the balance and surprising lightness of the weapon. Surely a sword ought to be heavier than this?

She swung it in a low, slow arc, and the blade made an odd, keening sound almost like a fragment from a mournful song- a lament or funeral dirge. As Anna moved the sword her eyes prickled with tears.

Finally, unable to bear either the weight of her emotions she put the weapon back in place and wiped at her eyes. Then she picked up her lantern and took a deep, shuddering breath. What had just happened?

She must never come down here again. If Saian found her she would be due some drastic punishment, perhaps the worst she had ever suffered. And her grandmother had a way of finding things out.

Might the old woman be waiting for her to do something with the sword, maybe even unlock some mysterious force inside it?

Suddenly fearful, Anna turned and left the hidden anteroom. The door shut in silence and once again disappeared, becoming nothing more than a seamless section of wall. Anna hurried back upstairs, worried that she might encounter Saian making her way down the steps, even though she would surely not return until the light grew poor and the market stalls closed.

Never go down there again, Anna reprimanded herself, but even then, she knew that matters would not be so simple.

II

"You seem nervous," her grandmother noted as they ate their dinner. As always Anna forced herself to eat the rotten parts of the vegetables from the market. Saian strongly disapproved of any wastage. *Only the rich get to pick and choose,* she often pointed out.

Anna shrugged and pushed pieces of boiled and partly mashed turnip and potato around on her plate. For a moment she thought she could hear a musical note in her head, pure in tone. The idea that the sword might be singing to her as it lay in the darkness below became so persuasive that Anna almost believed it for a moment.

"Have you broken something and tried to hide the evidence?"

"No, Grandmother." *Not recently,* she almost dared to say.

"I'll find it if you have. I look *everywhere.*"

"I know, Grandmother. I haven't broken anything. I promise."

"It would be an evil deed, to break something and try to hide the fact."

"Yes, Grandmother. It would."

"Do you not fear the evil that runs rampant throughout Toran and the wider world?" This was one of Saian's favourite subjects and it surprised Anna not one bit that her grandmother quickly latched onto an opportunity to speak of it.

"Yes. A little."

"A *little*? Murderers, rapists, and ill-doers in their many thousands lurk in the shadows," Saian grimly proclaimed. "Most men would revel in the chance to violate you. Your plain features would not put them off, I think."

Anna thought quickly. "Then I should like to be properly armed, Grandmother. I could carry out more errands for you if I could properly defend myself. I should like to be more useful."

The idea appeared to take Saian aback. "Oh! You'd like to be *more useful*?"

"If you'll let me," Anna said as meekly as possible.

The old woman sat back and tapped her hard, yellow nails repeatedly on the table. Perhaps she was already planning errands she could demand of Anna beyond her household chores, but the girl could not read her expression. Unnerved by the way Saian had moved the conversation, Anna quickly changed the subject.

"What do you think will happen to all the evildoers in Toran?" she asked. "After they die, I mean?" This was another of Saian's favourite subjects. Often, she would conjure a graphically detailed account of the hell such people would endure for all eternity.

But the old woman merely stared back at her, watchful and sunken-eyed.

"What do *you* think will happen?" Saian asked eventually.

"They... will burn for all time. Their punishment shall be eternal, for their sins knew no bounds, and so..."

"What do you think happens to *liars,* Anna? Deceitful children who try to hide their activities from their elders and betters?"

Fear stirred like a snake in Anna's stomach. "I... I'm not... liars would be punished too." Her voice shook.

Saian leaned over and seized her arm so quickly and violently that the old woman's foul yellow nails dug into her flesh. Anna cried out in pain and tried to pull away. Saian leaned nearer still, and Anna recoiled at the stench of old meat on her breath. "I have looked after you for most of your miserable life, you worthless creature." Her grandmother's voice had become low and menacing, every word ground out with spite. "But you have *deceived* me."

"No," Anna whispered. The look in Saian's eyes terrified her. "I swear I haven't."

Saian's fist crashed into her jaw, knocking her backwards. Her head smacked against the chair and for a moment Anna saw nothing but explosions of colour and shade. "I should have got rid of you years ago," Saian spat. "Vermin!"

Anna looked on in dazed horror as Saian seized a knife from the table. Her grandmother had a grotesque look on her face, a desperate hunger to hurt and mutilate. "*You held the sword.* What did it say to you? I'll have the truth. What did it say? *What did it say?!*"

"Please, Grandmother..." Anna was sure the old woman had gone mad. As she staggered to her feet, Saian stood up too. "I'll cut the truth from you if I must, girl." Her voice grew quiet. "I'll put out your deceitful eyes. I'll ruin you down between your legs. You'll plead for the pain to end, but I'll bring you back again and again, until finally I release you to Hell, where any punishment of mine will shrink to nothing before God's fearsome *judgement*!" Saian's face contorted with rage.

Anna screamed in fear as the old woman loomed nearer, but then a strength she had never known before coursed through her, reacting in violent fashion to this threat to her life.

She grabbed her own knife from the table, transfixed by the hateful visage of her grandmother, a woman so twisted with bitterness and evil that in that moment, teeth bared and face half in lampshadow, she barely looked human at all.

Anna rushed at her in a blur of energy and stabbed wildly again and again. The old woman's shirt and shawl became drenched in blood as her enraged screams filled the air. Finally, Anna stumbled backwards and dropped the knife, horrified at what she had done.

Saian screamed obscenities that Anna had never heard before. Her eyes bulged. Her rant became a breathless, wordless scream of utter hatred. She staggered forwards, blood seeping from her stab wounds.

Anna could no longer think coherently, but one dreadful fact screamed through her mind.

She had no choice now but to kill Saian.

Her grandmother lurched forward, eyes wide and malevolent. Anna saw that the old woman somehow still had the knife in her hand, and she darted to one side as Saian lunged lopsidedly. Desperately Anna picked up a chair and hit her as hard as she could.

Saian slipped on her own blood. She fell hard and her head cracked on the kitchen's stone tiles.

Anna stared in wordless horror as blood leaked from her grandmother's head.

Then came the silence.

Anna felt nothing at all now, only a sense of detachment, a dull calm. She picked up her knife and placed it on the table where it gleamed wetly in the candlelight. How had they not knocked the candles over?

The girl looked down at the caked blood on her hands. Vaguely aware that she ought to wash it off, she went to the pump in the adjoining room, but as she walked past a head-mirror on the wall Anna caught sight of her face, covered in a thick spray of drying blood. Her hair was also caked and darkened with it. But her eyes stared back, bright and alert.

Full of life, she thought.

Anna looked back through the doorway at the scene of their violent struggle and saw blood everywhere. The floor gleamed with it. The walls were splashed and spotted with the spray from the violence. In places it looked almost like an ancient script. Shadows made by the candlelight danced across the macabre scene as if rejoicing in its sheer horror. How could there be so much blood?

Anna walked slowly back to Saian's body, and jumped, startled as she heard herself speak. "You made me squat at the pump and wash in cold water. Do you remember, Grandmother? Even in the depths of winter you would stand there and watch me shiver. You enjoyed watching me, didn't you? So, I am going to make a bath of *warm* water and clean myself properly."

She heated pails of water over the large hearth where the logs were still glowing, then took them upstairs to the bathing room two at a time. Some of the water spilled, but now there was no one to shout at her for being so clumsy.

Anna found her other shirt and pair of trousers to change into. In the bathing room she removed her blood-soaked clothes and stared at herself in the full-length mirror, wide-eyed. *I look scared,* she thought as she wiped absently at her cheek, making a streak of dark red. *Look at my eyes, still full of the things they've seen. But I don't feel scared. Why not? Will that happen later?*

She remembered an occasion, perhaps a year ago, when Saian had forced her to stand here in front of this mirror, naked and shivering. *Look how ugly you are,* the old woman had whispered in her ear. *Skinny, ugly, wretched thing.*

"Skinny, ugly, wretched thing," Anna whispered, and traced a finger across a few of the scars gifted to her by Saian- a gouge on her right arm, a burn mark on her left breast, a cut on her cheek. All had hurt at the time, and yet the wounds had healed and faded and the old woman's words lingered on, as hateful and hurtful as the day they were uttered.

Anna bathed in haste but lingered long enough in the water to make sure she washed the blood from her skin and hair. She dressed in her clean clothes, then went downstairs. She had to get out of here.

Anna abruptly burst into tears as she looked at their unfinished meals.

"I'm *not* sorry! I'm not!" she sobbed, but somehow her protests just made it worse.

She was about to rush headlong from the house and get as far away as she could when she remembered the sword.

No, she thought firmly. She couldn't take it. That thing would bring her ill luck, as if she hadn't had enough of that her whole life.

And yet she had already turned and begun walking back to the stairs down to the cellar. She trembled and wiped sweat from her brow. "Don't," she mumbled, a half-hearted plea.

Anna began the descent, lamp in one hand as the other gripped the banister.

Her heartbeat quickened as she reached the bottom of the stairs and stood surrounded by the quiet darkness of the cellar. When she opened the concealed door, she imagined that the blade's strange, keening call sounded again, a cry of welcome.

She grasped the hilt of the weapon more forcefully this time, and something terrifying happened.

A powerful vision slammed into her mind, so intense that Anna saw nothing but its dreadful images.

A man and a woman knelt in a muddy field, shivering and naked except for cloths that covered their faces.

Six figures surrounded them, spaced equally apart. Five wore red cloaks over lightweight leather armour. The cloaks bore a narrow, dagger-like sign identifying their wearers as members of the Divine Knives- the elite fighters sworn to destroy the enemies of the Church and uphold its laws.

The sixth figure's head was bowed so at first Anna could not see its face properly. Then it looked up to reveal Saian, an expression of grim triumph on her face. The sleeve of her long, white robe fell back as she raised her hand, revealing a ceremonial dagger.

She swiftly drew the blade across the throats of their captives and blood cascaded down their bodies.

The vision abruptly vanished, and Anna stumbled backwards with a faint cry.

She hadn't properly seen the faces of the man and woman, yet she knew who they were. The revelation stripped away everything she had ever known, everything she had thought true.

Anna stood in the darkness of the cellar antechamber for a long time, her breaths fast and ragged in the dusty air. Perhaps hours passed. She couldn't move. She could barely think.

She didn't remember taking the sword before she headed back upstairs.

As Anna passed by the kitchen area, she saw that Saian's body had moved. For a moment, wordless terror almost enveloped her. The old woman had been so strong, so durable. It seemed entirely conceivable that she might haul herself up, ignoring her grievous wounds, and come after Anna again, powered by nothing more than sheer hatred.

But Saian had only dragged herself, forlornly, a short distance towards the knife that she had dropped when Anna struck her with the chair. Saian had stopped with the weapon still tantalisingly out of reach, her lips trembling, her scrawny arm outstretched. As Anna slowly approached, the old woman's baleful gaze followed her, but all her strength had fled.

"Do you know how much I hate you?" Anna whispered as she knelt nearby.

Not daring to draw closer even now, the girl continued, "I know what you did to my parents. Now I'm going to watch *you* die."

The old woman's mouth opened, but no sound emerged.

Anna waited until Saian stopped breathing, then plucked up the courage to check for a pulse, touching both her bony wrist and scrawny, wrinkled neck. When she found no trace of life, she exhaled slowly, stared once more into the old woman's now sightless eyes, and left.

When Anna opened the front door, snow covered the narrow street outside and more swirled from the night sky, so thick she could barely see the way ahead. Rumours had been rife of a cold winter coming- but so soon? Years had passed since she'd last seen any snow.

All the better to lose herself in though. Her footprints would disappear in no time.

Without her knowing, Anna's hand moved to clasp the hilt of the sword, and through the cold metal a vibrant, rippling warmth spread, as if something terrible had been set free- a snake or worm, dark and somehow fluid, moving within the weapon.

Fear finally caught up with her. She hastened along the increasingly narrow and winding passages away from Saian's house, through the swirling snow and into the depths of the dark city beyond.

III

Later that night, Anna came to a large church whose side door stood ajar. By now the cold had burrowed into her so deeply she was desperate to find anywhere with four walls and a roof, and even a church would do. She listened intently at the door for a while, heard nothing, and quietly walked in.

Tall, fat candles lit the interior, six near the chancel from where priests spoke, and six more on metal plates near the central aisle in the nave. The familiar, unpleasant odour of tallow hung in the air. Anna wondered why candles had been left lit without anyone around. Might someone return soon?

What would someone think if they saw her here, wide-eyed, and panic-stricken, shivering and frightened of every little night sound, and yet armed with a longsword? Her age would rouse suspicion further. She imagined a visitor asking, "Why's a girl of your age sitting here alone at this late hour?" or some other such nonsense, pretending to care about her.

Or maybe, if it was a man, he would decide she was there to be taken advantage of howsoever he chose. Anna's hand gripped the pommel of the sword more fiercely than ever.

The hour had grown late. Anna could not be sure but reckoned it wouldn't be long until first light, even though it was early winter, and dawn came miserably late.

She put thoughts of late-night worshippers and predators to the back of her mind. Few people attended church today- or yesterday, strictly speaking- the last trading day of the week, and none would arrive at this quiet hour with no priest in attendance. In Toran, and most other parts of Gharaan, Coinsday would have been marked yesterday, by copious amounts of drinking and debauchery throughout the city from the middle of the afternoon onwards. Even amongst the faithful, worship featured less prominently on Coinsday, a throwback to an old Gharaanian festival that pre-dated the Church, even though the Church sought to own it and dampen down its more excessive practices.

Anna leaned forward to rest her elbows on the back of the pew in front of her. She found herself automatically doing as she had been drilled to do for most of her life. Her hands pressed together, and her fingers intertwined. Then she noticed caked darkness behind her fingernails and silently cursed herself for having washed less thoroughly than she thought.

God sees everything, Saian had assured her, many times. *And he knows your most wicked thoughts.*

Anna would protest weakly that she never thought dreadful things- at least, nothing so dreadful that it ought to interest God- but Saian would select another aspect of her never-ending mantra about their all-seeing, all-knowing deity. Anna had consequently grown to believe that their God had a special, perhaps even perverse, interest in *all* things wicked, such as the idle daydreams of a child who imagined her grandmother's demise many times over.

Even at a tender age she had visualised those blackest of deeds every time Saian saw fit to punish or hurt her. Anna feared God's invisible, intangible eye, but whenever she knew wrong had been done, her internalised rage dominated that perpetual unease. She would play out many a dreadful vengeance in her mind- breaking her grandmother's bones one by one so that the unique pain of each crushing blow would be felt, putting out her eyes, skinning her alive and a whole series of other, ever more lurid fantasies. Of course, she could never dare to go beyond mere contemplation. Saian had been fearsomely strong even in her advanced years, and Anna was terrified that any act of revenge she attempted would turn into a desperate, impossible fight for survival.

And her suffering- the consequences of that failure- would last until her mind and body finally gave in to the torment.

"But then I grew up," she whispered to the empty church, "and my hate for you burned as brightly as ever. Did you never think that one day I might learn what you did? That day came, Saian. For years I wished a demon would come for you- but now it doesn't matter."

Saian would have killed her long ago if she hadn't liked the idea of keeping a servant. If Anna hadn't served a practical need, she would have died in that field alongside her parents, her blood soaking into the muddy ground. Nevertheless, she could not understand why she had been kept in Saian's guardianship- if one could call it that- for so many years. Why keep the daughter of her victims as a servant?

It had to do with the sword. A mystery that would not be unlocked anytime soon.

Anna lifted her head and allowed her eye to wander around the nooks and crannies and shadows of the church- the high, ornate ceiling, the altar at the far end, and the stained-glass windows, dimly visible by candlelight. The silence was oppressive, and Anna wished for a moment she had someone to talk to. But anyone wandering around at this late hour would likely not be someone to strike up a conversation with.

As she looked towards one of the higher windows and the scene it depicted- in the dim light she couldn't tell which story of the scriptures it told- Anna caught her breath. She felt certain that the picture had *moved*. A dark shape that formed part of the illustration-she couldn't be sure if it was a human or beast, if it walked upright or on all fours- had moved to the adjoining piece of glass in perfect silence, like ink or black paint spreading sideways.

As if to afford her a better view, the candles burned more brightly, their flames growing so tall they became longer than the candles themselves. The far-flung corners of the church were revealed a little more as the shadows shrank back, and Anna stared fearfully at the stained-glass depictions where she had seen the movement. The figure was now motionless, but she could not look away from the black and bristling creature that lurked at the side of the armoured warrior in the picture.

It doesn't belong there, Anna thought, although she had never seen this illustration before and had no idea what ought to be a part of it. It looked like nothing she had ever seen- a gathering of darkness and malevolence with no features other than indeterminate shape and a pair of deep red eyes like pools of coagulating blood, full of hatred and cunning.

Anna decided she was so tired she could no longer tell the real from the imaginary.

The candles now began to burn low, and the shadows they made grew deeper and larger. Anna had no desire to remain in this church in total darkness after what she'd seen, imaginary or not.

She hurried away from the diminishing light and out into the snow.

IV

Anna had experienced bitter cold many times, but never so deeply as she did that night. A few flakes of snow still spiralled down as she wandered street after street. Exhausted, she nevertheless dared not stay anywhere for long, fearful of falling asleep and freezing as she slumbered.

Very few people were out, and Anna did her best to avoid anyone she happened to see. Those who braved this grim early hour were wrapped in thick cloaks, eyes upon the way ahead as they carefully negotiated the snow and ice.

At one point she drew near to the Upper Town area over which the King's palace loomed, opulent and festooned with turrets and minarets. Light glowed behind some of the windows, and at the top of the towers great torches flickered on the crenelated walls, whose towers were crested with the Gharaanian flag- red and white squares arranged in a regular pattern. Anna looked on for a short while, but then turned away, not wanting to think about the people in the palace gathered around hearth fires or snug under piles of blankets or furs.

Somewhere further to the south, not visible from here, lay the Overchurch- the High Cardinal's vast seat of power. Anna had sometimes imagined the King's Palace and the Overchurch competing for the hearts of Toran's people. In some ways, they did.

Shivering, she hurried away and down towards the riverside area.

The Upper Southwater flowed through Toran after snaking through the deep valleys of the Spine mountains far to the north. The river was a tributary of the Southwater that cut through southern Gharaan and meandered along the mountainous border between Gharaan and Anphay before reaching the chilly expanse of the Southern Sea. Historically, the Upper Southwater was also known as the Great Blue, despite being neither great nor blue. In recent decades, the water had become dark and polluted. Even on a good day, the stench was unpleasant.

But at least it wasn't a place most people would think of coming to.

Anna stumbled along the muddy riverbank, threading her way between dilapidated fishing huts that had long since fallen into disuse. Nobody had fished here for many years. Anyone looking for something edible to ensnare from the river would need to head many miles north towards the foothills of the Spine, and that was where most of the fish eaten in Toran were caught.

Finally, barely able to keep herself awake, she opened the door of a hut that still stood intact and stepped inside. With any luck, no one would look in here. She could get some sleep and figure a way to escape the city when she woke.

Anna found some old sackcloth, covered herself with it, and leaned against the back wall of the hut, near the corner. Within moments she was asleep.

She woke to the sound of the door creaking. A figure stood in the doorway, framed in bright sunlight. It took a few steps inside and stopped.

Anna scrambled to her feet and peered at the newcomer, shading her eyes. The middle-aged man stared back at her. His face bore a cluster of scars and oddly coloured patches, as if he had been burned or suffered a debilitating skin condition. Parts of his scalp had no hair at all.

"You can't come in here," she said hesitantly.

He gave her an amused look. "I wouldn't have done, but I heard you snoring as I passed by. This your home?"

Anna placed a hand on the hilt of her sword, and he hastily took a step back and raised his hand slowly to placate her. "Are you on your own?" he asked.

"No," Anna lied. "My father will be back soon. You don't want to see him when he's angry. You'd better go." She stood up and grabbed her backpack.

The man moved so she could see him in better detail. He had an odd, mean look in his eyes that Anna didn't like at all. "So, the two of you live here in this little hut?" His smile made it clear that he didn't believe her.

"Go away," she hissed.

He gave her a considering look. "I could help keep you safe."

"I don't need anyone to keep me safe."

"I'll wait for your father, then," the man told her. "I should like to meet him."

"Please. Just go away." But he didn't appear to be about to, so Anna sidled around him to try to reach the doorway.

He moved to block her. "Don't go," he said quietly. "I can give you money."

"I don't want your money. I just want you to step aside."

"Don't be so hasty. I'm not going to hurt you. How about you earn yourself some easy coin. I'll bet you're hungry."

Anna tried not to think about that, but straight away she felt acutely the desperate emptiness in her stomach. The hesitation must have shown in her eyes, because he took another small step towards her and added quietly, "I'll show you what to do."

"No," Anna whispered. "No, I don't want to."

He lunged at her.

Anna dodged to one side and fumbled for her knife, for the sword was too large to be used in this confined space. She failed to pull her knife free and punched him in the face instead. Enraged, he pushed her up against the wall, knocking the breath out of her. Some of the mouldering wooden panels cracked.

Anna kicked him hard between the legs, and as he cried out, doubling over in pain, she managed to pull her knife free at last and thrust the blade into his stomach, twice, deep.

She grabbed her pack, ran through the doorway into the bright morning light, and fled along the riverside, every breath forced and sharp.

Anna ran until she could run no further, by which time she had left the riverside far behind and reached an area of waste ground. Wintry sunlight gleamed on ancient, crumbling stonework that rose above the snow. She knelt behind a half-fallen wall and tried to get her breath back, waiting for her heart's frantic pounding to slow.

A path led alongside some threadbare wooden fencing, towards a wide, muddy road. Once she had recovered sufficiently, Anna headed in that direction, glancing back frequently.

As she passed by a half-fallen wall of an abandoned house, she saw a traveller resting with a pack slung over one shoulder, dressed in a dark grey cloak and muddy, well-worn boots. The sound of Anna's footfall creaking on the snow made the other person turn sharply in her direction.

Anna was surprised to see that this young woman, who had allowed the hood of her robe to fall back slightly, had brown skin, unusual in Toran. Anna wondered if she might be from Wisteren, or maybe Hylios. She had seen less than a half-dozen such people in her entire life. According to the few books she had read about them, Hyliosen seldom left their own land, and only men were allowed to travel beyond their borders. The Wisterenes, whose culture was vastly different to the Hyliosen, were also rarely seen in Toran, mainly because the Church authorities considered them heathens at best.

Saian had harboured strong opinions of both peoples. The Hyliosen were *mad followers of a false God,* and she had reserved even more vitriol for the Wisterenes, who she claimed made un-speakable alliances with *faer* demons and coupled not only with the *faer* but with animals. Anna had never known what to make of the old woman's lurid descriptions but knew that while some religious texts agreed with those beliefs, others did not.

The woman watched her with wary, dark eyes. "Are you running from someone?" She spoke the common Theyan language remarkably well, but with an accent Anna had never heard before.

"No. Maybe. I don't know…" Anna looked nervously around, but the man hadn't stumbled after her. Maybe he had bled to death on the floor. *That would make two,* Anna thought bleakly.

"Someone tried to hurt you?"

"Yes. But I… I don't think he's… I mean, I wounded him. I didn't kill… no, I mean…" With an effort, Anna stopped herself from babbling.

"You have a knife in your hand," the woman pointed out quietly. "There is blood all over the blade. Some on your hands also."

Anna hastily sheathed the knife, for all the good hiding it could do now.

"Is anyone following you?" The stranger had an intent look on her face now and looked as if she might bolt any moment.

"No." *Not yet,* Anna thought.

The woman pulled her hood a little further over her head. "My name is Vashni."

"Mine is Anna. Where are you from?"

"Hylios."

Silence fell again. "Where do you live?" Vashni asked finally.

Anna shook her head despondently. "Nowhere."

Vashni stared at her for a long while. "Well," Anna said at last. "I'd better go."

"Where to?"

"I…" She hadn't expected that question. "I don't know," she admitted at last.

"Do you have money? For somewhere to stay?"

"No." A sinking feeling went through her. She hadn't been think-ing properly when she fled. She'd taken a sword she couldn't use but none of the money from Saian's coin jar. And she certainly couldn't go back now.

"I have a place for you."

"Where? A guesthouse or tavern somewhere?"

"No. Somewhere no one goes." Vashni shrugged. "Maybe you will see it and then decide you cannot stay there. Your choice."

Anna almost asked her why she would do such a thing- she was unused to acts of kindness- but thought better of it. "Thank you," she said awkwardly- and a little warily, for she wondered if Vashni had a hidden motive for helping her.

"But I must warn you," her new companion warned. "I know how to use this"- she moved her robe to one side to reveal a long, wicked-looking knife- "and I fight just as well without a weapon. Make any move against me, and I will kill you. You don't look like someone who will be missed or mourned."

V

Anna followed her companion along winding alleyways and narrow, pot-holed streets where snow and muddy slush lay thick. She stopped at one pile of snow to wipe the blood from her hands. Vashni spoke only to point out hazards such as patches of ice or debris.

At dusk, they came to an abandoned area not far from the city's northern edge. Amid this desolation a tall tower rose dark against the darkening sky. Grass grew long and thick all around, and shrubs emerged dark and twisted from the snow, half-hiding the remains of smaller buildings, rubble, and abandoned machinery. "Be careful,"

Vashni advised as she led Anna through the gathering dusk. "There are holes."

They reached the great stone tower with the sunset a faint memory in the west. The structure had fallen into disrepair, the south-facing wall having cracked in a number of places. As they arrived at a door in the wall, Vashni said, "People call this Henryn's Tower. Maybe you know the name, even if you don't recognise the place."

"I do." Anna peered up the wall, to the spire and the sky above where the five stars of the Huntress had emerged. "A priest called Henryn lived here once, maybe fifty or sixty years ago." She recalled what Saian had said about him. "He had three dozen or more followers. They practiced a form of faith which was frowned upon by the mainstream Church. One day the authorities came to arrest him on some charge or other, and Henryn and his people all killed themselves rather than be forcibly removed from this place."

"Divine Knives came for them," Vashni added. "Maybe they died by their own hands, maybe not. Where Divine Knives are involved, matters end badly."

Anna nodded soberly. The military wing of the Church had a fearsome and well-deserved reputation. For a moment the image of her parents surrounded by Saian and crimson-robed men of that legion flashed through her mind again. *I would love to kill them all,* she thought savagely.

"Once their bodies were removed, the tower was never used again," she recalled. "Except by those who needed a home, such as yourself. Some say it harbours the unquiet spirits of Henryn and his followers."

"They didn't make it as far as Hell then, if that's so. Are you afraid of this place?"

"No more than any other." Anna touched the stonework. "Maybe the tower was never knocked down for fear of angering the ghosts."

"I have lived here for months and seen no ghosts." Vashni pulled the door open. "I could not find a more peaceful place in Toran. It's not the dead I fear, Anna. It's the living."

She ducked inside and picked up a lamp that had been placed on the floor. She lit it, and ushered Anna inside. Then, Vashni took a thick plank of wood from where it rested against the side wall and placed it in the hooks for barring the door.

"Be careful on the steps," she warned, and set off slowly up a dimly visible spiral staircase.

The surface of the wall felt damp when Anna touched it. With some trepidation she began the ascent, taking care to walk at least several steps behind her companion.

They had climbed three circuits of the staircase and Anna's legs were aching when Vashni stopped at a door in the inner wall. The staircase continued into darkness. "What's further up?" Anna asked as her companion pushed the door open.

"Other rooms. One large room at the top. I chose this one. I don't wish to be high up. Sometimes the wind is too loud, and any-way there are many pigeons nesting in the top room. The roof is broken." Vashni placed her lantern on the floor, felt her way along a shelf to one side of the door and lit a second lantern which she placed further into the room. Anna peered around and saw an up-turned crate that Vashni presumably used as a chair, and further back, a ripped mattress next to which stood a bucket. A faint but persistent odour hung in the air.

"My home," Vashni said. Her dark eyes found Anna's. "It is not much, as you can see."

"It will be even colder here when the winter proper comes," Anna pointed out. "There might be more snow."

Vashni walked with one of the lanterns as far as the furthest wall, where the light revealed a fireplace. "I have this. But I may not use it. People might see smoke coming from the tower, at a distance. Some braver ones may come to investigate. I have not thought that far ahead. Most of time I don't think at all, except about how to find food. Some days I beg, but now I always choose the western quarter. I am kicked and spat on less. If I am lucky and keep my face hidden, I will have a couple of copper pennies at the end of the day, enough for leavings from the bakers, the butchers, the fruit sellers. But I hide if I see a flash of red somewhere in the crowds."

"Divine Knives."

"Yes. At least, I always assume so. Some days, I stay here until the deep night, and then I go out when the city is quiet."

"To steal?"

Vashni gave her a hard look. "No! I go to the fountains in West Lower Square, in the small hours. To bathe."

Anna was aghast. "People drink from those fountains!"

"Maybe they should not." Vashni shrugged. "I like to bathe. I like the feel of water. I like that there is so *much* water in this land."

Anna shook her head, baffled. She didn't want to think about bathing in cold water ever again.

"You can make it easier for us both," Vashni said. "We will go to purchase our food together tomorrow. But you must hide that sword in your robe. A young girl has no business owning such a weapon."

"It's mine," Anna told her, but Vashni wasn't listening. "I will hide my face and pretend to be your disfigured sister. Then *you* can talk. Better than my trying to hide the way I speak, which I cannot help."

Anna almost laughed at the plan, then reminded herself that she didn't have a better one.

"But tonight, I will know the story of your unusual sword, and the blood on your knife, and why you have no home. If we are to trust each other, you must tell me your entire truth, and I in turn will give you mine."

"Why do you need to know anything about me?" Anna could not keep the unease from her voice.

"Because I invited you into my home and you accepted," was Vashni's puzzling answer.

"Some of it may shock you," she warned.

Vashni gave her a scornful look. "Nothing you can say will shock me."

Anna hesitated. But then she reasoned that Vashni was a vagrant from a foreign land and couldn't possibly have any ties to the Church.

She began to describe her childhood in the home of the woman she had thought was her grandmother. Unwittingly, she gave Saian's name, and immediately cursed her stupidity- but the mistake was done, so she pressed on. The words came clumsily at first, but as memories swam back into sharp and painful focus, Anna's fluency increased, and she spoke at length of Saian's cruelty and fanaticism, and, despite her better judgement, their grim knife fight yesterday. Finally, even though she feared Vashni might think her mad, she described how the sword had seared her mind with an awful vision when she summoned the courage to hold it. "It showed me the fate of my parents," she said bitterly. "Saian killed them."

"Knowing this, what did you then do?" Vashni's intent gaze did not waver.

"I watched her die. That was yesterday. Then I ran away, and through the night I wandered around the city. Then, early this morning, a man came into the hut where I was sleeping, and he tried to force himself on me. That was his blood you saw. I stabbed him in the stomach. Deep. Twice."

"Good." Vashni nodded in approval. "That's a slow and painful way to die. He deserved nothing less."

But what do I *deserve?* Anna wondered.

She stared into the light of the lantern that Vashni had set between them. "I'm sure the sword belonged to my parents, but I don't know why Saian kept it."

"A trophy?"

Anna shuddered. "Maybe."

"Perhaps it isn't meant to be *carried* by you. Not as a weapon, at least."

Anna didn't understand. "What else could a sword be for?"

"Supposing it has a different purpose. Maybe it's meant to be used for something you do not know about. I am only guessing, of course. And you must still learn to fight properly- even if you don't use that blade."

"I *am*." Anna tried to sound convincing.

"We all learn, all the time." A look had entered Vashni's eyes that spoke of hard lessons. "We learn from the pain. Pain is the best teacher."

"Saian liked to hurt me," Anna murmured. "Sometimes she would hurt me while I was naked. I think she especially enjoyed that."

Vashni brought out the long knife Anna had seen earlier. She set about polishing the blade with an oiled rag. "Is that to stop it rusting?" Anna asked after a while.

"Yes. Weapons must be looked after, just as they look after us. Would you care to hear my story now, Anna?"

"I would. Is Hylios as terrible as the stories say?"

"That depends on whose story you hear." Vashni gave the blade a final wipe, touched it gently with a finger and put the weapon down. "Those told by menfolk, or those told by women. Not many women's tales have been heard. I would welcome the opportunity."

Vashni fell silent for a while, thinking. "I escaped from Hylios nine years ago, but very few women have ever left the land. Our lives are tightly controlled, our faces hidden, our voices unheard. It is a savage society that worships a savage God."

Vashni's voice had started to tremble. "I will begin now. But don't speak until I am done."

"I was born and raised in the baking heat of Ja'har, a city surrounded by desert," Vashni began. "It seems appropriate now that the day my chains fell happened to be the day after one of the holiest days in the year- its name is *rakun* in Hyliosen. That day drips with the blood of innocents, martyrs, and of course the guilty." She laughed. "Did I mention their savage God? I was savage that day, too. Anyway, God is only a gateway through which men freely indulge their worst desires, allowed by the mad priests who control society. I know that now because I learned Theyan after my escape. I learned it well. I read many books written by men- and, more importantly, by *women*- of other lands.

"Of course, I didn't think about such things back then. I was a girl, not much older than you are now, and I knew nothing of the wider world. Why would I? It was not for me to *know* things. Hyliosen society does not permit women to learn anything beyond their purpose as familial slaves. They exist to serve, and to reproduce.

"On this day, a small number of children selected by the priesthood for sacrifice are brought from the low houses of baked mud, usually the slums of Ja'har's western quarter. They walk in silence to their fate. To do otherwise extends that fate to their families, and so they take those measured steps to the gallows, heads bowed in submission to God, without so much as a stumble or a cry.

"That morning nine years ago, Anna... something inside me snapped. I reached my breaking point." Vashni looked steadily at her. "You have reached yours too. I see it in your eyes. I would see it even if you hadn't told me of the events that brought you here. You are frightened of your capacity to kill- but in time you will learn to value the freedom it has brought you."

Anna lowered her eyes. She no longer knew what sort of creature she was.

"I had no idea I would find my voice that hot, cloudless morning as the wind sighed around the family dwelling, carrying red dirt from the desert. Thinking back, I had no idea I even *possessed* a voice, a rage, an inner person. I was used to being beaten and worse, although the terror... that never changed. I never got used to it.

"I remained dutiful, silent except when commanded to speak. I did not meet the eyes of the menfolk in the family, unless commanded otherwise. I never uttered a word out of place. But no matter how submissive the nature of a Hyliosen woman, it does not make matters easier for them. My father and my brothers raped me, countless times. The Hyliosen men have much pride in their hierarchies and portray themselves as deeply honourable and pure. But behind closed doors, it's a very different matter. Did you know, there is no word for *rape* in the Hyliosen language?

"When I was fifteen, I gave birth to a son. It was no surprise that I had fallen pregnant. The men of the household argued and came to blows over who the father was. I certainly couldn't have told them. The boy was a wailing, weak infant prone to sickness. He died a few months later, from the disease you call deepcough.

"Have I grieved during the years since? I don't know. I am not sure I know how to grieve. At the time I had no idea what to *think*. I was too frightened. But on the day my son died, my father knew exactly how *he* felt, and he beat me for a whole morning, pausing only to wash, pray, drink some water, and tend to his sore fists.

"He left me for a week after that- even men know that women must physically heal so they can live to be used again. Then, one morning, he came to have his way with me. He lay nearby afterwards, tired and spent. *Contented.* He was smiling to himself. The salty stench of his seed hung in the air. And from nowhere, a rage took hold of me.

"A small stone statue representing God's image stood on the cupboard at the side of the bed. He would never have suspected that I might attack him. For a Hyliosen woman to... well, it never happens. But I *did*. I struck him, as hard as I could. I didn't knock him out at first, nor with my second blow. But with the third, the rage in his eyes died. Something indescribable soared through me. I had never felt so *alive*. As I smashed his skull to pieces with the likeness of his God, I felt like a God myself. And I carried on hitting him. I could not stop.

"At last, I knelt on the bedclothes, panting and shaking. Everywhere I looked I saw spatters of blood, pieces of his brain or his skull. I... came back down into myself and realised what I'd done.

"I remember it clearly, even now. I was so lucky that no one else was in the household at that time. I dressed in one of my brothers' clothes and burned my own in the cooking fire. I had trouble dressing at first. I wrapped a long scarf tightly around my breasts several times to help hide them, then I put on a loose-fitting shirt, a face scarf, and a wide-brimmed hat, the sort the men use in the desert. I tied my hair and hid it under the hat. I figured that in these clothes, unless I was questioned, I might be able to escape. I took a pack and filled it with some flasks of water and some fruit from the kitchen where I would have been working later that day.

"I had no idea where I would go, and to do this day I cannot say how I walked out of Ja'har. I was numb with fear and yet everything felt unreal. The dull roar of the markets, the sights and smells, the bells of the prayer houses and that dreadful wailing that the priests' assistants carry out as a call for the faithful. I reached the city gates and became one amongst the thousands who pour in and out of the city each day. There are far too many for the guards to check, and trade in Ja'har would be poor if those who wish to buy or sell were held up for a morning."

"I walked south for many days, following small tracks and avoiding any travellers I saw in the distance. At last I reached the abandoned land you call the Barrens. I didn't know its name back then. I didn't care for names. I just kept going south in the hope of something better. I found shelter in the days and walked during the nights when it was much colder. Luckily, it was spring, or what passes for spring there. In time, I came to the south-western corner of Asqabal, and I begged for food and water when I needed to. The people were suspicious for the most part, and sometimes they would send me away, but nothing happened that was more terrible than the things I had already known.

"Since then, I have lived in southern Asqabal, and the north of Gharaan, mostly near the Greatwater. The river fascinates me even now. So much water. In recent years I have lived further south and east- in Aun, and now in Toran. I am a stranger everywhere, so it doesn't matter where I live. I have no friends, but I cannot miss things I have never known. I like to see new sights where I can. No day passes where I fail to express my relief at being free. I am cautious, but not fearful.

"You see, because I lived a life so close to death before, now I taste life properly each day. Even if I must sometimes beg or do hard work that no one else will do. So, some days, if I am lucky..." She paused, appearing to search for an adequate phrase. Her eyes suddenly prickled with tears. "Some days, I have a smile inside me."

Vashni said nothing more. Anna tried to understand what it must have been like to live this woman's life. She had thought her own was terrible, but it barely compared with Vashni's nightmarish existence.

Suddenly she realised that she was crying, and as she wiped her tears away, Vashni looked up and laughed. "Why are *you* weeping? For me? I have already done that. Save your tears, Anna."

Anna said nothing for a while, dwelling on Vashni's grim story. "What do you hope for?" she asked finally.

"What do I *hope* for? I hope to remain free. But more than any-thing, I dream of one day returning to Hylios with an army at my back, to bring down the priests and the patriarchy."

Anna had no idea how to respond to that, but a chill went through her, for she saw that Vashni was entirely serious.

"The disappearance of a female in the family would likely not have been reported," Vashni continued, as if she had not professed her hope of overthrowing an entire nation a moment ago. "Women are not citizens in Hylios, so my brothers could easily have failed to report the matter of my disappearance. In any case, a disappeared woman is a matter of shame."

"Maybe they thought someone had broken into your house, killed your father and captured you for himself," Anna suggested.

Vashni pondered that, and slowly nodded. "That's a possibility. All the better if they thought so. Regardless, no one will have looked for me, and they certainly wouldn't mourn me." A bitter smirk creased her lips. "At least, not in any normal way." She took a sip of water from the battered flask near the bed, then offered some to Anna.

"How could you bear to go back?" Anna wondered aloud. "In your place, I would have kept running all the way to the Frost-wastes!"

"Because I swore to destroy the old hierarchy of Hylios- the cruelty, the slavery, the atrocities heaped by men upon women- and children- in the name of their foul God. How can I do that if I run to the other end of the world?" Vashni's words were spoken softly but held a determination that could have been etched in stone. *She really means it,* Anna reminded herself, which led her to the inevitable, sad conclusion that the woman was deluded. Anna knew very little about politics and warfare, but even she could see no end to the obstacles that would stand in Vashni's way. Armies cost a fortune, and what mad king or queen of anywhere would loan or sell her such a force, in so doing risking outright war with Hylios?

And who would follow her anyway?

Anna worried then if *she* might one day be like Vashni- consumed by the things that had been done to her. After all, in the wake of Saian's violent death, wasn't she already on that road?

But I'm not sorry, even now, she reflected. *I'd kill her again if I had to. I don't regret it.*

"It *will* happen," Vashni asserted, as if Anna had said otherwise. "I will *make* it happen."

To Anna's relief, they talked of other things after that. Vashni explained how she had taken every opportunity she could to learn as much as possible, especially the common Theyan language, as well as Asqabalese and Gharaanian, and even a few of the many Saanuese dialects. Anna was already in awe of Vashni's rich command of Gharaanian.

"For years, I struggled to communicate," her companion reflected. "Being unable to speak the language of those around you- *that* is true loneliness. But then I learned the words of the people around me."

A little later, Vashni shared a large bottle of daywine that she said she had bought for four copper bits. Anna found the taste harsh at first, but got used to it. Unfamiliar with the languid warmth it generated- and the fact that occasionally it made her want to laugh or cry for no reason- she found that it also made her drowsy after a while.

"Thank you for being my friend," she said later.

Vashni shrugged. "I am not sure we're friends yet. Perhaps."

"Yes. Perhaps," Anna agreed and gestured for the bottle. The wine tasted a little better than it had earlier. "Too much of this, and you'll regret it when your head feels like a beaten anvil tomorrow morning," Vashni warned as she passed the bottle over.

"I don't care about tomorrow." Anna took a gulp and didn't grimace this time.

"I used to think the same. Now, tomorrow is everything."

VI

Anna woke with a headache and disorientation the following morning, although the experience wasn't as bad as Vashni had forecasted.

She stole a glance at her companion, drawn to her faraway stare. Vashni's kindness had been the greatest she'd experienced in her life. Not only that, but it had come not from one of her fellow Toranians but a fugitive, a refugee from another realm. Someone even less welcome in this God-fearing city than she, Anna, was.

"Why are you looking at me?" Vashni demanded, without any shift in expression.

"I... I'm like you," Anna said without thinking, and immediately regretted her clumsy choice of words.

"You are *not* like me." Vashni's voice was laden with scorn. "Nor should you want to be. You are... how old?"

"Fourteen."

"I am twenty-four. You are not even a full-grown woman..."

"I am!" Heat rose in her cheeks.

Vashni sighed and looked her up and down. "Because you have a woman's shape? You know nothing of the world, Anna. A closeted life, miserable though it was, cannot prepare you for what lies ahead. *I* was not prepared. You don't yet have a woman's wisdom. That comes only with age. *I* haven't learned anywhere near enough yet. We all learn until we die, and that's the way of things."

Anna gritted her teeth at that condescension but held her tongue. It might even be partly true, she silently admitted.

Vashni abruptly changed the subject. "There is a guild dedicated to Theyan history, up on Masons Hill. We can try to find out about that sword of yours."

Anna felt uneasy at the idea. "Should we do that?"

"Of course we should. First, I'll give you money to buy us breakfast. It's easier if you do it. Many places will not serve me, even if I cover my face and hands."

Anna didn't want to go into a shop or near a market stall, worried that she might be recognised, but with an effort she swallowed down her fear. After all, Toran was a big city. Only Saian and a few of her friends had known her, and they didn't live in this area. Besides, what Vashni said made sense. Anna, with her pale skin, light brown hair and blue eyes, at least looked as if she belonged in Toran and had the accent to match.

They ate a breakfast of bread and cheese which Anna bought for two copper bits from an alehouse, after which they headed up Masons Hill, a lengthy walk that took them through the shadows of many austerely grand guild halls and churches.

Vashni pointed out a large, ornate building of grey stone blocks whose façade was fronted with four-sided pillars. The inscription above the wide-open main doors proclaimed that this was the Guild of Historical Studies. As they approached, Vashni pulled her hood further over her face.

Beyond the entrance archway stood the largest library Anna had ever seen, an area so vast that for a while she even put aside the suspicious glances occasionally being cast towards the cloaked, hooded figure and her young companion. They walked along aisles and past alcoves where people- mostly male and of advanced years- sat at tables to pore over documents or texts. Now and again a whispered conversation could be heard, or a quiet cough or clearing of the throat, but for the most part a heavy, solemn silence hung over this vast place. Each time Anna saw the white or black robes of a priest, a stab of fear went through her. But she recognised none of these men, and they paid her scant attention.

"This could take days," Anna murmured. "No. *Months*." Her gaze strayed upwards, towards high shelves reachable only by precarious ladders, and then the distant ceiling.

Vashni was not at all dissuaded. "We must make a start, then. Let's find the section on weaponry."

Anna and Vashni spent the morning and much of the afternoon looking through books about the history of Gharaanian swords, until at last Anna set aside the volume she had been searching through and put her head in her hands. "I give up," she sighed.

"Maybe we are searching for the wrong thing."

Anna looked up and frowned at her companion. "What do you mean, the *wrong thing*? It's a sword, Vashni."

"Yes, but supposing it isn't from this land at all." Vashni lowered her voice. "Supposing *you* are not Gharaanian. You said yourself that the woman you lived with..."

"Yes. I understand." Anna looked nervously around but there was no one nearby. "I hadn't thought of that. But that would mean we need to widen our search. God, we could be here for months!"

"Do you have something better to do?"

Later that afternoon they found a series of volumes about family sigils used in Asqabalese weaponry, and it was in one of these books that Anna, when she turned a page, found a symbol that matched the one etched into the hilt of her sword. There could be no mistaking it.

"This is it," she breathed.

Vashni sat a little nearer and together they carefully read the text that accompanied the drawing.

One of several Westriven family markings, generally applied to artistic works but added to weapons supposedly enchanted and to be used by a man or woman of Westriven blood. Depiction to left shows sword carried by senior members of family. Script shown often accompanies marking and is a variant of Old Asqabalese. No reliable translation yet found.

Westriven family members are senior courtiers to the Throne of Asqabal but separate in position and rights to the Sentai. Historically, they have been members of the ruling monarch's inner circle of advisors (known in Asqabal as the Inner Tower, a curious phrase not used elsewhere). [Note: possible translation issue]

Stories abound concerning the usage of this and other Westriven weapons that bear the markings. These, and the matter of the coloration and the arm and wing are beyond the scope of this treatise.

Anna could not believe the words in the book. Carefully she went through the text again. "This can't be right," she said at last.

"There's no doubt," Vashni whispered. "At least, why would the book be wrong?"

Anna sat in stunned silence for a long while. Her companion waited patiently at her side.

"We should go," Vashni said at last. "We can talk about this later."

Dusk had settled by the time they left the building. The companions hurried along as cold rain spat from the low grey cloud, turning what remained of the recent snowfall to slush.

After they arrived back at the tower, Vashni barricaded the door, and they headed upstairs. Anna stood fretting as Vashni lit a couple of lamps, then uncorked the half-bottle of daywine, took a swig and passed the bottle to Anna.

"Much to think about," her companion remarked after Anna had taken a gulp of wine.

"Is there?" Anna shook her head. "I think it's better if I forget all about this."

Vashni leaned forward and seized her wrist. "Consider carefully what you're saying," she said. "Why stay in Toran when you could claim your heritage?"

"Heritage? I can't even speak Asqabalese!"

"You know the common Theyan tongue, don't you? That's a good start, and my Asqabalese may be good enough to teach you a little. Besides, what else can you do, now you know?"

"What are you saying, Vashni? That I should take the sword to Char and present it to the Sentai? Why would they know or care about it? There is no longer a royal family in Asqabal. There hasn't been for as long as I can remember."

"You *could* stay here," Vashni admitted. "But you are almost as much an outcast as I am. And you've committed at least one murder, probably two."

"It's meant to be used by someone of the Westriven bloodline," Anna murmured, barely listening. "Maybe that's why it spent all those years down in the cellar. Saian couldn't use it but hoped one day to find a way of unlocking something. She kept me alive because I might be able to use it one day or unlock some secret inside it. A secret the Church might use for their own ends."

Anna sounded so confused and miserable that Vashni felt truly sorry for her. *I don't pity myself so much these days,* she mused. *As time goes on, I find others who suffer. Such is life.*

"I have never been to Char," she said, "but you should not go on your own. Obviously."

"If I *do* take it to the Sentai," Anna reasoned, "given who I am-perhaps I would be rewarded. Do you think?"

Vashni shrugged. She didn't know enough about Asqabal's court politics to make any judgement on that, although she thought it unlikely.

"So maybe *you* can come with me. We can look after each other. And I promise I'll share with you whatever reward I receive."

The Hyliosen woman kept her expression carefully neutral-something she had learned to do expertly from young childhood. She didn't doubt Anna's words, although perhaps her silence made the girl think she did, because Anna added earnestly, "I swear to God I'll share my reward!"

Despite herself, Vashni couldn't help but react. "Spare me your oath to God and such, Anna. A simple promise is good enough if kept."

"Maybe I have relatives in the palace in Char!"

Vashni shook her head. "Let's sleep now and talk about this tomorrow. You're exhausted."

Vashni sat and watched pensively as Anna drifted fitfully to sleep. The girl had latched onto a purpose of her own. Desperate for meaning, she thought she had found it. She believed her life would be transformed.

Perhaps it would. But transformations never happened in the way people expected or wanted.

The woman from Hylios knew that where courts and sorcery and kings and queens were concerned, nothing would be straightforward. The higher up in the hierarchy people were, the more they behaved like desert jump-snakes, vicious opportunists filled with poison.

And to think, nine years ago she knew nothing of this. Nothing of the world. She had assumed her life *was* the world.

Even now, it continued to open like a flower, with more to see the further in she looked. Vashni felt a terrible certainty that if she stayed with Anna, the girl would transform *her* life too, and perhaps not in a good way. Things would change, dramatically.

Vashni had seen the symbol of the red arm and black wing before. She couldn't recall where, nor did she know what it meant, but it had filled her with an irrational, instinctive fear the moment she set eyes upon it for the first time. And yet it had drawn her in, drawn her towards Anna.

The royal family of Asqabal and their circle of allies, even if they were supposedly disappeared from the world, were not the sort of people to casually associate with, if the history books were correct. And yet, might this path one day give her the chance to tear down the powers of Hylios? Sometimes that vow she had made energised her, no matter how far-fetched it might be. Sometimes it even felt *real*, tangible, a bright possibility that could happen if only she remained determined enough. All things were possible after all, even those that were almost impossible.

When she was certain that the girl slumbered, Vashni took off her boots and trousers and lay down next to her with a sigh.

Here and now, as she hid away in an abandoned tower, her dreams remained distant. The coin required to raise an army would be prohibitive.

Still, doing nothing was the surest path to failure.

One step at a time, she told herself.

Anna muttered something in her sleep and raised her hand in a fist cupped by the other hand, as if she fought someone in her dream. Vashni watched until the girl settled again, and then turned away.

They were headed down a dark path together.

V - The Abyssal Heart

I

Juli was not used to bad dreams.

She had always been blessed with the ability to rest for just enough time and wake refreshed and untroubled- something that apparently both humans and even *faer* found hard to do constantly. She wondered sometimes if her unusual nature might be the reason.

But since her arrival in Toran a week ago her sleep had rapidly deteriorated, and violent nightmares infected the little rest she managed.

Three days ago, she had bought sweetbalm from an Eastern Quarter herbalist, hoping it would improve her sleep and state of mind. An essence made from the root of the yellownut tree, sweetbalm's powerful properties dealt quickly with insomnia. Juli had never needed it before.

But it hadn't helped.

When sleep did come, her dreams were vivid, horrific depictions of people swallowed up by an ever-increasing void, an absence of light and hope. These episodes were both confusingly abstract and terrifyingly real. She felt the pull of a fathomless abyss. She heard the screams of untold millions.

Juli now feared that these perilous dreams were linked to the discoveries she made soon after arriving in the city.

She had an affinity for the lines of force that traversed the world and its natural formations, and which also weaved shapes in the homes and important buildings that both humans and *faer* had made. Power lurked in such meaningful architecture, and Juli sensed and saw that power, often in intense detail.

The Overchurch was a particularly auspicious building in that regard, for many different unseen lines ran through its multitude of faces and corners, forming a complex mesh of energy. Juli had studied these upon her arrival, surveying them from a distance. She sensed the conflict etched in this invisible pattern- a discord caused primarily by the Overchurch having been built upon the foundations and ruins of a previous structure, a great castle and underground network of tunnels made by *faer* and humans working together over fifteen hundred years ago.

It had fallen to ruin long before the Overchurch came to be, for the worlds of humans and *faer* had already begun to diverge, but the Church's decision to build on that site was no accident. The remains of the original work, most of it below ground now, had been augmented by the Church's builders, and- at a basic, visible level- assimilated as seamlessly as possible into the new structure. Perhaps that had been their crude way of conquering the old beliefs as they sought to demonstrate God's overarching power to their followers.

If blocks could be made to fit together then they belonged together.

But the lines of power wrought by the Church's masons were very different- how could they not be? They had been created for different reasons, and the Church men, who desired nothing more than the sweeping away every idea that posed a danger to their suffocating philosophy, assumed in their ignorance that by creating something alien on a site once sacred to others, they would conquer it.

Nothing was ever so simple.

The opposing forces made an inaudible cacophony in Juli's mind when she first approached and walked around the vast building, a

circuit that took almost half the morning. The lower, deeper structures reacted against those above them. The original site had also
made use of sorcery that even now ran through the deep foundations, a river flowing in the opposite direction to the faith that had
ushered in the daylit walls and spires far above.

Juli had visited Toran twice before and was used to the collision
of uneven, misaligned energies. But now something had changed.
Another, new force was at play, one she couldn't identify. It had distorted and subverted every line within and beneath the Overchurch.
It was growing, like an invisible weight pulling at a spiderweb.

This meant that sooner or later it would corrupt the vast majority who were normally affected only in subtle ways by the pull of
such powers.

Juli felt more afraid than ever before, and worried that only she
knew of this insidious new force.

Once again, she stood a way down the wide road that led from the
west-facing gates of the Overchurch, her pale, delicate face shadowed
by the hood of her cloak. Her hazel eyes surveyed the building as her
hands clenched into fists. She tasted the ebb and flow of competing
forces, complicated by the pervasive new power that grew within the
vast depths of the Overchurch.

But after only a short while, she turned and hurried away, unable
to bear that silent, unseen chaos.

That evening, Juli took supper in her room, and asked for a bath
to be prepared afterwards. After washing she changed into her spare
set of clothes which she had paid the housemaids to clean. Such
luxuries cost more than she would normally pay, but she had felt
unclean and desperate to scratch and scrub herself after standing in
the shadow of the Overchurch.

Afterwards, calmer at last, she stoked the fire in the hearth and sat near to the heat, mindful of the draughty windows and the mould that lingered in every corner of the room.

Juli was of a mixed and muddled heritage- born to west Saanuese parents of the Shasen tribe, steeped in lore taken from both human and *faer* cultures, which was not unusual in the north-west of Theya. Not for nothing was Saanu often called the Patchwork Land.

Her ancestry certainly included *faer* blood, although even her parents couldn't have said how much- the extent of mixing was never a matter of concern to them, and they retained few details of their family tree. Nevertheless, as a child Juli had shown an endless curiosity about her own nature. Even from the earliest years she remembered, that swirling mix manifested in her acute sensitivity to the natural forces and boundaries that held structures together, their relationships with time, purpose and the events that shaped such places.

Juli dreamed of the Overchurch that night, which was not unusual given its proximity.

But this time, her dream was far beyond anything she had experienced before.

She existed at a single point in some place within the Overchurch- perhaps the exact centre, for some small, faraway voice told her that to be in the middle allowed her to see from all vantage points.

Then she *expanded* and became assimilated into the structure and material of the building. She flowed like an impossible fluid across every inch of the floor, up the walls and over the ceiling. Within moments Juli *became* the room she occupied.

Now her skin had become the fabric that held the entire place together. She flowed effortlessly but without control, through every hole and past every corner of the Overchurch. The matrix of disparate forces guided her on that dreadful journey. Finally, she shrank back to her original, single place, a lone figure inside the building that she had become only moments before.

Then the terrifying transformation began again.

Then a third time.

A fourth...

Juli woke with a hoarse cry, desperately thirsty and covered in a sheen of sweat.

Who can help me? she asked herself numbly, shivering in the gloom as her skin cooled. *What can stand against the insidious blackness in that place?*

She glanced down at herself. Moonlight through the window partly illuminated her body, but for a moment Juli thought she had become transparent, faded, as if a part of herself remained trapped in that terrifying, cyclic dream.

Her instincts screamed at her to leave the city and get as far away as she could, but she knew that this implacable enemy could not be escaped in the fullness of time.

Might she call upon the *faer* and warn them? She had no right to do that, and the repercussions could be severe. To most, she was a mongrel, a dweller of the twilight, possessing some insight into secrets both human and *faer,* but with ownership and dominion over nothing. She observed- far more than she wanted to- but could never *belong.*

Juli knew how to make a Summoning, although she had never had cause to do anything so drastic. According to some *faer* laws- depending on which folk in which part of Theya those laws came from- for one such as herself to dare Summon was punishable by death. *Faer* law was mutable and depended on context and situation. If she conjured a cry for help, that call might be heeded, but she would as likely be punished for her insolence as helped. And their punishments could be cruel.

The *faer* way of looking at life was very different to the human way.

She must be as certain as possible that the changes in the Overchurch were worth their knowing about- and that they were real in the sense that they could reach out and twist and ruin the lives not only of those who lived in Toran, but others far beyond the city walls- human and *faer* alike. Everything that lived.

A Summoning would be a dangerous undertaking for another reason. Her blood would be needed, and because she was more human than *faer*, she would need a lot of blood.

That alone could kill her before she knew if it had worked.

Could any of the *faer* be Summoned to a place like Toran? Once, it had been a seat of great power. But that counted for nothing now.

The ritual could be carried out here in this room if she barricaded the door to make sure she couldn't easily be disturbed. The tavern was in the far west of the city, not near the Overchurch. Might it be easier to attract the attention of any *faer* presence from here?

She would think on it tomorrow, in some quiet place, and then, as the night grew late she would decide.

Late in the morning, dark grey clouds bearing sleet swept in from the south-west, and Juli took refuge in a Guild library, stepping out only for a quick luncheon. The place was occupied mostly by scholars and priests, except for a young girl and her hooded companion who sat some distance away from Juli and looked through book after book until two piles of volumes grew tall on their desk. Juli glanced at them a couple of times, saw the hooded woman's dark wrist where she hadn't pulled her sleeve down sufficiently, and wondered who they were. But for most of the day thoughts of the Summoning filled her mind.

With the onset of dusk, she hurried back to the tavern and allowed herself a few drinks and supper in the tap room before heading upstairs.

She would never know what might happen if she simply sat here worrying, Juli reminded herself. And inaction rarely brought rewards.

She brought out a small eating bowl she had carried in her backpack for months and sat with it in front of her, facing west. Taking the knife from her belt, Juli made a cut across her left palm and then her right, grimacing at the sharp pain. She took care to ensure the blood dripped into the bowl, although inevitably a few drops stained the floor.

Despite all the blood that fell, Juli knew it wouldn't be enough. She cut the fleshy part of her left forearm and held it over the bowl. This released so much blood that she began to feel nauseous. *More,* Juli implored herself, but her vision swam, and she almost slumped forward.

It would have to do.

Hesitantly she began to recite the chant her parents had taught her when she was barely five years old- one that supposedly brought the protection of nearby *faer* if her life was in danger- for that was the original purpose of a Summoning. She had never used it- after all, her family were fully accepted neither by the human communities nor the various and elusive *faer* of Saanu- and had no idea if it worked. Likely her parents had never known either. Until recently, she had barely thought about chants and Summonings and darkness spreading from under the Overchurch.

But this thread of hope was all she had.

Juli stumbled over some of the words, even though most were in the North Saanuese dialect, with a few Wisterene phrases and one or two supposedly from one of the many *faer* languages. She repeated the chant, trying to stop her words from slurring. Then she recited it a third time but couldn't tell if this attempt was any better. To her ears it sounded worse.

Juli uttered a low moan, unable to even start a fourth recitation. She imagined that the room had started to tilt to one side.

Then the blood in the bowl rippled slightly as if in response to an unfelt tremor. Juli stared at it, her vision swimming. Had she imagined that movement?

Wood sounded like brittle bone as it cracked in the fire. Somewhere else in the tavern, floorboards creaked. Laughs and shouts came from downstairs, a moment of uproar amidst the low, cacophonous revelry- but they may as well have been faint cries from another world. Imperceptibly, slowly, Juli's environment was changing- *adjusting* itself.

Sweat prickled her brow. Her raised pulse became a low boom in her head.

Everything slowed down, even the disturbance of her blood offering. The flames in the hearth grew languid, like tired drunken dancers. The remaining sounds became fainter yet, muffled and distorted as if a barrier thickened between Juli and the world of noise and light where she had spilled her hopeful blood.

Then she looked down again at the bowl.

Her blood had vanished.

Something detached itself from the shadows in the corner of the room. Juli shrank back uneasily as a human-sized but squat, oddly shaped being stepped forward. Dark and greyish green, it gleamed wetly in the fire's diminished light, as if it had been dragged from the depths of one of Saanu's great lakes.

The creature peered at her, baleful eyes unblinking. Then the toothy maw opened. "Why do you Summon me?"

"The... the Overchurch," she whispered.

The creature spat into the hearth and Juli scrambled further away as the flames momentarily climbed and roared as if in anger at that word.

"There's a darkness below it," Juli continued when she had gathered her composure a little. "It's seeping through the structure, through the old lines of power that your kind helped make. It grows larger, deeper. More powerful."

"*My* kind?" The words sounded scornful, even angry.

"Are you... are you not a *faer* being?"

"The word means nothing to me. There are a hundred or more races that you creatures call faer. It is your word, not ours. It comes from your ignorance."

The creature gazed intently at her for a long while. Finally, it knelt near to the fire. Juli thought she saw faces in the flames, and lips moving, although she heard nothing from the hearth but the crackle of burning wood.

"How can *you* know what happens in that place?" The words were ground out, dismissive and disbelieving.

"Sensing such things, before others can, is my gift. Or curse. Both." Juli trembled uncontrollably as the creature turned and crept nearer, and she caught an odour of old, dank wood and leaves, winter winds, and dark water. It had no place in the Church's city of brickstone and paved, lamplit paths. She wondered how much energy it had expended in coming here. Had the Summoning damaged or compromised it in some way?

"Maybe you question why your needy cry brought a being that fits poorly with your notion of the elder races. I had the misfortune of proximity. The nearest is always subject to the summons."

"Nearest." Juli nodded, now hugging herself because of the sudden cold. She tried to concentrate. "Where did you come from?"

"Deep in the mountains you call the Spine. I slept, but the summons cares nothing for sleep, Juli san-Derreth. I came, using one of the *short ways* which are known only to us."

"You know my name," she said, taken aback.

"It is in your blood."

"Oh." Juli began to realise how little she knew about the sorcery she had stirred into being.

"I will return here three days from now."

"Three days?"

The creature gave her a hateful look. "I must consult with others."

"Others..." she murmured. Her vision had almost gone, and she could barely speak.

Juli's consciousness faded away and she collapsed forward onto the floor, fresh blood from her wounds spreading across the boards.

II

Cardinal Aaron Blackwood knew that for a God-fearing man, doubt and uncertainty were part of a pious life. What worthy road was not pitted with challenges? Had an easy path ever taught a worthwhile lesson?

Yet he felt something far worse than simple worry whenever the High Cardinal summoned him to the Hall of the Interface.

Aside from the High Cardinal himself, only Aaron and the two other appointed Cardinals even knew the Hall existed- not counting the High Cardinal's mute and damaged assistant Pellin who went everywhere with His Holiness. Such ignorance was just as well, for the things that went on in that place were truly frightening- and the wider Church could not know about them. Lesser men would not understand the *means to an end* of the process, the absolute importance of that great unanswered question- a question that even the most devout, the strongest of faith, asked themselves.

What is the shape and form of the afterlife?

Or: *What is the nature of Heaven?*

The Hall lay on the forgotten lowest floor of the Overchurch. Hidden away down a labyrinthine set of dark and damp passageways, it made Aaron's old bones ache deeply, as if the innate moisture of the environment seeped into them and caused his marrow to blacken and rot.

But his physical health became a trifling concern in the Hall. Aaron instead feared for his soul, and no amount of meditation, no number of prayers and recitations, could sufficiently prepare him for the blackness that came.

He walked down numerous staircases and along corridors where mould spotted the walls and old books, implements and debris had been stacked. Some of this junk had been awaiting removal for decades.

Finally, he arrived at an ancient wooden door studded with rusted iron squares. He rapped on it using the great iron ring fixed to its surface. After a while, shuffling, scraping footfall sounded on the other side. The door opened slowly and a pale, disfigured creature leered into the lamplight.

The grotesque servant squinted at the Cardinal as if he couldn't quite remember who he was, then motioned for him to follow, without any hint of deference or protocol. Aaron wondered again why the High Cardinal kept and fed this simpleton. Pellin was mute as well as mentally damaged, capable only of grunts and a few other guttural sounds.

Pellin limped down the dank corridor that led to the Hall, shambling in his odorous, ill-fitting clothes. Like some goblin or badshape out of old *faer* tales, Aaron thought disgustedly as he kept at least half a dozen paces behind the High Cardinal's servant.

Aaron knew that a room ought not to have the capacity to frighten. Fear of that sort was a product of superstition about objects, which the Church had done its best to stamp out in the more enlightened parts of the world. But the Hall of the Interface filled his heart with a terror that he only just managed to keep hidden.

Over many decades, he had learned to keep his own counsel where needed, to listen and consider before speaking, and to be ever mindful of how he spoke or reacted in the vicinity of others.

That skill was never needed so much as in this dreadful place.

The distant ceiling, a patchwork of faded brown and yellow, was etched with markings. These were supposedly fragments of ancient artwork from centuries past, but to Aaron's still-sharp eyes they looked like scratches made by some awful creature. Sometimes he imagined that damned and dismal souls had made those gouges, fighting to stall their banishment to Hell- which was impossible, for souls in isolation had no corporeal form nor any ability to effect physical change.

Nevertheless, the idea still cleaved unpleasantly to him, especially when he considered the purpose of this room, which had given it its name.

High Cardinal Gorram Threnn stood towards the rear of the chamber, perhaps thirty paces from the entrance door. Thinner than in his younger years, grey and almost gaunt, he nevertheless remained tall and imposing. Pellin heaved his way towards his master and was still shuffling across the jet-black tiled stonework as Aaron bowed low and offered dedications to His Holiness.

"I am so glad to see you, Cardinal." Gorram's voice was rich and somehow melodious. Aaron had a gift for music and a keen ear for melody, and he had always found a strange beauty to the sound of the High Cardinal's voice. It would have pleased him and settled his nerves, had they met anywhere but here.

"We have much to ponder." Gorram's white and red robes rustled as he gestured to a small figure sitting bound with head upraised, in a chair, to the left and almost in shadow. "We are growing closer to the ultimate understanding. By tiny increments, it comes into focus."

Those words and the sight of the motionless figure- Aaron could make out few details from his position except that it was unclothed and of slight build- filled him with a crawling terror. *Lord God give me courage,* he thought faintly. *Let me rise to this challenge You place before me. Make me worthy.*

"That is indeed good news, your Holiness," he said aloud. The High Cardinal's cretinous servant was staring at him. With an effort he put the creature out of his mind.

"You are ever the architect of understatement, Aaron. Come here, so you may see the subject properly for yourself."

As the Cardinal made his way around to face the motionless figure and saw its physical state properly, he recoiled and almost gagged.

There had been others- so many others. Most were felons who deserved nothing more than to be marked as vessels for use in this important study. But this one...

"She's just a child," he whispered.

"Yes. Ten or eleven summers, perhaps." The High Cardinal might have been discussing the weather. "They see it differently, at the point of interface. The Great Light is not the same to all God's subjects. A child has a very different view to an adult. Clues to this are within the Elder Scriptures if one knows where to look."

Despite the unrelenting horror of the body in the chair, Aaron could not draw his gaze away from it. The girl had been clearly subjected to unimaginable torture prior to her death. Parts of her skin hung from the flesh like abandoned butcher's cuts. Her teeth had been removed. Nails had been driven through her forearms and ankles. Her eyes were wide open and bulged from their sockets. Aaron recalled from previous visits and involvement in the High Cardinal's studies that the eyes must always remain undamaged. They were, according to the scant information on the matter, essential for the delivery of the Great Light to the decaying minds of the newly dead. Thinking on that, Aaron had searched for information on how a blind man or woman who had lived a pious life would see the Great Light as they passed before it. Would it still be etched upon their soul somehow? What could it look like, to someone who could not see, who had perhaps *never* seen?

"May she suffer no more," he heard himself say.

"You misunderstand, Cardinal. The hand of God is with us here. Listen, and watch."

Gorram began to softly recite a prayer from the Elder Scriptures-*Andel's Crossing,* from the fourth book. It was seldom heard anywhere now, having fallen out of use. Gorram used the Old Gharaanian dialect, which Aaron knew passably well, and yet he found it difficult to concentrate on the words. Uttered at a reasonable pace, they nevertheless somehow contrived to merge into one another so that the prayer became a breathless rush of words, a chant that favoured sound and cadence over meaning.

And yet the sound, he realised, had an attractive rhythm. He did not want it to stop.

But Gorram's recitation did end, abruptly. Aaron blinked, unsure if it had completed naturally or not.

Then he felt something, tenuous as spider silk and cold as frost sweep over and around him. "What...?"

"Be silent, Cardinal, and observe." Gorram's voice cut like a knife through his fear.

An awful sound filled the air, a sudden and agonised intake of breath. The girl's chest rose and fell. Her head moved slightly, left to right and back. Her eyes did not blink. Aaron gazed at this sudden life- no, a travesty of life- in wordless horror.

The High Cardinal stooped so near to the prisoner that his breath steamed against the remains of her face. "Did you see Him?" The tremulous whisper was barely audible. "Did you see the Lord God's light? *Beyond* the light?"

The mouth opened further. A sound came from her, perhaps the jaw resetting itself. A long-drawn-out sigh emerged. The girl's chest rose and fell one more time, and then the body became still.

At long last, the High Cardinal straightened and took several steps back, displeasure showing on his face. "Four times," he said.

"Four times, your Holiness?" Aaron thought his own voice sounded faint and lost, which made awful sense. He *had* become lost, detached from himself, adrift on a sea of madness. Never had he seen a subject *return* to the tortured husk from which its soul had leapt. He had never expected to, no matter the High Cardinal's confidence that sooner or later one would.

"She has crossed the interface four times, Cardinal, in the last three days. I feel we are near to a breakthrough, and yet... we still have no words, no confirmation... only elusive clues as to what the mind sees on the other side. A pessimist might say there are no words to describe the shape of Heaven."

Aaron struggled to comprehend the enormity of what had happened. Finally, the High Cardinal had sent a subject through the interface between this world and the Great Light beyond and pulled her back through some miraculous means. A seldom-remembered prayer, or something hidden within it, had wrapped itself around that soul and brought it back to this desolate hall.

God had granted him that power- but why?

"There must be a reason," he heard himself say.

"Of course there is! Almighty God has set us upon this path accordingly. We must expect challenges and setbacks along the way." But the High Cardinal did not sound accepting of the challenge. He sounded almost mad with thirst for answers to great questions.

So, the long years of study, the trials and frustrations and the torture- the deaths, hundreds of them- had come to this. Not one of the tiny increments His Holiness had mentioned, but a vast step. A step towards God's light itself.

The High Cardinal had long espoused a theory that the prisoners had to be brought to that elusive precipice where life lay behind them and death before them. There *was* such a place, he asserted- half-bathed in God's light, a foot upon the threshold of Heaven. Meticulous torture was the only way to inch these unfortunates to that mystical foothold, and, in theory, keep them there.

Until recently, these were all condemned men and women, or destitutes who had simply fallen so far through society's cracks that no one would miss them. *Given to us by God, no matter their past,* Gorram had maintained, although not without careful searching and then bypassing the usual rules of law. The Lords' Council had looked the other way when needed. The subjects had all confessed their sins- the Truthseekers ensured that confessions were coaxed from even the most reticent- and begged forgiveness. Had they not, they would have been condemned and useless souls, with only the blackness of the Abyss awaiting them.

Aaron had never had any qualms about ensuring the Church's business continued unmolested in this way. He despised the Lords' Council, whose members paid lip service to the Church but were concerned primarily with their own creature comforts. That the Council's lords and ladies were so easily bought was proof enough of their Godless ways, no matter their observance of Holy days and

Church festivals. Provided such manipulation was done in the name of legitimate Church matters, he remained unbothered by it, and even engaged in it himself when obstacles needed removing.

But as time went on his disquiet regarding the Hall of the Interface and the things that happened here had grown. At Gorram's bidding, he had assisted in the torture of men and women down here in the dark. He had tirelessly written notes, conducted his own research, spent countless hours poring over ancient texts or simply meditating in the hope of enlightenment. Gorram had spent much more time doing the same. The two other Cardinals appointed under him- Irran Mayne of Aun, and Sanil Derrim of Timber Bay- had assisted as far as possible, although the areas for which they were responsible meant they were absent from Toran more frequently than Aaron so were less entangled in this research.

This dreadful secret.

Aaron looked again at the prisoner. She neither moved, nor breathed. Gone, again- but where?

"Your Holiness, I have a question, if I may," he said quietly. When Gorram nodded for him to continue, Aaron wondered suddenly if it might be better to say nothing. It would not do to have his faith brought into question. If this horror was indeed God's will, then He tested them severely.

The challenge was immense, but Aaron had maintained an unbending belief in the sanctity of the Church for many decades, from his childhood and through his ordination as priest at the age of only twenty-six, and his slow but sure ascent through the ranks of the priesthood- an unremarkable but tenacious climb that had gone broadly unnoticed.

He had outlived better men and worse men. He had lived for the Church, and all it stood for. If this were the path God had chosen for him- and it must be, for he would not have chosen it himself- then he must accept and walk that path even if his feet burned.

"Your question, Cardinal."

Aaron blinked and thought quickly. "I wondered how the prayer works. How it brings the... brings the subject back from the inter- face. That truly is a miracle." He swallowed, hoping his nausea didn't show.

The High Cardinal sighed. "I wish I knew. Truthfully, that is the only recitation I've found that pulls the subject *back* from the edge of the Great Light. There must be something in it, but I've yet to discover what it might be. You're familiar with that prayer, of course."

"*Andel's Crossing*, from the fourth book of the Elder Scriptures. It describes a great journey under darkness, so it seems pertinent. But others paint a similar picture."

"Just so. It's one mystery amongst many. Perhaps you can fathom it out when you return to your chambers."

"I will do everything I can to unravel it, your Holiness." Did his desperation to leave show on his face? He prayed not.

The High Cardinal silently indicated that he was free to leave. Aaron bowed, turned, and left as swiftly as he could without making an unseemly retreat.

The High Cardinal remained motionless as his servant ap- proached, dragging his feet over the stone. Pellin's worn boots scraped on the cold surface, until at last he stood facing his master. Spittle leaked from one corner of his slack-jawed mouth. His muddy, yellow-tinged eyes peered up at Gorram's.

After a while, the High Cardinal spoke, in the manner of a man who had just stirred from a dream. "Am I doing all I ought?" He nodded slowly, unaware that Pellin had performed the same motion at the same time. "Yes. We draw closer. Soon we will pierce the veil. An answer *will* show itself."

His manservant's hand moved down, suggestively. He uttered a faint, low sound in his throat as the High Cardinal knelt before him and with trembling fingers unbuttoned his trousers. Pellin leered down, a hard lust in his eyes.

For a short while the Hall of the Interface echoed harshly to the sounds of sucking and slurping, and Pellin's grunts of pleasure. Spittle dropped almost continuously on the High Cardinal's bald head.

Unnoticed by the two men, the prisoner's fingers moved, and drummed a faint rhythm on the arm of the chair, a slow but sure death rattle.

III

Aaron could not sleep. Long before the first light of dawn, he gave up hope entirely and went to read in his study. Even then he remained restless, unable to turn a page without looking up to stare into the middle distance. A while later he stood fretting by the window that overlooked one of the Overchurch's sheltered courtyards, as familiar structures slowly revealed themselves to the new day.

Sleep had proved elusive- but he *had* reached a decision.

Lord, I cannot believe that this is Your way, Aaron thought as he stared into the distance. From the elevated position of his quarters in the Overchurch he had a view over East Toran and much of the land beyond, fields and rolling hills that extended towards distant Timber Bay, hundreds of miles away.

I cannot believe that you sanction such misery, such wanton torture. What I saw in the Hall of the Interface yesterday was not the brink of some wondrous discovery, but a dreadful path that the High Cardinal has set himself upon. How can the head of the Church be oblivious to the horror done in Your name?

No, this is not Your work, Lord, and may You turn me to dust if I am wrong or deluded.

But I do not think I am.

His concerns must be heard by the only high-ranking member of the Church he could trust- Cardinal Sanil Derrim of Timber Bay. Sanil was not a friend- Aaron kept nobody close enough to consider them a friend- but they shared a mutual respect. More importantly, Sanil was a man of honour. Every priest and Cardinal claimed to be- how could they claim otherwise? But Aaron had spent long enough entrenched within the Church to know that far from everyone sworn to the Godly life was true to it.

The letter he planned to write and send could not be allowed to fall into the hands of the High Cardinal's many fervent sycophants- shallow, bright-eyed men who had a gift for saying the right things at the right time, but little else of substance. It would need to be carried and delivered by one of the Church's messenger birds, trained to go directly to Sanil or one of his highest servants who could be relied upon to pass it directly to his master without interference. Even this carried considerable risk.

Aaron then recalled that one of Sanil's priests was present in the Overchurch, due to return to Timber Bay tomorrow. Marim was his name. A solid, dependable sort, he could be relied upon to deliver a sealed scroll directly to his master with neither question nor comment. His loyalty to Sanil could be in no doubt.

The Cardinal spent almost the entire day in his study, forsaking breakfast and lunch and eating only some bread and fruit for his supper. His mouth felt dry, and he could barely consume his food, even with frequent sips of water.

He wrote his letter to the Cardinal of Timber Bay slowly, pausing to consider the weight and consequence of every word. In the wrong hands, his message would be considered treachery.

Some might even call it heresy.

And yet, when he finally finished what he had to say and sat back, hands trembling, Aaron did not feel like a heretic. He felt like a saviour.

Maybe a dead saviour.

IV

A thick sackcloth near the corner of the warehouse moved, slowly at first, then more violently as the sleeper on the mattress beneath woke and struggled to sit up.

Some of the building's other occupants were already awake, sitting in despondent silence and wrapped in the endless torpor of their existence. All were destitute, and many suffered from crippling addictions.

The man next to Siara, who had shared a little of his turnip *rasham* spirit with her last night, slept on, snoring loudly. His name was Rik, she recalled. He claimed to have once been a middle-ranking clerk within the Palace. "And I am still a respectable man," he had been at pains to point out, although his trousers stank of piss and much of his hair and most of his teeth had fallen out. He would sometimes lurch from lucid, rational conversation to senseless ranting in a breath. When he coughed, blood flecked his grimy shirt.

"I don't have long left," he had told her, unnecessarily. That grim fact, evidently, had given him reason to hasten along his ruinous road, *rasham* steadily washing away what remained of him, mentally and physically.

And that could be you if you don't do something about it, a warning whispered through Siara's mind, every day. Rik was far from the only reminder of that fact in this sorry place.

Siara hadn't expected to ever need this makeshift hostel for Toran's down-and-outs. The building had been bought and originally maintained by a group of Devotees of the Church- one of the few factions that Siara didn't entirely loathe- but they were seldom seen now, and the funds for maintaining the place had reportedly been stopped by a different, higher order within the Church.

Three weeks ago, her life had been very different. She hadn't been destitute. She had enjoyed a steady if modestly paid job as a scribe and translator in the Guild of Historical Studies. But her employment had come to a sudden, unplanned end through no fault of her own. The Guild authorities had explained how cuts to their funding had forced their hand and resulted in some workers losing their jobs. "The decision was made by the Lords' Council," she was told, as if a low-ranking foreign scribe could go marching into the palace and demand that it be reversed.

At first, she hadn't worried too much about this setback. The Saanuese were famously adaptable. She would find a way to deal with the situation.

Siara was well educated. She spoke Gharaanian with only the slightest Saanuese accent. She had learned some choice passages from the Church's Elder and Later Scriptures and knew the major points of modern Gharaanian history- they didn't care for anything older than the last eight hundred years, prior to the formation of the modern Church. The people of this land tended towards self-importance- those lucky enough to receive an education and help climbing the rungs of life's ladder, anyway- and they approved in no small way of foreigners who learned and appreciated their history, provided it showed them in the best possible light. Knowing a smattering of sayings from their holy books certainly did no harm either.

And so, Siara had been confident of finding new work. But her optimism ebbed away as the days wore on and her savings were whittled away to nothing. Only a matter of days later, she could no longer afford her lodging, and ended up as a beggar and a thief.

Her fortunes had changed with frightening speed, and yet the last three weeks had felt like three months.

Siara had never felt such continual, aching hunger before. She and her twin brother Tiam had grown up in a relatively well-to-do family of traders and craftsmen in the city of Aun. They had never gone truly hungry, and their parents had impressed upon the twins how lucky they were. Siara reflected ruefully that no matter their words, until now she had never appreciated her good fortune.

She felt ashamed, but necessity had long since overridden her embarrassment. The coins she thieved were nowhere near enough to find somewhere better to live or pay for passage home, but at least she could eat sometimes.

Siara had spent her last copper bits on food yesterday morning. She would need to find more money today. Soup kitchens set up by the Devotees dotted the city, but recently they were closed more often than open. Perhaps funding for those had been cut as well. Siara remembered hearing about an ongoing argument between Crown and Church about charity and where responsibility for it lay. From what she could tell, neither side wanted ownership.

Maybe she would have some luck if she went down to the Guilders Road market today. There would be crowds, fat purses, noise, distractions. Had it been seven days since the last one? Siara reckoned so.

She looked disconsolately down at herself. Her normally light brown hair hung limp, dark and heavy with grease. Grime and dirt clung to her discoloured shirt. She itched and stank.

"I'm still alive, though," Siara whispered as she left for the market.

Guilders Street teemed with buyers and sellers. Siara kept a keen eye on the morning's hustle and bustle and cut a careful path along the fringes so that people had less need to avoid the unwholesome creature wandering in their midst. Her breath steamed in the frosty air, and she had to shield her eyes from the low sun at times. She looked for suitable targets- easily distracted merchants with overfilled purses, especially those she overheard and identified as foreigners. At the same time, she kept an eye out for the city militia and especially for Divine Knives, although luckily there were none of them around this morning. That was just as well, given their brutal reputation.

Siara passed by the bakers' corner, where delicious aromas of fresh bread and sweet baked fancies newly out of the oven made her mouth water and her aching stomach rumble painfully. She willed herself to concentrate on the task in hand as she ambled slowly along. Certainly there were plenty of purses and bags here, although their owners had the good sense to keep one hand on or near their valuables. After all, thieves were the scourge of Toran. Thieves and beggars, and anyone whose life had taken a wrong turn.

Siara gritted her teeth in frustration and moved on. Patience was key.

Then, unexpected good luck came her way.

A loud argument broke out between two men in an adjacent aisle, and within a moment it descended into a fight. The combatants managed to wrestle each other into a butcher's stall, and people hastily scattered as meat and pieces of the wooden structure flew everywhere.

Siara knew this would be her best opportunity.

The knife was in her hand immediately. She cut through the cord of a small bag belonging to a stocky, dark-haired man nearby. She didn't stop to look properly at whoever she had stolen from. Like almost everyone else nearby, he was busy watching the two men rolling and grappling on the cobbles.

She turned to run, and an arm reached around her neck. Siara shivered as a cold blade pressed against her throat. "Give that to me," a man whispered in her ear. It wasn't the man she had stolen from- he had only now turned away from the fight, which had been broken up by two footmen of the city militia. Siara relinquished the bag, cursing her stupidity.

The grip on her neck lessened enough for her to turn slightly, and Siara's blood ran cold as she saw the red and white cloak and insignia of the Divine Knives. How had she not noticed this man?

Now she would likely die for her desperation.

Siara would have laughed, or maybe wept, if she hadn't been so frightened.

"We have a thief, Father," the Divine Knife announced to the man she had stolen from. His cold blue eyes surveyed Siara dispassionately as her heart sank at the word *Father*. Had she stolen from a *priest*?! Why had he not been wearing his Church robes?

This is the worst day of my life, Siara miserably decided.

The plain-clothed priest scowled. "We have no time for you to take her to the cells. The carriage leaves soon. Ask one of your men."

"As you say." The Divine Knife made a gesture, seemingly to no one in particular, and another of his faction appeared from out of the crowd. Siara still could not understand how she had missed them previously, in their bright colours on a clear morning. "Take this creature to the cells," the newcomer was told. "Have her charged with theft."

"Please," Siara managed to say. "Please, I'm just hungry. I'm a God-fearing woman, and I..."

"Save the begging for your day of judgement."

Handcuffs were fastened around her wrists, and she was marched away.

V

Ever since his arrival at the Palace in Toran, Lord Vayyin's instincts had pleaded with him to turn around and begin the long journey back home to his distant, wintry realm.

As he stood in front of the mirror in his bedchamber and fastened the buttons of his best tunic- this evening he had been summoned to an audience with King Ranith, after all, even if his Majesty cared little for protocol and formal dress these days- Vayyin's thoughts were of home and tasks long left undone. Should he sell the manor house that faced the bitter eastern sea and salt wind at Winden? He seldom visited the place, preferring the comforts of his castle on the edge of Southwood. But upkeep was needed at the castle too, and he had trouble keeping servants there for some reason. Some of the older folk in Southwood town said haunts hid there. Even the newly installed Priest of Southwood, a bluff and pragmatic man, found excuses not to enter.

There were always problems, but he would have preferred to be at home with matters to deal with, rather than here in this den of vipers, friendless and forever watching his back. Gharaanian simply by geographical limits, Vayyin was a man of Gharaan's distant south-east through and through, and the people of that area were an independent sort who clung to ways that long predated the Church. He observed religious ceremonies with a weary reluctance and often wondered at the shiny-eyed zeal of Toranians.

Before his audience with the King, Vayyin had the tedium of a Greater Council meeting to sit through. As a Lord of the Council, he would be expected to attend, as would all the landed lords and ladies of Gharaan's regions, from the wealthy and Godly north-west to the sparsely populated, threadbare south-east.

Those who could find no excuse to remain at home.

In past years, the King would have been a sharp presence, always interested in matters of the Council- or more exactly, in the petty whims of the Council Lords, not to mention the Church, which exerted a troubling influence on matters of law. A minor holy festival was imminent, so priests would circle like gulls this afternoon, making their case for additional funds.

But in recent years, the King's attendance had become less frequent. He made a grudging appearance only at events that required his presence- committing the royal seal to new laws or done deals. Meanwhile, rumours and whispers concerning the King's health flitted back and forth like little birds, some reasonable and others outrageous. Vayyin tried not to listen to these- his loyalty was to the King, not to the plotters and chancers forever jostling for position. For many years he had admired Ranith's resolve and independence in the face of an increasingly crafty and belligerent Church. But he couldn't help overhearing the latest rumours and found them concerning. The King's wits were failing him. He could no longer visit the privy on his own. He stared for hours at the walls and talked to imaginary people.

One consistent report was that he drank more now than ever before. Vayyin could believe that. King Ranith had been a shadow of his former self since the deaths of the Queen and his infant son and had turned increasingly to drink to dull his anguish.

With no line of succession, sooner or later the lords and ladies of the Council would meet to decide how to appoint a new King. The eventuality had been known for some time, of course, but the path forward remained unclear without any modern precedent. Ranith's line had ruled Gharaan for three hundred years since a disastrous war with Anphay had toppled the previous ruling family. But the King had not remarried nor had relations with any woman since the demise of his young family. Nor did he have any surviving relatives that anyone knew about.

Vayyin wished the King had shown more interest in solving the thorny matter of Asqabal. Many of the Council lords and ladies were complicit in the manoeuvrings and deals that went on between Gharaan and Asqabal's Sentai lords, and they knew Vayyin's feelings on the matter. He was not a pious man- he did many things that went against the teachings of the Church- but he had no liking for their north-eastern neighbour. In the distant past, the people of the Southwood region and surrounding lands had fought against out-worlders summoned by the Asqabalese to broaden and strengthen their power in the world. Some folk still commemorated those times, and even brought out their dark green banners on fayre-days, in open contempt of the Gharaanian red and white national flag. In those days, their land had been called Sheren. Its border had run from Saintscastle in the distant south, up to the remote north coast between Eastcliff and Timber Bay. Now it existed only in old books, and the thoughts of those who dared to remember.

Yes, he would be far safer ensconced within his castle. He was not well liked here- a man who cared little for etiquette and finery, and whose plain looks and shabby appearance- no matter what clothing he wore- set him awkwardly apart from his peers.

He was tempted to claim ill health, so he need never come to Toran again. Would the King bother to send for him by force? Would his absence be noticed? He was loyal, but quietly loyal. Was he ever truly needed?

Vayyin quite liked the idea of being forgotten about.

He finished dressing and made his way through the labyrinthine passageways of the palace to the eastern wing, and the Greater Council Chamber. About thirty other lords and ladies- although only five were ladies- of the Greater Council already waited, some at tables whilst others stood and conversed quietly in groups. Most clutched a cup of daywine and some picked at miniature pastries or honeyed fancies baked this morning. Servants deftly threaded their way through the gathering, keeping the Council refreshed.

The King, of course, was nowhere to be seen.

Maybe he's drinking, in the dark, Vayyin fretted. What state would his Majesty be in by the time they met later?

Events got underway once everyone had arrived and the ceremonial bell rang to begin the Session of Council. Vayyin listened sparingly as affairs progressed in their usual unhurried manner. He voted three times, with the majority, barely attending to the detail of the matter. Afterwards, wearied by the day's tedium he went to the drinking hall in the north wing of the palace, where he sat in a comfortable armchair with a large cup of Saanuese vintage for company. Vayyin had no wish to be drunk for his audience, no matter that the King might be- but neither did he want to sit through the meeting in cold sobriety. Somewhere in between might get him through the evening.

At last, not wishing to go- the wine had relaxed and comforted him a little- Vayyin departed to meet with the King.

To Vayyin's surprise, he was directed by one of the guards into an antechamber to the throne room- good-sized, but devoid of the greater chamber's vast oak ornamentation.

As the door closed behind him Vayyin saw the King sitting at the head of the table in the room. He began to bow, but Ranith responded immediately with an irritated sound. "Get up,

Vayyin. Don't prostrate yourself before me like those unbearable sycophants."

As Vayyin straightened a faint hope began to stir within him. Not only did he not sound like a lackwit, but King Ranith did not appear especially drunk. Perhaps he had downed a few cups of wine, but likely no more than that. His dark beard was trimmed, he sat up straight and his cheeks were pale, not flushed. Grey flecked his close-cropped hair and the lines on his face had deepened since the Lord of Southwood had last seen him. But he did not look unwell.

Vayyin thought the light was poorer than it ought to be. The corners of the room seemed too dark, and the lanterns, though they gave out as much light as they ought, also threw shadows upon the walls that had a particular blackness. Perhaps the plain furnishings and paintwork had something to do with it, but this room set him on edge and he could not say why.

"You're a worried man," the King noted as he sat back in his chair.

It's the light, Vayyin almost said. "I always have worries, Majesty."

"Well, speak of them, Vayyin. Everything you say here is in confidence. I have matters to discuss with you, but I would hear *your* concerns first."

Vayyin collected his thoughts. "Majesty, I fear many Lords of the Council grow... lax in their duties. There is widespread corruption..."

"That is not news, my Lord of Southwood. There has always been corruption. I expect nothing less of the Council. But they are at least consistent in what they do." The King seemed bleakly amused, and Vayyin blinked, taken aback by that raw assessment.

"You don't like Toran much, do you, Vayyin?"

"I..." He hadn't expected that either.

"Be honest, man. Speak your mind."

"Toran is... not entirely to my taste, Majesty." Vayyin tried to walk the thin line between tact and truth. "Too many people, perhaps. I enjoy the simple, rural life." *And I long to return to it.*

"Of course you do." Ranith rose and went over to a side cabinet to fetch a crystal decanter of rye spirit. He poured a glass for them both and handed Vayyin the more generous serving. The Lord of Southwood took a small sip and savoured the warmth as it spread down his throat and into his stomach.

"They do my bidding in name only and find ways to usurp the law," the King complained as he returned to his seat. "They are self-serving toads. A half or more are paid by the Church to serve the Church's interests. As if the archpriests don't have their own vote in Church matters! But you, Vayyin- *you* remain loyal, don't you?"

Could his loyalty really be in doubt? "Always, Majesty. I serve you and I serve Gharaan. If I can prove my..."

"You don't need to." Ranith took a grimace-inducing gulp of spirit and leaned back in his chair with a sigh. "But we must tread carefully in matters concerning the Council lords. Many have loyal subjects... most of those who live on their estates have far greater loyalty to their Lords than to me. Well, obedience may be a better word for it. Better a cruel lord than a distant one, perhaps."

Vayyin nodded politely.

"Well," his liege said. "To the Great Burning with them all. We are each measured against our deeds, at the last."

Vayyin hadn't heard the phrase *Great Burning* for many years. It was a phrase from before the time of the Church, although ironically the Hell that the Church liked to paint vividly in the minds of their faithful bore an uncanny similarity to it, and some within the Church even used the name themselves. Perhaps every power through history had threatened its subjects with a similar fate if they strayed from its ordained path. The phrase conjured up disturbing images of dark, fluid shapes that stepped through flames and reached out into the waking world. *Faer*, perhaps, or whatever primal forms they came from.

The *faer* had been allies of his ancestors, he uncomfortably reminded himself. Was that another reason why he felt so threatened by Toran and its power structures? He had never liked the Palace, but he liked the Overchurch even less.

The King wandered over to the cabinet to refill his glass. To Vayyin's relief he didn't offer him another drink. He would need his wits about him as he tried to find his way back to his room later. The palace was vast and much of it unfamiliar. He didn't come here often enough to properly learn his way around.

Vayyin had walked to his meeting with heart in mouth, full of unease- but he felt something more akin to confusion after his liege spoke up again.

"The rumours of my descent are all true, my Lord of Southwood. Tonight, something has awakened me- given back a sort of temporary life. It won't last, of course, nor should it. A loan is a serious matter.

"*You,* however, are destined for other things. I know you to be cautious and methodical. Your sense of self-preservation is strong." The King smiled. "You've turned as pale as a ghost, Vayyin. I should know- I've seen them."

The odd confession pulled Vayyin from his bewilderment somewhat. "You... you have, Majesty?"

"Ellinor, crawling across the great beams of our bedchamber, staring down at me with accusing eyes. Sometimes I see her in the sunlight, also. She's a pattern in the dust, severe on occasion, other times smiling- but always in pain, as in life. She and I will have a chance to talk again, perhaps. First, the two of us will go on a little journey. Come with me."

The King walked slowly across the hall to one of the minor entrances used by servants and led Vayyin down a passageway beyond. He stopped at a side door which he unlocked with a key to reveal steps that led down in a spiral. "The servants' quarters?" Vayyin wondered aloud.

"These are no one's quarters."

The two men set off down the spiral staircase. Lanterns held by brackets in the walls cast lurid shadows, as Vayyin stepped patiently behind the King. Ranith had bad knees whose condition was aggravated by the downward steps, but he bore the pain in silence and held grimly to the rope on the outer edge of the stairwell.

At the bottom of the stairs three passageways diverged. The King chose the one to the left and walked along with Vayyin now at his side. The Lord of Southwood longed to ask where they were going but didn't. He also wondered who had lit the wall lanterns that illuminated their way but didn't ask about those either.

After some time, they stopped at a side door which the King unlocked with another key. Vayyin had never seen so many keys, certainly not in the hands of the King. Had his liege so much as opened a door himself before? He couldn't remember. Such everyday things passed unrecalled. And now he might have a key for every room in the palace.

Ranith pushed at the door, and it opened reluctantly to reveal absolute darkness. The air smelled of must and mould and air that might not have been breathed for many years. "Take one of the lanterns," the King said as he peered into the gloom. "And Vayyin," he added as the Lord of Southwood carefully lifted a lantern from one of the wall brackets, "don't be afraid of whatever you might see in here."

The King's words failed in their intended effect. Vayyin's stomach tightened with worry. He even considered throwing himself to the ground and begging desperately for his liege to pick a more worthy ally. "Have courage," the King said casually. He might have been asking Vayyin to have a flagon of ale. "Remember, you need not fear things simply because you don't understand them."

That made good sense, Vayyin admitted as Ranith gestured for the lantern. But he and his fear had become inseparable.

The King, on the other hand, remained as calm and serene as Vayyin had ever seen him. His mood had changed as they went deeper into the palace, as if the younger, quietly confident Ranith had resurfaced- the man from before the deaths of Queen Ellinor and his infant son, before the drinking and the darkness. Vayyin could scarcely remember that time. He had been much younger then, too. Hadn't they gone hunting together once, in Southwood? He thought so but couldn't recall for certain. Why would the King have come to Southwood?

Vayyin followed carefully as Ranith made his way into the room beyond. "Close the door behind you," the King commanded. When Vayyin did so he noticed a subtle change in the room.

Faint outlines marking the edges of surfaces all around them emerged, as if their shapes and dimensions possessed a light all their own, for the glow that came from them was quite different to the soft illumination of the lantern. Although faint, it had a harsh, cold appearance. Like the light from another world, Vayyin found himself thinking, and shuddered.

"Walk with me," the King whispered. Vayyin followed him over the paved stone floor. It looked more like the smooth cobbled ground of a well-to-do city street than the floor of a storeroom, as if they had miraculously left the confines of the palace altogether. When Vayyin looked up the gloom appeared to stretch away forever. The air felt spitefully cold.

"How big is this place?" he whispered after a while.

The King did not reply at first. Vayyin had almost plucked up the courage to ask again when his liege said, "It's as big as it needs to be. A place from which neither *we* nor *they* can go any further."

Vayyin wished he hadn't asked.

As they continued through the forbidding chill, the Lord of Southwood became certain that someone or something monitored their progress. He opened his mouth to quietly warn the King, but Ranith pre-empted him. "There *is* a presence, Vayyin- but not malign. Not for the two of us, anyway."

In Vayyin's mind that unseen *something* pressed in ever closer.

Finally, Ranith stopped and placed the lantern on the ground in front of him. Its light had changed. The familiar warm yellow flicker had become green-tinged. Vayyin looked hastily away, certain that the light looked back at him.

The green light flickered as if a gust of wind suddenly blew within the lantern, and the flames became small and dim. From somewhere distant came a faint scraping, rustling sound. It was a noise that Vayyin thought might belong in Southwood's wintry depths. It reminded him of scare-tales from his childhood, of old, half-forgotten things.

He took an involuntary step backwards, but the King said to him without turning to look, "There's no way out, Vayyin- not until we're done here."

Vayyin's teeth chattered, and a violent shudder went through him. The air had grown so cold he could barely think.

The awful sound grew louder. Something terrible approached.

From out of the icy dark a painfully thin, translucent figure emerged. Over twenty hands tall, it reached towards them with angular and bony limbs that should have been too fragile to support its mass. Luminescent green eyes regarded them, set in a gaunt, colour-washed visage.

Paralysed with fear, Vayyin stared helplessly into the terrible, ageless gaze of this being. Its long, almost delicate hands ended in shapes that could have been talons or icicles or something else altogether. The creature and the King touched hands briefly and tendrils of faint green-hued light- or perhaps smoke- drifted into the surrounding darkness. Neither uttered a word- Vayyin did not know if this entity could speak, although a dark crack scarred its face where a mouth might otherwise be. Nevertheless, he felt certain that some unspoken understanding passed between them.

Then the vast being retreated slowly into the dark, almost as if whatever had sent it here now absorbed it back into a greater, unseen mass.

Vayyin drew a deep, shivering breath and followed the King as he turned and walked away- perhaps the way they had come, or a different direction. Vayyin no longer knew and couldn't even be certain that it mattered.

Sometime later, the Lord of Southwood found his voice. "Majesty, what was that creature?"

When Ranith turned to face him, Vayyin was shocked to see that the King's eyes held a greenish tinge and a flicker of light darted around in them for a moment. "An *arborian*." Ranith's voice sounded soft and almost dreamlike. "An ancient being of Theya, distantly related to other *faer* creatures, and a wielder of the old magic that once ran unbound the length and breadth of our world. Few remain now, and only in the hidden reaches. But they can come to places such as this, for the palace was built over the remains of something far older, far greater. As was the Overchurch for that matter, though the priests will deny it until the sun rises in the west."

Vayyin struggled to understand how *faer* creatures could appear in the depths beneath Toran. This would surely be the least likely place for such as them.

He flinched as the King clasped his hand. "Until yesterday, I would not have believed this either. They awakened me, Vayyin. They restored me. I now remember things I hadn't realised I'd forgotten."

"I've never heard of such things as *arborians*."

"No, and why would you? They exist beyond your horizon, absent from the world you think you know. Hundreds of years ago, man of Southwood that you are, you would have been raised to believe in them, maybe even pay respects to them. Or beings like them- the Old Ones, as I believe your people like to call anything *faer*." Ranith's grip on him tightened a little. The air remained desperately cold and yet the touch was like fire. Vayyin felt certain that a measure of that mad warmth had begun to pour from the King to himself.

Then, Ranith said quietly, "You might consider speaking of the things you've seen tonight."

Vayyin opened his mouth to vehemently deny that he would do such a thing, but the King told him, "No one would believe you, Vayyin. The Lords' Council regards you as a man on the margins, your territory a miserable frontier known only for fishing and for hunting things that no Godly man would ever eat. As for the Church- you pay them lip service when you need to- don't we all? But you're no more a man of their constructs than I am. Would you beg audience with the High Cardinal and tell him the King of Gharaan consorts with demons? In the eyes of the Church, everything from before *their* time is unholy in nature."

"I have no one to tell," Vayyin said, and he meant it.

"You, my Lord of Southwood, have been called upon. I did not choose you. *They* did, knowing your heritage. Others see through the *arborian's* eyes. The Old Ones- some of them, anyway. I brought you here so that they could see you and..." Ranith paused, frowning. "So they could *approve* you."

"Approve me." Vayyin almost laughed.

"Long ago, when my father was King and you and I roamed together on your estate- do you remember?- you called yourself a woodsman with a heathen heart."

The Lord of Southwood nodded slowly, a faint and distant memory coming back to him. "Good times," he murmured. "Care-free times. Why did I ever forget?"

He wondered if the night had passed, in the world outside this impossibly vast palatial realm. He longed desperately for sunlight- even winter's pale version.

The King observed his anguish and looked almost sympathetic. "The waiting will be difficult. Inevitably, you will question the path you're on. But you must also embrace who you are."

Vayyin could not hide his bewilderment. Ranith Cenoran, King of Gharaan and last of his line, had transformed from a self-pitying, drunken sot to an unearthly, mysterious man who made dark deals with ancient beings from Theya's hidden past. Could everything he thought he knew about the King be an elaborate pretence?

"And you, Majesty? Will you embrace who *you* are?"

"My time is almost done, Vayyin. They opened my eyes just before they close forever. Even they cannot undo the things that have happened to me. The things I have done to myself. But it's still a blessing of sorts- to be lifted up in my final hours."

"But..." Vayyin struggled to understand. "Why must you die? If that's the price, I want nothing to..."

"Hush. You need to sleep." Ranith's words implied that Vayyin must quickly find some reserves of strength for his as-yet unknown task.

They returned to the staircase and ascended to the antechamber where the King had received him. Vayyin thought it appeared longer than before, its ceiling higher.

Something was also different about Ranith's shape, he thought, although it was difficult to tell in the persistent gloom. Shadows seemed to extend one way but then another when he looked back at the light that cast them. He saw forms upon the walls and in the corners, that looked like tendrils and creepers shivering as if in anticipation of something. But when he looked again, they were nothing more than artwork or mosaic pieces that extended across the walls.

For a moment, the King appeared almost formless, a silhouette, but then as the light changed the Lord of Southwood saw the man he served- pale, rake-thin but bright-eyed and possessed of a bony, hard vigour. He did not look like a man about to die. He had the appearance of a man who might live forever.

"For now, I am not what others see. But *you* were able to cross the divide, faithful Vayyin. The Southwood blood knows the way instinctively."

As Vayyin stared fearfully back at his liege he felt certain that the King had grown a little, and his musculature was better-defined than moments before.

"Do I look well, Vayyin?" Even his voice had changed, its rough edges cut away. Vayyin fancied that it sounded like music.

"Better than ever, Majesty." *Don't die,* he wanted to say, and he found himself full of sudden desperation. They had both started to remember the old times. Vayyin wanted to remember more of them.

"Can you be ready for whatever comes?" The King's voice seemed soft, almost wistful. "Whatever they ask of you?"

Vayyin felt a nameless fear crawl through him, as if he stood on the edge of a precipice with the ground crumbling away beneath. He had time to remove himself from the limit of the land, and yet he stood there regardless, both repulsed by and drawn to the horror of his situation. *I'm going mad,* he thought, and almost sobbed. "What am I to do?" he asked helplessly.

"Tonight? Go to your quarters and sleep."

"But... I don't think I can find my way." Vayyin stared helplessly this way and that. This wasn't the same hall, he decided. He had never been here before.

The King laid a hand on Vayyin's shoulder, a gesture of reassurance that seemed laughable in the face of everything they'd seen this long evening. "It has been my pleasure to know you, Vayyin Morne of Southwood."

"Will I not speak with you again?"

"In another life, my friend." The King's smile was warm, knowing. "In another life."

Vayyin walked the palace corridors with his thoughts in tatters. Cold, silvery moonlight poured through the windows in some of the halls he walked through. He encountered no one and he heard no one. He feared he would become lost in this place he no longer recognised.

And yet he arrived at the door to his quarters, as if gently guided by an unseen presence. He managed a faint, tremulous smile and pressed his hand against the door to reacquaint himself with reality.

Exhausted, the Lord of Southwood nevertheless found himself too troubled for sleep, frightened beyond measure by the unearthly world he had glimpsed- a world of which he had become a part.

VI

"Courage," Vayyin said flatly to his reflection. The man in the mirror, stranded in early middle age, with stooped shoulders, veiny hands, and the beginnings of a rounded gut, peered reluctantly back at him, squinting slightly in the morning light that poured through the east-facing window. Vayyin judged it must be near breakfast time, but he had no appetite for the stodgy holy-cakes and honey-laced crispbreads that the people of Toran favoured. In Southwood he would breakfast on game or fish served with freshly baked bread.

"I have no courage," Vayyin added for good measure, and he looked away from his mirror-self, hating the innocuous, cowering creature that peered fearfully back.

He had no appetite either.

He felt disoriented and heavy-headed, as if he had slept for too long.

Vayyin opened the window, inhaled the cold morning air, and looked out over the complex architecture of the palace- blocks and towers and spires and columns whose purpose he knew next to nothing about.

I am a stranger here, he thought. *I will always be a stranger.*

He had another session of Council to endure today, but as soon as that was done, he would make arrangements for his journey home. His departure could not come soon enough. He could not recall a great deal from his meeting with the King but felt sure that he hadn't been instructed to stay.

The King had, it could be argued, not instructed him at all.

A faint sound made him turn, and he saw a paper being pushed under his door. Vayyin went to the door, picked up the paper, and on a whim, swiftly opened the door to see who had delivered it.

There was no one in the corridor.

Troubled, he returned to his room, closed the door, and opened the message.

Leave as soon as possible. Do not wait for Council business.

The message was unsigned but bore the unique imprint of the King's seal. Vayyin carefully folded and pocketed the note and went to find the courtyard servants, to arrange for a carriage to be made available and for his luggage to be loaded, not that he had a great deal. *My lucky day,* he thought, but he couldn't put aside his unease.

By mid-morning, his carriage was ready with belongings loaded. Vayyin, who had been pacing restlessly around in the cold, clambered in and sat down. Only then did he discover that he was not alone.

The robed, hooded figure sitting opposite him in the carriage was young, female, of slight build and delicate features. Hazel eyes gazed intently at him as he blinked in confusion. "What...?"

"Lord Vayyin," she said in a distinct Saanuese accent. "I'm to accompany you to Southwood."

Vayyin glanced out of the window, wondering if he ought to alert the guards. "Don't," she said quietly. "We need to leave here quietly, you and I."

"Did the King send you?"

"The King? No. It's not easy to explain, but I'll try to, over the coming days. It will take some time because I don't remember much about what happened yet. I waited, and then they came to me, and told me I had to leave..." Her voice trailed away as if she had lost her train of thought.

"Why are you here? Who sent you?" Vayyin persisted.

"My name is Juli." She leaned forward, looking into his eyes in such a way that Vayyin almost shrank away from her. Memories of last night began to trickle back through his mind.

"Have you ever felt," she whispered, "as if you were sleeping through your life, and now you've woken up into a different world?"

VII

Cardinal Aaron Blackwood watched helplessly, unable to look away from the man in the infirmary bed. As one might expect of a

Divine Knife, he clung grimly to life, although Aaron had only to look at the horror of his face to wish that the Lord God would put him out of what must be unbearable agony.

Where the bladesman's eyes should have been, black and singed holes gaped. The skin of his face had been mostly torn off. Whoever had attacked Marim and the Divine Knives guarding him, had clearly intended to visit as much agony upon them as possible. How this man had survived the attack and still lived after being brought back to Toran, Aaron had no idea.

Someone or something intended to teach them a lesson, he thought. But what lesson?

"They were just outside the village of Fallow, five miles east of the city, your Worship." The old priest who spoke, Father Dellamas, had seen much in his many years of service to the Church, but Aaron doubted that he'd seen anything quite like this. Aaron certainly hadn't.

Not outside the Hall of the Interface, anyway.

"Who could have done this?" They might never find out, but the question would not let him be. Even in God-fearing Gharaan, enemies of the established order lurked, especially in rural areas where the rule of law was sometimes weaker than it ought to be. Spies and agents of the Protectorate operated throughout the land, using every tool they could to try to destabilise Gharaan. The Asqabalese, meanwhile, colluded with demons. But both the Church and the Lords' Council were reluctant to do anything about them. Asqabal remained an important trading partner, even if relations between the two lands had cooled in recent years. Asqabalese gold had helped consolidate the power of the Church over the last few centuries, and the ways of those who ruled that land- which to Aaron's mind made them a more troublesome enemy than the heathens of Anphay- were conveniently ignored.

This atrocity might even have been the dark work of the *faer*, although the Cardinal could not understand what they might gain from it. When had any such creatures last set foot in Gharaan?

Best not explore that possibility yet, he decided. Half the priests, officials and servants in the Overchurch refused to believe they still existed.

"The priest in Fallow found little evidence left to gather, your Worship. Almost everything was burned, including most of the bodies."

Aaron felt certain that great evil had been at play here. "Deliberately," he said softly.

"I beg pardon, your Worship?"

"They left him alive as an example, Father. A man could not normally survive such torture. They wish to send us a message." *The scroll must have burned too,* he thought suddenly, and felt guilt and shame for the flicker of relief in his heart.

"Something odd happened in the city before they left, though," the priest remarked. "A young woman was caught trying to steal from Father Marim. She has been placed in the cells."

Aaron looked sharply at him. "Has she been questioned yet?"

"I don't know, your Worship. I don't think so, although she will likely attract more attention in the light of what happened in Fallow. The Truthseekers may need to be involved." Dellamas sighed regretfully, as if the Truthseekers were the last resort that Aaron wished they were. "Of course, it may simply be coincidence."

"Perhaps." Aaron wondered if he should arrange to question the thief himself. If the Truthseekers got to her first, there wouldn't be much left for him to interrogate later.

"As for a message, this seems an unfathomable horror to me, so the point of it is lost." Father Dellamas folded his arms and observed the tortured man in such an expressionless manner that Aaron felt stirred into further comment on his condition. "He is suffering greatly! Why is he being kept alive? We can do nothing for him now. Let him go into the Light."

Dellamas looked uncomfortable as he reluctantly met Aaron's eyes. "Ah. I do apologise, your Worship, that no one has told you. A request came directly from His Holiness the High Cardinal himself, for this man to be kept alive at all costs. It seems that, though he has suffered greatly, his will be a higher path. His Holiness has chosen him for something."

Aaron's blood ran cold. For a moment he felt unsteady, as if the floor had shifted beneath him. He grasped the bedpost for support.

The Cardinal could not remember what excuse he gave for leaving, but a short while later he sat at the desk in his study chamber, short of breath and tremulous.

Unlike many of his peers, Aaron was not a frequent drinker, but this evening he needed something to calm his nerves and help him nod off. He would not sleep otherwise.

He had one of his servants bring a bottle of dark red East Greatwater wine. Once alone he poured himself a glass and downed it in three gulps, barely tasting what was likely an exquisite vintage, for no people made better wines than the river folk. Then he sat wearily as the prickly warmth spread through his insides.

Should he interrogate the prisoner this evening?

The Truthseekers- always concerned with investigations into crimes against the Church and threats to its power- would already be hard at work piecing together this dreadful puzzle. But Aaron did not trust the Truthseekers, whose grim zeal masked a keen urge to obtain the best results to fit their investigative- they would say *protective*- work. Chief Inquisitor Xul Riverstead was a powerful player in the Church's wider structure, able to pull many strings behind the scenes. A Cardinal he was not, yet he may as well have been.

Aaron poured himself another glass, drank it in short order and poured the rest of the bottle. Conflicting thoughts milled around in his head. He wanted to weep at the horrors he had seen. He felt an urge to lash out. He wished he could gather those loyal to him and ask them what he should do, for he felt paralysed by indecision.

But as he finished his wine, the Cardinal of Toran realised blackly that no one with any power or influence could be trusted, here in the Overchurch.

He was alone, an old man who had tried to walk a righteous road but found himself sinking into ghostly darkness.

The shadowy form, a grotesque creature whose wet, filmy breath echoed harshly in the sparse, low-ceilinged bedchamber, pressed against Gorram. The High Cardinal's eyes closed and a faint smile flickered on his lips with each of Pellin's determined thrusts. His servant's ungentle, frantic efforts always reminded him of a boy he had bedded perhaps a decade ago. Gorram could not recall that youth's name, but he fondly remembered his boundless lust.

"What have I shown you?" whispered Pellin in his ear.

They observed this ritual every evening. It thrilled Gorram in a way he had never thought possible before he met this wonderful, frightening creature- a servant only in name, for he allowed Pellin whatever he desired.

"All things," he murmured. "All that can be, when the worlds are locked in place." He didn't understand those fearful words, at least not in a way that could be described. But he believed utterly in their importance. He believed in Pellin's curious ritual, maintaining his cover of a witless, mute imbecile in the Hall of the Interface, even when they were alone there.

Pellin slowed and then lay still, buried inside The High Cardinal. The manservant uttered a long, phlegmy sigh at his moment of release. Gorram sometimes imagined that Pellin's seed burned him terribly inside, working holes through his innards. That was nonsense, of course. He would not be alive were that so.

He wanted to know more about what had been done in Fallow- what was *necessary*, in God's name, awful though it was to sanction. But then Gorram's heart began to thump quickly as he imagined the ruin that had been wrought there- the blood spilled, the skin removed, the cries of agony. The bones extracted with their owners still alive and lucid.

"God save me!" he mumbled. "Why am I so drawn to it?!"

Pellin knew what he was thinking. Didn't he always? A warm, sweat-prickled hand reached around to fondle him. "Don't be ashamed," whispered that familiar, comforting voice. A coarse tongue licked the back of his neck. "We are only human. You and I do God's work. Picture them. Picture them laid out, their meat drying in the wind."

"Eyes missing," the High Cardinal whispered. "No path to Heaven. Only the one Divine Knife left. We walk towards the light. Is he the next step?"

"Oh, yes," Pellin murmured. "I should think so. I think the next step will be a *big* one."

The manservant's hand began a familiar rhythm, but Gorram had no need for further coaxing.

A moment later he rushed past the moment of no return. His sight came and went. His body convulsed. Pellin withdrew his hand, disengaged from the other man, and lay on his back in the darkness. He stared up at nothing, licked the salty discharge from his fingers and waited for Gorram to drift into the deep slumber that always followed their coupling.

Then he slipped away, silently. As always at this late hour, he had work to do.

VIII

Siara woke with the stench of putrefaction in her nostrils. Her eyes flickered open, and she stared up into a dimly lit room. She tentatively moved her arms, winced at the pain, and sat up.

Thick iron bars filled about half the opposite wall, and an iron door stood at its centre. A faint draught disturbed the stale, warm air occasionally. Enough could be seen of the area beyond to reveal a passageway, filled with shadows and flickering torches.

Siara's insides tightened like a knot. All logic pointed to her not surviving for much longer. There could be little doubt of her being found guilty. "Because I am," Siara murmured bleakly.

She cursed her stupidity.

If only she'd never come to Toran. If only she'd followed another path.

If only, if only.

The smell of rotting flesh grew more potent as the curious subterranean draught blew into her dismal cell. Siara guessed that the remains of other prisoners lay discarded in other cells nearby, slowly withering away. Clearly some trials were less than urgent.

For how long would she be left here?

Would she even survive long enough to be put on trial?

Someone imprisoned here before her had evidently tried to break through the wall on the left-hand side. Small pieces of stone had crumbled away and gathered on the ground. She went over to inspect the area, in hope more than expectation, but even that faint hope swiftly died. There was no way she could break through the wall.

Likely only another cell stood on the other side anyway.

A cluster of orange-brown fungus at the base of the wall caught her eye. It seeped a viscous liquid and a faintly acrid odour issued from it. Siara recognised the growth as rustscrape, a potently poisonous fungus. It struck her as ironic that it grew here, where the condemned might hope to take their own lives rather than face execution.

Then she saw a sharp piece of stone on the ground which could have been used to dig pieces from the wall. An idea occurred to her.

Rustscrape was almost always fatal once it entered the bloodstream. It could be handled, with care, provided the handler ingested none of it. She could wipe some of the fluid it exuded onto the stone, keep her makeshift weapon hidden and cut whoever came to collect her for trial.

If more than one guard came, that would make things more difficult. One only, and she might stand a chance.

Siara peered more closely at the piece of stone. It wasn't as sharp as she wanted, but it might draw blood, if she slashed hard enough.

Carefully she squeezed and rubbed some of the rustscrape secretion onto the edge of the stone, then stared doubtfully at her effort. It would have to do. Of course, it might be a long time before anyone came for her.

She waited for what seemed like hours with the stone hidden in her hand, the sharper edge facing outwards. Finally, exhausted, she put the stone carefully down and nodded off, leaning against the back wall. Sometime later, her slumber was disturbed by the jangling of keys and slow, deliberate footsteps.

Siara opened her eyes to see a guard of the regular city militia. He stopped outside her cell, and faint hope stirred inside her, mixed with dread. While he sorted through his keys, she picked up the stone and concealed it in her hand.

"Time for your trial," he said, a mean look in his eyes as he leaned to one side and peered through the bars. "Don't worry. It won't take long."

"Please," Siara said, getting unsteadily to her feet as the guard noisily unlocked the door. "I'm not a thief, I was just hungry."

"Hungry, were you?" he grinned, opening the door. "Come on, let's go. God, you really *are* a filthy creature, aren't you?"

Siara meekly shuffled forward and through the doorway. As the militiaman moved aside, glancing down at his keys, she lunged at him, slashing at his neck with the stone. It was enough to draw blood. The guard recoiled, eyes wide with shock. He moved a hand to his neck, and then grabbed Siara's arm so that she dropped the stone. He shoved her against the bars and drew back his fist, but then his legs buckled, and confusion filled his eyes. "What..." His knees gave way. He grabbed at one of the cell bars and tried to haul himself up but couldn't. His arms shook violently.

Siara stepped hastily back as the guard's body began to convulse. His eyes bulged. Froth leaked from his lips and dripped to the ground.

Rustscrape poisoning was not supposed to affect someone quite like this. He should have had a heart seizure, and then death would follow- not painless by any means, but at least it would come quickly.

This, however, wasn't turning out to be a swift death.

She pulled his dagger free from its scabbard, but he grabbed her wrist again. The touch was like fire. His eyes, bright with malevolence, found hers. He tried to say something but could only make choking sounds. His hold weakened.

Siara drove the dagger as hard as she could through his light leather armour and into his chest.

He stopped moving. The froth on and around his lips dried and became brown and dry. Almost the same colour as rustscrape, Siara thought, as if the fungus had multiplied swiftly inside him.

She carefully wiped the dagger, put it in her belt, then took the guardsman's keys, and stepped out into the passageway. She stood still and listened intently. No sound came from either direction.

Siara walked quietly along the corridor, pausing now and again to listen and peer through the bars of nearby cells. No other prisoners could be seen. Eventually she reached a sturdy iron door. After three attempts she found the right key for the lock and hauled the door open. Another passage led away into half-lit gloom, and she took a left turn at the next junction.

Despair began to claw at her. She had no idea how to escape this place. How large was the prison? And how could she find her way out of the Overchurch?

She reached a door at the end of the passage sometime later, still having heard only the sounds she herself made. Siara pulled the door open enough to pass through and stepped out onto a spiral staircase. Immediately the temperature plummeted.

She reasoned that heading upwards would be more likely to lead towards an exit and daylight, so she began to climb the spiral, which ended after a hundred steps or so, at an open doorway. More corridors led away left, right and centre, and not knowing what else to do, Siara chose one at random.

Then she heard men calling to one another. They were not near, but sounded as if they might be getting closer.

Siara fled down the passageway, passing several other junctions and archways that led into rooms and halls. "Find her!" a distant voice shouted. Heart pounding, she ran through a doorway to the left, up a staircase and then right at the top of the stairs, only to face a thick, ancient wooden door almost immediately. A massive lock had been fitted to it.

Siara cursed and turned the other way, only to hear someone approaching the base of the stairs. Their footsteps were not fast, but she had no time to head down the other passageway without being seen.

She was trapped.

In desperation Siara grabbed the huge lock and pulled at it. It didn't give way, but as she touched the surface a complex mechanism inside the lock moved, almost as if something lived inside the cold metal and reacted to her touch.

In a moment, the lock had snapped open and Siara removed it from the bolt, astonished.

She pulled open the door with a huge effort, hastily put the lock back on the bar- although surely it would still look tampered with- and squeezed through the doorway before pulling the door closed on the other side, so that she stood in absolute darkness.

To her amazement- and subsequent horror- the lock quietly snapped shut again on the other side.

What could an enchanted lock of all things be doing here in the Overchurch?

Now she really was trapped.

She heard the thump of more footsteps as a group reached the top of the stairs and started down the corridor towards the door, but they stopped well short almost immediately. "Heretic's Tower," one of them muttered.

"She'll have gone to the storage chambers then," another said. "There's nothing else down the other way."

"Don't take her to trial," the first man said. "Just kill her and be done with it."

"You sure?" The second man sounded uncertain.

"Truthseeker Jerrem said so."

"Why? No one has questioned her yet."

"Best if *you* don't ask questions either."

They headed in the other direction. As their footfall faded into silence, Siara exhaled softly and tried to calm herself.

So *this* was Heretic's Tower?

She had heard much about this place. Heretic's Tower had been long closed away to everyone for the best part of eighty years. By order of Lucas Errin, High Cardinal of that time, the tower had been locked and everyone forbidden from entering it until the end of time itself. Even the High Cardinal himself could not enter.

The Heretic in question was a junior priest by the name of Zan Erimson, an Anphayan by birth who converted to a follower of God and came to study in the Overchurch. He studied the history and usage of many trinkets and relics owned- and in most cases, stolen from around the world- by the Church. According to popular myth mentioned in Saanu but spoken of rather less in Gharaan, Zan had uncovered certain properties of one relic, which he noted in detail in his journal. This object, a crystal made from a substance that no one had been able to identify over the centuries, apparently caused him to suffer increasingly vivid visions whenever he spent long enough in its presence.

He wrote extensively about the things to which he bore witness, which included other worlds, some impossibly beautiful and others horrific beyond compare. The meticulously described creatures of these worlds often had their own deities. Some of these creatures supposedly could also see into the Abyss, and Zan wrote about this in disturbing detail, in the final chapter of his journal, titled *The Eternal Collapse / The Crushing Void.*

This chapter apparently so disturbed the priests who found and read his journal that they burned Zan's works and all his belongings, except the journal, which was submitted to the High Cardinal. Items were destroyed without being removed or even touched. Perhaps the priesthood had been too frightened to take them anywhere else, even as char.

The tower was then closed off forever.

They would have burned Zan also- alive- but the young acolyte was nowhere to be seen when the Truthseekers came for him.

Had High Cardinal Lucas Errin destroyed the journal when the Truthseekers brought it to him, little of this story would have emerged. But in his folly, he shared the details with his Cardinals, and inevitably some of those details were learned by other men within the Church. Illicit copies were made, most far from complete, and although time muddied some of its potency, the story developed an almost superstitious aura that meant it became the most infamous banned text across every God-fearing territory in Theya.

Of course, anything banned was still spoken of, in the shadows and behind closed doors.

Zan's behaviour had already grown erratic during his time study-ing in the tower, to the point that colleagues shunned him, and servants feared to wait on him. According to one version of events, he gouged out the eyes of a girl with whom he had been carrying on an affair- although Siara knew of an alternative story in which the girl had gone mad after witnessing the same visions as Zan, and subsequently gouged her own eyes out.

A vast search for the missing priest revealed nothing of his where-abouts. Those few within the Church who suggested he might have used the relic to escape to one of the worlds in his visions were dealt with swiftly and harshly. Perhaps because of Zan's alleged crimes, they had their tongues torn out- a common punishment for the worst kinds of blasphemy- and were then excommunicated.

Zan was never found.

Siara waited for her eyes to adjust to the darkness, but soon real-ised that there was no light here. After a while she plucked up the courage to move slowly forwards, and felt her way around the walls, slowly breathing in the stale, acrid air. She stopped at one point, momentarily fearful of the floor collapsing beneath her feet.

Her hand touched something strangely shaped. Siara instinc-tively flinched and pulled her hand back. When she dared touch the object again, she found nothing more terrible than the ornamental end of a bannister. She stretched one foot forward and touched the bottom of a staircase.

Siara held the bannister firmly and slid her hand along it, then slowly ascended the stairs, still half-fearing they might crumble. As she had expected- given that she had trapped herself in a tower- the steps turned in a gentle, wide spiral, and after a while, she came to a small, grimy window, through which other towers and high areas of the Overchurch could be glimpsed. Their black shapes rose against a dark sky, a few with faint lanternlight behind their windows.

Siara continued, surer of foot now as minimal light from other windows on the outer wall allowed her to see something of her surroundings. Dust lay thick underfoot, and a stench of ash grew stronger as she ascended. Doors stood in the inner walls, all of them locked. She didn't dare touch the locks, fearful of inadvertently stir-ring their internal workings into action.

What might happen if she didn't find a way out? Why had the entrance lock clicked shut? Why had it reacted to her touch at all? Surely the priesthood would never allow a device riddled with sor-cery into their stronghold. And she had no talent for waking such things. Her brother Tiam was the one with an unusual talent, and he had become a darkseer- a very different thing to a sorcerer.

Could she open the lock through the thickness of the door and escape back out the way she had entered? The idea sounded preposterous, but then the possibility of working the mechanism of a complex lock simply by touching it had been equally unthinkable.

But even if it were possible, she would need to wait until they'd given up looking for her. One of the men had mentioned a Truthseeker. Why would a Truthseeker be involved in the trial of a common thief?

Siara wondered if the men had been looking for someone else all along.

The door at the top of the stairs lay open. The side that would have faced the room beyond had been burned to charcoal, as had part of the room itself. By the faint light the blackened remnants of furnishings and other objects came into view. The remains of a bookcase lay in a collapsed heap against one wall, and a table and chairs stood by the window on the far side of the room, surprisingly intact. Cobwebs festooned the area, ghostly threads dimly visible in the half-light.

As her view of the room improved further, Siara saw that its contents had not been destroyed completely. Smaller bookcases with volumes on their shelves remained mostly intact. She had as-sumed- along with presumably everyone else over the decades- that the priests had made certain nothing could be recovered. But their efforts were incomplete. Perhaps they had simply set the fire and then hurried away, fearful of this place.

Rain began to lash against the windows, flung by a tempestu-ous wind that howled around the tower. Siara swallowed, suddenly aware of how thirsty she was. When had she last drank anything? She imagined lifting her head to taste the rain, letting it pour over her face and down her throat.

Then, something incredible happened.

Water began to drip from somewhere in the middle of the shadowy ceiling. At first, only single droplets descended, but in a short while they merged to become a small but continuous stream.

For the first time in decades, judging by the dryness of this place, the roof of Heretic's Tower leaked.

Siara walked unsteadily to where the water fell and lifted her head. She opened her mouth and drank thirstily, oblivious to the harsh, almost metallic tang. A condemned woman shouldn't care if the water was dirty or contaminated. She gasped and almost choked as the cold liquid washed down her throat.

Finally, she stepped away, her thirst quenched. The stream of water slowed to a drip and then stopped entirely.

There was magic in this place, Siara decided. Here, in the Overchurch!

Might it be harmful?

She peered again into the murky heights of Zan's study chamber and tried to determine exactly where the water had dripped from, but she couldn't.

Her mind raced. She had imagined the sensation and taste of the water when she saw and heard the rain. And then it leaked through the roof. Now the water had stopped even though the rainstorm remained as powerful as ever.

And at the tower entrance, the lock had opened for her when she desperately imagined getting through the door.

Siara tried not to imagine her body slowly rotting away here to lie undiscovered for decades, perhaps even centuries.

She couldn't give up. The tower had drawn her in for a reason, and the key to her escape must lie somewhere here. Maybe she could try to work the lock at the bottom of the stairs again- if that was possible through the thickness of the door- but she needed to escape the Overchurch, and the chances of being discovered were far higher outside the tower.

Surely something in this room would be her salvation, if only she could find it. She walked carefully around the chamber, and meanwhile the sky gradually grew lighter outside, allowing her to see much more.

Her eyes fell upon the dusty books once again. Carefully Siara opened and began to read from a few that had not succumbed to the long-ago fire.

An accomplished student of many Theyan languages, Siara nevertheless struggled with many of the words in these books. Some had been written in Old Gharaanian, others in an obscure variant of Asqabalese that she barely understood at all. The subject matter, insofar as she could tell, varied from geography to ancient history, from theological principles to the study of powerful magics, covering matters that the Church would certainly have banned Zan from studying had they known about them before his studies spiraled out of control. How had he smuggled such books into the Overchurch? Had he written some of them himself?

Siara thumbed her way through page after page until her vision swam and her head dropped. Despair set in. Why was she sitting in a locked tower reading ancient texts?

She could try opening the locks in the inner doors, although surely the priests had blocked every possible exit. But perhaps something in the inner rooms might help her escape.

Siara shook her head miserably. What were the chances of her eluding all those who were searching for her *and* finding a way out of the Overchurch? And if she miraculously escaped, what were the chances then of escaping Toran?

No money and no friends, she reminded herself.

And no luck either.

She reached forlornly for another book, not knowing what else to do, and was surprised at the weight of this volume. Setting the plain leather-bound book down with an effort, she cautiously opened it.

Siara could not understand, let alone believe, what she now saw.

Instead of pages, a book-shaped container of black, writhing liquid lay before her.

She stared in mute disbelief until the mysterious fluid began to seep in tiny rivulets from the edges of the book, as if brought seething from a dark well in another world. Siara gave a cry of fear and scrambled to her feet, then backed away as far as the wall behind her, terrified that the liquid darkness would follow her.

Throughout Zan's study, tools, books, ornaments and glassware glistened faintly, as if the objects of this place were being imbued with new life or at least new purpose. As the dark liquid spread, they became brighter. A faint monotonous hum started, an indication that the fearful contents of this place had stirred from their long slumber.

"What have I done?" Siara whispered, horrified. "What have I *done*?!"

IX

Pellin's dreams had not been entirely his own since the *hyyr* merged with him years ago. Instead, for at least part of each night he had become a willing, enthralled passenger in the abstract dreams of the *hyyr*, which itself had only experienced such a thing as dreaming since its occupation of Pellin's inner darkness. Its previous hosts had been overwhelmed, their minds washed free of all the things that had made their personality. But Pellin was stronger. More importantly, he was fascinating- a human creature with such boundless imagination, such dedication to his own advancement and the demise of others. For the one and only time in the untold millennia of its existence, the *hyyr* entered a symbiotic relationship with its host. Pellin, supposedly a withered and cretinous outcast, made a useful shell, and the *hyyr* in turn had given the creature in which it lived a new life of its own.

Pellin had never been an imbecile, but he *had* been truly mute- the High Cardinal had chosen him from among a gathering of street dwellers to be his bed-boy for that reason, perhaps worried that a more able youth might speak of their arrangement to someone. That had happened once before, although the claim had never been treated seriously and the boy had died mysteriously a matter of days later. Before the *hyyr* encountered him, Pellin had been the shuffling, submissive servant he still appeared as to everyone but Gorram. He dressed the High Cardinal, fetched things for him, ran errands, cleaned. He serviced the old man's urges reliably and skillfully enough for Gorram to keep him. There was, after all, nothing wrong with his tongue.

The *hyyr* had mended Pellin's damaged vocal cords and given him a voice. It had, of course, already shown Pellin that it was one of God's highest servants, a spirit of great power, and so Pellin revealed to the High Cardinal one day that God had blessed him and given him the power of speech. Pellin's thrill and joy were genuine, as was Gorram's dumbfounded awe at the evident power of his deity.

A day later, Pellin showed the High Cardinal another gift from God. With only a little effort he could put his hands to his face, twist his skin and underlying flesh, and reveal an altogether more pleasant visage- handsome, even. It was still recognisably the same man, only made far more pleasant to look upon. And the process could be reversed, so that anyone outside Gorram's chambers would see only the mute, retarded gargoyle of a man they had spent years shunning.

"He has remade you in his image," the High Cardinal had whispered, transfixed, as he moved his hand gently across Pellin's face. That had been the moment when Pellin, at the silent insistence of the *hyyr*, had asserted himself. "I am God's messenger," he had said. "You will remain High Cardinal, but the two of us are now partners, equals behind closed doors. God has great plans which I will reveal. You and I, Gorram- we will help to reshape the world."

And they would- or at least, Pellin would. The High Cardinal's usefulness would find its limit one day, and likely before God's great plans reached fulfilment.

The *hyyr* had shared its recent past with Pellin- the last eight centuries. The preparation of the Church and its vast hierarchy for the imminent changes had taken hundreds of years and remained an ongoing, painstaking process. The *hyyr* remembered and shared the memory of the subtle influence it had exerted through that time, the delicate changes wrought to pull the Cardinals of each era slowly but surely in the right direction. Passages in the Scriptures were altered in subtle ways over time, and entire parts imbued with minor but effective sorcery, to help fulfill the plans of the *hyyr*- which were ultimately the plans of its master.

Pellin often derived amusement from wondering what Gorram would think, were he to realise that each sacrifice in the Hall of the Interface brought nearer an entirely new Age, one that had been centuries in the making.

The paradox of a *hyyr* that had never dreamed, sharing the body of a man who dreamed frequently and violently, made for a curious, subconscious arrangement.

This night, Pellin drifted through blackened, withered landscapes, swam in lakes of thick, languid blood that never quite congealed, walked on perilous paths above fathomless chasms filled with the restless, writhing forms of condemned mortal creatures. The colossal scale of each desperate realm almost overwhelmed him. The equally vast imagination of the entity with which he shared his body and mind conjured new scenes in moments, each glorious vista melting into the next.

One such evolution took place now, so that within a short while Pellin walked on an unsteady yet satisfying surface made from the naked, mutilated forms of a million creatures- not only human but also humanlike *faer,* and *gobanneth, flammar, myrmai, aren han* and many others. Amongst them too were the higher beings of doomed Ilentra- *xyrral* and *schiaan.* Pellin, having never yet encountered any such creature, nevertheless knew them because the *hyyr* knew them. The *hyyr,* more ancient by far than any of these beings, knew their history, their society, the structure and intricacy of their corporeal forms. The *hyyr* had existed for millennia before these races even came to be.

Pellin slowed his pace as he traversed this landscape of ruined flesh, until at last he crouched and then began to crawl, dragging his way across the still-weeping morass of trapped souls to heighten the pleasure of his journey.

Something savage and brilliant- an immense light- cut through the dream and pulled him mercilessly from the hellish contours of that world.

Pellin's eyes flickered open. He kicked off his sweat-dampened bedclothes and sat up.

A force of considerable power had been awakened nearby- a power that had torn him from his sleep and lit a flaring beacon in his mind.

"*Oh,*" he whispered.

He had already determined its nature, because the *hyyr* had. Its proximity shocked him. That one of the *arterrim* had been hidden here in the Overchurch!

He got dressed, the *hyyr* part of him whispering urgently. "But where?" he said aloud.

There could be only one place, they decided together. The one part of the Overchurch where no one had set foot for decades.

Someone had broken into Heretic's Tower.

Pellin grinned in the darkness. He would access that place, find the interloper, and tear them to pieces.

And claim one of the three *arterrim* for himself.

VI - Fools' Errands

I

First Protector Ferrim paced restlessly around the hall, each measured step echoing harshly, his stony countenance giving no hint of his thoughts. Kaya Moorcroft waited for him to speak.

Kaya had developed vast reserves of patience during her slow rise through the ranks of the Protectorate. She had occupied her position of High Commander for a year and had somehow- against her own expectations- survived the inevitable purge that followed Ceiran's recent replacement as First Protector. Granted, she had been no ally of Ceiran's, which might have helped, although Kaya preferred to think it was her reliability, her competence, her experience. She was not a member of *any* faction.

Perhaps Ferrim, somewhere inside that grey, emotionless shell, valued her for that.

Kaya half-admired the new First Protector's understated ruthlessness, although it wasn't necessarily a trait that best served such a political station. How long he would last was difficult to say. He had been elected from a field of five who put their names forward to be considered by the Grand Assembly, and his win, though comfortable, was hardly overwhelming. Ferrim had always been coldly considering, and perhaps manipulative, although Kaya had never thought he possessed the required intelligence to be an effective First Protector. Time would tell, she supposed.

She hadn't voted at all, and often wondered how Ferrim had received almost a half of all votes cast.

Would he make sensible use of those around him with many years or even decades of experience? His predecessor had kept his own counsel in most matters, and maybe that had contributed to his downfall. Certainly it had helped stir suspicion.

"The trail has grown cold." Ferrim's voice was like iron. "You would have told me if you'd heard even the vaguest of rumours."

"Of course." Did he really think she wouldn't?

"He must be found, no matter the cost. He will have plans for us."

"Maybe he's been reduced to planning his own survival rather than our downfall," Kaya suggested.

"Don't by naïve, Kaya. He craves the demise of the Protectorate."

"That won't happen."

"No, of course it won't. But he will nevertheless seek to damage us however he can." Ferrim stopped pacing at last and sat at the central table. Even then, his nails tapped the marble surface restlessly. "Still," he remarked, "at least we learned of Arc Thendrin's part in his treachery. The intercepted messages were of *some* use."

Kaya nodded soberly. She sometimes wondered how Arc had been allowed to remain in the Protectorate for so many years, whilst better men and women failed and left the ranks in disgrace. He had rarely shown his face at Assembly gatherings, and not at all in the last seven years. It wasn't unusual for Protectors to stay in foreign lands- often undercover- for years on end, but Arc's lengthy disappearance had spread more rumours than any other.

Kaya had been initiated as a junior Protector as part of the same intake as Arc Thendrin, and their paths had met often in their first few years, although she would barely have considered him an acquaintance. Intense and yet distant, he had often given the impression that he was concentrating on something no one else knew about.

Perhaps Ceiran had engaged him in furtive errands even from the start.

"I need you to take on this task," Ferrim said bluntly, interrupting her thoughts.

"You want me to find Ceiran?"

"Not only that, High Commander. I want you to find and execute him."

Even in her initial shock, Kaya quickly recognised the manoeuvre for what it was. The very existence of a female high-ranking officer made Ferrim uncomfortable. Perhaps he saw her as a threat, no matter that Kaya had no desire to become First Protector. By sending her on this mission, he moved decisively against the renegade former leader, *and* all but ensured Kaya's demise. What hope would she have against Ceiran, a natural magician of rare power and sharp intellect? He could melt into the world unless he wanted to confront her.

"I have every confidence in your ability," Ferrim remarked earnestly. "I would not have asked this of you unless I believed you could rid the world of this man."

Liar, she thought savagely.

Kaya forced herself to speak, and with decades of practice, kept her voice reasonably calm. "What resources can you give me to help in this?"

"You will have a companion on your journey."

"Do I need one? I'm not the sort who grows lonely with age."

"His name is Tiam. He works for us as a darkseer."

Kaya frowned. "Yes- I've seen him. He's a bit young, isn't he?"

"He is very good at what he does."

"Be that as it may, why do I need a darkseer with me? Is he to interrogate Ceiran's vengeful spirit if we find and put an end to him? I fear that would be beyond anyone's capabilities." The light-hearted words spilled from her mouth even as she felt a noose of dread tighten around her heart.

"Nothing so dramatic- and darkseers don't communicate with spirits. They have an uncanny ability to study and find useful information in the residues of people- the *living*, not the dead- the ripples they make in the how-why and what-if of our existence, as they go about their lives. Beyond that, I know relatively little of how they work. But he *is* good at finding those who might otherwise be difficult to find. At the moment, all we know is that our former leader is most unlikely to be in Fort Cailan."

"Perhaps we should have played the long game, waited until Ceiran finally returned and then have him summarily executed."

"In normal times, I would quite agree. But he has vanished *because* of the chaos he's sown." Ferrim scraped his manicured nails irritably on the granite table, and Kaya almost shivered at the sound. "We digress. Together with your more... traditional strengths as a senior Protector, the two of you have every chance to exact the justice demanded by the Grand Assembly."

The Assembly had called for Ceiran's head, Kaya recalled. They hadn't specified who should bring it back to Fort Cailan. That, unfortunately, was for Ferrim to decide.

You make it sound easy, she almost said. This mission would almost certainly end in her death- and Tiam's for that matter- if they were unlucky enough to find the former First Protector. Ceiran's powers were formidable, and Tiam did not sound as if he would be useful in a violent situation.

"Understood," she said briskly, her face a mask of nonchalance. "Is there anything else I should know?"

"Tiam will meet you in the main courtyard at first light tomorrow. Take whatever funds you need from the treasury, within reason. I have authorised your visit with the countsman. Horses will be made ready for you before you leave tomorrow morning."

After all these years, she would be gone in less than a day. The High Commander didn't know whether to laugh or cry. "One more thing. What if we can't find him?"

"You can't fail, Kaya." Ferrim sat back and regarded her coolly for a short while. "There is far too much at stake here. Don't return until you've dealt permanently with Ceiran of Witherport."

II

That afternoon, Kaya was alone in the practice yard working on her swordplay and exercises- both needed more frequent attention these days- when Lord Commander Strommen found her. Dark-haired and slender, he was about her own age and of ordinary height and build, but somehow he always seemed more imposing than he ought. A dependable but enigmatic man of few words, some called him surly and withdrawn. Kaya respected him more than she did Ferrim and often thought the only reason Ferrim had been voted in as First Protector was because Strommen declined to put his own name forward- although he had retained his position as effective second-in-command in the Grand Assembly.

Strommen waited until she paused to rest before walking towards her. Kaya sheathed her sword, breath steaming in the chilly air. Much of the practice yard still lay covered in frost where the sun had not yet landed.

"I hear you've been handed a death sentence," the Lord Commander remarked without preamble.

Kaya laughed despite herself. "My punishment for living, I suppose. The First Protector wishes to be seen doing something about the thorn in our side. I understand that."

"I have something for you, Kaya." He handed her a plain silver ring. Kaya frowned and turned it around as it glinted faintly in the light. For a moment she saw a single character etched on the inner surface but when she turned the ring over again it was gone. "What's this, Strommen? You're not trying to propose to me, are you?"

"Had the First Protector chosen me, I'd have kept this for myself. But you will have far greater need of it."

"Should I wear it?" Kaya looked guardedly at him. "Is this a *faer* artefact?"

"Could be."

She took a sharp intake of breath and moved the ring carefully in her palm. "How did you come by such a thing? What does it do?"

"It was given to my great-grandfather as thanks for a service my family performed. Apparently, the ring may be given once only, outside the family to whom it was bestowed. So, it's yours now."

"What does it *do*?" Kaya repeated.

"It has protective qualities. Supposedly against outworlders, but also tricksters such as... the thorn in our side. I've never needed it as much as you likely will."

"It's safe to wear, Kaya," he added when she looked doubtfully at him.

Cautiously she slid the ring onto her middle finger. It fitted snugly. "What *did* your family do?" she asked.

"Long story. I'll tell you if you come back." He paused and regarded her expressionlessly for a moment. "Good luck."

"Thank you," she said, but Strommen was already hurrying back into the relative warmth of the fortress.

Kaya decided not to wear her Protector's cloak when she departed– she and Tiam would be engaged in *quiet business*, and although there were undoubted advantages to wearing the insignia of her rank, and the immediate deference this elicited, their mission might have numerous surprises in store and could take them into Saanu or, far worse, Gharaan. Anonymity would be essential in the Church's lair.

Although anonymity likely wouldn't prevent Ceiran learning of their hunt, she reminded herself.

Kaya looked up and saw a crow staring down at her from the fence, eyes hard and inquisitive.

Maybe he already knew.

The following morning, Kaya spotted Tiam as she stepped through the archway from the officers' quarters towards the main courtyard. She leaned against the sandstone wall, tied back her straw-blonde hair, and watched him for a while. An athletic youth of a little over average height, with shoulder-length brown hair, he spoke with the stable hands for a while and then began saddling one of the horses, which it was certainly not his job to do. One of the boys stood nearby and watched him with an uncertain expression, perhaps thinking about intervening. The young darkseer was known by many around the fortress but had no official rank, so the servants were never sure when to defer to him.

Then Kaya realised that Tiam was doing nothing more than adjusting the straps and saddle, moving them this way and that, only to stare at his strange handiwork and walk around to the horse's other side to repeat the exercise.

She strolled to within several paces. "What are you doing?" she demanded.

Tiam jumped, startled. His brown eyes blinked in confusion, then he clearly recognised her and gave a hasty bow. "High Commander Moorcroft! I beg your pardon, my Lady."

My Lady?! "And I know who *you* are, Tiam. The darkseer in whom First Protector Ferrim places so much faith."

He shrugged, embarrassed. "I'm to help you howsoever I can." His Theyan was excellent, spoken with only a slight Saanuese accent. East, Kaya thought. Aun, maybe.

"Yes, and I'll need all the help I can get." She stared at the nearby stable hand until the boy hastily bowed and made himself scarce, then turned back to her companion. "You didn't answer my question. What were you doing with the saddle and straps? They were already just so. Are you training to be a stable hand? Looking for a less spiritual vocation?"

"They needed to be moved. They were not quite right."

"Not quite right." Kaya shook her head and decided not to pursue that line of conversation any further. "Tiam, I assume you've been told why we're leaving Fort Cailan at this unseemly hour, on a long journey with winter approaching?"

"The Lord Commander briefed me, my Lady."

"Enough of your *my Lady* nonsense, please. As you'll soon find out, I'm far from most men's idea of a *lady*. I'll bet Strommen's words were indeed brief."

"He doesn't waste them," Tiam noted.

Kaya looked her mount over. The black mare had a calm, stoic look that the High Commander liked. As a rule, she found horses far more agreeable than people. She called one of the stable boys over again. "They've both been fed and watered?"

"Yes, High Commander."

"Good. Tiam, let me be honest with you." She waited until the stable hands had gone about their other morning duties and then continued, "Likely neither of us will survive this mission. If we *are* to survive, however, we will need to use our respective strengths cleverly. Or to put it simply- you find, I fight."

"As you say, High Commander." He looked ill at ease.

"Call me Kaya if you please. This is a place of unbearable formality. That's one aspect of the road that will lighten my heart."

"May I also say I'm grateful to have been chosen for this task..."

"Are you? I got the impression that the First Protector has no one else with your particular set of skills. Your *gratitude* is hardly the point."

"I'd wanted to be of help to you for a long time. I hadn't thought to sacrifice myself in so doing."

Kaya shrugged. "Life is a set of weighted dice." She put a booted foot in the stirrup and mounted her horse, not as lightly or gracefully as she once had. "Don't be grateful."

A short while later they ushered their horses slowly towards the distant outer gates of the courtyard. "We'll take some hot breakfast at the North Arch," she said, referring to the great exit in Fort Cailan's northern perimeter wall. Several inns and stalls around there sold early meals to travellers in and out of the fortress city, so there would be plenty of choice even at this miserable hour. Kaya and Tiam waited for the night guards- sleepy looking fellows near the end of their shift- to open the courtyard gates, and then they were through, away from the Fortress of the Protectorate and into the surrounding city.

"Tell me how it works," Kaya said as they headed slowly through the cold, empty streets. "This odd talent of yours. The *darksight,* some call it. It all sounds very mysterious."

"I don't know much about the *how* of it," he confessed. "But sometimes I gain a sense for how people have affected things as they pass by, or how objects have been changed by someone. It's as if they leave a sort of residue, a ghost of whatever happened at the time. I picture how things happened. Sometimes it's very clear, almost as if I'm there watching."

"I can't imagine what that must be like."

"And can't describe it properly. But I've never thought of it as a mystery. It's been my constant companion for as long as I remember."

"Your childhood must have been interesting," Kaya remarked.

Few people were about at this early hour, with the sun a faint promise in the east, but a few food sellers were set up and trading at the North Arch as Kaya had hoped. Her mood improved a little once they'd breakfasted on fresh meat pasties and honey cakes. She took her time about her meal, enjoying the substantial breakfast but wishing somewhere in Fort Cailan sold the delicious saltfish she remembered from her childhood in distant Hopesfall. River fish never had the same pungency, so she never ate them.

When the sun rose into the azure sky, they had already left the city behind and headed along the Great North Road past fields and farmsteads, towards the rolling wooded hills of northern Anphay. Far to the east the distant peaks of the Needles, the natural border between Anphay and Gharaan, made faint shapes. Snow already covered much of those mountains and would soon come here too. Even parts of northern Gharaan had already seen snow in the last few weeks, and that was *very* unusual.

"Where are we going first?" Tiam asked as they rode slowly towards the forested uplands.

"I thought Barrows Field. That's where *he* was last seen by any reliable witnesses, although that was some weeks ago. By the way- and I shouldn't need to tell you this- we never mention him by name unless the two of us are alone and cannot be heard. Actually, don't speak his name at all. Who knows what may happen."

"May I ask something regarding... the former First Protector?" Tiam ventured.

"I'll tell you everything I know, if it helps you find him."

"Where was he last seen?"

Kaya looked askance at her companion. "Barrows Field, Tiam. Are you still half-asleep?"

"No, I meant where in the town. A tavern? Maybe a market? A whorehouse?"

Kaya couldn't help but smile at the idea of a whorehouse. Ceiran had been notoriously celibate, with no carnal interest in either women or men. "To my knowledge, his last verified location was the Two Bridges Tavern. You think we should go there?"

"It's a starting point. I may discover something that helps us."

Kaya shivered and drew her plain cloak more tightly about herself. Maybe it would snow later today, or tomorrow. It was cold enough.

They stopped at a river crossing around midday to stretch their legs and allow the horses to drink. "Does the Grand Assembly think he's under the control of outworlders?" Tiam wanted to know as he stood watching the water.

"Their view is, he's a traitor and must be brought to justice," Kaya said bluntly. "I don't know if there *is* any thinking beyond that. Clearly, it's no great stretch of the imagination to suppose that outworlders have used him to aid their cause. We now know he has been helping the former Queen of Asqabal."

"I thought she disappeared many years ago."

"Well, now they both have. And the ruling family of that realm have consorted with outworlders for centuries. So that makes for a very... *unfortunate* alliance."

Tiam refilled his water flask from the river, upstream of where the horses were drinking. "Why would he do this?" he mused. "What could he gain from it? He has a reputation as a clever man. Why put trust in demons who will take whatever he offers and kill him when his usefulness has passed?"

"Those are all good questions, Tiam. No one knows."

The darkseer continued to reveal himself to be a man who questioned accepted ideas, which Kaya liked. "How does someone like that just disappear?" he pondered later that afternoon as they rode along the wide track between seemingly endless rows of pine and larch. The sky had grown leaden, and Kaya reckoned the snow would arrive before nightfall.

"How does he disappear?" she repeated.

"Well, we know what he looks like. He's a distinctive man. Tall, and walks with a limp. He's bald and has scars and tattoos all over his face. And he has *very* dark eyes."

"Black, Tiam. His eyes are black. They weren't always. That was one of many penalties he paid for his victories."

"So, he killed some outworlders, but now he helps others? That makes no sense either."

"I don't know a tenth of the things he's done. The limp was another badge of honour if you could call it that. Not to mention the wounds that people never see."

"Well, then. He can't very well hide in plain sight."

Kaya pondered that for a while. "You see this Protector's sword?" she said at last, tapping the hilt with a gloved finger. "Like all the others, it's forged from the fires of the Deep Flame, the inextinguish-able furnace gifted to the people of Anphay by the *faer,* more than a thousand years ago. The White Fire, some call it. You see a Protector do something extraordinary, it's often because of the great power burned into their blade, a small part of the Deep Flame itself. We train for many years to be able to wield and control these weapons, so that the force within them can be levelled against outworlders.

The demons burn in the sorcerous heat. That is what we live for- the defence of Theya.

"The man we hunt- and perhaps a few others across the world- are different. They have innate magic, of a kind." Kaya gave him a considering look. "Some might say *you* do."

Tiam shook his head. "A sixth sense, is all it is."

"Anyway, according to much of the hearsay down the years, he has a certain ability to... bend the perceptions of others so that what they see and what they *think* they see are two different things."

"Useful."

"Useful, and dangerous, if true. It would make matters even more difficult. Someone once told me that he knows his way around the entire world, even places he's never been. I don't think *that's* true, but likely it came from something that is. Many stories have a certain muddied truth to them." She sighed. "You see, Tiam? We're at an instant disadvantage because we can only guess what we're up against."

Kaya was not like other Protectors- and Tiam had already known enough of them to last him a lifetime. She appeared not to be driven by anything or compelled by any protocol or arcane rules of the Grand Assembly. In fact, High Commander Kaya Moorcroft didn't seem to care much about anything, which made it even more perplexing how she had risen through the ranks.

Maybe she was simply very good at her job, although in the convoluted world of the Protectorate that seldom counted for much by itself. The First Protector clearly thought her expendable.

Tiam had been fascinated by her for much of the last six months, since his arrival in Fort Cailan. He had observed her from time to time, passed by her in corridors, listened to her voice. Every occasion was a clue about this enigmatic, formidable woman, and yet those clues together added up to frustratingly little.

His twin sister Siara would have laughed at him and pointed out that once again he was starting to fall for someone beyond his reach and would suffer for it. He'd done it before. *You never learn,* she had told him.

Kaya spoke perfect Theyan. Protectors needed to master languages as part of their training, but many- most of whom were Anphayan- retained a harsh Anphayan accent. He wondered how *his* enunciation of the language sounded to her. Did he speak with a more pronounced Saanuese accent than he suspected?

Tiam shook his head despairingly at his errant thoughts.

Kaya had her blonde hair tied back still, and her cloak- an ordinary travelling woollen, not the standard Protector issue- tied with a belt due to the breeze. She stared straight ahead, severe, seemingly as cold as the weather coming their way. Tiam imagined Siara's amusement if she could see him now. *You think she'll melt for you?!*

He sourly reminded himself to cease such flights of fancy. He was young enough to be her son. He was neither a Protector nor from a notable or landed family. He wasn't even Anphayan.

Aside from those clear obstacles, those who knew anything about Tiam tended to be cautious, even suspicious, around him- and more so if they thought he was paying them closer attention than they wanted. It was almost as if Protectors believed he could see and hear the shadows of vanquished demons inside them. Perhaps a few really did think he could, but Tiam had no knowledge of such things. Those shades and voices were, he reckoned, nothing more than artefacts etched into their minds. When demons were slain, surely they stayed slain. Nothing came back from a strike through the heart- or whatever such creatures had in place of one- by a blade forged in the Deep Flame. An entity was either dead, or alive. It could not be both.

This being a sensitive subject, however, Tiam wisely kept his philosophies on the matter to himself.

Kaya sensed his eyes upon her and threw him a questioning look. The darkseer swiftly returned his attention to the road ahead.

"How many outworlders have you killed?" Tiam ventured later.

"Two." Kaya stared into the distance, perhaps remembering. "It doesn't sound like many. But not many find their way into Theya. Not outside of Asqabal, anyway. The frequency of their incursions tends to be... overstated."

Tiam had always thought it odd that the Protectorate gave them such a religious-sounding label. "That's the name for them in Saanuese, too. More or less. The actual word is *asharilla,* meaning dark devils."

"It's all a figure of speech. Where they're from and what they are isn't the point. What they *intend* is. This world hangs in the void, and the void is full of demons trying to reach in."

"How do they survive in the void?"

Kaya threw him an amused look. "Has anyone ever told you that you think too much?"

"Yes," he admitted.

Her expression changed. "Well, never be ashamed for being a thinker, Tiam. Were the world ruled only by those who consider before acting... anyway, I've been lucky. Maybe this sword is lucky too. I don't know. Without it, they'd have ripped me apart in moments. It took years for me to learn to control this weapon. Even now, it sometimes feels like it has a life of its own. The enchantment of the Deep Flame does that."

"You and the sword are partners," he noted.

"Mortal creature and inexhaustible force." Kaya smiled bitterly. "Hardly fair, is it?"

Kaya found that her defeatism changed to something else during the afternoon. Rather than wonder what would happen if or when they encountered Ceiran, she considered what would happen if they *never* found him. The idea would not let her go. Might Ferrim lose patience and send someone in her stead? Might he even send someone to dispose of her and Tiam? He'd given them no deadline, but no one's patience was infinite.

"Be honest with me, Tiam. Do you really think you'll be able to track him down?" she asked that evening. They were cooking squirrel over their fire, this being the one creature Kaya had managed to hit with an arrow today. Archery had never been one of her more auspicious skills.

"Honestly, I don't know. I might have a better idea when we reach Barrows Field."

"Maybe he doesn't leave a trace." Kaya's tone was morose. "Best that we never find him."

Tiam looked questioningly at her. "Best that we never find him," she repeated. "Don't you agree?"

The young man was clearly caught between what he wanted to say and what he felt he ought to. "Better for us, certainly," he ventured at last.

They sheltered for the night in a wooden hut a short distance off the trail. Some logs and kindling had been left by whoever used this place before them, so Tiam and Kaya at least enjoyed a decent fire that evening. A small, covered outbuilding stood next to the shelter and they blanketed the horses before leaving them tethered with enough food and water.

Kaya remained withdrawn after that, saying no more than she needed to, and Tiam decided it would be best to leave her be. To pass the time, he focused his energies on their immediate surroundings, wondering how much he could glean and if any of it would be useful. He allowed his back to touch the stone wall behind him. He placed his hand upon the ground. Then he closed his eyes and allowed his sense of this place to drift. Soon vague, opaque images came to him, like fragments from a dream. He saw a lone traveler, short and middle-aged, wrapped in furs, staring into the fire he had made. At one point he ate some dried meat and drank from a bottle. A stiff breeze blew around the hut, sighing against the stones. The man wiped at his eyes. Was he tired, or weeping for some reason? Tiam couldn't tell.

The vision *felt* three or four days old, he reckoned. The traveler had long gone now. How many others had this ancient stone hut seen over the decades, even centuries?

A strange melancholia stirred within him. Tiam detached himself from the scene he observed, to stare instead into their fire. Soon, that too would be history.

III

The following afternoon they reached the town of Barrows Field. The Two Bridges Tavern proved easy to find on the main road, and while Kaya went to the stable across the road to arrange shelter for their horses, Tiam looked at the walls, windows, and sign of this unremarkable inn, wondering if he could find even a hint of what had happened when Ceiran was here. He touched the walls and then the door. He concentrated on the drab, peeling sign as it creaked in the chilly breeze. Something was wrong with it, he decided, although he couldn't say what. It looked old, faded- and yet he felt sure it had changed recently. How could that be?

Tiam touched the handle of the door and immediately flinched, stumbling backwards. For a moment he felt sure that he'd seen something dark and formless- a space, or a gateway, he couldn't be sure- in place of the door. The vision swiftly disappeared.

Might it have been something to do with Ceiran? Tiam doubted it. Usually, the causes and effects he sensed could be linked with particular people. This sudden flash of darkness had no link to anything or anyone, as far as he could tell. It didn't belong here.

Unnerved and feeling colder than ever now, he drew his robe closely about himself and waited for Kaya to join him.

Only one room was available, so Kaya bought it for the night and then they sat in the mostly empty tap room downstairs. The Protector bought them a meal each- tender cuts from a suckling pig slowly roasted over a hearth at the far end of the room which had been set up as a makeshift kitchen- and two large tankards of strong ale. Her mood improved a little, although she asked nothing about this place, the last known whereabouts of the former First Protector. Tiam thought that was a little odd.

"May I ask you something?" he ventured after a second tankard each.

"About myself?"

"If you don't mind..."

Kaya moved a silver half-sun across the table. "I don't want to talk about me. How about you buy us another couple of ales, and then we can talk about *you*."

Tiam wasn't sure he liked the sound of that. When he returned with their drinks Kaya gestured for him to speak.

He hesitated at first. "I'm not sure there's much of interest to tell you..."

"Let me be the judge of that."

"Well, I'm from Aun in Saanu..."

"I thought you might be."

"My family name is Bearswood. My parents are crafters. My twin sister Siara is a student of history and languages. She works as a scribe and translator but recently she found that she could be paid more if she travelled to other lands." Tiam shrugged wearily. "She found work in Toran."

"You're not happy about that," Kaya noted.

"No. But she's a grown woman." Tiam took a long draught of ale. "She can look after herself, as she likes to remind me."

"And what about you? Do you like being what *you* are?"

He didn't know what to say. "I don't know any different," he ventured at last. And he quickly changed the subject after that, for an image of the fathomless darkness he had seen earlier swam to the surface of his thoughts again, like a slowly spreading stain.

Tired after another day in the saddle, they went upstairs to their room while the tavern was still filling up with revellers. Tiam stood and stared around the room as Kaya sat on the bed and stripped down to her underclothes. A quick glance in his direction showed that he was trying his best not to look at her. "The room is a little small," he remarked.

Kaya smirked at him. "The *bed* is big enough for us both. Provided you can keep your hands off me, I don't foresee anything terrible happening. Do you?"

The young man removed his shirt and trousers and climbed into bed. Kaya blew out the candles, then lay back and stared up at the faint shapes of the roof beams, pondering the formidable task that lay ahead. Tiam fell asleep in moments and began to snore faintly.

Kaya didn't remember falling asleep. When she woke later, the room was still dark. She got up and padded over to the window. The sky had begun to lighten.

Tiam shifted and muttered something quietly in his sleep. The High Commander glanced back at him. She wasn't sure what to do about the darkseer. She had been surprised, after their first day together, when she realised his attraction to her. In some ways, the attention was not exactly unwelcome, but it made a complication that she could have done without.

"What *should* I do about it?" she murmured, knowing full well that protocol demanded she do nothing at all, and ignore the fact.

Then again, what did protocol matter now?

Kaya watched her companion in silence, listening to his steady breathing. Then she turned away, having suddenly realised she was smiling.

"Which direction ought we take?" Kaya asked Tiam over breakfast.

"They're all the same," was his unhelpful response.

"East? West? North? South?"

"East," he said with a shrug. "Truthfully, I've found no hint that Ceiran was ever here. We've no trail to follow." Then he asked his companion, "Why didn't you ask me yesterday?"

"Probably, Tiam, because I don't really want to know."

The morning began brightly enough and they departed Barrows Field in sunshine, but during the early afternoon thick clouds arrived, gloomy with the promise of snow or sleet. The Protector, increasingly angered by their situation, declined an evening meal or even ale in the next village, and retired to their room. Tiam read her mood and remained downstairs to drink.

Kaya seethed helplessly as she lay down on the bed and stared up at the ceiling. What had she done?

She ought to have resigned her position. But then she would likely have met a mysteriously sudden end. No one of her rank simply *resigned* and got away with it. Certainly no one given a task of this magnitude responded by resigning and still expected to live.

Kaya tried to formulate a plan to extricate herself from the mess she had fallen headlong into but could not come up with anything resembling a solution.

Her mood grew black and despairing.

She pulled the covers over her and drowsed, stirred sometime later by Tiam stumbling into the room. Kaya heard him undress as she lay with her back to him. Tiam slipped into bed with a sigh and immediately found his way over and pressed against her, then ran a hand through her hair. "No," Kaya reprimanded him, and was surprised when, instead of persisting with his drunken advances- which would have ended badly for him- Tiam mumbled an apology and rolled onto his back with a resigned sigh. *Polite young man,* Kaya thought, and even smiled a little in the dark. A *polite young man* was exactly what her father had hoped she might bring home one day.

Well, that horse had bolted long ago. She had no home to speak of and her father had been dead close to fifteen years.

Kaya was surprised to find, when she woke the following morning, that she had opted to take a running leap into the dark, perhaps because her other options led only to death or misery. Her desperate choice would mean a life of shame as a fugitive- or at least, it would mean a life of shame if she cared about it. But she didn't. She had no family or close friends to shame through her actions.

Kaya watched Tiam until he stirred and his eyes opened. "Where do you want to go?" she asked.

"What?" He sat up on one elbow, rubbed his eyes and stared blearily at her.

"Where do you want to go?"

"I have no idea where he could be. I don't think I'll be any use to..."

"Never mind *him*. Never mind the whole damned Protectorate." She lowered her voice to a whisper. "Do you want to *live*?"

IV

Theo collected the last of the broth from his bowl with a hunk of stale bread and finished his meal as he watched Devotee Alum's continued prayers. The Devotee- who had dedicated his life to travelling through remote areas in pursuit of enlightenment and to spread God's word- prayed at sunrise, noon, and sunset every day, or as close to those points as he could estimate if the weather was inclement. Three prayers a day was considered appropriate for a fully trained Devotee. Theo preferred one long prayer late in the evening before he slept and shorter ones throughout the day as the mood took him. Alum was not a stickler for hard and fast rules and allowed him the liberty. Besides, Theo had not yet been anointed as a Devotee. A year or more of training still lay ahead of him.

The first rays of the morning shone on the Devotee's bald head as he knelt and faced the rising sun. Theo admired his mentor's unflinching dedication and used it as inspiration whenever possible. God knew he had sometimes wearied of their long journey, through remote settlements mainly along the border between Gharaan and Saanu and on towards the Needles, near to the heathen land of Anphay. The weather in the northern foothills of the Needles was bitter at this time of year, and frost covered the ground most mornings. Theo would rather have gone into the wilds of west Saanu. It rained more there, but the climate was a little warmer.

He, Alum and to a lesser extent Parrik, the Divine Knife who travelled with them, would spread the word of the Lord amongst the people they encountered in the settlements they visited. Sometimes, if their words found a receptive audience the long days were worthwhile, but this far south and close to Anphay, many of the rural folk clung to customs that had roots in *faer* mythology and superstition. Border folk, they called themselves, no matter that they lived in Gharaan. Their beliefs were a confused patchwork, taking some ideas from the Church and others from backward traditions.

Theo had never had the grim misfortune of encountering a *faer* creature, and couldn't even be certain they still existed, but Alum assured him they did. Although they no longer possessed a frightful hold over the world, the Devotee warned that they waited in the darker corners of Theya to take it back again for themselves. Even more worrying, the Protectorate were in league with the *faer* in many covert ways.

Theo had enjoyed his days spent training for his vocation in Toran but had to admit that Alum was right- these remote settlements were exactly the places where they must spread the word of God. "It would be slothful," his master had pointed out, "to wander along the paved streets of Toran or Timber Bay, enjoying the attention of those who already live in His Light. We are meant for the harder path, Theo. But the harder path…"

"…is the virtuous path," Theo had finished.

Parrik had placed his various weapons on the grass in front of him and waited for Alum to complete his morning prayers. Once the Devotee stirred, stretched, and returned to the embers of their campfire to make his breakfast, the dark-haired Divine Knife began his own ritual, sharpening each weapon in turn. Theo could not believe that any of those blades had dulled since their previous honing, but dared not question Parrik, whose sullen demeanour could easily flare into something worse. The acolyte couldn't understand the Divine Knife at all.

And yet this was a man of God, apparently.

Perhaps Parrik harboured some ill will at being assigned as a guard to Devotees. Amongst the ranks of the Divine Knives, this was considered one of the least worthwhile tasks, even a humiliation.

Theo tied back his hair and began reading from his book of the First Reckoning, one of the older sacred texts. His was a copy, of course, and an abridged edition at that, given to him by Alum shortly after they met two years ago.

Meanwhile, Parrik completed his sharpening and went to work through his swordplay exercises, much to Theo's relief. The sound of metal scraping on metal always set his teeth on edge.

Alum settled next to his understudy and contemplated the rolling foothills that stretched away east towards the great central plains of Gharaan as the rising sun illuminated them. "Praise His Light, it's going to be a beautiful morning," he declared. Theo had never known anyone as relentlessly optimistic as Alum, who took any hardship in his stride- even welcomed it sometimes- and possessed seemingly boundless energy. "Praise Him," he absently agreed, turning the page of his book.

"I feel a resonance in the air this day," Alum declared. "A *significance* of some kind. Our path is leading us somewhere special, Theo."

Theo nodded and gave a polite smile. "I hope and pray so." He didn't point out that his mentor had said much the same thing every day since their departure from the Devotees' mission in Aun.

Although he preferred to think before speaking and often chose not to speak at all unless he had something worth saying, Theo nevertheless enjoyed being amongst people and watching how they went about their lives. He had liked Aun, a city where many different cultures somehow managed to exist side by side. Aun had been a good place to learn about people and their places in the world.

Alum, who possessed a more single-minded nature, found that cities made him restless, and during their tenure at the mission he had made no secret of his desire to set out on the open road- or more accurately, seldom-trodden trails- spreading the word of God in the more far-flung corners of the world as he had done years before.

No matter that in such places there were few people to listen to His word.

Alum called out to the Divine Knife. "Are you ready for the ascent into the mountains proper, Parrik?"

Parrik, who had discarded his light leather armour and under-shirt and was now performing press-ups, ceased his exercises and looked up. "The border is difficult to know unless we follow the Southwater. The map shows the parts where the river goes into Anphayan territory. Keep to the map as a guide, I say."

"Do they guard it?" Alum rejoined, undaunted. "Is there any-thing to guard?"

Parrik spat distastefully. "Anphayans are not the only heathens lurking hereabouts. The mountain people are scarce now, but not extinct. More's the pity."

"Praise God," he added unconvincingly when Alum frowned at him.

"Why does the border not follow the river through the moun-tains?" Theo asked. "Would that not make more sense? A border that cannot be mistaken or crossed accidentally?"

"Yes, Theo, it would. But life is rarely simple, and those who make the laws of lands contrive to make it even less so." Alum finished his breakfast of bilberries- picked yesterday but still good to eat-and hard bread. The berry juice had stained his fingers dark. "The weather should be set fair for the day. We'll make good progress. Do you think the clouds look different today, Theo?"

The younger man peered into the eastern sky. Only half a dozen clouds dotted the horizon, and they looked the fair-weather sort as Alum had already alluded to. "No," he said at last, wondering if the question might have meant something else, or was intended to catch him off-guard, not that Alum ever showed interest in such tricks. "At least, I don't think so."

"But the air *does* feel a little different." Alum took a long, deep breath as if to taste that difference.

"Mountain air *is* different."

The Devotee smiled and went to wash the breakfast utensils in the stream nearby.

The three men walked for the entire morning, the path taking them on a gradual ascent through the foothills of the northern Needles and along an increasingly rocky route. The land fell away on both sides as the path wound across hillsides of tough grass punctuated with bare rock. Around midday, they stopped for a brief rest at the crest of a hill, with the nearest of the Needle mountains rising sharply before them. Snow had fallen here recently.

"Two paths," Alum noted, pointing to an area a few hundred paces ahead where the way forked left and right, the right-hand path taking a steeper, more direct route up the mountain whilst the left continued flat before descending gradually into a shadowed valley.

"Left, if we want the river," Parrik grunted. "No need to go up into the high mountains, Devotee. No one lives there to be converted. Unless you want to meet the mountain men."

"River it is," Alum replied, flashing a smile. "Some small settlements cling to the Southwater. I'm sure we'll find a welcome there."

"Depends on what you mean by *welcome*."

Alum appeared not to hear him. "We'll be at the river by nightfall, if the weather stays…"

A flash of brilliant white light cut through the sky.

Theo's sight had gone. He panicked as he felt the ground tremble beneath him, and then a blast of air threw him backwards along the path. The impact on the ground knocked all the breath from him. As he tried to sit up his sight gradually returned. Bursts of afterlight shimmered and fizzed at the edges of his vision. His back hurt where it had hit the rocky path. When he breathed in a sharp pain cut through him from the base of his spine up to his left shoulder.

Alum and Parrik were also on their knees as they looked south towards the mountain heights. Parrik appeared unhurt, but Alum had a large cut on the side of his head, from which blood seeped. He swayed slightly as if he might collapse to one side at any moment.

Theo looked in bemusement at the colour of the sunlight, the way it fell, and the length of his shadow. "No," he muttered distractedly. "That's impossible..." *How can it be late afternoon already?* he wanted to say.

"Theo!" Alum's voice was cracked with emotion. "Theo, *look!*"

The acolyte's gaze followed Alum's shaking fingers.

High in the region of the mountain before them, winged figures circled, their shapes dark against the late daylight. As Theo watched in disbelief, one drew near enough to be seen in greater detail. It landed on a precipice, and looked towards them, scaled limbs and great golden wings glittering in the sun, long tail curled against the rocks.

"God be praised," Theo whispered.

He had seen pictures and paintings of these beautiful, mythical beings so many times. Their images hung in tapestries on the walls of every holy building. They were a cornerstone of the Church teachings, a promise of better times, of justice, of a great reckoning for unbelievers and a joyous celebration for the faithful.

And yet, as the eyes of this mesmerizing creature caught his own- even over a great distance- Theo felt a pang of terror that confused and shamed him.

For what true man of God could feel anything but bliss, as he looked upon the prophesied angels?

V

The sea foam rose and churned against the barnacle-crusted rocks, and with the fall of the water the heads of two swimmers were revealed.

The friends laughed spontaneously, ducked beneath the water one more time, and then rose to climb effortlessly onto one of the jagged rocks.

Uelene smoothed back her hair and took a deep breath of the cool salty air. Behind them the dark cliffs of Saanu's western edge rose, more than eight hundred hands high. Before them the ocean stretched away. No one knew for sure how far the Western Ocean extended. The *myrmai* with whom Uelene had lived for the last five years said that somewhere far to the west lay the submerged Lost Lands, fabled realms that had sunk below the sea many thousands of years ago in a disaster known as the Cataclysm, about which almost nothing was now known.

She looked down at her body and silently marvelled- as she so often did- at the subtle yet miraculous ways in which it had evolved during her time with the *myrmai*. Her fingers and toes had become slightly longer and wider, her torso tighter, smoother, and yet more muscular. She could remain underwater for far longer than ought to be possible for any human.

Then again, she was no longer entirely human.

That was the price that rare people such as herself- *adaptive* was a term used in some lands, but she was more than that- paid for the continued company not only of the *myrmai* but other *faer* folk- *flammar, heralyn, gobanneth, tremannin* and many others strewn across the far-flung reaches of Theya. Even Uelene had no idea how many distinct races there were.

She sensed Shaelyn's watchful stare and favoured her with a smile. Shaelyn was not her *myrmai* name, but it was the closest approximation to it that a human could pronounce, and she appeared to like it well enough.

"When you take the ceremony?" Shaelyn demanded. Her lidless, dark grey eyes fixed Uelene intently. The *myrma's* grasp of Theyan had grown considerably over the last year, as Uelene redoubled her efforts to teach her. Her own skill in the *myrmai* language was far less advanced despite her best efforts.

An honour bestowed on very few humans down the ages, the ceremony of *remaking* gave an outsider full acceptance into the *myrmai* society. In Uelene's case it would mean much more than that, for as an adaptive she would inevitably become more *myrma* than human over time. Her fluid nature all but demanded it. Perhaps the *myrmai* had decided to allow her the ceremony because of that. Not that any of them reminded her, except for Shaelyn who made a point of mentioning the ceremony almost daily.

"Soon, I think." Uelene found herself lost in the horizon again as her thoughts wandered. What would it truly be like, to become as one with these folk and eventually lose her humanity? For her, such a loss would be easier than for most. She had no family, no human friends, no ties to anyone or anything. She was an outsider and had been for almost as long as she could remember. Perhaps that was another part of the price that adaptives must pay.

Not only that, but Uelene had found that her deep understanding of people had the effect of repelling her from them. Often, she saw such grotesque ugliness in human nature that her insight into people's thoughts and secrets was a curse. What she had seen, could never be unseen.

She would not miss humanity and all its pointless horrors.

"No think." Shaelyn's words were blunt. The caress of smooth, webbed fingers against her hair made Uelene shiver. "*Do,*" Shaelyn added forcefully, as if Uelene might not have worked out her meaning already.

What was stopping her from taking the ceremony? She loved being amongst the *myrmai*. They had all but accepted her already, and the ritual would simply make that acceptance complete. Sometime after, with the passing of years, she might become almost indistinguishable from them, and live and die beneath the waves, never again walking amongst humans.

"Catch me," Shaelyn invited. She flashed a grin full of sharp teeth and slipped from the rock and below the roiling surface of the water in a single deft movement.

Uelene knew she couldn't catch the *myrma* unless Shaelyn allowed her to, but she also knew that Shaelyn *would* allow her. In the cool darkness they would become lost to both the human and *myrmai* worlds for a while.

She sank into the ocean, and for the rest of the morning Uelene forgot about the ceremony and all it entailed, and lived only for the moment, carefree.

Early in the afternoon, Uelene sat on the rocky beach eating mussels and clams that she had collected. Shaelyn had gone with her family to hunt fish in the open depths- something that Uelene could not physically do- which gave her the opportunity to mull not only the matter of the ceremony, but deeper, existential matters. Whether she was human or *myrmai* was not important, Uelene decided as she tied back her long brown hair with some strands of seaweed and began her lunch. She must forget the past, the constraints and definitions with which she was born. Those limits had not made her, and they could not define her.

If she was destined to join the *myrmai*, and her identity as seen by the outside world changed, then so be it.

Uelene blinked in surprise as she realised that she had made her decision. She *would* take the ceremony. Shaelyn would learn of it first, of course, and then...

She became aware that she was no longer alone on the beach. But it was not a *myrma* that she sensed. It was a human.

Uelene turned and scanned the multitude of cracks, crevices, and caves in the vast cliff. Her eyes fell upon something- little more than a shadow- in one of the larger caves. "I see you," she called out warily.

The figure stepped forward to the cave entrance, and Uelene felt a pit open in her stomach. She had hoped never to encounter this man again.

He limped towards her across the pebbled shore, jet-black eyes regarding her without expression. His face bore almost as many scars as tattoos, so many that barely an inch of unblemished skin remained. His plain black cloak flapped in the cool sea breeze.

Ceiran made a sight as fearsome as it was unwelcome.

"I don't know why you came all the way here," Uelene remarked at last, struggling to regain her composure. "I doubt you've come to plea for an audience with the *myrmai*."

"They won't speak to me." Ceiran's voice sounded brittle and harsh like iron, the sound of a man who lived his life in pain. "The Old Ones shun me. I'm tainted by those I've vanquished, Uelene. We both know the price. The outworlders' darkness is a part of me."

"Then you'd better be gone from here before the clan return, tear you to shreds and leave your remains for the gulls to feast upon."

Ceiran smiled at that. "Let's not waste time on pleasantries. I sought you out because I need your help."

"I am done helping you, Ceiran. You deceived me. I nearly died taking that child to the Faering. Besides which, the *faer* knew her nature at a glance, and they demanded a heavy price for allowing her into their realm."

"Which was?"

"That's between me and them. But you never told me the truth about Imogen."

"I told you what you needed to know. Anything else and you might not have agreed. In fact, Imogen is the reason I'm here."

"I'm not interested. If you want to help the half-demon mongrels of Asqabal, do it yourself."

"Strange to hear one such as you use that word," he remarked. "I see you've begun the change."

"And I intend to complete it."

"Imogen left the Faering recently and headed out into the Barrens. Her mother- as far as I'm aware- sensed that something had happened..."

"Yes. Kick one Omerian and they'll all limp," Uelene shot back.

"...and sent a Protector I had assigned to her out north to find the girl. Imogen was brought back to Waters Green, but then she escaped."

"This sounds like a disaster of your own making, Ceiran. You need to assign better men and women to such missions."

He ignored the jibe. "No trace of her was found until I sent someone with sharp enough senses to the area. It seems that a *xyrral* has taken her to Char. Inevitably, she will soon be crowned Queen of Asqabal."

Uelene did her best to look unsurprised at that. "This is an interesting story, but it sounds complete."

"Hardly. Our problems have only just begun. You're as aware of Imogen's nature as anyone, Uelene."

"That was seven years ago- she'll be a young woman now." Uelene looked down at her unfinished lunch. Somehow her appetite had fled.

"Through those who seek to manipulate her, or independently, she will become a tool of immense, frightening power. I need *you* to gain her confidence. She must be ready, and on the right path. All the great powers of Theya must be ready and united. Oblivion is nearer than anyone knows."

Uelene stared at him in astonishment and then laughed. "You're a desperate man, Ceiran."

He walked as far as where wavelets crashed gently against the shore. "The world will be ruined beyond recognition. Nothing will be as it was."

Uelene shook her head. "I don't believe you."

"And I don't have time to argue the matter with you." In a moment he stood next to her, and before Uelene could muster any kind of defence, he had seized her head in his hands.

She had no recourse against the horrors that poured through her mind.

Humans, outworlders, *faer* and every other being throughout Theya, fled before a vast, fathomless darkness, an abyss that sought to snuff out all life save that which it could remake in its own image. Nothing could stand against it because factions had fought one another almost to the point of annihilation, ignorant or unknowing of the far greater threat gaining in power all the while.

Uelene was sent hurtling into the midst of that chaos, into the unimaginable agony and misery of millions, into the ruin and desecration of the world. Demons with neither form nor substance- not outworlders but born of something far, far worse- slipped from place to place, stirring mayhem, urging those they corrupted to engage in horrific, depraved violence against others.

The sky grew dark, and unspeakable creatures the like of which she had never imagined made the world their own. Over time, all of Theya became unrecognisable, its lands and its people now changed and ruined. Nothing of what had once been still existed. Uelene stared into a world become an abyss, an absence of all hope.

Finally, Ceiran released her, and Uelene sank to the shore, weeping.

"Go to Char and do whatever you must to guide Asqabal's new Queen. Likely she will have been crowned when you arrive." He half-turned towards the cliff. "You may want to find some clothes to wear."

"I hate you," she whispered as he limped away. "I swear I'll destroy you for this."

"Come for me when our work is done," he invited her without looking back.

Uelene crawled back onto the rock and looked longingly out to sea. Her dreams lay in tatters, if she chose to leave the *myrmai* and do as Ceiran demanded. They would not allow her to return. No one was ever invited a second time.

I could forget he was here, Uelene thought. *I could take the ceremony, and in time become one of the* myrmai. *Even Ceiran can't follow me to the ocean depths.*

But as much as she strove towards that course of action, the vision that had assailed her would not let her be. It remained sharp, a fragment of black glass in her head.

Uelene thought back to her journey with Imogen seven years ago. Only during the days after their departure did Imogen's unique nature- the Omerian blood sang through her veins more powerfully than Uelene had thought possible- manifest itself in strange and terrifying ways.

The child's nightmares- where she even brought faint but horrifying residues of those dreams into the waking world- were only the start. Imogen's despair and rage at being separated from her mother ate away at her to the point that the mad darkness lurking inside her often rose like bile to the surface. Uelene employed every subtle power at her disposal to prevent the girl from losing control. The worst part of it was that in between those times, Imogen- who remembered little of such terrors- showed herself to be nothing more than a confused, despondent young girl, who simply missed her mother.

Her sheer *normality* made Uelene's heart ache, for the child was anything but normal.

As Imogen's mother had pleaded, Uelene invoked one of her more potent powers before they reached the Faering, causing Imogen to forget everything of her former life. The child would remember something of the aftermath, as Uelene rested from the ordeal, but almost nothing before, until or if she met her mother again. The adaptive had questioned the wisdom of this from the beginning, but it was not for her to tell Alianne what she should do, and certainly not Ceiran, who had echoed Alianne's command. He had paid her well, and she'd needed the money desperately back then.

So, she had done as bidden, with a heavy heart.

Uelene had no idea what the *faer* would do as she brought Imogen to the edge of their realm. Their ways could change like the wind. She knew only that a price would be demanded if Imogen was to be allowed into the Faering at all. They would already have sensed the sort of creature that approached their border, and Uelene would be duty-bound to pay the price, if they didn't refuse her immediately.

The *faer* gatekeepers appeared- three of them, gnarled and angular members of the *aren han* race. Uelene bowed, offered her respects, and explained Imogen's situation. She pleaded sanctuary for the girl. They listened in silence, offering no hint of their thoughts, and then they disappeared into the Faering's tangled fastness to confer.

Uelene's dread concerning the price that might be levied became so great that she even considered taking Imogen away from the Faering, perhaps back to Alianne, thinking to pretend that the *aren han* had dismissed their plea.

But then one of the creatures returned and whispered words across the wind that filled Uelene with dread.

We allow this creature you bring to our realm, but a toll will be due.

The *aren han* did not however reveal what the toll would be. The two others reappeared, and together they led Uelene and Imogen along the winding paths of the Lower Faering to the edge of Greenwood, which happened to be the nearest sizeable settlement. They waited long enough for some of the women to appear and see the *faer* folk with Uelene and Imogen. Then they vanished into the dusk.

As commanded by the girl's mother, Uelene told the Elder of Greenwood only as much as she needed to know- that Imogen required a haven in which to grow and learn. "I am her mother," she added, although no one had told her to say that and to do this day Uelene had no idea why she'd said such a thing. "Promise me she'll be safe here."

She mentioned that they were Gharaanian- Imogen's accent placed her there after having spent many years in the land, and Uelene, who happened to be Saanuese by birth, could take on any accent she chose. The Elder granted Imogen a place of learning in

Greenwood- perhaps because the *faer* had already allowed Imogen into the Faering. If the *faer* allowed something, then the women were generally inclined to do likewise.

Uelene discovered the toll exacted by the *aren han* sentinels weeks later.

The creatures had somehow made her barren.

Over the following months and years, Uelene spent her blackest moments wondering what their reasons had been for inflicting such devastating cruelty. Perhaps, in their view, she had brought a demon child into their realm, and the price for that would be the loss of her ability to conceive a child herself. Then she would wonder why they had allowed Imogen into the Faering at all. To study her? For some reason so obscure that no human could ever guess it?

And soon she will become Queen of Asqabal, Uelene thought.

She had only ever been a small player in this. Now she was being pulled back into the mire of Ceiran's plots and machinations. Knowing what she knew- for there could be no doubting the vision- could she still turn her back?

There was, however, something she dreaded even more.

She would need to bid farewell to Shaelyn.

VI

The *myrma* stared back at her for so long that Uelene wondered if her friend might not have understood what she'd been told. She was thinking how to put it to her using different words when Shaelyn said, "No."

"But I must go. There is something important I must do. I'm needed." Uelene shook her head in frustration. How could she make Shaelyn understand? Perhaps she couldn't.

Then the *myrma* sighed and bowed her head in defeat. Droplets of water ran down her smooth skin. "As you say. You go, you go."

"Thank you, Shaelyn." Uelene exhaled softly, relieved. "I don't wish to go. It's the last thing I want. But..."

Shaelyn pointed to the water. "Swim. One more time."

Uelene nodded sadly. A moment later they dived into the water.

She sensed Shaelyn dive a little further down towards the ocean floor and followed, her eyes quickly adjusting to the gloom. Uelene's emotions as she swam after her friend were bittersweet. She had enjoyed her time here and had especially taken pleasure in Shaelyn's company and friendship- but this would be their final time together.

Shaelyn waited for her near a cluster of rocks and coral. She beckoned Uelene nearer, and in the near silence of the deep water, Shaelyn clasped her arm. Uelene looked into the eyes of her friend. She saw sadness, anger...

No, Uelene realised, and a chill went through her. She saw a fury so intense that it terrified her. Abruptly she tried to break free of the *myrma*'s hold, but Shaelyn maintained an iron grip on her with one arm, and her long, muscular tail had coiled around Uelene's legs.

She isn't going to let go, Uelene realised in horror. *She'll keep me trapped here until I drown.* She shook her head in a desperate plea, but saw no mercy in her friend's eyes, only murderous intent. The *myrma*'s grip intensified. Uelene struggled desperately and eventually managed to pull an arm free. By now a crippling pain spread through her lungs. Almost blindly she struck at Shaelyn's head, and the blow was enough for the *myrma*'s hold on her to weaken. Uelene struck at her again, wriggled free and swam as fast as she could towards the distant light.

Uelene gulped for air as she reached the surface and struck out for the nearest rocky outcrop. As she clambered onto the rocks, something sharp dug deep into her leg. Uelene let out an agonised scream and looked back to see Shaelyn's razor-sharp teeth buried in her flesh. She kicked as hard as she could with her other leg, but it took three blows with her heel before Shaelyn's hold weakened enough for her to pull away.

Hobbling and in desperate pain, Uelene managed to scramble from rock to rock, slipping several times and gashing her legs and arms on barnacles. At last, she reached the shoreline, but Shaelyn was not far behind. Uelene grabbed the largest pebble she could find, turned, and shouted, "Shaelyn, I beg you! Let me go!"

But the *myrma* went for her, face twisted with such hatred that Uelene sobbed in terror as she flung the stone as hard as she could.

It struck the *myrma*'s wide, flat forehead straight on, and she fell back on the rock. Uelene felt certain that she had only knocked Shaelyn out for a short while, yet she was too exhausted to move any further. She sat shivering on the rock, and as her shock gradually subsided her physical pain grew even worse. Blood on her legs and arms mingled with salt water. Uelene watched Shaelyn intently, fearful that the *myrma* would stir and come after her again. She would be too weak to defend herself.

But Shaelyn did not move. Uelene crept nearer. She flinched as Shaelyn finally rolled slowly onto her side.

"Why?" Uelene whispered as she looked down at her friend.

The *myrma*'s lips moved. She said something, but Uelene could not hear her words above the churn of the sea.

Then Shaelyn's eyes darkened from grey to jet black. "No!" Uelene cried, for the total darkening of the eyes was a sure sign of a *myrma*'s passing.

A dreadful sound arose from beneath the waves. Uelene had heard the dirge of the *myrmai* only twice before. She clapped her hands over her ears, but nothing could prevent the call of a hundred or more seeping into her. They had immediately sensed the death of one of their own. They would arrive in moments and when they did, they would see that murder had been committed.

She must flee now or die violently on the rocks.

Uelene dragged her way to the nearest cave and staggered on into the dank gloom. Her breath echoed harshly as she found the hidden entrance to a passageway that would lead her up to the clifftop. She worked her way through the darkness of the rocky tunnel for a long while, pulling herself along in agony. Her breaths were short and sounded like the gasps of a cornered creature as she struggled through the salty, earthy gloom.

She had almost reached the top- a faint dot of light issued from somewhere up ahead- when a much louder cry than the earlier lament came echoing through the rock. Such was the fury of the *myrmai* call that Uelene froze helplessly in the dark, her shaking limbs bereft of energy.

She pictured the *myrmai* swarming through the cliff tunnels, determined to shred her with their teeth. Somehow, she summoned the will to drag herself onwards.

Uelene emerged from the tunnel exit, shivering, and streaked with blood. She found herself in a thicket of windswept trees and bushes, about a hundred paces from the cliff edge. If she fled eastwards, away from the cliff, soon she would be in territory that the *myrmai* could not reach.

She staggered out of the wintry copse and made her way across the undulating grassland, her progress painfully slow. The wind whipped at her bloodied body. She moaned incoherently as she stumbled along.

Sometime later Uelene curled up to sleep in the briar-tangled ruins of a long-abandoned homestead set alone in the bleak, windswept plains, far from any human settlement. She dwelt bleakly on the ruins of her life, and the supposed end of the world.

Let it come regardless, Uelene thought miserably as she drifted into a fitful slumber.

Let it all fall to ruin.

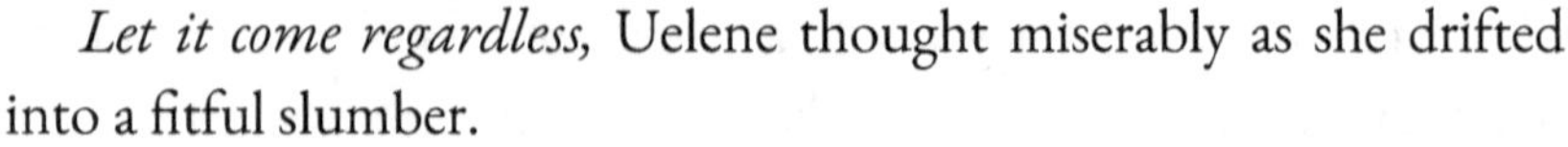

Book Two of the Heralds of Misfortune, provisionally titled *The Blood That Shines,* will be out soon.

Join the author's newsletter to keep up to date with all the latest news about the series: https://www.simonwilliamsauthor.com/

If you enjoyed *A Symphony of Wings,* please take the time to rate and review on Amazon!

www.ingramcontent.com/pod-product-compliance
Lightning Source LLC
Chambersburg PA
CBHW072053190726
48294CB00005B/1495